DARK H

HOME

A POST APOCALYPTIC JOURNEY

BOOK ONE — SETTING OUT

DARK HIGHWAY HOME

A POST APOCALYPTIC JOURNEY
BOOK ONE — SETTING OUT

LARS H. LARSEN

SETTING OUT

Cover Design: www.getcovers.com
Editing: Enchanted Ink Publishing
Book Design and Typesetting: Enchanted Ink Publishing
Publication Assistance: Self-Publishing Services,
selfpublishingservices.com

ISBN: 979-8-9874111-0-0 (E-book)
ISBN: 979-8-9874111-1-7 (Paperback)
ISBN: 979-8-9874111-2-4 (Hardcover)

CONTENTS

DECEMBER 2023

DAY ONE

GRID DOWN. GETTING READY.
SETTING OUT. MASON. TENT LIFE.

ONE

had the Land Cruiser sailing along in the interstate's slow lane at sixty-five, fifteen miles per hour under the speed limit. Big rigs had been blasting by all day, buffeting her about as they shot past, heading south doing eighty or ninety, some pulling up to three trailers in the states that allowed it. I'd been at it since five this morning, and she was running flawlessly. So well, I knew she could effortlessly take me across the country if I wanted her to.

I'd left my family's ranch outside Whitefish, Montana, yesterday morning, and after spending the night at a motel in Salt Lake City, had set out again early this morning. I was currently southbound on Interstate 15, headed toward my final destination, Las Vegas, Nevada, the site of our company's annual year-end gathering.

My restored, tan 1972 Toyota Land Cruiser, achieved its best gas mileage with a cruising speed of fifty-five, but wanting to arrive early in Vegas, I'd been keeping the speed at sixty-five, sucking up gas at an absurd rate. It's 350 miles from Salt Lake City to Las Vegas, and according to the road sign ahead, I had another 120 to go. I'd already filled up twice today, the latest a few miles back in St. George, Utah.

The desert landscape was incredibly beautiful in this part of the country, and the interstate ran through deep canyons and arroyos formed by long-dry ancient rivers. It was mid-morning and the sun now high enough to illuminate the vivid reds and pinks of the rock formations that presented themselves out to the far horizons. I'd driven through several rain squalls, and the air was filled with that wonderful sweet smell of a post-desert rain shower.

I'd gone through my iPhone's entire music library, twice, and I was now hitting the radio's search button in hopes of finding a decent classic rock station. It kept landing on country music, Spanish speaking, and Christian talk shows—all three a big no-no. I was ready to give up and go back to the iPhone's music when it landed on an NPR station out of St. George.

It's Tuesday, December 12, 2023. I'm Noah Cranston. Here are today's state, national, and international headlines.

In Utah news, the US Supreme Court yesterday refused to hear an appeal by lawyers representing a group of nine Russian citizens whose ski resort properties had been confiscated by the US Justice Department's Task Force KleptoCapture in May of 2022. Lawyers for the owners claim that property, valued at one hundred seventy-five million dollars, mostly in Park City, Utah, and Aspen, Colorado, were illegally confiscated by the government. In August of this year, a federal judge in Salt Lake City ruled that the US government, under internationally imposed sanctions, was entitled to the proceeds from the sale of the properties. Many Russian citizens, politically and financially linked to the now-imprisoned Putin, have had homes, ranches, airplanes, yachts, and bank accounts seized in the aftermath of the unsuccessful invasion of Ukraine by the Russian military.

This news was of interest, as a large, internationally known quarter horse breeding ranch outside Kalispell, Montana, had been seized in July of 2022. We later learned that it was owned by a Putin-backed Russian oligarch using an overseas shell corporation. My father, Neil Kristen, had been approached by the Montana Department of Revenue shortly after to gauge our interest in a possible future purchase of the entire operation. My father had said he'd be very interested. But the owner had sued to halt any possible sale, had been granted a stay, and to my knowledge nothing had come of it. Maybe now something might happen.

In national news, the CDC today announced that its Global Response Team, which has been tasked with slowing the spread of the hyper-contagious omicron BA.5 virus, has identified sixty-seven new positive cases . . . all sixty-seven in and around the town of Pecos, Texas. The sixty-seven infected have been isolated as per last year's national mandate policy. The CDC has also confirmed that fourteen contact tracer teams have been deployed across the US in search of individuals that came in contact with members of the infected group. The original number of infected was seventy-five, eight of which subsequently died. "The time span from initial infection to hospitalization to death is just incredibly fast," says Dr. Sinja Schmidt, Director of infectious disease at Harvard Medical School. "We watched these individuals go from first symptom onset to hospitalization in less than three days. And in all eight cases, death occurred within four days of those symptoms' first appearance."

These are the first reported infections and deaths in the US in four months. The CDC has confirmed that fifty-eight of the sixty-seven infected are members of the same church group. All fifty-eight had chosen not to be vaccinated or boostered.

A big rig pulled alongside, and the driver tapped his horn. I looked up and was greeted by the male driver and his female co-pilot giving me thumbs-up along with big smiles. I waved back, mouthed a slow thank-you, and they sped off ahead. This happened several times a day. The thumbs-up was for the Cruiser, not me.

Ten minutes later, I came to a halt behind a mile-long line of vehicles stopped for a highway construction flag man. I watched as a few dozen dump trucks filled with paving gravel crossed the median from the northbound lanes and formed up on the southbound fast lane's shoulder. Many of the drivers ahead of me had taken the opportunity to get out and stretch their legs. Leaving the engine on and driver's door open, I joined them on the roadway. I continued to listen to the radio broadcast.

In other news, the Biden Administration announced today that the much-needed electrical grid hardening and security upgrade will be completed by mid-January 2024, a month from today. During the spring 2022 Russian invasion of Ukraine, in retribution for Biden's harsh economic sanctions, Russian state-sponsored hacking groups, along with their Chinese counterparts, had made digital incursions into the US electrical grid and disrupted power to sixty-eight million American households for eighty-three hours. "It was a lesson learned," said Elizabeth Sisan, spokesperson for the Department of Energy. "Our electrical grid was often the target of foreign hacking attempts, and unfortunately, many were successful. Under the infrastructure bill passed in 2021, rebuilding our bridges and updating our electrical grid were deemed as priorities over all others. Americans can be assured that soon our grid will be protected against unlawful digital intrusions and any natural catastrophes, such as solar sun flares or other electromagnetic pulse events."

There is a noteworthy bit of news out of China today: US intelligence agencies report that due to the Stealth Omicron, the Chinese military has lost in excess of forty percent of its 3.1 million active-duty land, air, and sea-based personnel, whether to death or incapacitation. The World Health Organization confirms this news and says that China's vaccine has been found to have an efficacy rate of less than eighteen percent. Total civilian deaths in China remain unknown, as the Chinese government hasn't released official numbers, but is believed to be as high as thirty-five percent of its population.

And now we have NPR's Jennifer Tobin joining master gardener Cecelia Santos on the art of successfully growing tomatoes in containers . . .

Ten minutes later, the flag man flipped his sign from the red stop to a green go. Five minutes after that, I passed him, drove over three miles of freshly graded mixture of dirt and gravel, and got back up to speed after hitting pavement.

It had been a tumultuous two or three years, what with the Covid pandemic, Black Lives Matter marches, China's aggressive stance in the South China Sea and toward Taiwan, the 2020 presidential election, the January 6 insurrection and its subsequent congressional investigation, and Russia's invasion of Ukraine. And if all that wasn't enough, Putin ordered the detonation of a low-grade battlefield nuclear device on the Polish/Ukraine border (which his generals had refused to do), Putin's subsequent removal from power by the Russian military, and his life sentence in a Siberian gulag followed by democratically run elections.

And last but not least, with Putin in prison, China no longer had an ally. Not one. Well, maybe North Korea. And it lost its major source of oil, as the new Russian leadership turned off the spigot that was supplying China's industrial and military complexes.

Aside from China, things had settled down these past few months, both domestically and internationally. Business was returning to pre-Covid levels, and with the exception of Kim Jong-Un of North Korea, most of the world's sociopathic leaders had been killed, imprisoned, or were headed for trial. Russia had resumed shipments of oil and natural gas to Europe and Great Britain, and the economic hardships that had played out during the Russian invasion of Ukraine had all but disappeared.

So, I guess a segment on growing tomatoes didn't seem out of place.

But I had no interest in growing tomatoes. I bit the bullet and went back to my iPhone music.

TWO HOURS LATER, I'D SELF-PARKED the Cruiser in the hotel's parking structure and had checked into my company-supplied suite. The cybersecurity company I worked for, Securetech International, supplied its upper-level executives with suites, as we conducted several days of individual and group meetings with our respective team members. I was one of three domestic senior vice presidents, and I was responsible for all sales, customer service, and marketing for the western United States and Canada—basically, everything west and north of the Rockies. We had a regional office in Seattle, which I managed. Including me, our group consisted of six team members in Seattle and another four admin support staff in the company headquarters in Atlanta.

Once a year, Securetech gathered the entire company in Las Vegas, minus twenty-seven well-compensated volunteers who remained at company headquarters holding down the fort. We were in Las Vegas to work on next year's goals and budgets, review new products and features we'd be introducing in the new year, conduct annual employee reviews, and most importantly, hand out very generous year-end bonuses.

We worked. We ate, a lot actually, in catered hotel ballrooms and at restaurants that closed their doors for the night and then reopened for us alone. The company owners, Renee Knowles and Ben Ives, also gave each employee one thousand dollars to gamble with during the company's casino night. It cost the company big bucks to put on these annual meetings, but we were very profitable, and the company owners were not shy about sharing those profits with our team members. Needless to say, we were one very happy company.

This year, Securetech was flying in 210 domestically based employees to Las Vegas. Our 110 team members who made up our international division would gather the following week in London.

We were here to work, but I must admit, it was more about having fun and carousing. Ben and Renee participated with the team members and had as much fun as everyone else.

This year's gathering was special for us, for after a three-year absence due to the original coronavirus and the loss of four fellow team members to Covid, this would mark our first get-together since December 2019.

Due to federal and state vaccine programs, the country had experienced months of declining deaths due to Covid or one of the four variants that followed in its footsteps... the Covid menace had gone from front page headlines to back page mentions. Europe was once again overrun with tourists filling hotels, restaurants, and famous local landmarks. Vaccines and boosters had done their job. China, on the other hand, hadn't fared nearly as well, as its leaders had refused all foreign offers of help with vaccines and boosters. The death toll there was rising, not falling.

Here in the US, I hadn't seen a mask on a face in months.

TWO

During day two of our meeting, my college roommate and fellow ex-Special Forces service member, Burt Casey, had called with some particularly good news . . . my new Barrett .50-caliber rifle had been received and was ready for pickup. Burt, along with his father, Chris Casey, own Desert Tactical and Surplus, the largest gun and tactical supply store in Las Vegas. Heck, maybe even the largest in the western United States.

In a proud and somewhat breathless voice, he'd said, "Master Sergeant Jon Kristen,"—that's me, and it's ex-master sergeant—"I've got it assembled and lubricated. We even took a quick trip out to the desert and zeroed it in at three hundred yards. Beth and I then set up seven hundred, twelve hundred, and fifteen-hundred-yard metal targets and had at it. It's fun and very accurate, dude. We put a Nightforce optic on it and a Harris bipod.

"It wasn't easy with the post-pandemic shortages, but I was able to get you fifteen ten-round magazines, along with one hundred twenty rounds of Hornady A-MAX .50 caliber, with a promise of another eight hundred rounds of decent ball ammo by tomorrow afternoon. I may, just maybe, be able to acquire a few hundred rounds of some Nammo .50 from a local source."

"The Nammo are from Norway?"

"Yes. And by the way, the rifle comes in a wheeled Pelican Storm Case."

"Thank you for putting this together for me. And thank Beth, too." Beth was Burt's wife. The three of us attended the University of Utah together and had shared an off-campus home in the Avenues neighborhood close to campus. "And thanks for zeroing it in. That's awesome."

And I meant it. It was awesome. Owning a Barrett had been a dream of mine for most of my post-military adult life. The United States government had supplied me with a loaner Barrett and spent tens of thousands of taxpayer dollars training me in its proper utilization—their word, not mine. I'd put that training to good use in multiple tours in Iraq and Afghanistan.

Now, I planned on using that experience at our ranch's shooting range. The covered shooting benches were located a quarter mile east of the ranch's runway and hangars. The range had sixteen lanes: ten rifle, three pistol, and three shotgun and skeet. The rifle lanes were set at one hundred yards to a whopping 1,760 yards . . . one mile. I hadn't had a weapon capable of reaching targets in the furthest two lanes. The Barrett would change that.

Our ranch hosted semiannual, five-day, long-distance shooting clinics each year, in the spring and fall. Classes were taught by ex-military instructors and snipers. The clinics were attended by law enforcement, military branches, intelligence agencies, and a few lucky civilians who were chosen by lottery. The thirty students stayed at our ranch's all-inclusive guest lodge. I'd been known to teach a class or two. Burt had been a guest instructor as well.

"Wait, I almost forgot," Burt had said excitedly. "We received the suppressors for both the Barrett and your Colt this morning. We were able to get you the new QDL model for the Barrett and the SureFire SOCOM for the Colt. We charged your credit card this morning for the rifle, ammo, and all the other goodies. Good thing you've got a high limit, because even after our very generous family-and-friend discount, it's still friggin' expensive."

"Ouch. Can't wait to see my next credit card statement." I didn't ask Burt what the final number was, but I figured somewhere in the neighborhood of nineteen to twenty-three thousand. The ammo alone was a tad over five dollars per round, double since Biden took office and the demand-driven national ammo shortage became a reality.

"You drive down in the Cruiser?"

"Yep. Can't fly commercial with that ammo. And the rifle, while flyable, takes too much paperwork."

"I look forward to seeing it. You bring your Colt? If so, I can have the store's gunsmiths take care of the barrel mods needed to handle the suppressor."

"I did. It's up in the rooftop cargo box." I had a custom-built metal luggage-supply rack installed on the Cruiser's roof. Half of the rack supported a black fiberglass Thule cargo box, which was weatherproof and lockable. The box was low in the front, getting taller toward the rear, and was somewhat aerodynamic. Thanks to my father's insistence, the Thule currently held the Colt AR, my Glock .40-caliber handgun, a small faraday bag protecting a few electronic items, my plate carrier, and a well-stocked get-home bag. I humored my dad and let him put together the get-home bag. I didn't share my father's passion for being prepared, but I was smart enough to know not to criticize or belittle his efforts.

"I'll try and drop the Colt off tomorrow during one of our afternoon breaks. But these meetings can be pretty time consuming, and it may be that I won't be able to get away until it's over in two days. I look forward to seeing you, Burt. It's been too long."

"Sounds good. I'll see you sometime in the next day or two. Call me and let me know when you're coming so I can be here. Beth is going to want to see you, too. Later."

IT WAS NOW FOUR IN the afternoon on the third and final full day of our year-end gathering. I'd just wrapped up the last of my team member reviews and the handing out of the year-end bonus checks. The reviews were overwhelmingly positive, and our team was solid for next year. It had been a long day, and I was ready to head down to one of the hotel's larger indoor/outdoor meeting rooms where the Securetech management executives meet each afternoon to review the day's events and work on the next day's agendas.

Tonight, there would be our last company dinner followed by the company's casino night. But first, it was time for my own annual review. I rode the elevator down to the meeting room level and walked a long, tunnel-like hallway to Securetech's executive meeting suite. Our meeting room was a conference room with its own private outdoor patio and pool. Renee Knowles, our company co-owner, was waiting for me poolside. She was wearing a white polo shirt with our company logo on the front and white Bermuda shorts. She was sitting on a large beach towel with her feet dangling in the water.

Renee spotted me and waved me over. "Hi there. Take your shoes off and join me."

"Hi, yourself. Great place for a meeting." Removing my shoes and socks, I rolled up my khakis and put my feet in the cool water. It was December, and the weather was still warm and in the low seventies. It certainly created a near-perfect day.

Ben Ives, Renee's business partner and Securetech's co-founder, was standing on the other side of the pool. He spotted me and waved hello. He was in his usual business attire: Hawaiian shirt, cargo shorts, and flip-flops. Ben was four years older than Renee, had premature gray hair that stuck straight up and out like Albert Einstein's, stood six feet tall, and was thin and wiry. At first glance, Ben appeared to be an older surfer dude, but he was anything but. Ben was a brilliant programmer and coder but was also very socially adept and had developed friendships and contacts around the world. Early in his career, he taught at MIT, which was where Renee and he met, and was soon put in charge of the school's prestigious UROP (Undergraduate Research Opportunities Program). He was such a positive presence that the school gave him an open invitation to return anytime he wishes. I liked Ben, but more importantly, I respected him.

Renee was a year older than my thirty-four. She was tall, coming in at five eleven, five inches shy of my six four. She was lean and muscular from running marathons and nightly gym workouts. Strikingly deep-blue eyes complemented the facial features that could only have originated from a Nordic gene pool. She had long blond hair, which she wore in a perpetual braided ponytail. She was tan from the outdoor running. She had beautiful skin, which makeup had never touched. She wore no jewelry, not even earrings. She was also one very smart cookie.

Oh, did I mention the fact that she was drop-dead gorgeous? But she never played that card; instead, played the cute nerd. She was a computer geekette at heart and was one of the country's brightest software coder slash engineers. She started this company with Ben Ives in her late twenties and had grown it into one of the world's largest, most innovative computer systems security companies.

Renee and Ben, along with a large team of Securetech engineers, created the toughest next-generation firewalls and EDR (endpoint detection and response) programs available today. We counted among our larger customers most of the major domestic and international airlines, and since the SolarWinds hack by the Russians, we now protected federal government agencies such as the US Treasury, FBI, CIA, and NSA—yes, even the NSA. We also kept watch over the country's largest retailers and big-box stores. We protected some four thousand medium to large US cities and municipal computer systems. Hospitals counted on us to protect their patients' privacy, while biotech firms relied on us to protect their billion-dollar research and development data. We operated in another twenty-two countries and, except for a few of our intel packages, offered most of our products and services to them as well. We did not do business with nation-states that harbor or support terrorist and hacking groups—think China, Russia, Iran, and North Korea, to name a few.

It was a huge undertaking and took a good amount of dedicated people doing good work. And not one of our customers had had their systems hacked or hijacked and held for ransom while under the protection umbrella of Securetech. This couldn't be said for our competitors, which was why we were currently experiencing incredible growth, both domestically and internationally. In December of 2020, we notified the National Cyber Security Centre and the UK, Canadian, and US intelligence services that eight of our clients had experienced attempted breaches against them, orchestrated by Cozy Bear, the official Russia-supported cyber security unit. None of the attacks were successful. The Russians and Chinese went after two of our biotech clients and three of the world's largest pharma companies, also our clients. None of the attempted breaches were successful. Each of the five firms led the worldwide effort in producing a Covid-19 vaccine, an Omicron vaccine, and subsequent boosters.

Being devoted to the company as she was, Renee had no time, or desire, to become mired (her word, not mine) in a long-term relationship. Renee personally hired me right out of the military six years ago, and over those years we'd formed a special bond. I was single. She was single, and as such, Renee and I enjoyed each other's company in more intimate settings. During these annual meetings, we were usually able to find a few alone hours and had taken several vacations together over the years, the latest being two months ago in Cabo San Lucas, Mexico. Other than Ben, our relationship wasn't known to anyone at the company.

Renee caught the attention of one of the roving meeting waiters and ordered a sparkling water with ice. I asked for Woodford on ice.

"No champagne today?" I asked. Champagne was the only alcoholic liquid she touched and did so whenever a social opportunity presented itself. She was a self-professed champagne snob, and I'd seen the two large built-in wine coolers in her high-rise Atlanta condo, which chilled her large collection of bottles.

"I'm going alcohol-free until I'm in London next week. How were today's team reviews?" she asked.

"All positive. We're good headed into next year. My people are solid, and I don't see any issues. Our key accounts are happy and have renewed for another year with some for another two years. Monica Andersson is doing a great job managing her territory and is a wizard at signing up new accounts."

The waiter appeared with our drinks. I continued to review the day's meetings and reviews. Renee was a good listener and asked great questions. We sat there for over an hour discussing my team's performance and Securetech's as a whole.

Renee reached behind her and grabbed an envelope, which she handed to me. "I'd give this to you later when we're alone, but we should complete the public show. It's your bonus check." She put out her hand and shook mine. She smiled, kicked the water with her foot, said, "Ben and I value your contribution to the company, but more importantly, we both trust you . . . completely. If your schedule allows, we'd like you to fly to Atlanta next week and meet with us to discuss the details of the new position of President, USA Operations. We feel that you're the right person for the job. Congratulations."

Dumfounded, I simply stared at her, although I managed a quick peek inside the envelope—$75,000! *Astonishment* was a better word. Being handed such a large bonus check, then being told a promotion to president was in the works, had caught me completely off guard. Pleasantly so, of course.

Seeing the look on my face, she smiled, said, "Because of the tremendous growth in our international business, Ben and I feel we need to focus more of our own efforts there. But we can't do that until we have the right person in place here in the States, someone we can trust taking over most of our North American responsibilities. And we feel that someone is you. If you're interested, of course."

My mouth must have hung open in surprise, for Renee smiled, hit the top of my head with her knuckles, said, "Hello in there."

Recovering, I said, "I'm interested. Heck, I'm more than interested . . . I accept. I'll make sure my schedule is cleared and fly out next week after I know you've flown back from London. Thank you for the trust and confidence you and Ben have shown in me. And thank you for the check. It's very generous." A check that large meant a good-sized chunk of the mortgage on my condo in downtown Seattle would be paid off.

Renee stood. "Well, you deserve it. Give some thought to who you think should be your replacement."

"Shall we promote from within?"

"For sure. Now I've got to go up to my room and shower. Big dinner tonight—we've taken over TAO Asian Bistro. It should be good." She leaned in and lowered her voice. "Give me a five-minute head start, then knock on my door. We'll shower together. Sound good to you, Mr. Kristen?"

I stood, and we performed a professional hug, this for the sake of our fellow Securetech colleagues who might be watching.

"See you up there," I whispered in her ear.

She smiled, turned, and walked toward the hallway leading to the elevator banks, shaking hands and offering quick hugs along the way.

Across the pool, Ben was in a meeting with another team member, but I caught his eye. He gave me a thumbs-up and smiled. I mouthed a thank-you and grabbed the waiter for another Woodford.

THREE

As promised, dinner at TAO had been wonderful. During dessert, Ben had dinged his wineglass, and the dining room had fallen silent. He and Renee then announced the creation of the new position of President of North American Operations. They had me stand, and Ben introduced the new president to the assembled domestic team. I gave a very brief speech where I thanked Ben and Renee for the opportunity, spoke of the important work done by all, next year's new menu of services the company was introducing, and then thanked each of my team members, by name, for making me look good.

After a half hour of congratulatory hugs and handshakes, all 210 of us, each armed with our thousand-dollar seed money, made our way to the private casino the hotel was providing us. And best of all . . . a Vegas rarity, a no-smoking casino!

I found a place at the craps table next to Renee and Ben, and we spent the next five hours placing bets and moving chips. Ben and Renee, being smarty-pants, overanalyzed bet percentages and generally lost.

By five in the morning, I, on the other hand, had parlayed the original thousand into something bigger. A lot bigger . . .

$27,000. I wouldn't say skill played an important role in the night's success—I was hot with the dice and pure luck was beyond doubt the main ingredient.

Renee, standing next to me at the table, suggested we quit playing and have an early breakfast at the hotel's Grand Lux Café, in my opinion, one of the best places for breakfast in Las Vegas. I grabbed my chips, tipped the croupier, and we made our way to the casino-side café.

A hostess greeted us and sat us at a four-top out on the indoor patio overlooking the hotel's main casino.

We ordered breakfast, and while waiting for our food to arrive, I went to the cashier's cage across the patio and cashed out my chips. The total was $27,380.00. Wow, just wow.

"Do I need to fill out any IRS forms?" I asked the cashier.

"What games were you playing, sir? Slots, keno, bingo, or a poker tournament?"

"It's all from craps."

"Then you just got lucky again, sir. For whatever reason, the IRS doesn't require you to fill out their W-2G form when the winnings are from a table game like craps, roulette, blackjack, or baccarat. No one besides the IRS understands why. It's just the way it is. But they do require you to declare these winnings on your tax return. If you'd won on a non-table game, I'd have you fill out the W-2G form, and the casino would withhold twenty-five percent of your total winnings."

"Are there alternatives to taking cash or a check?" My father was constantly nagging at me to buy and hold gold, and I figured now would be as good a time as any.

"Not here at the cage, but the jewelry and coin shop next door will exchange cash for gold. It'll cost a few percentage points, but it may be worth it to you."

"Thanks. I'll do that. Have a good day."

"You too, sir. You're certainly off to a good start," she said as she pushed two piles of hundred-dollar bills under the security grill. I grabbed the piles and managed to carry them next door. Estelle, the store manager, was happy to see me as I entered and even happier when I exchanged twenty-four thousand in cash for nine one-ounce South African gold Krugerrands. I also bought four quarter-ounce gold American Eagles. Her profit for three minutes of trouble was almost six hundred dollars. I'd left myself with eight hundred in cash, the most I'd ever carried.

I always wanted to own gold, and now I did. It felt great to have the weight in my pocket. All thanks to a super-hot craps table and my dad's endless nagging.

I rejoined Ben and Renee. Our food was delivered a few minutes later. Other Securetech workers had shown up for an early morning breakfast, and four of my team members were sitting at the table behind us—Kris Edwards, Monica Andersson, Jim Ventura, and Kathy Lin Canberra.

Monica Andersson was my Washington, Oregon, and British Columbia territory manager. She was the company's number one producing territory manager and happened to be Securetech's oldest employee, age-wise, at fifty-four. She was five seven with long, dark-blond hair. She usually streaked her hair with dark blue or red, but this morning she'd gone all out with purple. When she started with Securetech, she was overweight and out of shape, but after her husband of thirty years left her earlier this year, she joined a gym, and over the next nine months lost eighty pounds. She was now vibrant, strong, and happily single. With her full blessing, I referred to the new Monica as Monica Two. She reminded me of Cher, but better looking. And blond . . . with purple streaks. Monica was also my choice to succeed me. If she accepted, that is.

Kris Edwards covered Colorado, Utah, and New Mexico for us. Kris was short at five four and was in her mid-thirties. She was also blond, with deep blue eyes that could bore into you if you stared at them for long. She was a beautiful woman, with high cheekbones and what was best described as a cute little button nose. Renee and I had nicknamed her Miss America. As beautiful as she was, she was also ultra-conservative, didn't care to socialize with other team members at these gatherings, and was prudish and much too serious. But boy oh boy, could she sign up customers. But most hurtful . . . she didn't seem to appreciate my sense of humor.

Kris was famous in our company for writing a letter to Renee and Ben after I'd interviewed her for an open position and didn't advance her to the final interview stage. In her letter, she wanted to let them know what a colossal mistake I'd made by not selecting her for the position. Further, she would make it her life's mission to secure a position with our main competitor at the time and make life hell for us in her part of the country. I liked the letter and hired her the next day. Microsoft was not happy I'd recruited one of their top salespersons. Kris was going to make my life a living hell when we announced Monica as my replacement.

Kathy Lin Canberra was our Montana, Idaho, and Wyoming territory manager. She was thirty-two, five feet five, Asian American, and a gym rat, sporting cut arms and legs. She had long, thick black hair which was usually corralled in a ponytail. She was a wonderful salesperson, had an outgoing personality, and was smart, smarter than anyone I knew, smart up there on par with Renee smart. Besides handling her own territory, Kathy handled most of Securetech's more complex sales calls, travelling the country helping local salespeople with larger accounts. Her husband, Bradley, was a senior-level attorney at Amazon. They'd been trying to get pregnant with no success. They were both avid backpackers and were always camping in one forest or another.

Jim Ventura was our California, Nevada, and Arizona territory manager. Standing five nine, Jim was muscled-up from daily gym workouts and was an amateur bodybuilder/ weightlifter who had won several statewide competitions. He was bald and sported a year-round tan from living a block from the sand in Newport Beach, California. Jim was my only territory manager who didn't physically work out of our Seattle office. He was one of Renee's first hires and had told me point blank that he felt I stepped into the position he should have been offered. I'd been told he didn't care for me, which was fine, as long as he respected my position and kept his business up to snuff—which he did.

THE WAITRESS WAS POURING US a refill on coffee when the lights went out . . . not just in the café but throughout the entire casino. Every lightbulb on every slot machine went dark, and the slots' incessant carnival-like sounds went silent. The gaudy neon lights which lit up the casino gambling floor went dark too. The constant hum of overworked air-conditioning units fell silent. The only sounds were people gasping in surprise.

It was pitch dark, as dark as a deep cave, and I felt the waitress grab the back of my chair to steady herself. A few seconds later, the emergency battery-operated exit lights flickered on. The lights were located on the casino's outer perimeter walls and did little in offering light to the casino's far interior where we were sitting.

The waitress flicked on a lighter, and its flame cast enough illumination for her to make her way to the kitchen. All along her path, I could see the concerned faces of our fellow patrons.

Shocked silence was slowly being replaced by questioning voices. I took out my cell phone, and for the first time in the six months I'd had it, its screen was blacked out. I pressed the power button with no result—the phone was dead.

I held up the darkened phone, asked, "Does anyone's cell phone work?"

Phones were checked, and no one reported a working phone.

"How about Apple iWatches? Any working?"

A chorus of nopes and nos came back at me from the darkened restaurant.

Uh-oh, I thought. This wasn't looking good. Power outages happen from time to time, but I'd never heard of a power outage killing cell phones and watches. And if it was just a power outage, then why hadn't the emergency generators kicked on?

"The generators should kick in pretty soon. Let's hang for a bit and see what happens," I said to Renee and Ben, who both thought it was a good idea.

Several seconds later, a distant but loud boom sounded, followed by a shock wave that reverberated through the casino floor.

"What the hell was that?" Ben questioned, his hands gripping the edge of the table as if needing to feel something solid and known.

And then another boom and shock wave. And another. And then more.

Questions were being asked but no one had good answers. I was detecting unease now, but it remained subtle and under control.

Another boom and shock wave hit.

"Do you think we're under some kind of attack?" Renee asked, her voice barely above a whisper.

"It's certainly possible," Ben answered, "but how do you explain dead cell phones and iWatches."

I thought I knew what had happened but kept my opinion to myself.

I could see our waitress weaving her way through the tables, headed in our direction. She was holding several lit table candles. "We use these at night, but I don't see why we can't use them now," she said, setting one on our table. She smiled, but her happy facial expression couldn't hide the worry in her eyes.

"For our bill and the table behind us," Renee said to the waitress, handing her two one-hundred-dollar bills, saying thanks and to keep the change.

We half-heartedly pecked at our food. Four or five minutes had gone by and still no power. The exit lights were starting to dim as the batteries slowly drained down. I wanted to know what was happening outside, so I stood, said to our group, "Who wants to head outside and see what's going on?"

Besides our two tables, I could make out a couple dozen hands raised in the air. Monica dug in her purse and pulled out a small pen-sized flashlight. "Look," she said, "it even works." Light flooded her table, and we all clapped and shouted out, "Yes, Monica!"

"Here, Jon, lead the way," she said, handing me the flashlight.

"Okay, everyone, you may want to stay behind me," I suggested. "And I know this may sound corny, but let's hold hands as we make our way outside. We have a distance to go to get to the main check-in lobby. Let's try and stay together."

Without hesitation, we formed a conga line and made our way from the casino floor toward the hotel's main lobby, Renee's hand in mine.

FOUR

Some minutes later, we emerged into the chilly, early morning desert air in the hotel's covered outdoor parking check-in area. We stood together in shocked silence as we took in the scene unfolding in front of us: cars with hoods up, the owners peering under them, a long line of taxis in the pickup lane all dead, cars stopped in the middle of Las Vegas Boulevard with the owners standing idly by as if waiting for them to magically restart. And only silence where there was usually a loud and constant din of a noisy, vibrantly alive Las Vegas.

All the world-famous Vegas neon lights were out, every single bulb, tens of millions of them, dark and dead, as far as the eye could see. And up and down the Las Vegas Strip, black smoke and flames were rising from below-ground electrical transformers. Hundreds and hundreds of them.

In the distance, toward Harry Reid Airport, we could see thick black plumes of smoke rising into the air. I knew then that those were planes that had fallen out of the sky and were most likely the source of the booms and shock waves we'd heard and felt earlier. Those planes could each carry hundreds of passengers whose lives had most likely ended in terror. If I remembered my trivia correctly, at any one time in the US, there were roughly nine thousand planes in the air carrying a little over 1.2 million passengers. And if this event was national in scope, then they'd probably all just perished.

Renee wrapped her sweater tightly around her to ward off the desert's morning chill. "You have any idea of what's happening?" she asked, grabbing my arm and hugging it to her.

"I do, and it's not good," I said, taking my sports coat off and draping it over her shoulders.

Ben had overheard. "You thinking what I'm thinking?" he asked, eyes glued to the scene in front of us.

"If it's an EMP, then yes," I answered.

Renee looked from me to Ben, said, "EMP, as in electromagnetic pulse? Seriously?"

"Yes. This could be the real deal," I said. "The electrical grid is probably down."

"So, our cell phones are forever toast?" she asked.

"Yes, and not just cell phones. Everything that runs and is controlled by a computer chip is now toast and will never work again," Ben answered, gazing at the dead cars and fires up and down Las Vegas Boulevard. "Which means all electronics, transportation—planes, trains, automobiles—are pretty much useless now."

"And no way to communicate," I added.

Monica and Kris both looked at their dark, dead cell phones and nodded in understanding.

"How'd this happen?" a visibly upset Kathy asked. "Maybe the electrical grid was hacked again?"

"I'd say yes to that possibility, except our cell phones, watches, and all these cars appear to be dead," I said.

"Only a couple of things could cause this kind of widespread outage," Ben answered, "and that's a nuclear detonation or a solar flare. I don't think it was a solar flare, as we'd have heard about any unusual solar activity."

"I don't see a mushroom cloud." This from Jim Ventura, our California manager.

"Me either," Monica seconded.

"The detonation most likely occurred in the upper atmosphere. We would never have seen it," I explained.

Jim appeared puzzled. "What about radioactive fallout?"

"There won't be any if it detonated beyond our atmosphere," Ben answered.

"How widespread do you think this is? Do you think other parts of the country or world have been affected by this EMP?" These questions from Monica.

Ben considered the questions, answered, "One well-placed blast over the Midwest could, theoretically anyway, take out the electrical grid for the entire country . . . probably most of Canada and northern Mexico as well. But why stop with just one? If it was me, to make sure the job was done right, I'd send three or four. Whoever did this to us probably did it to other countries as well."

"Who would do this?" Renee asked.

"Well, North Korea would be a good guess. From what I've read, they have the capability of sending missiles our way with a payload onboard. But they haven't mastered the art of reentry survival. However, they could easily have them detonate in space," I said. "Then there's Russia, China, Iran, and a host of other countries that can put together something like . . ."

". . . I'm going to go with a terrorist group," Ben stated, cutting in. "Probably funded by the Iranians."

"But we just did a prisoner exchange with the Iranians and we lifted some of the harsher sanctions we'd imposed a few years ago," Kathy said. "Why send missiles now when relations are getting better?"

"I agree with you, Kathy. But don't forget about China," Renee said. "After Putin lost power, China was left on their own. The new government in Russia cut off oil to China. I just read somewhere that China has lost some forty percent of its armed forces personnel to the Delta and Omicron viruses. China is weak now, and I'm sure they blame us for their problems."

"All good points," Ben said.

Renee put her hand to her mouth as if in sudden realization, said, "We have over two hundred employees here. How the hell are we going to get them home?"

No one volunteered an answer.

"We're not," I finally said, breaking the silence. "Because we can't."

"We have to, and we will," Renee stated firmly, head up and posture stiff.

"How?" Ben asked. "Except for a few old prop airplanes, nothing is ever going to fly again. Cars, buses, trains, and trucks don't work, at least more modern vehicles operating with onboard computers won't."

"Then we'll wait for the police or military to do something. I mean, this is what the government is supposed to take care of. Right?" Jim asked.

"Wrong. Do you see any firefighters battling these fires?" Ben responded. "Their trucks depend on computer chips—to start the thing, let alone being able to spray water on a fire. Same thing with police cars. And as far as government assistance . . . forget it. They're in the same boat we are. How are they going to get help to us when they're waiting for help themselves?"

"So, what you're saying is we're suddenly living back in the eighteenth century," Kathy said. "Horses and buggies and outhouses."

"Good analogy," I replied. "And very true. Especially the outhouse part, as there are no more working water and sewage treatment plants."

"I need to grab my stuff from the room and get to the airport," Kris said, tears starting to flow. "I have two little kids at home, and I need to be with them."

"No, you're not," Ben said gently. "There are no working aircraft to take anyone anywhere. For years, maybe even decades."

Renee walked over to Kris and hugged her tightly. Kris offered no resistance and fell into Renee's arms.

After a few minutes of silence, I caught Ben's and Renee's attention and had them walk with me away from the others.

"You do know we're screwed, right?" I said, more of a statement than a question.

Seeing them nod agreement, I continued. "You've got two hundred employees here with no way to get home. The hotel is going to run out of food in a few days, and then what? The water has probably already stopped flowing, as the treatment plants and pumping stations are toast. The government isn't going to be of any help, at least not any time soon. The police aren't going to be able to quell the lawlessness that's bound to happen. At first, they'll be out there trying to keep the peace, but at some point, the officers are going to want to return to their families and homes. As food supplies disappear off store shelves and home pantries empty, desperate and hungry people are going to do desperate things. Like killing for a bag of rice or a bottle of water."

I took a good look at the growing crowd and saw dozens of fellow team members. "What I suggest you two do, is gather together the entire group right now, as best you can, and tell them what we think has happened. Speak frankly about what will likely happen in the next few days and weeks. Get some of the managers together and start working on some kind of game plan that will get them home, but more importantly, a plan that will help them survive. Maybe work up a plan to walk home. Or head to the local bike shop and get ahold of a bunch of bikes."

"Seriously, Jon? How are we going to feed two hundred walking or biking people, let alone protect them?" Ben asked. "This isn't Sherman's March through the South where they ransacked every plantation and farmhouse along the way."

"Well, maybe it is," I replied. "Within a few days, you'll start to see people killing others as starving folks who haven't prepared for an event like this find themselves willing to do anything to feed themselves and their families."

"Wait! Wait! Wait!" Renee shouted out, grabbing ahold of my arm. Realizing others could hear, she brought her voice to a near whisper. "Ben, the Feds are going to come for us. Remember the program review meeting we had in DC? Part of the operational terms is that they know where you, me, and the thirty off-duty team members that run the site are at all times. They would have been advised of our whereabouts before we left Atlanta. They know we're here. They need the Kentucky facility, now more than ever. They need us, guys!"

"What are you talking about?" I asked, not understanding.

"She's talking about the server farm we designed, built, and run for the federal government," Ben answered. "It also houses a Summit supercomputer, which is the second fastest computer in the world."

I looked at them both and put my palms up as if waiting for a further explanation.

Renee looked at me, said, "This is something we would have shared with you had you flown out to Atlanta next week."

"With your new position, you would have been given overall responsibility for the project," Ben added.

"I accepted the position, guys, now tell me. Please."

"Sure," Renee answered. "Ben, you want to explain, since it's more your project than mine?"

"Six years ago, the Office of Strategic Services approached us looking for help in building a super-secret, super-secure server farm," Ben began. "They wanted every federal agency, including all branches of the military, to have duplicate software and database storage. They didn't completely trust the cloud-based storage available at the time and wanted a hard backup of the backup's backup. Every night, that day's government business, every single bit of it, is automatically encrypted and downloaded to Securetech headquarters' servers. And then encrypted again and transferred to the secure server farm. Since the SolarWinds hack by the Russians, it's . . ."

"Where is it?" I asked, interrupting Ben. "Sorry for cutting in."

"No worries," Ben replied.

"A little west of a small Kentucky town named Knifley," Renee answered. "The locals think it's a storage site for government paperwork, so they aren't curious and don't seem to care about it. We purchased fifteen hundred acres of forested land and leveled one hundred. It took two and a half years to build and is ultra-secure, and most importantly, it's EMP proof. The entire building sits forty feet underground and is completely lined with a special lead coating . . . it's akin to a giant faraday cage. A faraday cage is . . ."

"I know what a faraday cage is," I said. "I have a small faraday bag sitting in the cargo box on top of my Land Cruiser."

"Are you some kind of prepper?" Ben asked me.

"Not at all. But my parents are and have been for years . . . as long as they've run the ranch at any rate. And my dad bugs me about protecting things, and bugs and bugs me until it's just easier to do what he suggests."

"Always good to be prepared," Ben said. He then turned his attention back to Renee.

"You really think the Feds will come looking for us?" Ben asked, getting back to the discussion at hand.

"There's a rotating group of workers at the site. Thirty people on for a month and thirty off for a month. We have housing for a hundred team members on-site, food and other supplies to last years. The facility is totally self-sufficient—we even have our own pulse-protected hydro-electric plant, which is why we built next to a lake.

"But both shift managers are here in Vegas along with the lucky thirty that had the month off, which makes the site leaderless. The Feds know we're here, and I bet they are probably already planning on getting us home."

"How will they get here?" I asked. "I mean, they use airplanes, trucks, and cars like we do."

"We're talking about the federal government, after all. They must have prepared for this at some point," Renee said.

"So, we wait, is that what you're suggesting?" Ben asked.

"I think that's probably best. But I don't know how many Securetech team members the Feds will be able to transport," Renee said. "Could be the thirty plus the two managers or just the managers and you or me, Ben."

"You think we could demand that all two hundred of us are given transportation back to our homes?" Ben asked. "I mean, we have something they want and need. Us."

"We can certainly ask. Do I think they'll provide it? No, I don't. Do we wait for the Feds to contact us?" Renee asked. "And how long should we wait?"

"I say we wait until six tonight," Ben answered. "Eleven hours or so. If, as you say, they know we're here, they probably have a team being assembled now to come get us."

They both looked at me.

"You're looking at me why?" I asked.

"The three of us are the company leaders, and I want to know what you think," Renee said.

"I've waited a lot longer than twelve hours at airport gates for a flight. I say let's give 'em until six tonight."

"What shall we tell the rest of the team members?" Ben asked.

"Everything, except the part about the server farm. We can't breathe a word of that," Renee said. "But I don't see why we can't say that there will be a possibility of a ride home from the Feds."

"What about the thirty server farm workers and two managers that are here? Do they know to remain quiet?" I asked.

"Oh yeah," Renee answered. "Security is a huge concern at the farm and has been drilled into them. We've all signed ironclad government nondisclosure forms."

"What possible reason can we give that would explain the Feds giving us a ride home?" Ben asked.

"We tell them we've been working on a project for the government and that they need us back in Atlanta to complete it," Renee said. "The truth, or a version of it, is always best."

"I agree. Let's assemble as many Securetech team members as possible in the main lobby . . . say in an hour or so, and explain the situation," I said. "Tell them there's a chance that they might have a ride or flight back east."

"Okay. Good suggestion," Ben said.

There was an abandoned taxi next to us, and I hopped up on the hood and then the roof. I cupped my hands together, shouted, "Attention Securetech team members, we have an announcement to make in an hour in the hotel's main check-in lobby. That's the lobby right inside these doors. Please let other team members know. It's important."

I jumped to the ground and rejoined Renee and Ben.

"At this point, I don't know what else we can do but wait," Ben said.

FIVE

I t was an hour later, and the hotel's large main check-in lobby was packed with anxious-looking Securetech team members. Word of the meeting had spread to non-Securetech employees as well, and there was a fifty-fifty mix of Securetech team members and the random guest or hotel employee present.

Renee, Ben, and I stood in front of the hundred-foot-long check-in desk.

"I don't think it's a good idea to mention a possible ride home with this mixed group in attendance," I said, glancing at the assembled crowd. "Maybe provide an idea of what we think has happened and then ask our team members to relocate to one of the ballrooms for more information."

Ben and Renee both agreed. Ben then stood on the priority check-in desk and waited for the room to quiet down. Which it soon did. He began speaking.

"You've all no doubt noticed that the power is out."

Many people chuckled or exchanged comments, the main one being, "No shit."

"What you're probably thinking is that this is a temporary power outage, not unlike last year's power grid outage we experienced at the hands of Putin's old Russia and the Chinese government."

"It'll come back on," someone shouted out. "Just like last year's outage."

Ben shook his head. "I wish it was like last year's outage," Ben answered. "But it's not. What's most likely happened is an electromagnetic pulse event. This is more commonly referred to as an EMP event. An EMP can be caused by two things: a solar flare or a nuclear explosion.

"You'll remember this one. Back in February of 2022, NASA reported that a mundane geomagnetic space storm, better known as a coronal mass ejection of plasma from the sun, rendered forty newly launched SpaceX Starlink satellites useless. But we saw that ejection two days before it arrived. If it was a solar flare this morning, we would have heard about it. We didn't. No, we think this morning's event was caused by a nuclear explosion in the upper atmosphere, most likely above the Midwest."

The lobby was stunned into almost total silence, with only quiet gasps heard throughout the large space.

"What makes you think it was an EMP?" someone in the crowd asked.

"Good question. How many of you have power in your cell phones or Apple Watches? Ben waited as the crowd brought their phones out and checked the screens, then turned their wrists and saw a blank screen. "Anyone? No one. Right? And bad news, folks, your phones, iWatches, iPads, computers, cars . . . anything with a computer chip has been rendered useless and will never work again. This means no airplanes, cars, buses, or any vehicle newer than the early seventies are working. Your credit and debit cards are now useless. Have you seen the parking lot and roadway out front? The cars and trucks are dead and will never run again."

"Any idea when the power will be restored?" a uniformed hotel employee shouted out from the back of the lobby.

"Another good question. If I had to guess, perhaps in ten to fifteen years."

His answer was met with silence. And then the room erupted into dozens of questions being hurled in Ben's direction.

"Bullshit! How can that be?" was the one question that could be heard above the rest.

"Let's work it backwards, shall we?" Ben said, sounding like the college professor he once was. "Your home gets power from the pole behind your house or under your home's front yard. On that pole or underground utility box is a transformer that steps down the voltage so your electrical panel hiding behind artwork on the wall in your house or garage can handle the delivered power. Those transformers and power lines are now toast—literally. Those power lines lead to neighborhood power substations. You know the ones I'm talking about. The ones surrounded by chain-link fences with weird-looking towers, coils, and metal boxes containing transformers inside the fence line? There's like sixty thousand of them in the US alone."

"There's one two blocks from my house," someone shouted out.

"Even small towns have two or three of them," Ben said. "Those are also now crispy critters."

"Seriously?" a man in the back asked.

"Have you looked down the street?" Ben asked him.

"Well, no," came the answer.

"If you had, you'd have seen hundreds of fires. Most of the fires are transformers burning. But let me put it this way: of those sixty thousand substations . . . all that's needed to shut down the entire electrical grid is for nine of them to fail. Nine, people. In this case, all sixty thousand most likely failed."

There was silence in the lobby as each of us tried to comprehend the extent of the possible damage.

Ben let the silence go on for ten seconds, then continued the lecture.

"The substations are fed via stepped-up high-voltage transmission lines. These are the power lines that are a hundred feet off the ground and held up by those huge robot-looking steel towers? Burned and most likely sitting on the ground, which caused hundreds of thousands of fires that are probably raging out of control as we speak."

"How do you know all this?" a woman in the middle of the lobby asked.

"I'm an electrical engineer," Ben answered. No one questioned Ben's qualifications.

"Now we're at the power plants, whether it be coal fed, oil, natural gas, wind, solar, or hydro—such as the Hoover Dam a few miles from here. Those are all run by computers, which manage a zillion more transformers.

"All useless. Garbage. Throw it all out. Now, all of this, which we call the electrical grid, took one hundred and forty years to build. And that was when there were manufacturing plants to build all those wires and transformers. There are tens of millions of transformers that need to be built to replace the ones that burned out a few hours ago. And then three million miles of transmission lines to carry the power from plants that have to be rebuilt. And how are we going to be able to manufacture all this when there's not one factory up and running?

"It will take years to get the first manufacturing plant operational. So, yeah, fifteen years. Probably more."

The crowd digested the news. "What were those loud booms we heard and tremors we felt right after the power went out?" a woman asked.

"Airplanes falling out of the sky," Ben answered, which produced more gasps.

"How will we get home?" someone asked.

Another asked, "I live in Los Angeles. How am I supposed to get home?"

"The answer to both those questions is walking," Ben said. "Gather as much water and food as you can carry and get going. It's good weather for walking."

"What about the government? They'll take care of us."

"I doubt it. The government is in the same predicament we are. How are they going to get here? But if you think waiting for the government to arrive is the right thing to do, then wait. There's always a chance they'll show up.

"That's all we know. Securetech team members, follow me into the Venetian Ballroom for further information."

Ben jumped down off the desk and led a procession of a hundred and fifty or so Securetech team members down the hallway and through a large set of open double doors. Two hotel security guards with flashlights stood behind Securetech team leaders checking to make sure all who entered were employees.

Renee and I followed the crowd into the ballroom and spotted Ben.

"Well?" Ben asked us.

"What you said was on point," I answered. "Short and to the point."

"Maybe so, but this next part is going to be the difficult one. I could be getting their hopes up to just let them down."

"Give them credit for understanding your position. Just give it to them straight," Renee said, putting her hand on Ben's arm and giving him a reassuring squeeze.

"I fear that I might just be blowing smoke up their behinds," Ben said.

SIX

We watched the last of the team members enter the ballroom. The security guards then stepped out into the hallway, and the doors were shut behind them. There were many exits from this ballroom, and each one had an Exit Here sign that was still providing some emergency lighting. The room was dark, but not pitch dark.

The stage that had been set up for yesterday's Securetech events was still in place. Ben made his way up and stood on the audience-side of the speaker's dais.

"Okay, everyone, listen up," he said. "I didn't want to say this in front of non-team members, but there is an outside chance that the federal government will be coming for us. There's a project we've been working on in conjunction with the Feds, and we're fairly confident that they'll want us back in Atlanta working on it. Does that knowledge translate into actual transport? Who knows? We're waiting to see if they show up."

"And what if they don't show up? How do you propose we get home?" one of the Atlanta-based product managers asked.

"That's a good question, Helen. But I don't have an answer for you right now. Let's all just cool our jets and wait for word.

There are many team members not present. Do me a favor and try and locate them and have them come down here to wait. The hotel has generously provided us with bottled water and snacks. That's it for now." Ben made his way to the back of the room where Renee and I waited. "Now we wait," Ben said. "Fingers crossed someone shows up."

"Renee, who would have a master list of our employees and their assigned rooms?" I asked.

"That would be Louanne Phillips. She's the redhead standing next to the exit doors. Why?"

"Might be a good idea to have her check the names of those present here in the ballroom, then send security to the rooms of the missing employees. They need to get down here."

"Good idea, Mr. President of North American Operations," she said, walking off to make it happen.

"Renee, don't forget the company's two pilots," Ben said. "They need to get home too."

———

IT WAS NOW EIGHT IN the morning. Renee and Ben began working the room, answering questions and trying to put folks at ease.

As is the case with most corporate affairs, regional teams stick together, so it was no surprise that seven of my team members made their way to where I waited. They grabbed chairs and set up a semicircle away from other employees.

It was now two hours later. We'd been shooting the breeze and killing time. Security had woken many team members who had slept in late, but there were still a few missing.

"Any idea where the rest of the team members are?" I asked the group.

"Where we should be. In bed," Monica answered.

"I agree, but you should wait here in case the Feds do show up and we have to move fast. They're not going to wait for stragglers."

"What's this project that Atlanta is working on?" Kathy asked.

"I don't know the full answer to that. Sorry."

Which was a small white lie, and it didn't feel right as soon as I said it.

Ben and Renee finished a conversation with a group of Atlanta-based programmers and walked over to us. They grabbed two chairs and joined our group.

Twenty minutes later, the main ballroom doors opened, and a dozen men and women dressed in black with black helmets and night-vision goggles streamed into the room. Each carried a short-barreled machine pistol with green laser sights, their green targeting beams dancing around the ballroom. Even though they weren't dressed in military fatigues, they were very well trained and were probably ex-military, or at the very least, government trained.

"Well, hell, that was fast," Ben said.

The dozen formed a large circle by the doors and waited a full minute before a middle-aged Black woman in a black business suit with no-nonsense black shoes stepped into the room. She had silver hair that barely touched her shoulders and had a contrasting light-gray scarf around her neck and shoulders. The woman was nondescript in every way and was someone you wouldn't think twice about—perfect for security work.

"She looks familiar," Ben said as we watched the woman stop in the center of the security circle.

"That's because we've met her," Renee whispered. "In our offices, before construction began in Kentucky. She's in charge of national project security."

The woman put on a pair of thick black-framed reading glasses. "I'm looking for Renee Knowles and Ben Ives," she said, reading from a piece of paper. "If present, please step forward."

She removed her glasses and scanned the room.

"Showtime," Ben said, raising his hand. "Let's hear what she has to say."

"Good luck, guys," I said.

Renee and Ben strode to the middle of the circle and shook hands with the woman. The three then turned and strode out of the ballroom. The armed men remained in place.

Forty minutes later, the three returned. Renee pointed to me and gave me a come-here wave. I joined the three in the circle.

"Jon, this is Wilma Patterson. She's in charge of project security for the government's Strategic Security Services department. The person who handles security for our Kentucky facility is in Europe, and they don't know when she'll be able to return. Ms. Patterson is filling in for her."

We shook hands and nodded in greeting.

"We have good news and bad news," Ben said. "The good news is that Ms. Patterson has one working pulse-proofed C130 at her disposal. It's a stretch version and can carry one hundred and twenty-eight fully equipped soldiers."

"Or close to two hundred civilians," I said. "Maybe more if you limit their luggage to a single carry-on."

"Very good, Mr. Kristen," Ms. Patterson said. "Excellent guess."

"I've been in a few, Ms. Patterson."

"I'm aware," she said.

"Well, that is good news," I said. "Our team members get a lift back east. But let me guess what the bad news is—they're only flying in one direction. East."

"Again, impressive."

"They refuse to budge on this point, Jon," Ben said. "This C130 flew in from San Diego to pick up a group of congressmen and their wives. Then agent Patterson learned of its arrival and commandeered the congressmen's ride. There are a bunch of pissed off politicians."

"Serves 'em right," Renee said. "But we refused to leave without our team members. Agent Patterson has agreed to allow the plane to stop in St. Louis to drop off Karen Kemp and her team members. It will then go on to Atlanta."

"Our employees are getting rides back to Atlanta. That's the important thing," I said.

And Renee with them. I felt an ache in my chest and knew I would miss her something fierce.

"I am truly sorry, Mr. Kristen," Agent Patterson said. "This was not my decision. The poop rolled downhill from a very high mountain on this—something along the lines of fuel conservation. But from what I've learned from reading your file is that you're a very capable guy. You'll get home."

I lowered my voice. "What's going to happen to the Kentucky workers' families?" I asked, directing the question to Wilma Patterson. "I assume you're going to want all sixty team members living full-time at the facility. Are you going to provide for the families while our team members are away in Kentucky?"

"I asked the same question," Ben said.

"And the answer is yes," Renee said. "Family members will be provided food and shelter at a government-run VIP facility. Congress, Senate, cabinet members, their key staffers, and all their families, will be their full-time roommates."

"Well, that's good," I said. I figured nothing ventured, nothing gained, so I took a shot. "If my Seattle-based team members want to fly to Atlanta, will you take them?"

"How many?"

"Four."

"We can make that happen," she answered.

"Ben, if they flew with you, could you provide food and shelter for them?"

"I . . . uh . . . guess we . . . Yes, we could figure something out," Ben answered.

"Thank you. Ms. Patterson, can you share with us any information on what caused the blackout?" I asked.

"I haven't heard anything official yet, but an EMP event would be my guess."

"That's what we figured as well. Let me tell my team members that there's a seat on the plane for them and a place to live in Atlanta."

She nodded. "You have two minutes."

I nodded a silent thank-you and walked back to my group.

They listened as I explained that there was a seat on the plane going to Atlanta should they want it. Without getting into too much detail, I then told them I had a working vehicle in the hotel's parking structure and that I planned to drive to Seattle. "I have room to take five passengers."

"There's nothing for me in Atlanta," Monica said. "Besides, I've been there a couple of times and didn't really care for the place."

"I have two kids waiting for me at home," Kris said. "It's out of the question."

Kathy said she'd stick with me. Jim remained silent.

Four of our group were our Atlanta-based support admins and would be among those flying home.

"Attention, everyone," Ben said from the stage. The room quickly quieted down. "We have transport back to Atlanta with a stop in St. Louis. There is a C130 waiting for us at Harry Reid Airport."

The room erupted in applause.

Ben motioned with his hands to quiet down. "Go back to your rooms and pack a carry-on bag or backpack. Only one. There is a weight limit that this aircraft must adhere to, and you can't be bringing on a bunch of luggage. You have one hour to get your stuff and get back down to this ballroom. We leave in one hour and ten minutes. Wear comfortable shoes, as we're walking to the airport. It's not far, maybe four miles. These gentlemen and ladies will be escorting us. The vehicle transport that brought them here has left for another hotel and is unavailable to us.

"Louanne and hotel security were able to get forty-five additional team members down here, but we're still missing another nineteen. If you see other team members, tell them. The elevators aren't working, so you're going to have to hoof it up and down the stairs. The room door locks are electronic and are not working—find a maid's cart and ram it into your door. If that doesn't work and you can't get into your rooms, then forget about it and get back down here. You cannot be late. Go now. Oh, wait one—a couple of additional things. Don't tell anyone that's not a Securetech team member about the plane. And this pains me to say, but leave all electronics here—they will be checking luggage and backpacks before boarding. They're useless now, anyway, and would only be dead weight. Okay. Go now, please."

Ben hopped down off the stage and walked over to me. I told him that Kathy, Monica, and Kris were sticking with me. He said they would be in good hands. "Thanks, Ben."

I was getting antsy standing around. I knew what I needed to do and just wanted to get at it. Taking care of my team members—or at least getting them headed in the right direction before all hell broke loose—was a priority.

I turned back to my four team members that wouldn't be flying today.

"Okay, guys, here's the reality we're facing. There are no planes, cars, buses, or trains that are going to get you back to Seattle or Southern California. There's no police or any kind of protection for you. Three days from now, maybe even two, this is going to be the Wild West again, and everyone is going to have to fend for themselves. It's going to be bad . . . especially for women."

"What do you mean?" Kris asked, sounding puzzled and biting her lower lip.

I thought about what to say and how to say it. It was going to be awful for the next few months, and women were going to be easy targets unless they hardened themselves. Prepared for and expected the worst from everyone they encountered along the way.

"There will be no law enforcement available to keep bad people in check. Hell, make that bad people and good people, now able to live with a sudden anything-I-want-to-do-with-no-consequences attitude. As a woman, you'll be highly prized. If you let your guard down, for even a few seconds, you'll be taken and used in ways you can't imagine. You'll be traded for food, survival gear, or weapons."

Looking at Jim, I said, "Men will be shot with no questions asked. Their wives, girlfriends, or sisters, food, and belongings taken from them."

I stopped to make sure they were listening. They were. So were Renee and Ben, who had ambled over.

"I figure the next couple of days will remain somewhat calm as most people will think this is another cyber-attack on our power grid and will try to wait it out. When the power doesn't come back on by day three or four, they're going to panic as their food and water begin to run out. Stores only have a three- or four-day supply of food on the shelves, as they count on twice-weekly deliveries from central warehouses. When they realize there's no more food or water at the stores, they're going to look for it elsewhere, starting with their neighbors and unlucky passersby. In a week, there will be total anarchy here, and you won't even recognize the place."

"I'm waiting for the government in the form of FEMA to show up," Jim said. "I'll take my chances with them. I have friends here in Vegas I can stay with until help arrives."

Jim shook hands with Ben and me, nodded to the women, turned, and made his way out of the ballroom.

"He won't even be able to get into his room, will he?" Kathy asked.

"Probably not," Ben answered for me. "Those doors are electronically controlled. The only way he can get in is to hope his roommate is still inside, have a security guard let them in with an old-fashioned key, or break it open."

"Okay, listen up," I said. "I'm going to run to the parking garage and get a crowbar we'll use to force open those room doors. Sandy, that's the name my little sister gave to my Toyota Land Cruiser, is a pre-electronic one, a 1972 model, and will run just fine. I've restored it, and it will take us home. It'll be tight, and with this many people, uncomfortable, but we'll get there. Kris, Monica, and Kathy, you've got a seat with your name on it. I can take two more.

"You guys choose who gets the other two seats. I'll leave it up to you who'll join us. But you have to decide within the next ten minutes. And choose well; you want someone that will be a team player and has some physical stamina.

"And this will not be anything like a fun and family-friendly road trip. The chances of us making it will be slim and the odds only getting better if you listen and do exactly as I say. No questions asked. You just do. I've done these kinds of road trips in Iraq and Afghanistan, and it's dangerous and is going to take some time. If you . . ."

"Like I said before, I'm in," broke in Kris. "Get me home to my babies. My husband and my parents are there and will take care of them until I get home."

"Me too." This from Monica.

"I trust you, Jon. So, I'm in," Kathy said.

"If you'll let me," Renee said, "I want to go with you."

TAKEN ABACK, BEN AND I both stood there speechless, though my heart missed a beat or two. Does happiness rate a missed beat?

"Renee, we have a plane waiting for us. What are you thinking?" Ben finally sputtered out.

"It's fine with me," I said before she could answer Ben.

"What the hell, Jon?" Ben said, giving me a hard staredown and putting his palms up in question.

I was overjoyed that Renee and I would face whatever was ahead of us together.

I turned to the other three women, said, "I'm going to get that crowbar. We'll then go to each of your rooms and wait while you gather some belongings. Stay right here for me. It shouldn't take me longer than five minutes."

Four heads nodded in the affirmative.

"Ben, you'll watch over them while I'm gone?"

"You bet. Go."

Renee turned to Ben, said, "Ben, you'll be fine. Besides, you're more familiar with the operational side of the farm than me. I'll figure a way to get in touch with you there. I prom . . .."

I didn't wait to hear any more of the conversation between the two. Ben was a capable guy and could handle anything that came his way.

Using Monica's flashlight, I ran out of the ballroom, down the hall to the lobby, and then outside. I weaved my way among the dead cars and taxis to the self-parking garage. I sprinted up the ramps to the third floor, where the Cruiser was parked. I looked around and, seeing no one nearby, scooted under the driver's door and grabbed the spare key in the magnetic hide-a-key case.

Key in hand, I unlocked the driver's door and slid behind the wheel. Crossing my fingers, I put it in neutral, depressed the clutch, inserted the key, and turned it. The engine caught on the first crank of the starter and hummed as it always did. Not wanting to attract attention, I turned it off, reached under the driver's seat, and retrieved the crowbar. I thought about grabbing the Glock out of the rooftop cargo box but decided things wouldn't go bad that quickly. It was only ten in the morning, and most people were still sleeping or just waking up.

I locked the Cruiser, pocketed the key, and hustled back to the ballroom.

I found Ben, Renee, and the three women where I'd left them. Wilma Patterson was having a heated conversation with

Ben and Renee. The conversation abruptly ended with my arrival.

"Jon, Ms. Patterson is not happy with my decision to go with you," Renee said, grabbing my arm and bringing me closer. "But she's allowing me to remain with you as long as we promise to make a real effort to get to Kentucky as soon as it's safe to do so."

Renee brought her right hand up and handed me a small electronic device.

"That is a very special emergency locater beacon," Ms. Patterson said. "You push that button, and a signal goes up to a series of pulse-protected satellites, which then activates a red light and alarm on a console deep in a mountain somewhere in the southeast. Push it again, and you'll be able to verbally compose a text message and send it to the same console. The text is limited to a hundred words. Pushing that button will start a series of events that will lead to a small elite military unit being sent to your location. You and Renee here want to pave a path back to Seattle then onto Montana and Kentucky . . . be my guest. But don't let anything happen to her, Mr. Kristen. And don't push that fucking button unless it's absolutely necessary."

"Heard and understood, ma'am," I said. "Is this thing also a GPS tracker?"

"Yes. We'll know where you are at all times. But know this, the only reason I'm going along with this is the fact that I've read your file and know you have a good shot at getting there."

With that, she turned and walked away. "You have one hour, people!" she shouted to the room as she exited through the two ballroom doors, six of the twelve armed personnel following close behind.

Ben turned to me. "Take good care of her. I want to see her again in Kentucky or Atlanta," he said. "Now get going."

Ben and Renee hugged and whispered parting words of encouragement to each other. Ben pushed away and kissed Renee's forehead.

"Jon, you could fly with us to Atlanta," Ben said.

"And leave my people to fend for themselves? I couldn't do that and sleep at night."

"I get it. But I had to ask. Please push the damn button if you find yourself in a situation you don't think you can get out of," Ben said. "But understand that it could take some time for them to get to you."

"Got it, Ben. If I don't see you before we leave, thank you for everything. I'll take good care of Renee. Scout's honor." I held out my hand, and ignoring it, Ben came in for a hug.

"Don't let anything happen to her," Ben whispered in my ear. "Good luck."

I turned and addressed the ladies.

"Stay either right beside me or directly behind. Your job is to always keep me in sight. Always. You do that and I will get you home. If you're behind me and get in trouble, or even see or sense trouble, speak up. And always keep your head on a swivel. Are we clear on that?"

Four heads nodded in unison.

"Okay, we now have one spot available. Who shall it be?" I asked the group.

Monica spoke up. "We seem to have forgotten Melissa." Of course. Jeez, how could I have forgotten her? Melissa Drake was our Seattle office manager. Melissa was twenty-three and a recent hire. While only being with us for a short two months, she'd proved her worth many times over. She'd organized the office, and me, to where we were a much smoother-running organization. She also rode her bike to the office every day and was in great shape. At five nine, she was slender and lean. She had jet-black hair cut very short on one side of her head and long on the other. She had a bunch of small stainless-steel hoops that ringed the perimeter of her right ear, had a small metal nose ring, a tongue stud, and another ring on her left eyebrow. I sometimes wondered how she got through the TSA's checkpoints without setting off every alarm the machines had. I thought at times she resembled Lisbeth Salander, the lead female character in the movie *The Girl with the Dragon Tattoo*, minus the piercings and tattoos. Then again, for all I knew, she might have had the tattoos.

"She needs to be with us. Do you know where her room is?" I asked the group.

"She's my roommate," Monica answered quietly. "I seem to have forgotten her in the mad rush that's been this morning. I guess I'm not a good roommate."

"Don't be too hard on yourself . . . I forgot as well. Let's go. The elevators aren't going to be working, so let's start at the highest floor and make our way down. Give me your room numbers."

Monica's was the highest on twenty-seven. Holding hands again, we wove our way through the lobby and casino to the emergency stairs at the very back of the main floor. We made it twelve stories before Kris asked for a rest break. Bending over at the waist, she put her hands on her knees and tried to catch her breath.

"Sorry, guys, but I have two kids and have no time to take long runs or a nightly hour or two at the gym," she explained, chest heaving in an effort to get air into her lungs. "I'm in fairly good shape, but this is really, really hard. Just a warning . . . I'm about ready to puke."

"Take two," I said. "Let's move to the side and let these people get by."

Dozens of guests were streaming down the staircase, many asking if we knew what was happening. Rather than having to explain, I replied with "power outage."

While waiting for Kris to catch her breath, two Securetech employees showed up. We briefly explained the situation with the power. We told them to go back up to their rooms, pack a single bag, and get down to the main ballroom. And pronto. Neither had roommates still in the room, so we detoured to the twenty-first and twenty-fourth floors. I had the ladies wait in the corridor outside the stairwell. I kept them in sight while I crowbarred opened the doors for the two fellow team members.

I was shocked, pleasantly so, at how easy it was to open the doors.

We made it to the twenty-seventh floor without having to stop again. Monica led us to her room, knocked, and a few seconds later, a sleepy-eyed Melissa answered the door— opening the door from the inside must be a manual function and not dependent on electrical power.

She came awake at the sight of Renee. "Did I miss a meeting or something?" she asked.

She stepped aside and held the door open for us. We streamed in, and Monica packed a carry-on while Renee filled her in on what was going on.

"We have one spot left," Renee said. "It's yours if you want it."

"You bet," Melissa quickly answered, not asking any questions.

I stepped down into the sunken living room, slid open the drapes, and took in the view from twenty-seven stories up. Their room faced the airport, some four or five miles away, its terminals and runways clearly visible.

Crash sites, flames, and black smoke rising into the still morning air, with only tail assemblies and landing gear recognizable, seemed to be everywhere. Most of the planes must have been on final approach, for several had crashed in a straight line leading to the runways. More were burning on the other end of the dual runways, with two more a quarter mile from the runway's end, one crashing on takeoff onto a golf course, and the other ending up on a freeway motel's rear parking lot.

Scattered throughout the airport were planes on taxi-ways with doors opened and emergency slides deployed. Cargo doors were open, and I could see crew members handing down stowed luggage to waiting passengers. Hundreds more were walking on runways, most of them headed in the direction of the terminals.

Sitting all by itself in a remote tarmac parking area was a gray, unmarked C130, its rear ramp down and ringed by six or seven armed guards.

To our right, I could see down the entire length of Las Vegas Boulevard—Caesars Palace, Bellagio Hotel & Casino, Aria, and the others. The Latitude Hotel, with its signature rooftop rollercoaster, was burning out of control, flames spitting out of windows, the rollercoaster leaning at a precarious angle.

Kathy and Renee walked over and took in the view.

I pointed to the Latitude, said, "The rollercoaster is about ready to come down."

"I wonder if the hotel was hit by a plane," Kathy said.

"I bet you're right," I answered. "Something had to ignite that fire, and jet fuel would certainly do it."

"There it goes," Renee said, pointing.

We watched as the rollercoaster tipped over and fell to the ground, landing two hundred feet below on dozens of cars, cabs, and airport shuttle buses parked below.

Renee turned to Melissa, said, "There's a plane taking our team members to Atlanta. There's a seat for you if you want it."

"Thanks, but I'll stick with you guys," she answered, checking her cell phone. She shook her head and threw it on the bed.

"Then pack a bag with essentials only," I said. "Change into jeans and sneakers if you have them. Monica, get out of that dress and put on something you can travel in. And ditch the heels. Bring all the socks and underwear you have, too. Toothbrush, toothpaste, and hand soap. And take all the towels and blankets you can carry. Then take the toilet paper, even the roll on the dispenser. Oh, and grab a pillow or two. Finally, raid the minibar of everything, booze and snacks, and put it in a roll-on bag. We can go through it later.

"You have fifteen minutes. I'll wait out in the corridor so you can change."

I stepped out to the corridor and shut the door behind me. Five seconds later, the door opened and out came Kris, Renee, and Kathy.

"That was a test of your instructions, wasn't it?" Kathy asked. "The one where we always keep you in sight."

"Yep, and you passed."

A few minutes later, Monica and Melissa emerged ready to go. Over the next hour, we visited my room on seventeen, Renee's on sixteen, and Kris's and Kathy's on ten. We needed the crowbar on all of them.

While waiting for Kris and Kathy to pack, the rest of us went to the window and took in the view. Renee pointed down the street, and there were our team members walking to the airport, wheeling suitcases behind them or with backpacks on. Surrounding the group were the armed guards. From this high up, I couldn't pick out Ben or Wilma Patterson.

We made our way down the concrete stairs, and even lugging luggage and backpacks, the going was much easier. We emerged out on the casino floor and headed to the self-park garage. We marched up the ramps and came to the Cruiser. I opened the driver's and passenger doors, then went around to the back and swung the spare tire to the side and opened both rear doors.

"The Cruiser's nickname is Sandy—named by my younger sister, Abs, after one of our ranch horses that could climb hillsides like the Cruiser. There are two inward-facing jump seats back here, ladies. Each one folds down and holds two people . . . you decide who goes where. But first, who here knows how to fire an AR-15?"

Melissa's hand shot up. "I grew up in a gun family. Both of my brothers and dad have one."

"Good, you're riding shotgun and will carry the AR whenever we're in the Cruiser. Do you think you could shoot at someone? Be honest with your answer."

"Yes, I think I can if the situation requires it."

"All right then. Ladies, pile the roll-on bags in the back and squeeze in where you can. We're making a stop a few blocks away, and we'll rearrange there." I reached up and unlocked the black fiberglass Thule cargo carrier. Once unlocked, the rear rose on its own, and I grabbed the AR and Glock. Both were loaded with a full magazine each. I shut and relocked the storage case and handed the AR to Melissa, who was already seated in front.

"Charge it, please. Let me see that you know how."

She released and dropped the mag, checked it and the empty chamber, then reinserted the mag, giving it a good smack to make sure it was fully seated. She released the bolt carrier, and once the safety was off, the Colt was ready to fire. Her finger never touched the trigger.

"Nicely done. Safety back on, please." I reached over her, placed the Glock on the center armrest, and then shut her door.

"Jon, we have a problem back here," Renee said.

SEVEN

hree men were standing next to the four women. All three were in their late twenties, and looking them over, I figured they were security, though nothing they wore gave any indication as to their actual duties. They were dressed in pressed khakis and white polo shirts, the shirts sporting the casino logo. They were clean-cut and had gold-and-black hotel name tags over the right chest. They were bunched up together—if they were street fighters, they'd forgotten the golden rule: spread out.

Mike, the bigger of the three at maybe six two, spoke up. "Our cars aren't working. Can you give us a ride? We live about ten miles from here."

"Sorry, wish we could, but we're full up, as you can see," I said. "Besides, ten miles is an easy walk for you guys. You probably cover that distance during a shift."

"I don't think you understand, mister," Mike said. "We need a ride." The smaller of the three turned his wrist, revealing a steak knife in his hand. He held it out for us to inspect. "Give us the keys."

"Really, guys? That's it? One knife? I've got to say, I'm not exactly shaking in my loafers."

"Yeah, really, asshole. And we're through asking nicely," Rob, the smaller one, said. "There's three of us and one of you, unless the women want to jump in. Which could be fun."

"Turn around and walk away," I said.

"Or what?" Rob asked.

The third guy, an Asian—his name tag said "Po"—was smaller than Mike but slightly taller than Rob, backed up as if not sure he wanted any part of what looked likely to happen.

"Last warning," I said.

"Give us the keys to the fucking Jeep," Rob hissed, lips pressed together and his face turning red.

"Jon?" Kris asked, stepping away from the three.

"This will be over soon, Kris. I promise. And, Rob, never ever call a Land Cruiser a Jeep. That's just plain wrong. And I do my best to correct a wrong."

"You do, do you? Well fuck—" Rob began to say.

I always try to tone down fight impulses with calm banter, but all bets are off once a weapon appears.

Before he finished his sentence, I took two quick steps toward Rob and with my right foot kicked the knife out of his hand. Then, with the full force of my forward momentum, I sent my elbow into his throat. He went down hard, right on his ass, gasping for breath, both hands clawing at his throat. I'd tried not to hit him too hard, but it's almost impossible to judge just how much force to use.

I turned to my left, and as I knew he would, his larger friend came at me with a swinging right hook aimed at my head. If he'd connected, it could have done some damage, but the move left his midsection unprotected. Before he reached me, I ducked low and, using my full body weight and shoulder, swung a hard right to his stomach. With my left, I threw an uppercut to the bottom of his chin. He doubled over and ended up on his hands and knees. He was in front of but facing away from Renee, throwing up his last meal. Renee swung her leg back and sent it between the guy's thighs, soccer kicking him in his unprotected testicles. Ouch!

Po turned and started to walk away.

"Stop right there, Po," I said, pointing to his two friends on the ground. "Get back here."

Po stopped, walked back, and stood over his two buddies. He was shaking as if waiting for a punch he must have thought was sure to come.

I high-fived Renee. Kris, Kathy, and Monica were staring open-mouthed at the two prone men writhing on the ground. I wasn't sure if Melissa was even aware of what had just taken place.

"Ladies, this is the kind of thing I warned you would start happening. Others are going to want what we have: a working vehicle, our food, our supplies . . . really anything of value. We have to protect what's ours at all costs. Our ability to get home is dependent on it."

I pointed to Mike, lying at Renee's feet, said, "Po, please help the ladies here move these two pieces of shit out of the way so I can back out of the space without running them over. Kris, get the knife and throw it in the back."

Po, Monica, and Kathy each grabbed an arm or leg and dragged the two to the adjacent parking space. Through clenched teeth, Mike cursed at Renee and called her some very nasty names. She just smiled at him, which pissed him off even more. Rob, still clutching his throat, wisely stayed silent. Po ran away.

We loaded up, made our way out of the parking structure without further incident, and turned right onto Las Vegas Boulevard. We had plenty of people staring and pointing at us, but no one approached. There were dead cars everywhere, some still occupied by their owners, but more often than not, abandoned, hoods left up. It was easy going, as it was still morning and not nearly as crowded as if the pulse had happened later in the day. We saw no police or fire personnel anywhere despite the numerous underground electrical transformer fires we passed. I didn't see any buildings on fire but figured it was only a matter of time.

I turned left onto Spring Mountain Road, and while we had to dodge stalled cars, the going was still pretty good. At Decatur, I turned left again and then made another left into the first parking lot on the left. I pulled up to the lot's security gate and honked. All told, we'd been gone from the hotel for less than three minutes.

On the other side of the chain-link security gate was a parking lot that looked capable of handling a hundred cars. Beyond the parking lot was a huge concrete-sided warehouse at least thirty feet tall with six sunken freight docks, all with fold-out weather shelters, three ground-level metal roll-up doors to the left of the docks, and a double-metal entrance door to the left of those. Over the entrance door were big black letters spelling out "Desert Tactical and Surplus, Main Entrance."

Embedded in the ground and spanning the width of the entrance doors were a series of thick stainless-steel security posts that looked capable of stopping an Abrams tank. Then more concrete walls. For security, there were no windows at ground level.

"You think anyone is here?" Melissa asked, sounding more than a little skeptical.

"This is my friend Burt's place," I said. "We were college roommates and later served two tours in Afghanistan together. That's his old Jeep parked inside the gates. He would never have left that here overnight. He's here."

"This place is huge," Renee said. "I've seen smaller Walmarts."

"It is big. Burt's dad bought the building from FedEx, who had been using it as their southern Nevada distribution center. The interior is over one hundred thousand square feet of retail and warehouse space."

While we waited for Burt to let us in, I turned in my seat and looked back at the women. "What happened back in the parking structure was nothing compared to what could happen and probably will happen once we're on the road," I said. "Next time they'll have guns and won't flash a knife. Those three snuck up on each of you and, yes, you told me, Renee, which is a good thing. But you should have seen them coming and said something sooner. When we're actually on the road, I'll teach you how to set a perimeter watch. Every time we stop, you hop out, take a knee, look outward, and cover 180 degrees in front and to each side of your position."

Kathy cut in, said, "Like in the movies when soldiers hop out of a helicopter, fan out, and take a knee?"

I smiled, said, "Exactly like that."

The middle metal roll-up bay door slowly started rising. And there was Burt, pulling hand over hand the bay door's manual opening chain. Securing the chain, Burt turned and walked toward us. He inserted a key into a large lock and walked open both sides of the security fence. Once fully opened, he waved us through. He closed and locked the gate behind us and came up to my window.

"Jon, good to see you. Who are your friends?"

I introduced him to the ladies. Once introductions were made, he had us drive inside the warehouse. I cut the motor, and the bay door slowly closed behind us. I hopped out, and Burt and I embraced.

Burt was quite a bit shorter than me at five seven, and I had to stoop for the hug. Burt had curly red hair, and thousands of freckles covered his face and arms. Constantly ribbed as a kid, he taught himself to fight and he was the toughest, physically strongest person I knew. He couldn't weigh more than 170 pounds, but he was all lean muscle and packed a lot of power in such a small frame. He powered through Afghanistan and everything it threw at him, only to come back to the States to find that he was unable to handle "normal" life back home. He was diagnosed as suffering from PTSD and had been in therapy for three years. The VA hospital had some of the best and most dedicated therapists in the country, and they had really helped with his struggles.

"Well, I bet our fathers are pretty proud of themselves about now . . . both always said that this would happen someday, and here it is. It's pretty fucked up," he said as he watched the women pile out of the Cruiser.

"It's a clusterfuck, for sure," I replied. "It's not bad out there now, but that's going to change in a day or two. And as far as my dad's concerned . . . while probably not happy his favorite reality shows are off the air, he's most likely now sitting on his porch with a smile on his face, patiently waiting for his kids to show up.

"Is Beth here?" I asked.

"Not yet. She'll be here later this morning along with her parents and four brothers. My dad and mom are in San Diego on a buying trip, and I'm not sure when they'll get here. Dad's driving his old pickup, so I know it's running."

"Sorry, that's some bad timing."

Burt shrugged. "He'll be okay. He's got a hidden gun locker under the back seat of his truck, and as usual, he's loaded for bear. California and their ridiculous gun laws won't stop him. And he's put in an auxiliary fuel tank, so he's not going to have to hunt down gas."

Burt stood back and took in the Land Cruiser. "You really did an outstanding job of restoring it," he said. "It looks brand-new. You're going to cry like a baby the first time you take it off-roading and scratch the heck out of it."

"Thank you. I'm glad you like it. But scratches are the least of my worries."

"I hear you. Are you driving these ladies back to Montana or Seattle?"

"Seattle first, then Montana."

"You've got a long drive ahead of you. Let me get the Barrett. You're going to like it."

I wanted the ladies to do some shopping, and I asked him if it would be okay. I held my breath waiting for his answer— our ability to get home safely was riding on it.

"Of course," he answered, looking up at the ceiling. "There's plenty of light coming through the skylights, so they'll be able to see just fine."

I let out a sigh of relief. "I know cash and credit cards are worthless now, but I have some gold coins to give you." I filled him in on my winnings of a few hours ago and the gold coins I'd purchased.

"Jon, in a week this place will be destroyed, as it'll be a prime target for every asshole in Vegas. Like your dad, my dad knew the day would come when we'd have to leave. So, a few years ago he went to a military auction and bought himself three humongous 1960s-era, M35 6x6 military cargo supply trucks. Each one has a twenty-four-foot, triaxle, enclosed cargo trailer hooked to the back. We've been restoring them, and they're parked in the rear lot, gassed and ready to head out.

"Once Beth and her brothers get here, we'll start loading them up and empty the store of all the weapons, ammo, and as much of the other stuff as we can. But we'll never get it all. We can protect it for only so long before we'll have to head out. So, have at it. Have them take whatever they want. No charge. I'd much rather you have it than the scavengers that'll be rolling on in after we leave."

"Thank you, my friend, that's super generous of you. Are you going to head to the family ranch in Utah?"

"Where else? It's perfect for us. It's more of a compound now. Multifamily setup . . . kind of like your family's ranch in Montana but minus the luxury part."

"Don't know if I'll ever make it out to Utah, but hopefully someday. You still have that water tank on the roof?" His father, like mine, were preppers to the extreme, and that included storing hundreds of gallons in long-term storage.

"Yep, help yourself. Plenty to go around."

"You sell those blue five-gallon plastic water storage containers? If so, we could use six of them. And the red plastic five-gallon gas cans, too."

The women were standing watching us. Melissa was cradling the AR in her arms like Burt and I had back on patrol.

"We have dozens of them, so again, help yourself to both the water and gas," Burt answered. "You know where the water spigot is, and the gas is in the back with the rental ATVs. The gas storage tank works on gravity so there won't be an issue filling them."

Burt turned and headed toward the sales floor.

While Burt was off getting the Barrett, I had the women gather around me.

"Okay, here's what we're going to do. Burt has greenlighted us to shop for the things we need. First, I want you to get to the backpacking section and grab the largest backpack you think you can carry with a heavy load. Make sure it's in camo or black. That backpack will carry everything you bring—no more roll-on luggage or carry-ons. We have very little room in the Cruiser, so these backpacks are it. Everyone with me so far?"

A chorus of yeses came back at me.

"Once you get your backpack, head to the clothing section. I want you to strip down to undies and bra, or, uh, whatever it is you're wearing, and try on long camo pants with belts, brown T-shirts, and camo shirts . . ."

"Look, I think he's blushing," Renee said, smiling and pointing to me.

"He is looking a little red in the face," Monica said. "What if we're not wearing any 'whatevers'?"

"Okay. Okay, let's get serious here," I said in mock seriousness.

"Try everything on and make sure it fits, then get a size bigger and keep them on. Grab an extra set of everything. Grab an extra military olive-brown T-shirt, preferably long sleeve. If you don't have more than a few pairs of underwear, grab at least five more hiking-type underwear. Same for hiking socks. And find jog bras if they have them."

From somewhere on the sales floor we heard, "We do, aisle twenty, toward the back of the store," Burt shouted out.

"Thank you, Burt," I shouted back.

"Next will be cold-weather jackets. Make sure they fit well and that the fronts zip up snugly. It gets cold at night in the desert, and we'll be headed for some mountains and possibly snow. Then find some gloves, knit ski hats, and balaclava face masks, all in black or camo."

"All those items are on aisles thirty and thirty-one," Burt shouted.

"You heard the man. Then head to the shoe department and pick out some hiking sneakers, and make sure they're dark-colored and not some bright neon ones. The next stop will be the hat area."

"Melissa, you know what a boonie hat is?"

"Sure do."

"You all need to get a couple of boonie hats in traditional camo or desert pattern. Make sure all your hair can fit underneath by trying them on. This is important, as we want to make you look like men. At least from a distance."

"Go do that now. You have thirty minutes."

No one moved.

"Go on. Go."

I stared at them, and realization came. "Ah . . . my rule on being in sight of me at all times. Exceptions are okay if I say so, and this is an exception. Go!"

And off they went. Including Melissa with the AR.

"Melissa! Stop!" I shouted.

She stopped and turned, looking back at me with a puzzled expression.

"The rifle. Bring it back, please," I said. "It's more important that you get outfitted. You can put it in the front seat. Barrel up, please."

"Well, duh," she replied as she hustled back to the Cruiser, deposited the rifle, and took off at a full run in the direction of her teammates.

I unlocked the Thule cargo carrier on the roof, removed my bug-out bag and plate carrier. I ditched the loafers and stripped out of my dress slacks and white button-down shirt with the Securetech company logo over the pocket. I stepped into my well-worn desert camos and put on my olive-brown long-sleeved T-shirt. I wore these during two of my four deployments to the Middle East, and it felt great to be wearing them again. Both pants and T-shirt felt a little snug for my liking. But heck, it'd been six years and at least they still fit.

I finished dressing by putting on socks and my equally worn combat boots. Tucking everything in and cinching my belt, I then went to the rear of the Cruiser and emptied the aft seating area. I deposited the carry-on luggage, pillows, purses, and all the other stuff on the warehouse floor. The women would have to sort through all this and decide what they were going to keep by stowing it in the backpacks. We'd keep all the mini-bar riches.

I slipped the plate carrier over my head and settled it on my shoulders. The rig had been with me throughout all of my overseas deployments. It was dirty and ratty and just about perfect in my eyes. It held four thirty-round 5.56 mags and four Glock, gen four, fourteen-round .40-caliber mags. I grabbed the Glock and slipped it into the cross-draw holster built into the rig over my left breast. I secured the bullet plates and then bounced up and down, testing for noise.

Burt came through the sales floor door with the Barrett's Pelican case in tow. Seeing me bouncing up and down, he said, "Man, does that bring back memories—good times and bad."

Burt hefted the pelican case into the back of the Cruiser and unsnapped all three of the press-and-pull latches. He raised the lid, and there it was . . . sitting pretty in custom-cut black foam. The buttstock, receiver, trigger assembly, scope, and bipod were together, but the barrel was detached and could easily be reconnected. The weapon was in desert-brown earth color, identical to what I had overseas. There were five loaded magazines and the suppressor nestled alongside the barrel.

"I've got the other ten magazines in my office," Burt said. "I'll get those for you in a few minutes."

"That is one beautiful sight," I said, running my fingers over the barrel. "I haven't laid eyes on one of these beauties since I turned mine into the quartermaster in Afghanistan. Thanks again for putting it all together for me."

"You're welcome. You wanna fire off a few rounds?"

There was a twenty-five-yard indoor range in the back of the building and a hundred-yard, two-lane, semi-enclosed outdoor rifle range behind that. I'd fired off thousands of rounds in both during numerous summer college breaks.

"I wish we had time, but we've got to get a move on. The shit is only going to get worse as the day wears on."

Burt scanned our belongings scattered on the garage floor, asked, "What are you doing for weapons? Besides the Barrett, I don't see anything other than your Colt and Glock."

"I was hoping to buy some from you."

"I'll tell you what. You give me three of those Krugerrands and I'll outfit those ladies, and you, with Colts fitted with Eotech red dots with flip-to-the-side 3x magnifiers, Glocks, plenty of extra mags for both the Colts and the Glocks, chest rigs with plates, and best of all, night vision for each of you."

"It's a deal," I answered, handing over three of the one-ounce Krugerrands. "But how'd those Eotechs and night vision units survive the pulse?"

"A big-ass faraday cage. And wait until you see the rifles. Let's go into the armory and lay it all out."

I closed and latched the pelican case. I followed Burt into the front half of the store and watched as he unlocked a large metal security door. Light streamed into the enclosure from two skylights set thirty feet up on the ceiling. Inside was row after row of rifles and shotguns. There had to be six or seven hundred rifles of every type and caliber.

"Impressive, Burt. You going to transport all these up to Utah and start your own army?"

"You think this is a lot? . . . We have triple this number already up in Utah. And yes, we'll be taking all these with us. But let me show you the rifles I'm giving you."

At the very back of the room was a super-sized Liberty Fatboy gun safe. Burt spun the dial, and it clicked open to reveal at least thirty desert-brown Colt M4's, the military's AR. Each had the Eotech red dot sights with the flip-to-the-side magnifiers that he had mentioned. Taking one out, he handed it to me, said, "Tell me what's special about these, good buddy."

It took me all of two seconds. "Holy shit! It's an M4A1." The A1 version was selectable for semi or fully automatic. "How?" I asked.

"We're licensed by the Feds to have these," he explained. "For a price, we let people shoot in fully automatic mode on our range out back. We also train the Las Vegas Police Department in their use. We bought these directly from Colt. Let's grab six and put them on the table out front. Your AR is nice and all, but I'm pretty sure you'll want one of these puppies."

"You really need to ask? And I'd like one more for Melissa. But if you've got non-A1 M4s in there, I think the other women might be better off with that model." M4s could fire in semiautomatic as well as in three-round bursts, which made them much easier to control.

"We do," he answered.

Before walking out of the armory, we grabbed five brand new Glock .40-caliber handguns, model 22s, still in their black plastic carry cases. We lugged the lot out to the garage bay and set them on a large ten by ten wooden equipment assembly table. Burt went back to the armory and reappeared ten minutes later with a dolly loaded with a full manufacturer's carton of ninety-six Magpul 5.56 magazines, two cartons of Federal 5.56 NATO ammo, each carton a bulk pack of twenty-five hundred loose rounds, two bulk cartons of a thousand rounds each of .40 caliber for the Glocks, and an extra twenty-five magazines for the Glocks.

"Supposedly there's a national ammo shortage," I said. "But apparently not today."

"We always keep a large supply on hand, even though our retail store shelves are empty and our website says out of stock.

Every time a democrat is elected president, there's a run on ammo. We've got millions of rounds up in Utah waiting for us.

"I also have the .50 caliber for you," he said, reaching behind him and bringing out boxes of ammo. "I was able to get the Nammo, but only 240 rounds. Here's 120 Hornady A-MAX rounds—these are eight dollars per round and should only be used for long-distance shots. Here are two hundred rounds of armor piercing. I had hoped to get eight hundred rounds of bulk .50 but only got my hands on four hundred rounds of Lake City."

"This is incredible," I said, separating the ammo boxes by brand.

Burt wasn't done. He turned and headed back toward the retail floor. "Come on, let's grab plate carriers for each of the ladies. Follow me."

We made our way to the sales floor and passed by the women as they tried on hiking shoes. We entered the tactical area and selected five rigs pretty much like mine but minus the armor plates. "We have plates, too, and can outfit these with lighter-weight inserts," Burt said. "They won't stop a 7.62 round, but anything under that and it's all good. Sound like a plan?"

"You bet. Thanks."

We spent the next twenty minutes inserting and securing the bullet plates. Once done, we carried them back to the assembly table in the garage bay.

"Now for those night vision units."

In the far back reaches of the garage bay was a large walk-in, restaurant-sized freezer. Or at least it looked like one.

"We had one of these on base in Afghanistan if you remember. It looks like a freezer, but it's a faraday cage. Dad bought this one from a deactivated military base in Arizona. I've already checked, and all the contents made it through the pulse."

Burt opened the door, turned on a flashlight, and rack upon rack of small electronics came into view, all neatly arranged.

"This is my dad's pride and joy. He's been collecting this military stuff for years, and here it is. We have dozens of night vision goggles and headsets, so let's get you six of 'em."

He took six boxes off one of the lower shelves and handed them to me. "These are brand-new and are the latest fourth-generation sets—they've just started supplying them to our guys overseas this past month. They're battery-operated, and I can give you lots of replacement batteries, or we can set you up with a solar charger. Your choice," he said. "Or both."

"Let's do both," I answered. "Having these night vision setups, I'm thinking we're going to be able to do most of our traveling at night. We can charge them during the day with the solar panels and use the replacement batteries if need be."

Burt then said, "Almost forgot. Those Eotechs on the six M4s need replacing, as I'm sure they were fried in the pulse." He bent low and grabbed six boxes housing the red dot sights.

"We don't need new flip-to-the-side magnifiers, as they're not electronic," Burt explained.

Walking out of the faraday cage, I noticed a short stack of boxes just inside the door. "Is this what I think it is?" I held up one of the boxes so Burt could see.

"Why, yes, it is," he said matter-of-factly. "A Pulsar Trail XP50 thermal rifle scope, if you want to be specific. I can let you have one. The rest are for Dad and Beth's brothers."

"Fantastic, Burt. Thanks! That's like a three-thousand-dollar scope."

Burt laughed, said, "Actually, double that. They're one of the better civilian thermal scopes out there. You're going to have to zero it in, but you can do that at the range out back when we're zeroing in the new Eotechs. We can also zero it using the Barrett—the scope's computer saves specs for multiple weapon platforms and ammo loads. You only have to fire three or four rounds to zero it to a particular weapon. While we're back there, we can teach the ladies firearm safety and how to fire the Colts and Glocks."

We carried everything back to the garage and added it to the table.

Looking at the pile of weapons, ammo, and accessories, I said, "I feel like I'm back overseas getting ready for a recon op."

"I hear you, buddy, but I wouldn't trade my life now for any of that shit over there. No do-overs for me."

"You're going to get into it here, Burt. They're going to be showing up here in the next few hours hoping to buy or steal any weapon they can get their hands on. I hope you're ready. We can hang until your people get here."

"Appreciate that, Jon. And I'll take you up on your offer."

"Consider it done," I said.

And at that moment, the women walked up. They were fully outfitted in desert camo, boonie hats, and hiking shoes. Each had a backpack stuffed to the gills with who knows what.

"Well, hell, Master Sergeant, I guess you've got your squad ready to go," Burt said with a chuckle.

As they stood there waiting for instructions, they couldn't help but see the weapons piled on the assembly table.

"Are those for us?" Monica asked.

"Yep, I answered. "And we'll get you outfitted later, but now you need to drop your packs and head over to the camping department . . ."

". . . which is back through the door you just came out of, then turn left," Burt cut in with. "I'll go with you, ladies. I'll help you pick out some good quality sleeping bags, sleeping pads, tents, cooking stoves, pots and pans, plates, utensils, and most importantly, some Mountain House freeze-dried meals . . . my personal favorite being their beef stroganoff."

Burt turned, and with the women trailing close behind, headed off in the direction of the door leading to the retail store.

"Thanks again for all this, Burt," I said to his retreating back.

Not breaking stride or looking back, Burt raised his hand and waved. "No hay problema, mi amigo," he said.

While they were getting the camping gear together, I found the water and gas cans. I filled the five water containers first and had just come back from the rear of the building pushing a dolly with six full gas cans when the women showed up.

They spread out the gear, and it was a lot of stuff. Camo sleeping bags. Camo two-man tents. Backpacking stoves and lots of Coleman one-pound propane tanks. And five extra-large army duffel bags stuffed with Mountain House freeze-dried breakfast and dinner meals . . . there had to be hundreds of them. And last but not least: three Costco-sized packages of toilet paper and one large package of paper towels.

"For filtering water, we have a Platypus gravity water filter," a smiling Kathy said, holding it up for my approval.

"Most excellent, Kathy," I said.

"I have the same model we use for camping," she said, leaning down and picking up a solar shower kit. "And for showering, we have a solar shower. I have . . ."

"We are not going to be taking showers," I said, cutting her off.

"Try and stop us," they said in unison.

Having grown up with three strong females, I learned not to argue with a stubborn woman, let alone a group of them, so let it go with, "We'll see. If we come across a water source, maybe. But water will be for drinking and cooking," I said.

"We grabbed you a sleeping bag and pad," Renee said. "Along with a two-man tent. Of which I'm the second man, er, woman."

The rest of the women had big smiles on their faces as if sharing a secret.

"They know, Jon. About us, I mean. Seems pretty much the entire company has known," Renee explained, pulling my head down and giving me a big wet kiss on the lips.

EIGHT

I put the women to work loading magazines. First were the 5.56 mags, all ninety-six of them, followed by the Glocks. The Glock magazines were much harder to load, so Burt provided the women with manual hand loaders which helped a lot. I'd load the other ten .50-caliber magazines later.

"You're never going to get all this stuff in the Cruiser, even using the rooftop rack," Burt said, taking in the huge pile of weapons, ammo, food, packs, and everything else scattered on the warehouse floor. "Not if you want to bring the women along, that is."

"I guess I could yank off the covered portion of the roof rack and put the jerry cans up there, though it might make the Cruiser a little top-heavy," I said, sounding slightly defeated.

"Don't give up so easily. Follow me. I have an idea."

We walked to the far-right rear of the warehouse, where two rows of trailers holding one, two, or four rental ATVs were parked.

Burt stood in front of a black, two-axle trailer holding four ATVs.

"The ATVs didn't survive the pulse, but the trailers certainly did. It's sixteen feet long, seven feet wide, and has thirty-six-inch metal sides so it's going to securely hold all your gear . . . and then some. Please tell me you have a trailer hitch on the back of the Cruiser."

"I do."

"Two-inch ball?"

"Yes again."

"Phew . . . perfect. Storage problem solved. Let's get these useless hunks of metal and plastic rolled off and wheel it over behind the Cruiser."

We lowered the trailer's rear loading ramp, released the tie-down straps that secured the ATVs to the trailer, put the four into neutral, and pushed them down and off the trailer. Once on the incline ramp, they picked up steam and shot across the garage floor where they crashed into the warehouse's cement wall. Fiberglass and plastic shattered and flew everywhere.

Burt laughed, said, "As Beth likes to say . . . whoopsies!"

Leaving the wheeled trailer jack in the down position, we maneuvered the trailer across the warehouse floor and positioned it behind the Cruiser. I retrieved the ball mount and hitch pin from the rooftop cargo box and slid it into the Cruiser's receiver. We lifted the coupler and settled it on the trailer ball, then clamped the latch closed. I cranked the jack up, secured it in its travel position, and crisscrossed and connected the safety chains. I opened and shut the Cruiser's rear-facing doors to make sure there was room for them to open. They did. All good.

"Having two axles is going to allow you to carry a lot of weight." Burt pointed to the pile of camping gear and weapons, said, "All this stuff will only take up a third of the trailer's available space. Try and put the heaviest items up front. And don't connect the wiring harness . . . you don't want the brake lights shouting out your location. In fact, I think you should disconnect the Cruiser's brake and rear running lights for the same reason."

"Great idea, thanks."

"This is going to kill you, good buddy, but you should probably spray paint those beautiful chrome bumpers and hub caps flat black. If the sun catches those shiny bumpers, they'll reflect like crazy."

Burt walked over to a workbench and came back with screwdrivers and two cans of Rust-Oleum spray paint. He threw the two cans at me, and I missed them both. Laughing, he climbed in the rear of the Cruiser and disconnected both running and brake lights on the left and right rear.

I shook the cans and painted both the front and rear bumpers the flat black. The hubcaps were the stock Land Cruiser chrome jobs and painted up nice. I had a Warn winch on the front bumper, but it was covered by a black vinyl weather cover.

The women had finished loading the magazines, and I had them join me at the rear of the trailer.

"Let's get this trailer loaded up . . . heavy things up front and then working back toward the rear," I said, lifting one of the red plastic gas cans and placing it up against the trailer's front bulkhead. "There's plenty of space for everything, so don't double stack. That way we can get to it quickly if need be.

"In fact, leave a foot-wide aisle down the middle so we can get to everything without having to climb over stuff. Gas and water cans at the front, then ammo cans and cartons. Your backpacks should be placed next to the ramp for easy access. If there are items you want to remain on your person, take them out of the backpacks now and stow them in your pants cargo pockets. Weapons, loaded magazines, and chest rigs like the one I'm wearing, leave on the table."

While the women were loading the trailer, I took Melissa aside and had her put on a plate carrier. Lifting it over her head and settling it on her shoulders, I showed her how to adjust the retention straps. We loaded the magazine pockets with four, thirty-round 5.56 and three, fourteen-round Glock mags.

"How's it feel?" I asked. "I put bullet plates in the back and front. Even though they're lighter-weight models, it's still got some heft to it."

Melissa shrugged. "It's a little heavy, but not bad. Heck, if it stops a bullet, I'm happy to carry around the weight."

I had her bounce up and down a few times checking for noise.

I inserted a loaded clip into the Glock and charged it. I then slipped the weapon into her rig's quick-draw holster over her left breast. "I should have asked, you right-handed?"

"Yes."

"Glocks don't have a safety, so . . ."

"I know, Jon."

"Okay, good. Just an FYI . . . we're staying here until Burt's wife and family arrive sometime later this morning."

Spotting Burt, I asked him to join us.

"Burt, I'd like to send Melissa up to the roof and provide some eyes on the parking lot and street." I pointed to a set of stairs. "Those go to the roof?"

"Yep," Burt answered. "There's a metal access hatch that simply unlocks with a twist of the closure. But you'll need some comms if you're going up there, Melissa. Be right back." He turned and headed into the faraday cage.

"Melissa, grab the rifle closest to us. Then reach up in the cargo carrier on Sandy's roof and grab the rifle sling and bring both back to me."

While Melissa was getting the rifle and sling, Burt came back with a handful of Midland fifty channel two-way radios. Putting them on the table, he said, "We use these when we go shooting in the desert. They're fully charged, and you can recharge them with the solar panels. We've put nine-inch flexible antennas on them, as it helps with the range—they have a thirty-six-mile range in open terrain but much less if obstructions like buildings and hills are in the area. Your chest rigs have a shoulder pocket that you can put them in, but keep the speaker volume low so the world doesn't hear you. They come with boom mikes and earpieces, but I can't find them."

I was overwhelmed by Burt's generosity and told him so.

"Listen, like I said before, I'd rather you have all this than the hordes that will invade this place once we leave."

Burt then showed Melissa how to use the two-way radio. "Set it to a higher channel, like forty. We'll set the rest of them to forty as well, and if you see something that concerns you, key the mic and let us know what's happening. Then release the mic and wait for our response."

"Do I get to say over and out?" she asked, smiling.

"Of course," I answered. "That's part of the fun of it all."

I then showed her how to set up, adjust, and use the two-point sling. "Keep the rifle cradled in your arms like you were before. The sling will help with the weapon's weight and allow you to quickly bring the weapon up into a firing position.

"This is the military's version of the civilian AR-15. You and I will have this model. It shoots either semiautomatic or fully automatic." I showed her the selector lever with the two settings. "The other women will have the M4s, which fire semiautomatic or three-round bursts."

Burt saw me setting Melissa up with the sling, said, "We've got bunches of those two points. I'll make sure each of the ladies gets one."

"Thanks," I answered. I found a screwdriver and took the fried Eotech off the rifle and replaced it with a new one we'd grabbed from the faraday cage—it wasn't zeroed in yet but would be good enough for now. I threw the old one in a nearby trash can. "You put that red dot on your target and you're going to hit it."

I then showed Melissa how to turn on the replacement unit. "This will stay on for three hours and then shut off automatically to save battery power. Just turn it on again when it eventually turns off. If you want to bring an object in closer, then flip this magnifier up behind the scope."

I had her flip the magnifier up and down a few times to get her used to the motion. Melissa then started for the stairs, and I called out after her. "It's only been six hours or so since things went to hell, so there's probably not going to be any problems, but if you see something, say something. Okay?"

"Oh, I will, trust me," she replied as she headed up the stairs.

"I'll relieve you in an hour or so. None of us has slept since yesterday, so we need to make time for some shut-eye."

"I have cots in the camping department you guys can use," Burt said.

What didn't he have?

THE LADIES MADE QUICK WORK of loading the trailer. We slipped a dark-green water-repellent tarp over the entire load and secured it in place with a bunch of bungee cords. Half of the trailer's sixteen feet had been used.

"Lots of free space for any goodies you might pick up along the way," Burt pointed out.

Burt and I set each of the women up with chest rigs and comms. Burt then took one of the rifles and led them to the shooting range for a quick thirty-minute crash course on firearm safety, shooting basics, and instruction on how to use the Eotechs and flip-to-the-side magnifiers.

Burt had them fire half a magazine in semiautomatic and finish off the remaining rounds in three-round bursts. He then switched to the Glocks and let them fire off a full magazine.

He then put them to work reloading the emptied magazines.

While Burt was busy with the shooting lessons, I zeroed in all the new Eotechs that we'd put on the Colts. I then wheeled the Pelican case to the one-hundred-yard range and assembled the Barrett. Burt had already zeroed it in the desert, but the Pulsar thermal scope needed to be zeroed.

Ideally, a Barrett should be zeroed in at several hundred yards, but this was what I had. I was hoping the Pulsar's computer would help with future ranging and drops. I put on ear protection and fired off four rounds. Bullseye on the third and fourth round. I then put the suppressor on and fired off the balance of the magazine. What a sweet setup this was.

I took the Pulsar off the Barrett and installed it on the new M4. It took a few minutes of fiddling with the computer before I had the rifle ready to fire. After seven rounds, I had it zeroed in. I then screwed on the SureFire suppressor and fired off another five rounds.

I removed my ear protection and fired one last round. While much quieter, it was still loud. But if I fired at an object two or three hundred yards away, the object would never hear it.

BY THIS TIME, WE WERE all dragging butt, and it was pretty obvious we needed some sleep. We set up six cots next to the Cruiser and, once the women had taken off their chest rigs, fell instantly asleep. Burt went into the retail store and came out with six blankets and covered each woman.

Our comms squawked, "Burt? Jon?" This from Melissa.

"Go ahead, Melissa," I answered, keying my mic.

"We've got a group of seven guys out front starting to climb the chain-link fence," she said, sounding anxious.

"We'll be right up," Burt said, both of us grabbing an M4 and four loaded magazines.

We double-timed it up the stairs and emerged into the brilliant sunlight on the building's roof. We spotted Melissa, and a few seconds later, we were standing next to her glancing down at the street. Sure enough, seven men were attempting to climb the parking lot's ten-foot wire security fence. They appeared to be unarmed.

"You know them?" I asked Burt.

"Nope."

All three of us turned when we heard footsteps behind us. Four women were running toward us, chest rigs on and M4s in hand.

"We thought you might want some backup," Renee offered.

"Thanks," I said. "Spread out, ten feet apart, safety on, selector set to three-round bursts. Fingers off triggers."

"Stop where you are and get down off the fence," Burt shouted down.

One of the men who was just about ready to throw a leg over the top of the fence stopped and shouted back, "Sir, we know this isn't just a power outage and that it's probably an EMP. We want to buy some rifles and ammo and protect our families. Please let us in. Please!"

"Sorry, but we're closed and not reopening," Burt shouted back. "Try down the street at Harver's Gun Shop. Now get off the fence."

"We have cash," another shouted.

"Cash is useless now, friend. Again, get off the fence."

Burt looked over at Melissa, said, "Well, we did ask nicely to get off the fence and even suggested another shop. You want some practice with that weapon?"

"Sure," she answered, though she didn't sound thrilled at the idea.

"Then take the safety off, put the fire selector on full auto, and put a group ten or fifteen feet to the left of them," Burt instructed. "Finger off the trigger until you're ready to fire. It's going to pull up on you, so aim a little low."

Melissa did as he said, aimed, and pulled the trigger . . . twice. The sound cracked loud in the silence that was now Las Vegas. Dirt, concrete, and fence debris exploded where the bullets impacted. The men jumped down onto the sidewalk and scattered every which way.

"Excellent job, Melissa," I said, offering my palm in a high five, which she accepted.

Melissa was jumpy with adrenaline, and the rifle's muzzle was bouncing every which way. Wary of touching a heated barrel, I took hold of the Eotech and moved the rifle until it was pointed down toward the street. "Safety on and finger off the trigger, please."

"Oops, I forgot. Sorry," Melissa said as she fumbled with the safety lever.

"No need to be sorry, kiddo. It's only natural to be pumped after an exchange," I explained. "Just remember to always keep your finger off the trigger after you're done firing, and then set the weapon to safe."

"Happens to all of us," Burt added. "Take a few deep breaths. It'll help."

"Let me take over up here, Melissa," I said. "Go get some shut-eye. We have some cots set up downstairs.

"You other ladies do the same. Thank you for coming up. You did well in responding the way you did."

Renee offered to stay with me. I thanked her but told her I'd rather she head back down and get some much-needed rest.

With that, they left the roof and headed downstairs.

Burt followed them, and I was alone on the roof.

———

EVEN THOUGH THE SUN WAS shining brightly, it couldn't have been more than fifty degrees out—cold enough to see your breath.

Everywhere I looked, fires were burning—hundreds of them. With the fire department out of commission, the fires would only be spreading. The sky was thick with acrid-smelling black smoke, and I figured every electrical transformer in Las

Vegas had probably caught fire. The transformer two buildings down from Burt's was smoldering, the black guts melted and pooling like lava on the ground under the street-side pole.

It was now noon, and I was dead tired. To stay awake, I continuously walked the full perimeter of the roof. From this height, I had a commanding view of the surrounding streets, and it was while walking above the front parking lot I spotted four pre-seventies 4x4 trucks headed toward the building. Each truck's cargo bed was loaded with what appeared to be personal belongings.

I took a knee and rested the M4 on the roof 's three-foot raised concrete bulwark. I flipped the Eotech's magnifier up and glassed the lead truck, which had slowed and turned into the driveway, stopping in front of the locked rolling gate. Beth, Burt's wife, was in the front passenger seat and was looking up at me. She waved. I lowered the rifle and waved back.

I keyed the comms, said, "Burt, Beth is out front. She's in the first of four trucks."

Burt clicked back in acknowledgment, and I heard the roll-up door open. Burt soon appeared and opened the parking lot gates. All four trucks drove through and entered the building. I heard the roll-up door close a minute later.

"Jon, come on down and say hello to Beth," Burt said over the comms. "I'll send one of Beth's brothers up to replace you. You need to get some rest."

I responded with a simple, "Roger that."

I made my way down the stairs, and Oliver, Beth's younger brother whom I met years ago when he was just a kid, came bounding up. We met at the midway landing.

Shaking Oliver's hand, I said, "Good to see you, Oliver. Been a while. I wish it was under better circumstances."

"Good to see you, too, sir. Let me take an overwatch position up top. I'll catch up with you later." He then ran up the rest of the stairs, disappearing into the sunlight.

"Jon! Come on down here and hug me already," Beth shouted up the stairs. She was standing at the bottom waiting for me. As soon as both boots touched concrete, she hugged me tight . . . chest rig and all.

Beth was Burt's opposite. While Burt was quiet and reserved, Beth was outgoing and gregarious. Beth was also tall and skinny as a rail with an unruly mass of light blond hair. Unable to have kids, Beth poured her energy into making life easy and enjoyable for Burt. They both worked hard on Burt's PTSD issues, and Beth was his rock. They made an unlikely couple but loved each other to death. Most importantly, they were truly best friends.

Beth was still hugging me thirty seconds later. "Release me, please," I pleaded.

Beth let go and took a step back, looking me up and down.

"Gosh, but don't you look good," she said, flapping her hands around as if she'd touched something hot. "All handsome and manly in your war getup. The women must be lining up waiting to take their turn at you." She grabbed my stomach with both hands and squeezed. "And you still have those abs going on. You still weigh 220?"

In college, Beth and I started watching our diet and doing daily crunches together. Both of us turned our soft stomachs into hard six-packs, although mine were now more of a soft-outline six-pack.

"Last time I weighed myself, I came in at 230. And thank you, honey. You're looking good yourself," I said, laughing. She was wearing light blue surgical scrubs with the St. Rose Dominican Hospital logo over her right breast. Beth was a trauma surgeon on staff at the hospital and was in medical school at the University of Utah, where we all lived together in an off-campus rental house.

Taking my hand, she guided me back toward the sleeping women, said, "My husband told me to take you to bed, but I bet one of those ladies would be a little upset with me. So, which one of these lovely ladies is yours?"

"What makes you think any of those is mine?"

"Just an educated guess."

"Funny, honey," I said, laughing. "Four of them work with me, and I'm going to try and get them home to Seattle."

"And the fifth?"

"She's the owner of Securetech and yes, smartass, we're together," I said.

"I knew it."

"Can we catch up later? I need some sleep," I explained, taking off my chest rig and setting it down next to the last open cot.

"Sure, we'll be quiet and let you get some sleep."

I took my boots off and lay down on the cot.

I said, "Thanks, Beth. Will you tuck me in, too?"

I never heard her answer, as I was already fast asleep.

THE FIRST THING I DID after opening my eyes was to check my watch. It was a self-winding model, MWC military dive watch, and was unaffected by the pulse. Its glowing green time marks said it was ten after eight. As it was dark in the warehouse, I assumed it was eight at night. That meant I'd slept for just shy of seven hours. Good.

I swung my feet to the floor and got my boots on. I slipped the plate carrier over my head and, seeing the other cots empty, made my way into the retail store. I found everyone sitting around a long table enjoying spaghetti. A hissing Coleman lantern hanging from a ceiling light fixture provided illumination.

Burt spotted me and patted the chair next to his. "Hey, Sleeping Beauty, grab a plate and take a seat."

"Smells wonderful," I said, leaning forward and filling a plate with still-steaming spaghetti. My stomach growled as I dug in.

"Where's Kathy?" I asked the group, casting aside proper manners and loudly slurping up the last few inches of a long piece of spaghetti.

"She's upstairs on the roof," Renee answered, grabbing a napkin and wiping my face. "I can't take you anywhere."

At the table were five of our group and Beth, Burt, Beth's parents, Charlene and Edward Sullivan, and their four sons Oliver, Dwight, Alexander, and Glenn. Glenn's wife, Vicki, was at the far end of the table helping their two three-year-old identical twins, Constance and Lauren, spoon spaghetti into manageable portions.

Between bites, I looked over at Burt. "Anything from your parents?" I asked.

"Not yet, though I don't know how Dad would be able to get in touch with us," he replied, wiping his mouth with a napkin and pushing his empty paper plate forward. "The pulse happened early morning before rush hour, and I would think the freeways should be fairly empty. If he didn't run into any issues, he should have pulled in here two or three hours ago. I'm hoping he went by his house to grab a few things before heading here."

"They're going to be fine," Beth said, having overheard our conversation. "If anyone can take care of themselves, it's your mom and dad."

"Have you started loading the old army supply trucks and their trailers?" I asked.

"We have," he answered. "We've got the entire armory and faraday cage contents loaded up and are working on the ammo and magazines now. By the way, I put the other ten .50-cal mags on your driver's seat."

"Thank you. Any further issues with people wanting in the store?"

"A few, but Oliver and Dwight took care of it."

We sat quietly talking and catching up for another forty-five minutes. Renee grabbed my hand and squeezed and didn't let go. It felt strange, a good strange to be sure, to be holding hands in front of people we knew after hiding our relationship for so long.

I slid back my chair and, standing, addressed the group.

"I can't thank you enough for the generosity you've shown us today. You're a good man, Burt, and you've got a great family here with you."

"You seem to have forgotten the three Krugerrands," he said, holding up the three shiny one-ounce gold coins. "You're the generous one."

I reached out and, before he could react, grabbed the three coins out of the palm of his hand. "I think I was overly generous, and I'll keep two of them."

"Not so fast, buster," Renee said, swiping them out of my hand and giving all three to Beth. "I think it best the ladies take care of the gold."

"Fair enough," Burt said, laughing.

"And I think it's time we get going," I said, addressing the four women in our group. "You ready to roll?"

"We want to take a shower before we leave," Monica blurted out. "We haven't showered since yesterday morning, and we're feeling more than a little disgusting."

I spread my hands out, said, "Come on, ladies. Showers? We went weeks without showering in Afghanistan. Besides, there are no showers here."

It was Beth who ruined that argument. "We sell a Coleman propane-fired hot water shower, don't we, honey?" she asked Burt.

"Yep, there are a few still on the shelf in the camping section. Be easy to set up in the back of the building," he offered. "We can run a hose from the water spigot no problem."

"See, Jon, problem solved," Beth said. "Ladies, let's get you cleaned up."

The ladies marched off to shower, first stopping by the Cruiser to take a few confiscated Venetian towels and a bunch of the hotel's mini shampoo and liquid body soap bottles.

Beth's father, Edward, spoke up first. "You should know by now, Jon, that saying no to one woman, let alone a whole pack of them, will get you nothing but painful frustration. Learn from my years of experience, son."

We all laughed at that. Burt then said, "Alex, if you're done eating, can you please go up to the roof and relieve Kathy so she can take a shower too?"

"Will do," Alex answered, grabbing an M4 and a chest rig, and then running up the stairs.

Burt reached into his back pocket and took out several folded-up road maps. Handing them to me, he said, "We sell road maps for all the western states, and here are Nevada, Arizona, Utah, Idaho, Oregon, Washington, and Montana. I also drew you a map with directions to our place in Utah should you ever venture out that way."

"Thanks much. I hate to ask anything more of you, but by chance do you have a national map which shows interstate highways?"

"We do. Planning a cross-country road trip?" Burt asked.

"Renee and I need to get to Kentucky or Atlanta at some point."

"Long drive. I'll get you a map for every state. Dwight, can you run over to the map section and get a map for each state? Minus the states he already has. And grab the folded waterproof map of the US Interstate System."

"You bet."

"And maybe a Canadian map if there is one," I said. "Please."

"There is. It's on the far-right rear of the rack," Burt said.

"Thank you, Dwight," I said.

"Have you thought about the route you're going to take to Seattle?" Burt asked, watching Dwight make his way to the store.

I unfolded and spread out the map showing all the western states. With my finger I traced our route.

"I figured we'd head north on Interstate 15, and if things are okay, continue up until just south of Provo, where we'll turn west on Highway 50 . . . I want to avoid Provo and Salt Lake City at all costs. Then turn north on 93, which runs up to Twin Falls, Idaho. From there I'm not sure. We'll have to see once we're in the area."

"You're going to have to deal with St. George and Cedar City on your way up 15," Burt said, "but it's only been fifteen hours into day one of the blackout, so you might just have an easy go of it."

Beth's father walked over and put his finger on Las Vegas.

"If I can make a suggestion," he said. "You may want to head up 15 as planned, and if things are dicey, then get on 93 where it hits the 15. That way the only semi-large town you'll have to deal with is Ely. There are a few much smaller towns you'll pass through: Alamo, Ash Springs, Sunnyside, and Majors Place, which is where you hit Highway 50 and up to Ely. But those towns are truly small and shouldn't present a problem. That entire road is not that well-traveled, and I don't think you'll have to deal with a bunch of dead cars and trucks blocking your way. One thing though, there are some mountain summits and hills you're going to have to contend with, but I imagine your Toyota is built for long, steep stretches."

"Well heck, Ed, that sounds like a plan to me," I said. "Anything that helps us avoid people, I'm all for. Thank you, we'll do it."

I ended up taking a shower at the insistence of Renee, who had come back from her shower, wet hair and all, saying she was feeling like a new person.

I relented and had to admit I felt a lot better.

"I'm putting the Coleman shower in the trailer along with a large, grill-sized propane tank," Burt said, a big grin on his face. "Happy woman equals happy travels."

"Once again, Burt. A huge thank you. You've made this trip possible."

NINE

An hour later, after the goodbyes and hugs were said and done, I helped the women double-check their weapons. Each had their rifle charged but with the safety on. I then had them turn on their night vision goggles. The goggles, four tubes sitting in front of their eyes, were held in place by webbing that fit over their heads. Burt turned his flashlight off, and the women got their first taste of nightlife, military-style.

After the oohs and ahhs, they settled down.

We loaded into the Cruiser, me driving, Melissa riding shotgun, Renee and Kathy on the jump seat behind Melissa, and Kris and Monica behind me. I started the engine but stayed in place for a minute while Burt raised the warehouse roll-up door.

"Okay, this is how this is going to work," I began. "This method of travel has taken me hundreds and hundreds of miles over hostile countryside, and I'm still in one piece. Melissa, your job is to scan the 180 degrees in front of us. Renee and Kathy, you'll scan behind us and the driver's side. Kris and Monica, you'll be responsible for the rear and passenger side. You see something, say something.

"We'll take stretch breaks every hour or so. When we stop, everyone piles out and drops a knee fifteen feet out from the truck, space permitting. If I say "close-in," then take a knee right next to the Cruiser.

"Place your rifle's buttstock on the floor and let the barrel rest on your chest and shoulder. Leave your right hand free to grab your Glock . . . It's dark out, and the Eotechs and their red dots aren't going to help much at night, so the Glocks might be better in short distance exchanges," I explained. "Also, if we do get into a shooting match at night, look for muzzle flashes and aim and fire at them. "Everyone ready?" I asked.

A unanimous yes was the response.

"Okay. Hold on," I said, honking the horn at Burt and the assembled group as they waved goodbye. I let the clutch out, and we were off. Edgar had opened the parking lot gate, and I turned right onto Decatur. Buildings flashed by in an eerie greenish glow of the night vision. I saw no one on the streets.

The Cruiser felt heavy and sluggish with the additional weight of people and trailer. But as I went through the gears, she showed her low-end torque prowess and leaped ahead.

"To be honest, I'm a little frightened," Kris admitted.

"Me too," Kathy seconded. "Actually, beyond scared."

"Well, while I'm not exactly scared, I admit to being nervous," I said, "But if we don't take unnecessary chances, you listen to me and do everything I tell you, we'll be okay . . . I promise. And once we're off these surface streets and on the interstate, things should be much safer."

We drove north on Decatur and two blocks later turned right onto Sahara Avenue. If I remembered correctly, the northbound 15 on-ramp should be about a mile ahead on the left.

This area of town was mainly warehousing, auto repair, body shops, and those businesses that catered to the Las Vegas resorts, hotels, and casinos. Being commercial, I didn't expect to see anyone out and about, but there were dead cars on the road, which I was having to maneuver around. This constant lane changing was really slowing us down.

"There's a traffic light ahead, and the intersection is clogged with dead cars. I don't see a way around them," Melissa said.

I scanned ahead, and sure enough, we were going to be boxed in. I came to a quick stop and considered our options. The median was thick with bushes and trees, and there was no way we could drive over it and continue in the opposite lanes. I didn't want to back up with the trailer and reverse course. It was Monica that came up with the solution.

"Go right into that gas station and cut the corner through their lot," Monica suggested.

"Let's do it," I said, turning into the darkened gas station. "Everything look okay, ladies?"

"Yes," came a chorus of replies from behind me.

We had just passed the first set of pumps when a group of ten or twelve men and women poured out of the gas station's broken glass entrance door. They had their arms full of drinks, bags of potato chips, and snacks. They didn't appear to be armed.

"Get your Glock out, Melissa," I said. "Roll down your window, and when I tell you, fire off a single round over their heads. You have a round in the chamber?"

"Yes, good to go," she answered, rolling down her window.

Seeing us, the looters stopped dead in their tracks and started yelling for us to stop. "We need a ride," they shouted. "We need to get back to Los Angeles!"

We were in first gear, rolling through the station at seven or eight miles an hour. "I'm not stopping, guys, so be ready if they try to storm us."

Seeing that we didn't plan on stopping, the looters started throwing water bottles at us. Thirty feet to our front, one big guy, maybe even a football player in his day, stepped into our path and stood his ground, palm up and facing us as if he were a traffic cop signaling us to stop.

"Fire off a round, Melissa. Now."

She extended her arm out the window and fired a round into the night sky. The other looters ran back toward the station's store, but football player man stoically stood his ground.

We were now twenty-five feet from the guy and quickly closing the distance.

He threw several family-sized bags of chips into the air and charged us. He was fifteen feet from the front bumper when Melissa fired another round, hitting him in his left foot. He dropped to the ground, and with mere inches to spare, I managed to swerve around him. We exited the station, turned left on the side street, and then right back onto Sahara Avenue.

"I aimed to his right to scare him off but hit him," Melissa said, sounding shocked. "I didn't mean to hit him," she said matter-of-factly. Melissa still had her hand and Glock hanging out the window.

"You did fine, Melissa," I said, putting my hand on her shoulder. "Now get your finger off the trigger, bring the weapon back inside, and holster it. And remember that you have twelve rounds left in that magazine."

"We have people running toward us on the right," Kris shouted. "There must be thirty of them."

I sped up and slipped in front of the crowd before they got to the street and attempted to block us. A second later a shot rang out, and I heard it impact the steel roof rack. There were no follow-up shots.

"The fuckers just shot at us," Monica exclaimed.

"Good thing they're shitty shooters shooting shots." This from an excited Kris.

"Say that five times in a row, and I'll give you the bag of chips that landed on the hood," Melissa said, laughing, relieving some tension and then pointing to the bag of Frito Lay potato chips resting between the hood and windshield.

We all laughed at that, Kathy even trying to say it five times but only managing two before mangling it.

"What would you have done had they been able to block our path?" Kris asked.

"What we did in the gas station—fire a round over their heads."

"And if the whole bunch of them had run at us?" Monica asked.

"Run them over," Melissa answered.

"Really?" Kris asked.

"If we couldn't stop them with gunfire, then yes, I would have run them over," I answered. "Without hesitation."

In the greenish glow of the night vision, I saw the signs for the Interstate 15 North on-ramp. I drove under the freeway, slowed, and turned left onto the ramp. This section of the freeway was elevated, and I brought us to a stop at the top of the ramp. I opened my door, stepped onto the tubular running board, and scanned the road ahead. Seeing no one, just abandoned cars and semitrucks, I got back in and set out.

But not before Melissa grabbed the potato chips.

WE DROVE ON IN SILENCE, slowly leaving the huge, darkened resorts, hotels, and casinos behind. We were still on an elevated freeway as we drove north on Interstate 15 through North Las Vegas. Avoiding dead vehicles, I cut right or left as necessary, steadily making progress.

Everywhere I looked there was the brilliant glow of hundreds, perhaps even thousands, of fires burning across the city. The night vision picked up people walking on surface side streets and even more congregating and running into and out of big-box stores that lined the freeway.

The further we went, the more big-box stores we saw, most located at the bottom of off-ramps. Hundreds of people were milling about in the store's parking lots. Fast food restaurants had already been broken into and were in the process of being stripped.

"It hasn't even been a day, and people are already going nuts," Monica observed, her gaze steady on the scene unfolding below us.

"Why are they already going nuts?" Kris asked. "If Ben and Jon hadn't explained that what we're experiencing is an EMP, I would have figured the country's power grid had been hacked again. I mean, why not wait a day or two before looting stores and restaurants?"

"Because their cell phones, computers, and cars aren't working," Kathy answered. "Based on that alone, I think most people realize what we're experiencing is not a simple power outage."

"If it's like this now, what's it going to be like in five days? Or even a month?" Melissa asked.

"In five days," I answered, "those people down there are going to be killing each other for bottled water and food scraps. In a month? Most of them will be dead."

"I can't even imagine having to kill someone for bottled water," Kris said.

"When you haven't had a sip of water in two days, you'd be shocked at what you'd be willing to do to satisfy the thirst," I replied.

"I couldn't do it. Ever. Kill someone for what they have," Kris came back with.

"Well, hopefully, you'll never have to find out one way or another," Renee said.

We passed the exit for the Las Vegas Motor Speedway, and through the night vision, I could see dozens of people milling about the vast parking lot. Even from a quarter mile away, several pointed at us as we drove by on the elevated freeway.

I wasn't going fast, and the tires weren't loud, so something had to have alerted them to our presence.

I rolled down my window and stuck my head out. Cutting through the usual rush of wind, I heard something flapping behind us.

"The tarp covering the trailer must have come loose," I said. "You guys in back see anything?" I asked.

Renee answered first. "Yep, driver's side rear tie-down has come undone."

A half mile further up, I downshifted and came to a stop in the fast lane. Leaving the engine on but setting the parking brake, I hopped out and checked every direction but saw no one within the farthest range of the night vision goggles. Fourth-generation night vision like ours had a detection range of about four hundred yards, but a recognition range of two hundred yards. It was a moonless night, so the range might not even be that much.

Before I could walk back to the trailer, Kris spoke up, "I'm sorry, but I have to pee." This was followed by "Me too" from the rest of them.

I guessed now was as good a time as any to teach them how to set up a perimeter watch.

"Okay, from now on this is what we're going to do when we stop," I said. "Once we're stopped, you're going to exit the Cruiser, and depending on where you're seated, that will be your outside area of responsibility."

I walked around the front of the Cruiser and opened the passenger door. "Melissa, you're in front, which means you're responsible for the area in front of the Cruiser. Take your rifle and follow me." I took five large steps away from the front of the truck, which was probably fifteen feet, more or less. "Take a knee here and face out. Safety on and keep your finger off the trigger. Turn your comms on and make sure the volume is low. You see something, you say something. Got it?"

"Yep, no problem."

I repeated the procedure with the rest of the women.

Once they were in position, I keyed the comms and asked for a check-in.

They all checked in, and I went to work on the tarp.

"I still have to pee," Kris said over the comms, followed by four more of "Me too."

"Okay, Kris," I said.

Kris stood and walked to the shoulder of the roadway, then started slip-sliding her way down the embankment.

I keyed the comms, said, "Kris, get back up here, please. You do your business where we can see you."

"I won't be able to if everyone is watching," she answered.

"Don't care," I answered, adamant. "We'll look away, but everyone pees or poops within sight of each other. Like it or not, that's the way it's going to be."

Kris walked back up the embankment, dropped her pants, and squatted in the slow lane. She held the rifle awkwardly in her left hand.

Finished, she said, "I forgot toilet paper. Can someone bring me some?"

Jeez, what next?

"We've got company coming up the on-ramp, maybe a half mile back," Monica's voice barked over the comms. "No headlights, maybe a motorcycle from the sound of it."

"Kris, pull your pants up and get back on perimeter. Now!" I yelled, not bothering with the comms. "Monica and Kathy, get ready. The rest of you, watch your areas."

"It's so dark, chances are he's not going to see us until he's almost on top of us," Kathy said.

"Good point. Monica and Kathy, come over by me," I said. "Kris, come back to the Cruiser and hug the rear fender. Melissa, make sure you're protected by the front bumper. Let's let this guy have plenty of room to get past us."

Thirty seconds later, a slow-moving motorcycle with two people aboard appeared in my NVs.

"Let 'em through," I said.

"He's slowing down," Monica said. "And now he's stopping."

And they had, about seventy-five feet behind us. The rider put his left foot down while his passenger, a woman, started to dismount. The bike looked to be an older Triumph.

"Turn the engine off," I yelled.

They were both visibly startled. The woman let out a loud yelp.

The driver reached out to his handlebar and turned off the engine. "We mean you no harm and aren't armed," the driver shouted back. "My name is Brandon, and this is my fiancée, Ruth."

A hand came off the driver's waist and gave us a tentative wave.

"Put the kickstand down and get off the bike," I said. "Then I want you both on the ground, facedown with helmets off."

The driver put the kickstand down and helped the woman dismount. Both took their helmets off, then lay face down on the pavement.

"Please don't hurt us, mister. We found out this morning I'm pregnant with our first. We just want to get home," the woman shouted, pleading. "We were in the base hospital and had just gotten the good news when things went dark. We set out for home but ran out of gas by the racetrack. Luckily, someone let us siphon gas out of their car. And, well, here we are."

I went over to Monica, whispered, "Go pat them down. Thoroughly."

"I'm sending someone over to search you. If they find any weapons, we're going to take them and disable your bike," I said.

"You won't find a weapon, sir," the man said, addressing the darkness.

Monica walked over and, putting her rifle over her shoulder, patted both down, nodding in the negative. She went back to her original position.

The man glanced up and saw the night vision goggles. "You men military?"

Not answering his question, I said, "You can sit up but remain on the pavement."

I walked over and stood five feet away. I moved the M4 to my side and took out the Glock.

"Master Sergeant," Brandon said, spotting my stripes, "I'm an active-duty flight lieutenant temporarily based at Nellis Test Range. You men on some sort of recon?"

"We're headed up to Seattle," I answered, flipping up the NVs. I keyed the comms, said, "Stand down, but return to positions."

Five clicks came back at me. I left the mic open so the ladies could hear the exchange.

I reached down and offered the woman a hand. She took it, and I helped her stand. Brandon stood and offered his hand to shake. We shook, and he wrapped his arm around Ruth.

"I'm curious, why'd you stop, Brandon?"

"I had to tinkle," Ruth answered for him.

Out of the darkness came hearty laughter.

I BROUGHT FOUR OF THE women back behind the trailer but left Melissa on a loose perimeter patrol. We spent fifteen minutes talking to Brandon and Ruth. Brandon turned out to be an Air Force A-10 Warthog pilot and Ruth an Air Force master mechanic.

"I'm at Nellis conducting in-flight testing on two new weapon systems for the A-10," Brandon told us. "But before my posting here, I flew two-hundred-plus sorties in A-10s over Afghanistan, supporting ground brothers such as yourself, Master Sergeant."

I nodded, said, "You Hog drivers saved our bacon more times than I can tell you, Lieutenant."

"And I'm chief mechanic for the A-10's new weapon system platform," Ruth offered. "I install 'em, and Brandon flies 'em."

"You have any information on what's happened?" I asked.

"We do. Like Ruth said, we were at the base hospital when the power went out," he said. "The base commander gathered everyone together at the base theater and told us that he'd heard from National Command at the Pentagon. Seems that two nuclear devices had detonated—one over Colorado and the other over Ohio. Both in the upper atmosphere."

"How did he hear from the Pentagon?" I asked. "I just assumed that most electronics were fried, meaning no communications."

Ruth was the one that answered my question.

"I can't speak for the other branches of the military, but for several years the Air Force has been reinforcing its infrastructure, meaning its planes, radar installations, comms systems, anti-missile defenses to protect against EMPs. I know because I helped install some of the counter-measures."

"He also said there were four missiles that had been detected headed our way and that our early warning systems had seen them," Brandon added. "Our antimissile defense systems got two, but the third and fourth slipped through and detonated. And no big surprise . . . those four missiles came from North Korea."

That asshole, Kim Jong-un, finally did it.

"That little shit wasn't just after us," Ruth said. "He also sent another six missiles out to Moscow, London, Brussels, Paris, Rome, and I can't remember the sixth. But they all detonated in the upper atmosphere, so they're all in the same boat we are."

"The sixth was somewhere over Israel," Brandon added. "Maybe Tel Aviv."

"I notice that China and Iran were spared a present," Renee pointed out.

"Interesting you say that, ma'am. The Pentagon thinks that it might have been China that supplied the missiles to North Korea and that they may have their sights on North America and parts of Europe," Brandon said, "which is why they had the missiles detonate in the upper atmosphere—so as to preserve the spoils."

"More folks will likely die from lack of electricity than a surface nuclear blast," Ruth said.

"Several intelligence agencies reported increased signal traffic after Biden's people reported the rebuilding and reinforcement of the power grid was nearly complete," Brandon said.

"But North Korea no longer exists, because no sooner than we'd seen those missiles coming our way, we sent a few right back at 'em," Ruth said, rubbing her stomach like most pregnant women seem to do. "And not just us, but Russia and Israel sent their own as well. And they were surface blasts, not atmospheric."

"That's the only good thing I've heard so far," Monica said.

Renee shook her head. "Not so good, Monica. South Korea is now living in a cloud of radiation. Seoul has eight million people living within a hundred miles of the North Korean border."

"China must know we'd retaliate if they try and invade the United States. Though they may think we're unable to, due to the EMP," Brandon pointed out. "The Pentagon thinks China acted now, since President Biden has made reinforcing Taiwan's air defenses a priority and couldn't risk waiting."

"Like you said, President Biden announced a few days ago that our power grid upgrades would be completed next month," Kris said. "Maybe that's why they hit us."

"Good point, ma'am. I'll tell you one thing, if the Chinese send ships to the West Coast, they're going to run into a bunch of A-10s that are ready to go, already pulse-proofed and loaded for bear," Ruth said. "They even have the latest anti-radar jamming equipment. The Chinese will never see 'em coming."

"Never personally attacked a naval ship before," Brandon said, "but I know what I can do to a heavily armored tank, and a ship is thin-skinned in comparison."

"I wonder if the two that got through were supposed to have detonated that far up?" Renee asked, changing subjects. "And were the other two going to reenter the atmosphere and hit the ground?"

"Don't think we'll ever know the answer to that question," Brandon said. "And it's scary to think that four nuclear bombs might have hit anywhere in our country."

I hated to break up the conversation, but we were burning up darkness and felt we needed to get going.

"Listen, you two," I said, "we've got to get a move on, but if you ever want a safe place to raise that child of yours, my parents have a large ranch outside Whitefish, Montana. Get yourself to Kalispell. Once on Highway 93 and after the sharp left turn in town, go five miles, and you'll come to Skyles Lake Lane. Turn right, and two miles past the trail head, you'll see our ranch entrance on the right. We're two miles from the road. We're just west of Whitefish Lake up by its smaller sibling, Beaver Lake. But ask anyone where the Kristen Ranch is and tell them I sent you.

"Heck, we have a six-thousand-foot concrete runway on the property you could land an A-10 on if you wanted. We even have two pretty big hangars: one holds twelve planes and the other six, all corporate jets larger than your itty-bitty A-10. We could probably get twenty-four or thirty in the two hangars."

"Kristen Ranch west of Whitefish Lake by Beaver Lake," Ruth repeated. "Sounds good, sir. Thanks."

"Never know, we might take you up on your offer," Brandon said, helping Ruth onto the bike. "If we do someday show up, it'll be by air. We'll look for the runway and hangars." He slid his right leg over the seat and started the engine. "Stay frosty, guys."

And they were off.

TEN

We headed out a few minutes later.

Silence filled the Cruiser's interior. I was trying to digest the news we'd just learned, and I imagined the others were doing the same. What was in store for us, our country, or for that matter, the world? Earlier, Ben had laid out a probable timeline for recovery, and if anything, from what Brandon had told us, Ben's timeline was pretty spot on. At this point, I had more questions than answers. How would we grow food? Produce medicines, communicate, keep the peace, raise, educate, and keep our children safe? Coming to grips with all this was going to take some time.

A few minutes later, the mileage sign for Highway 93 appeared in the greenish-glow of the night vision—six miles.

"Once we're on 93, we should be able to pick up speed," I told the women. "I can't imagine too many people were on this road so early in the morning."

"If that's the case, there not being many folks out and about, can I turn off my night vision and close my eyes?" Kris asked. "My eyes hurt."

"That should be okay, but let's get on 93 before we turn any off."

"Missiles with nuclear warheads?" Kathy asked. "I thought once Putin was locked up in a remote gulag somewhere, this kind of worry was a thing of the past. Boy, was I wrong."

"North Korea had to know the countries that were hit would retaliate," Monica said. "I mean, how stupid to think they could get away with attacking us."

"It's so stupid, it makes me wonder if maybe China snuck a submarine or two into North Korean waters and fired them off," Renee said. "Can we tell which silo a missile is fired from?"

"Good question," I said. "Maybe someday we'll find out."

A few minutes later, the turnoff lane for 93 North appeared in the NVs. I merged right onto the ramp, which went up and over 15 and then headed back down where it faded into the darkness of the desert.

"Okay, Kris, go ahead and turn off your night vision. You too, Renee." This left Monica and Kathy covering our sides and rear and myself and Melissa the front. "Let's do one on, one off watch rotation starting now."

Earlier at Burt's, I'd plotted our route and figured we'd stop for the day a few miles south of Sunnyside, Nevada—just shy of two hundred miles up 93. If the road was somewhat clear of dead cars and trucks, and with our night vision on, I thought we could safely make our way at a steady forty to fifty miles an hour. We needed to take advantage of the relative calm of night one of the blackout—the going would never be better than this. No doubt most people were still thinking this was temporary, not unlike the days-long power grid hack of last year.

We saw several groups of people walking south on the shoulder. Most were families with the father and mother toting wheeled luggage behind them with children setting the pace in front. The entire family stopped when they heard us approaching, the parents peering out into the night, grabbing their kids, and stepping further back onto the highway's shoulder. By the time they were able to see us, we were whooshing on by.

The road was straight, with few bends. It did follow the topography of the land, so it was hill after hill, up one side and down the other, with the low points crossing desert arroyos and then vaulting skyward, sometimes a good hundred to two hundred feet up before dropping down the other side. I was uneasy when cresting these hills, as I didn't know what we'd encounter on the other side. It wasn't until we were heading down that I could see what was ahead in the greenish glow of the NVs. For now, this was working, but in the days ahead, when more people were out and getting desperate for food and water, this cresting and blindly heading down without really knowing what lay ahead wasn't going to work.

We made good time and an hour and a half later stopped on a high portion of the roadway for a restroom and stretch break. The women poured out of the Cruiser and, without being told, formed a perimeter ring. One at a time, with the others covering their positions, they dropped pants and did their business.

I went back to the rear of the trailer, lifted the left rear tarp corner, took out my M4, and booted up the attached thermal scope. Once it was fully operational, I slowly scanned a full 360 degrees. A few hundred yards to our left, and according to the sign we passed a few miles back, was Upper Pahranagat Lake, its water shimmering in the scope. And other than a semitruck a few hundred yards ahead of us, I saw nothing of concern.

What an amazing piece of technology this scope was. It could see anything producing a heat signature up to eleven hundred yards out. It had a built-in ballistic calculator and range finder. With just a little bit of work, I could hit a target up to five-hundred yards with the M4 rifle and up to the limits of the scope, or eleven hundred yards, with the Barrett. This baby was going to help keep us safe.

I scanned again and, not seeing any threats, keyed the comms. "Okay, ladies, relax and take fifteen. You can turn off and then take off your NVs but keep your rifles and chest rigs on."

The women made their way to the back of the trailer and with flashlights dug through backpacks and duffel bags in search of the trail energy bars we'd collected in Vegas. I kept overwatch by scanning with the thermal.

A few minutes later, Renee appeared at my side. She wrapped her arms around my waist and hugged me tight, whispered, "I haven't had a chance to talk to you about me tagging along. I know it's a little late to be asking you this, but are you really okay with having me here?" She tilted her head back and looked me in the eyes. "Like, *with* you? Like the two of us together? I mean . . ."

". . . like a couple?" I finished for her.

"Yeah, like a couple. When I heard that the plane was only flying east, all I could think about was that I might never see you again."

I tilted her chin up and gently kissed her.

"Other than the world falling apart, I am a very happy guy. From the moment back in Vegas when you said you'd like to come with us, I've thought about the *us* factor, and I like it. A lot. And I'm glad you're here with me and that we're facing this ordeal together."

"Does that mean that I can stay with you, no, make that *live* with you, in Montana?" Renee asked.

"Yes, we'll live together. My parents are going to love you," I said before kissing her again. "My mother is going to love you like a daughter. So watch out."

We stayed in place, hugging and kissing.

I completed another scan, and all was good.

Renee hugged me tighter, grabbed my rear, and pressed herself against me. I tried to get to her boobs and, thwarted in my attempts, said, "Your chest rig doesn't exactly lend itself to romance . . . all I get is a hard Glock and a couple of rifle magazines."

Renee laughed and, breathing heavily in my ear, said, "You've got something to look forward to when we stop for the night, mister."

She released me and, smiling, turned around and backed into me. She reached down and brought my hands up to the sides of her chest rig, slid them into the rig's open sides, and planted my palms on her ample breasts.

I happily kneaded away like a kitten on its momma's stomach while Renee moaned softly and ground her rear into my front.

This was getting a little out of hand. I whispered in her ear, "If we continue with this, I won't be able to stop. And we need to get going."

Renee sighed, said, "You're right. Can't wait for later, Master Sergeant."

"Let's load up and get going," I told the group. "Resume night vision rotation."

I made my way to the Cruiser, and a question came to mind. "Anyone here know how to drive a manual?" I asked.

"A manual?" Kris asked. "What's a manual?"

"It's a transmission," Monica answered. "For a car. Like what's in the Cruiser, where you have to manually change gears."

"My father used to laugh and say a manual transmission is a Millennial anti-theft device," Melissa said.

"I like your dad's sense of humor," I said. "And it's very true. Very few younger people know how to drive a stick shift. Anybody know how?"

Monica, Renee, and Kathy all said no.

Which left Melissa, who said, "I sorta kinda can. My brother has a 1970 Chevelle, which he's let me drive a few times. It has four on the floor . . . if I said that right."

"Okay, good," I said, feeling relieved that we had someone who could drive the Cruiser if need be.

"Pile in, everyone. Melissa, give me your rifle and get behind the wheel. It's time for a quick refresher course."

I did another 360 scan with the thermal and again came up empty. I got in the passenger seat, asked, "Melissa, you know which is the brake pedal and which is the clutch?"

"Yes."

"Okay, this is a four on the floor like your brother's Chevelle. Let's see if you can do this on your own, then we'll work on whatever needs help. Go ahead and start it."

Melissa depressed the clutch, wiggled the gear shifter, and found neutral. She turned the key, and the Cruiser came to life.

"Good. Now release the parking brake. We're on level ground up here and have at least a hundred feet before the roadway dips back down, so we're probably not going to roll."

Melissa released the brake, and of course, the Cruiser rolled forward.

From the back, Kris said, "Please don't kill us, Melissa." Kris was in no way joking or having fun with Melissa.

"No back-seat drivers, bitch," was Melissa's reply.

"Kris, comments like that are not welcome," I said. "If you have nothing constructive to say, then don't say anything." I felt like I'd stepped into my mother's shoes.

"I don't know why you don't continue driv—" was as much as Kris was able to get out.

"Shut up, Kris. Now!" shouted Renee. "Or I swear to god I'll slap some sense into you."

"You think you can tell me what to do? Well, no fuckin—"

Whack. The sound of open palm against cheek was unmistakable in the tight confines of the Cruiser.

For several seconds, there was only shocked silence.

"We all good now?" I asked the group a half minute later.

I heard four yeses.

"Kris?" I asked, waiting.

"Good to go," she finally replied, her voice cracking with barely suppressed emotion.

"Excellent. Okay then, Melissa, put your foot on the brake and stop our rolling."

She did, and we stopped with a jolt.

"Now, with the clutch still in, put it into first gear. Now slowly let the clutch out and then out completely," I instructed. We were now moving. She still had her foot on the clutch pedal. "Take your foot off the clutch pedal. That's called riding the clutch, and that will quickly wear it out."

Melissa let the clutch out, and the Cruiser slowly crept forward at a stately five miles an hour. "The Cruiser is meant to climb off-road trails, so the gearing is very low. Don't give it much gas . . . just let it idle along. Okay, now let's try and change ge—"

"I think I have this," she said, interrupting me. "Let me try it on my own."

"By all means. Go for it."

Melissa gave it gas and smoothly played the clutch and gas pedals, getting up to third gear in no time. We soon reached the bottom of the hill. "It's getting it moving from a stop that's hard," she said. "Once we're moving, it's easy changing gears."

"We've got a steep hill ahead, so keep it in third and let's climb to the top. Don't let the RPMs drop . . . That's called lugging it and is bad. Once we're at the top, stop."

At the top of the roadway, Melissa brought us to a smooth stop. I got out and scanned the road ahead with the thermal scope. Nothing was out there.

"Hit it," I said, hopping back inside and shutting my door. Which she did, this time making it to fourth gear and keeping it there until the next hilltop.

The distance between hilltops varied, some one mile, some three or four. But we made good time, even stopping at each hilltop and scanning the highway ahead. We kept this up for the next hour and a half until we crested a hill just south of the town of Alamo. Melissa stopped, and I performed my usual scan. We'd come across a few people walking, but they'd been single adults or family groups, and what I now saw in the scope was puzzling. A small child, not sure if it was a girl or boy, was slowly walking toward us down the center of the road, maybe three hundred yards out.

Melissa, who had her night vision on, saw the little figure at the same time I did. "There is a very young boy walking toward us, and he's alone," she said.

I stuck my head inside the Cruiser. "Let's stop here and set up a perimeter. Please set the parking brake, Melissa."

Once they were in position, I keyed the comms, said, "Let's let him come to us. Be watchful, everyone." I raised the M4 and carefully scanned the area to the rear and sides of the advancing child. Nothing. Using a child to lure someone into an ambush wouldn't be unheard of.

"A child out here alone is beyond weird," Monica said.

"Maybe the car he was in had an accident when the pulse hit," Kris added.

And then it was Renee's turn. "We're not going to leave him out here, are we?"

"No," I answered. "Kris, you have kids, would you go meet him? Maybe take off the night vision goggles so you don't scare him."

"Will do," she replied.

Kris removed her NVs, put them on the hood of the Cruiser, and waited for the boy to close the gap.

It was hard to tell the boy's age in the green glow of the night vision, but judging from his height, I'd guess maybe three or four years old.

He was holding a stuffed animal in his right hand and was barefoot. He had on a short-sleeve T-shirt and pajama bottoms. He was looking down at the road and appeared to be concentrating on each step.

He was ten feet from Kris when she kneeled down and softly said, "Hi there, honey."

The little boy looked up and walked right up to Kris. Without hesitation or saying a word, he hugged her as if holding on for dear life.

"My name is Kris. What's your name, sweetheart?"

"Mason," came a quiet response. "I'm cold."

"One of my friends will get you a blanket," Kris said.

"On it," Renee said over the comms.

"Is that a rabbit you have there, Mason?"

"Uh-huh."

"What's his name?"

"Charlie," he answered, holding the rabbit up for Kris's inspection.

"He's very cute," Kris responded, then asked, "Mason, where are your mommy and daddy?"

Mason raised his arm and pointed back in the direction he'd come from.

"Why are you walking alone, honey?"

"My mommy told me to run, and I did, but my feet hurt, and I can't run no more."

Renee walked up to them and draped a large bathroom towel around the boy's shoulders. "Hi, Mason. I'm Renee."

"Hi."

"Do you know why your mommy wanted you to run?" Kris asked.

"I was sleeping in bed, and I woke up because I heard a really loud noise. I looked out the window, and Mommy was outside the car on the ground, and two men were with her. Mommy's friend was on the ground sleeping. Mommy saw me looking out the camper window and told me to run. She looked really scared, and I was scared too, and I just ran and ran until my feet hurt too bad."

"Do you know the two men, sweetheart?" Kris asked patiently.

"No."

I'd heard enough. "Kris, carry him to the Cruiser and let's get going."

I grabbed Kris' night vision off the hood and helped her load Mason into the back.

Getting into the passenger seat, I said to Melissa, "Stop a hundred yards from the top of the next hill. Kris, you stay in the Cruiser with Mason. Renee, Monica, and Kathy, when we stop, set up a three-person close-in perimeter. Melissa, you stay in the

Cruiser and watch me. Move the Cruiser forward when I tell you, and stop when I tell you. You three on perimeter, move alongside the Cruiser.

"Everyone good?" I asked.

A unanimous yes was the answer.

"Let's go, Melissa."

Melissa made her way slowly down the hill and up the next, stopping just shy of the hilltop. I slid out and quietly closed the passenger door while the women did the same in the back. They fanned out around the Cruiser as I walked up a hundred yards to the top of the hill. I raised the night vision goggles and scanned the roadway with the thermal scope. Clear.

I motioned for Melissa to move forward with me, and we repeated this routine down the hill and up the next. I had her stop just short of cresting the next hill. I raised the rifle and thermal scanned the next half mile. Down in the low valley, perhaps a half mile further on, glowing bright red, were two vehicles. I also saw four bright red human-shaped blobs ... only three moving.

I turned back to Melissa and ran my hand across my throat, indicating that I wanted her to cut the engine.

I keyed the comms, said, "Okay, listen up. There are two trucks up ahead and four heat signatures ... only three moving. It's got to be Mason's mom and the two men. This is the real deal, so no fuckups or hesitation. Safeties off and set it to three-round bursts. Melissa, set yours on semiauto. Fingers off triggers.

"Melissa, set the parking brake and then put it in first gear and leave it there. Leaving it in gear acts as a backup parking brake."

"Okay."

"You know what those men are doing to Mason's mom, and we can't let that go. We're going to get Mason back to his mother," I said. "Melissa and Renee, you're going with me. You both stay at my side. Don't leave unless I tell you to. Kris, stay where you are with Mason. Kathy and Monica, take positions in front and in back of the Cruiser. Move out twenty-five feet and continually scan three-sixty with your night vision. You see anyone approaching, let me know. There could be more bad guys out there other than the two down below."

Melissa and Renee ran up to me, and we slowly crested the hill. We made our way down the other side toward the two trucks, which I could now see were an older-model VW camper and a sixties-something four-by-four pickup truck. The four-by-four was parked in such a way as to block the road.

As we got closer, we could hear a woman crying. We were fifty yards away, and I could see in the green glow of the night vision a woman on her back, on bare pavement, being raped . . . one man between the woman's legs and holding a wicked-looking knife to her throat while the other held her hands over her head. Two rifles were leaning against the camper's front passenger door. The driver's door was open, and I figured that was the door Mason had opened to run away.

The woman was begging them to stop. I then heard her say, "Please, Barry, stop. Please. I won't say anything to anyone if you stop now."

"You always were a fuckin' bitch, Margo. In high school you wouldn't even talk to me," the man between her legs shouted, thrusting harder.

"I only want to get my son and get home," the woman said, pleading. She looked up at the man holding her arms above her head. "Scotty, we grew up together and were friends. Why are you helping this asshole do this?"

Scotty didn't have an answer as he remained silent.

I stopped, took a knee, and had the two women come closer to me.

"Renee, I want you to take a knee right here," I whispered. "If for some reason those two get past Melissa and me, you will need to put them down. Can you do that?"

"Absolutely," she whispered back.

"Okay. Once again, safeties off and fingers off triggers. And, Renee, select three-round bursts. Do you need help with getting your weapons set?" I asked them. Hearing no response, I added, "Now is not the time to be shy."

"I'm good," Melissa said, voice full of strong confidence.

"I'm ready, Jon," Renee answered.

I nodded. Melissa and I left Renee where she was and continued down toward the assault, getting within thirty feet of the VW camper's rear end. The trio were in front of and to the right of the camper. Staying here and taking a shot would risk hitting the woman. A better angle would be from their right to left, even with them, with me at the three o'clock position shooting toward nine o'clock.

I whispered in Melissa's ear, "Position here. I'm moving to their right and will fire from that angle. Only fire if I miss and they try to get away or fire back."

"Got it."

"You're fuckin' dead, bitch. Your daddy is never gonna know what happened to you," Barry shouted. "We're gonna bury you out here when we're done having fun with you."

The two men continued to overpower the woman. The three active bodies were in close proximity to each other, so close that even well-placed single rounds might be too dangerous. I crept into position, took a knee, raised the night vision goggles, and put the thermal scope's reticle on Barry's head. The range finder kicked in, telling me I was ten yards from the target, but at this range, I didn't need a computer. The crosshairs glowed and pulsed red.

The fact that Barry had a knife to the woman's throat sealed his fate.

I waited until Barry's head came a bit higher and pulled the trigger. In the scope, I saw his head explode in a red mist, bits of heat, thousands of them, flying off into the night.

The woman screamed and tried to push Barry off. Scotty's brain didn't have time to tell the rest of him to let go of the woman. A half second later, I scoped Scotty's head and repeated the firing sequence. The top of Scotty's head disintegrated into a mass of flying heat, and his body immediately collapsed on top of the woman.

The woman became hysterical as she tried to wiggle her way free of the three or four hundred pounds of dead weight now piled on top of her.

I keyed the comms. "Melissa, I need you down here. The rest of you keep watching for anyone that might have heard those shots. Renee, you're still on overwatch."

I approached the tangle of bodies, said, "Miss, calm down. It's over. You're safe now." I grabbed an arm and pulled Scotty's body off her chest.

Melissa appeared beside me and took over by saying, "We're here to help you." She bent down and offered her a hand up. "I know your name is Margo. Mine is Melissa, and this big guy is Jon."

I walked over to the man who I assumed was her husband and checked for a pulse. Feeling none, I went and searched the two dead men, finding wallets with Nevada addresses in the town of Alamo, which was just a few miles north.

Margo had managed to free herself from the men and, not believing Melissa, started crawling away.

"We found Mason, Margo," Melissa said in a calm, reassuring voice. "He's fine but needs his momma."

Hearing her son's name stopped the woman's backpedaling. She stood and asked, "Where's my son?"

Margo was lean and toned. I guessed her height at five- six or seven and one hundred thirty pounds. She had small breasts, long brownish hair, and a perky Nordic ski jump for a nose.

The thermal scope was still showing glowing bits of brain matter over her torso. The camper's passenger-side sliding door was also covered in it.

"He's safe with our friends back down the road a bit," I answered as I walked over to the four-by-four. "We'll bring him to you. Give us a few minutes to get that done."

"Why don't you gather your clothes?" Melissa suggested. "You must be cold."

For the first time, the woman seemed to notice her nakedness. She turned and slid open the camper's sliding door, asked, "Is Kurt dead?"

"Whoa. Stop," I said, stopping the woman from climbing in the camper by grabbing her arm and gently pulling her back. "Sorry, but let me check your camper first. May I?"

"Sure, but you won't find any weapons if that's what you're worried about."

And like she said, there were none.

"Well, is he dead?" the woman asked again, gathering her clothes and a towel.

"I'm sorry, your husband didn't make it," I answered.

"He's not my husband. He's my ex-boyfriend, who tried to run off when these two losers blocked the road and came at us with guns. I'm sorry he's dead, but he's my ex for a reason, and I won't miss him."

"Well, okay then," Melissa said.

"Do you see any sign of Barry's brother, Sam? The three of them had stopped another car before we drove up. I saw it parked next to their truck. They were unloading stuff from the car and putting it in the back of their truck. I don't know what they did to whoever was driving the car."

"The only vehicles here are your camper and their four-by-four," I said. I raised the thermal and completed a 360 scan of the surroundings.

"I don't see any bodies in the area. Maybe Sam took the driver with him."

"Let's get you rinsed off before you put clothes on . . . We don't want Mason to see you like this," Melissa said. "You have any water in the camper?"

"Yes, in the front cup holders."

Melissa took the two rifles leaning on the front passenger door and handed them to me. One was a decent Ruger 10/22, one of the most popular .22-caliber rifles in the world. The other one was an off-brand AR of dubious quality.

"Looks like you two have all the weapons and gear you need," she said, looking us over. Pointing to the two rifles, she asked, "Can I have those, please? I think the country is in for a world of hurt, and I could use them. And knowing those two assholes who raped me, I bet there are more weapons and ammo in the back of that piece-of-shit truck."

A piece-of-shit truck that was now worth its weight in gold. Literally.

"Yes, you can have the rifles. We'll hand them over to you when we're ready to leave. I'll check the truck, and you can have anything we find," I replied. "Heck, just take the truck."

"Not interested," she answered. "This is a 1968 Volkswagen Westfalia, and I'll keep it, thank you."

Melissa backed out of the camper with two water bottles. "It's going to be cold, but we need to get you cleaned up." While those two were busy with that task, I keyed the comms and told the others I was on my way back up and not to shoot. I reached Renee, and the two of us made our way up to the Cruiser. I called the other women back and told them to bring their weapons to safe and to walk alongside the Cruiser. After taking one last 360 thermal scan, I slowly drove down the hill, parking twenty feet behind the VW.

The night vision picked up Margo, who was now cleaned and dressed.

"Kris, keep Mason in the back with you," I said. "He shouldn't see what's down there. We'll bring his mother up to you."

I had Margo follow me to the back of the Cruiser. I opened the rear doors, and there was Mason, his arms open wide, waiting for his mother. She spotted her son and let out a sob of relief.

"Thank you all so much. I can't begin to tell you how much I appreciate you bringing him to me," she said, hugging him tightly, tears streaming down her face.

"Don't cry, Mama," Mason told her, wiping her tears away. "Charlie and I are okay."

"Margo, do you have socks and shoes for Mason in the camper?" Kris asked.

"Yes," she answered, putting Mason back into Kris's arms. "Let me get them and his favorite jacket. Be right back, Mase."

I caught up with Margo at the camper's sliding door. "Mason shouldn't see the three men. Maybe you should drive up a bit and then carry Mason well wide of all this. I'll check out the truck and load the camper with anything I find in the way of weapons or supplies. Sound good?"

By way of replying, she hugged me tight and kissed my cheek. "Thank you."

"You're welcome." I untangled myself from her embrace and started searching through the men's truck. And sure enough, after making my way through six inches of empty Big Gulp cups and Burger King wrappers, I found two more ARs and a shotgun along with an old Baretta handgun. There were several boxes of ammo for each weapon, along with a dozen assorted magazines. I also found four cases of Costco-brand water bottles.

Margo had moved the camper thirty feet past the truck, and I loaded the weapons, ammo, and water in the camper's rear seating area.

Margo had carried Mason wide of the carnage and was now buckling him in the front passenger seat.

"Seeing as how you knew those two men, I'm guessing you live up the road in Alamo."

Finished buckling Mason in, she turned, answered, "Yep, born and raised. My dad's the Lincoln County Sheriff, and their main office and jail are in town. Those two clowns were frequent visitors to my dad's facility."

"You want to bring those three bodies back to Alamo?" I asked.

"Fuck no, leave them here for the coyotes and buzzards. In two days, they'll be gone." She strode back to the two dead men and kicked both in the crotch. Glancing down at her handiwork, she laughed, said, "Well, thank you, Lord, for small favors . . . Barry was wearing a condom."

I handed her the key to the four-by-four. "This truck is now a valuable commodity. I suggest you have someone drive out here and take it back to your house. Stash it in your garage if you have one."

"Dad is first and foremost a rancher, and we have a huge storage garage that's big enough to hold a hundred of these trucks. But that truck is well known in town, and someone will wonder why Barry isn't with it. I'd rather you disable it, and we'll leave it here."

"Okay," I said. "Be right back." I drove the truck away from the highway and parked behind a small hill. I threw the keys out into the desert. I took the Glock and put a round into each tire, then put a round in the gas tank.

"We need to get going," I said. "We'll follow at a distance to make sure you make it back to town. But let me wash down the camper's sliding door of the blood and other stuff."

It took four bottles of water to get it cleaned.

"Does Barry's brother live in Alamo?" I asked.

"Yes, two ranches over from ours."

"How are you going to deal with him?"

"My dad will make sure Sam never takes part in another hijacking."

Margo got in the camper's driver's seat and turned the motor over. The starter motor strained and then slowed. I was going to ask if there was a problem when the engine suddenly caught. She revved the motor to what must have been its redline and released the clutch, and the van lurched forward, leaving behind a cloud of black smoke. A smiling Mason waved to me as I walked back to the Cruiser.

I keyed the comms and brought the women back to the Cruiser. They loaded in, Melissa in the passenger seat. "Night vision on, safeties on. Keep a good watch," I said.

ELEVEN

We followed one hundred yards behind the camper. Margo had her headlights on, and I used her VW's taillights as a guide going forward.

From the back, Kris said, "You killed those two men. Why?"

"I wish I wouldn't have had to," I replied.

"You could have warned them and let them go," she said, pressing the point.

"Let them go so they could kill and rape someone else, Kris. Really?" Melissa answered for me. "Besides, you weren't there. You didn't see what happened."

"They killed Margo's ex and would have killed her when they were done with her," I said. "They never would have let her go. In fact, one of them told her she was dead and that her father would never know what happened to her. He had a knife at her throat and was going to kill her. They might have even gone after Mason. Living in the same town, it would have been impossible for them. Plus, they hijacked another car before she came along. There was a third man there who took off with the car and perhaps the driver and whoever else was in the car with them."

"Kris, if it had been you down there on the ground being raped, would you have wanted them to be allowed to leave?" Monica asked.

Kris didn't answer.

We fell silent then, each of us dealing with what had happened in our own way.

Ten minutes later, we crested a low hill, and her headlights lit up the small town of Alamo off to the left. Up ahead, both lanes were blocked by an old John Deere tractor with a long, low-slung hay hauler trailing behind. At least a dozen armed men manned the blockade.

I stopped a hundred yards back and watched Margo drive up to the assembled group. They must have recognized the VW, as none raised their rifles.

Margo came to a stop, jumped out of the camper, and embraced one of the men. She stepped back, said something, and then pointed back toward us. The man she'd hugged glanced our way and motioned out to the darkness for us to come forward.

I wasn't going to just blindly trust them, so I stayed put.

Margo turned and ran back to us. Reaching the Cruiser, she came to my window.

"My dad wants to thank you for bringing us home safely. They have this roadblock here and another up the highway at Edythe's Road on the north side of town. He'll send a deputy with you to make sure you have freedom of travel through that northern barricade. I didn't tell him about Barry and Scotty, but I do plan on telling him later."

"What did you tell him?" I asked. "And any sign of Barry's brother?"

"That we ran out of gas a few miles back and you put a couple of gallons in our tank. And no sign of Sam. But we passed the road to his ranch a couple miles back. I'll make sure my dad knows about Sam."

"Works for me," I said. "Give me a couple of minutes. I'll see you up there."

"Oh, okay," she said slowly, as if mystified as to why I wanted her to go ahead without us.

"Just a minute or two, Margo. I want to speak to the group first," I explained.

Margo nodded and walked toward the roadblock, where the men awaited her return.

As soon as Margo was out of earshot, I turned to the women. "Melissa and Renee, when I tell you, please exit the Cruiser, fan out with ten feet of separation, and take a knee," I instructed. "We're shrouded in darkness this far out, and they won't see you. Safeties off, but this time set the selector to full auto on yours, Melissa, and Renee, yours on three-round bursts. Make sure your comms are on.

"If you see me put my left hand above my head, point your weapon above our heads at the eleven o'clock position, pull the trigger, and immediately release. One volley should probably do it. If you see me turn toward you and give you a come-here wave, come to me. Understand?" I asked.

Both women nodded.

Margo was just reaching the barricade when the two women exited the Cruiser and took a knee.

"I'm going to stop twenty yards out where there's still some darkness," I said to the three remaining women. "I want you three to set a close-in perimeter." Then I added, "Safeties off and three-round bursts. All good, ladies?"

Three affirmatives in answer.

"I'm scared," Kris said. "Is this what's going to happen every day?"

"Just breathe and try to relax," I said. "I don't think anything is going to happen here. And until we get you home to Seattle, yes. It's probably going to be like this, and most likely a lot worse."

I put the Cruiser in gear and slowly crept forward.

I learned the hard way to never approach a non-US-manned checkpoint without having set an overwatch first. Afghanistan was like a classroom with lessons learned every day.

I stopped, and the three ladies exited the Cruiser. With their backs up against the tires, they set up a close-in perimeter.

I cut the engine and stepped out. I left my rifle with the thermal scope inside the Cruiser but undid the Velcro strap that secured the Glock in my chest rig's holster. I started walking toward the barricade.

Margo and an older man approached. We met halfway.

Margo made the introductions. "Dad, this is Jon. Jon, this is my dad, Ken Stokes."

I put my hand out, and we shook. Margo's dad released my hand, said, "Margo tells me you got her going again out there in the desert, and for that, I'm most appreciative, Master Sergeant."

Ken Stokes and I stood the same height. He was pushing the far side of sixty, had longish silver-gray hair sticking out of his black Stetson hat, was as rail thin as his daughter, and if his grip was any indication, was strong as a man half his age. He was wearing pointy cowboy boots, blue jeans, and had on an opened blue jean jacket with a light-colored wooly collar. Clipped to his belt on his right hip and oriented in a left-handed cross draw position was a black semi-automatic pistol.

"Happy to have helped, sir," I said.

Ken Stokes pointed to a deputy standing behind and to his right. "This is Jeff Stills. He's my second-in-command. When you're ready to be on your way, Jeff will accompany you as far as the next barricade on the north end of town."

Deputy Stills touched the front of his Stetson and tipped his head in greeting.

"Deputy," I said in acknowledgment.

"Why are you blocking the highway, Sheriff?"

"Soon enough there's going to be thousands of folks from Las Vegas streaming up this highway looking for food and water," he answered. "Water we can give them, but food is another matter. This roadblock will allow us to keep things orderly when we turn them away."

"Makes sense to me. If food is a problem," I said, "I suggest you send a team with bolt cutters and open some of the two dozen or so semitrucks we saw abandoned between here and the junction of 93 and 15."

"We've got a few men who are leaving at first light to do just that."

"May your efforts prove fruitful, Sheriff."

"Margo tells me there are six of you, but I only see one . . . you. Are the other five lost out there in the desert, Mr. Kristen?"

"Just being cautious, Mr. Stokes."

"Of course." Stokes turned and faced his people. "Relax, boys, everything is fine. We're going to let these folks through and escort them to the next barricade."

A young man, perhaps an older teenager, standing on the hay hauler, spoke up. "I can't be sure, Sheriff, but I think they might have a trailer behind that rig. Might be worth takin' a look."

"Don't be a complete fool, Darrel," the sheriff shouted, admonishing him. "Don't you realize they have . . ."

The comms came to life, loud enough that Margo and her dad could hear. "We have four people approaching the Cruiser's nine o'clock . . . two hundred yards out and closing," Melissa said.

"I'm not part of this, Master Sergeant," Ken Stokes said, putting both palms up.

"Dad, what's going on?" Margo shouted, clearly confused.

I took a step back and put my hand on the Glock's grip but left it in the holster. I looked at Stokes, said, "I'm going to have my people put a stop to those four men out there by firing a warning volley. One only, sir. The next will be a stopping volley. Do you understand?"

"Yes," Stokes answered. "Margo, please quiet down. Darrel, what the fuck have you done, you moron?"

I keyed the comms, said, "One of you put a volley over the heads of the four approaching men."

One second later, a quick volley on full auto thundered out of the dark. The men manning the barricade instinctively ducked, some even falling off the hauler. Shouts and curses came from the darkness that was the surrounding desert.

The comms chirped. "Retreating," Melissa reported.

"You have automatic weapons," Stokes said.

I wasn't sure if that was a statement or a question but answered with, "Several."

"Jesus Christ!" Stokes exclaimed. "What a clusterfuck. Jeff, have someone take that idiot Darrel to the jail and stick him in a cell. And keep him there until I find out what he's up to."

Watching two men herd the offending Darrel off to jail, I turned to the sheriff, said, "Listen, we helped your daughter and want nothing in return other than to be allowed to pass. Now we can do this the easy way, or we can do it the hard way."

Margo said, "Dad, he's a good guy. Don't let this become something it isn't."

"Don't worry, pumpkin," he said, putting his arm around her shoulders. "Nothing is going to happen here."

Turning, he yelled to the assembled men, "Point your weapons down. Now."

I keyed the comms and asked if we were clear. "Yes," came the reply.

"Sheriff, I'm sorry, but I'm going to ask that you have your men put their weapons on the hauler and then step back fifty feet toward town. That includes you, sir," I added.

"I understand. Not a problem," he said, taking his gun out and walking toward the hauler, where he placed it among the other weapons. "I repeat, I did not have anything to do with that bullshit, Master Sergeant."

"I believe you, Sheriff, which is why you and your men will see the sunrise."

The sheriff and his men retreated the requested fifty feet. "I'm pretty sure what's happening is the result of an EMP, but have you heard anything about how it all started?" the sheriff shouted in question.

"I have. One sec," I answered, putting up a finger.

"Melissa, please make your way down to the Cruiser."

"Two nuclear weapons detonated, one over Colorado and the other over Ohio. Four were sent by North Korea. We intercepted two, but the other two slipped through. North Korea sent out six other missiles, hitting the world's major players. All, that is, except China. The consensus is it was China using North Korea as its proxy. For its efforts, North Korea has been vaporized off the planet," I added, repeating what I'd been told.

Margo put her hand over her mouth, said, "Oh my god."

Stokes was a little more understanding of the situation. "China might try and attack us?"

"Who knows," I said. "It's too much to think about."

The comms came to life with Melissa's voice. "I'm back."

"Good. All of you load up and come on down. Melissa, drive slowly on by me and continue up toward the next barricade, then stop one hundred yards short and wait for me. Renee, provide overwatch and walk parallel to us as we head north to the next barricade."

"Will do," Renee replied.

"Sheriff, please have someone move this tractor so we can get by without having to drive off-road," I said.

A moment later, we all heard the Cruiser start up at about the same time as the tractor moved off.

Melissa slowly drove by us a minute later.

I turned to the deputy, said, "Take a walk with me, Deputy. Good night, Margo, Sheriff. Good luck to you," I said, then added, "And stay away from those weapons until we're gone."

Stokes removed his hat and combed his fingers through his hair, replied, "Will do. And good luck to you and your group, Master Sergeant."

"Bye, Jon," Margo said. "Thank you for everything."

Deputy Jeff and I walked behind the crawling Cruiser.

"Where are you headed, sir?"

I considered whether to answer but could see nothing wrong with sharing our destination. "Montana via Seattle," I answered.

"A long journey in the best of times. Now, who knows."

"It's going to take some time," I admitted. "What about you, Deputy. You have a family?"

"I do. A wonderful and beautiful wife. We have three kids, all under six."

"You plan on staying here, or do you have a safe place to hunker down somewhere else?"

"My wife wants to leave tomorrow for her parents' place in Idaho. They've got a six-hundred-acre farm just outside a town called Gooding. They're Mormons and are very well prepared for just this kind of scenario. She guessed it was an EMP, and she's been proven correct."

Off to our left was a darkened Valley Truck Stop with a half dozen semitrucks sitting alone in the far reaches of the back parking lot. I could hear trailer refrigeration units rattling away, keeping their perishable cargo cool . . . *No computer chips in those things*, I thought.

There were dozens of people milling about with just a single deputy standing guard in front of the entrance to the minimart inside.

"You have a vehicle that's running?" I asked.

"We do. A fully restored '68 F-250 Crew Cab four-by-four. I also have a dual-axle trailer."

"I love those beasts," I said, "Gas or diesel?"

"Diesel."

"Nice. It'll suck fuel like a thirsty cowboy at the end of a hot, dusty day but will get you to Idaho. Do yourself and your family a favor, Deputy—pack up and head out this morning while it's still dark. You'll have another day of relative calm, but after that, it's going to get nasty."

The comms squawked alive. "Barricade ahead," Melissa said, stopping the Cruiser.

"Renee?"

"Looks like just a couple of men sitting on an old ride-on mower with a fertilizer spreader behind it," she reported. "No one else around that I can see."

I looked over to Deputy Jeff, who shrugged. "You use what you have," he said.

"They're going to take your truck from you, Deputy. Best leave soon."

Deputy Jeff stuck his hand out, and we shook. "I'm hearing you. Stay frosty, Master Sergeant." He touched the brim of his hat and walked up to the barricade. A minute later, the lawnmower started up and moved off the roadway.

I pointed to the truck stop across the street, said, "If you haven't already done it, you may want to consider confiscating those semitrucks with the fridge units still working. Besides what's in them, you'll be able to store other things. Got to be folks in town with insulin or other meds that need to stay cool."

Before he could comment, I keyed the comms, said, "Come on down, Renee. Time to get out of town."

———

RENEE CLIMBED IN THE BACK, and once the rear doors were shut, I quickly drove north. A few miles up I saw a large paved driveway on the left. The drive led underneath a ranch entrance, in this case, two stone columns which held thick logs jutting up in the air. Hanging between the two upright logs was another log which spanned the width of the driveway. A wooden sign hung beneath the log stating the name of the place—Long Horn Bed & Breakfast. A metal plaque on the right-side stone column stated that spa services were available.

Further up the drive and glowing huge in the greenish glow of the NVs was a large, almost mansion-sized building. It looked very upscale. I pulled up parallel to the entrance and stopped.

Kathy was the first to comment. "Hello, bed, I could use you right now."

"Maybe make a reservation for a facial and pedi for later in the day," Monica added.

Renee laughed, said, "Why go for just a facial and pedi. I'd go for the whole works: warm stone massage, a body wrap, a Watsu treatment, craniosacral therapy, and finish with some reflexology."

"I know what a couple of those things are," Melissa said, "but not sure the others sound appealing—and they actually sound painful."

Then Kris spoiled the mood. "I don't know how you can talk about spas and facials when we're in the middle of fucking nowhere and who knows how far from home. We watched two men killed in cold blood and then another dozen or so a few miles back come close."

I was ready to let her have it but bit my lip.

Instead of berating Kris, I said to the group, "While I appreciate a good massage as much—" was as far as I got.

"As long as it includes a happy ending?" Melissa asked sweetly, interrupting me.

And we all laughed at that.

"What's a happy ending?" Kris asked. "And why is everyone laughing?"

Renee explained to an unamused Kris what a happy ending was.

"That's disgusting," Kris said. Then she announced, "I have to pee."

And once again laughter filled the Cruiser. Even Kris joined in.

"You have to have the smallest bladder of any human I know," Kathy said.

"I know," Kris said. "Sorry. It really pisses me off."

Which brought even more laughter.

I stepped out and scanned the area with the thermal. Once I was sure we were alone, I told the women they could pile out.

On her own, Melissa grabbed her NVs, took a knee, and provided overwatch while the other four women dropped their pants and did their thing. When all were finished, I gathered them around Melissa, who maintained her position.

"I know you're all tired and sick of being cooped up in the Cruiser, but if you're up to it, I'd like to go another hundred miles to south of a town called Sunnyside. We'll find a dirt side road somewhere and off-road it a mile or two from the highway and make camp. We'll sleep in late, maybe spend the entire day there, and then resume our travel once it's dark again. Sound good?" I asked the group.

Before anyone could answer, Melissa said, "We've got a single man walking up the drive from the building. He's got a rifle."

"Okay, you all know what to do."

The women set up our usual perimeter watch. I waited until the guy was fifty feet out. "Stop right there," I shouted.

Startled, the man let out an involuntary yelp and stopped in his tracks.

"Place your weapon on the ground and approach us," I said. "We mean you no harm."

"Well, that's nice and all," he said into the dark, placing his rifle on the ground, "but my heart's beatin' so fast I'm likely to die of a heart attack before you could shoot me."

The man slowly approached and stopped when he saw me and the Cruiser.

"Renee, will you please search him for weapons?" I said, flipping up my NVs. Which she did, finding none.

"Sorry to have startled you like that, sir. We stopped for a quick stretch and will be on our way."

"No problem, son. Stay here as long as you'd like." Pointing across the road to a mailbox, he said, "In all the excitement today, I forgot to check the mail. My name is Walter, and along with my wife, Sally, own and run this little bed-and-breakfast."

Walter appeared a bit older than my father at sixty-five and stood at least six feet. His head was covered by the obligatory Stetson hat and sported longish hair tied into a ponytail.

I introduced him to our group, and he invited us in, saying he had two vacant rooms.

"Thank you for the offer, Walter, but we need to get a move on," I answered.

"And pass up a spa treatment. Come on, Jon," Monica chimed in.

"Sorry to say, but we haven't heard from any of our staff," Walter said. "The closest one lives in Alamo, which is nine miles back down the road. So, the spa is unfortunately closed."

"And it might stay empty based upon what we've heard," Kathy added.

"Which is?" Walter asked.

Kathy filled him on what we knew. When she was finished, Walter took his hat off, drew his fingers through his hair, said, "Well, fuck the proverbial duck. I figured it was somethin' more than a power outage when our cell phones died and the cars wouldn't start. And we've had folks walkin' by all day askin' for food and water. We tried to be accommodatin' to all who asked, but we're runnin' low on food and stopped handin' it out . . . We have six rooms full of guests who checked in before the power went out that we feel obliged to feed, but we're goin' to have to ask them to leave soon. And some folks get upset when I say no to the food—hence the rifle."

"In a few days, you're going to have hundreds if not thousands of people headed north out of Las Vegas. This is the shortest route up to Idaho and Montana," I said.

"And this place will be a target on everyone's radar," Renee pointed out. "It screams food and water."

"You have any family that can come and help you, or better yet, a safe place to head out to?" I asked.

"Our son lives and works down in Alamo and has a restored truck that should run," Walter answered. "He's married to a gal whose family farms land up in Idaho. I'm a little surprised he hasn't shown up yet checkin' in on us, but he's probably busy down there."

"By chance is your last name Stills?" I asked him.

"It is. Is that a lucky guess, or do you know somethin' I don't, son?"

"Nothing untoward, sir. I met your son down in Alamo. His truck does run. I hope I convinced him to leave today for Idaho."

"Well, if he does head up there, he'll stop by here first. Sally and I can hitch a ride. But boy oh boy, it's goin' to kill Sally havin' to walk away from all this."

"Better to walk away and live, Mr. Stills," Renee said. "It's going to get ugly, sir. Heck, it's only day one, and it's already turning ugly."

"Okay, folks, I need to tell Sally what you've told me and come up with a plan," he said, putting out his hand and shaking all of ours. "Good luck to you all. May God help us."

TWELVE

We were soon back on the road and making good time. Dead semitrucks, cars, and pickups were parked haphazardly along the way, but none blocked our path. We were able to average thirty-five to forty miles per hour. I had the group turn off their NVs to conserve battery power, and I was the only one with a unit powered up.

We passed people walking alone and in groups. Most were pulling wheeled luggage and headed north, where earlier they'd been heading south. Again and again, we were on top of them and whizzing by before they knew we were there.

Power lines were down, and the tops of wooden power poles with transformers still glowed brightly in the NVs and thermal scope.

Darkness was our ally, but daylight would drastically change the equation. In daylight, we would be visible and vulnerable. We would be a highly viable target for those who were desperate for transportation, food, and water. Our trailer would look like a big-box store on wheels. Even two days into the darkness, as we began to call it, folks would be thirsty and hungry and willing to do anything in order to quell the thirst that was slowly killing them.

The road continued to rise and fall, but the dips were shallower and the distance between hilltops farther apart. I debated the need to thermal scan ahead as we had earlier and decided to rely solely on my NVs. My rationale for doing so was thinking a roadblock would more likely be set up near a town rather than out in the middle of nowhere. So far, so good.

A road sign told us we were a mile from a town called Ash Springs. A few minutes later, we crested a hill and the town lay before us. We stopped, and I scanned ahead with the thermal. All appeared clear with no dead vehicles or roadblocks, and I took advantage of the downhill grade to build up our speed to sixty-five. We flew past the town and up the next hill.

A road sign off to our left announced that the next street would bring us to the famous natural hot springs. I told the group what the sign said.

"There's our spa," Renee said.

"That's true," Melissa said, then added, "However, that is not the kind of spa I was hoping for."

A few miles further on, the road took a sharp right bend, and a mile beyond that we came to an intersection where we had a decision to make: Off to the left was Highway 318 North, which would take us past two very small towns and a hundred miles or so further on connecting us to Highway 6. Once on Highway 6, it was a short twenty-two mile shot to Ely, Nevada.

If we continued straight on Highway 93, it would take us some distance east before turning north and taking us through the larger towns of Caliente, Panaca, Pioche, and eventually hitting Highway 50 just east of Ely, Nevada.

Taking 318 North would keep us away from those larger towns and was definitely a shortcut.

So 318 North it was. There was the occasional dead car or pickup, but there were no semitrucks to be seen. And we soon learned why . . . This may be a shortcut to Ely, but the road was steep, climbing higher and higher. My ears popped in response to the higher elevation. We encountered tight, twisty roads with hillsides coming down to the roadway on both sides.

The road leveled out, and we passed the tiny town of Hiko, population 119, this according to a road sign south of town. Another sign north of town told us that the next services were sixty-five miles farther north in the town of Sunnyside, Nevada. It was just south of Sunnyside that I planned to stop and make camp for the day.

We encountered no more abandoned vehicles, and the first fifty of those sixty-five miles flew by quickly as the road remained fairly straight and level. Vague outlines of the occasional trailer and ranch house showed in the peripheral edges of my NVs, but nothing else as we sped along.

We made one pit stop, and stepping out into the early morning high desert air, we were quickly chilled. With the increasing elevation, it became much colder, and I guessed it was close to forty degrees out.

"Look at all those stars!" Renee exclaimed.

We all looked up, and it truly was a spectacular sight. Crystal clear skies with no moon at all and those twinkling stars that appeared close enough to touch.

"I've never seen so many stars in my life," Kris said.

"With no cars or trucks burning fossil fuels, industrial smokestacks idle, and no jet airplanes spewing carcinogenic-laden soot, comes crystal-clear skies," Monica pointed out.

"The fact that there is no light pollution helps, too," Kathy said, craning her neck for a better view of the night sky.

"I hate to be a Debbie Downer," Melissa said, "but we're almost there, and I for one want nothing more than to pitch a tent, lay out my sleeping pad and bag, and fall into a deep, deep sleep."

A chorus of "I second that" followed, and we hit the road again. I turned the heater on as we quickly made our way north.

So far today we'd traveled just under two hundred miles, and I'd been watching the gas gauge slowly move toward the big

E. I would soon need to grab three of the five-gallon jerry cans and fill the tank.

Twenty minutes later, I spotted low hills off to our right that appeared high enough to hide behind.

I turned off the road, and the Cruiser had no problem negotiating its way around and between the low hills. The ground was hard-packed and rocky, and I doubted that we'd left any blatantly visible tire tracks. A half mile in, I rounded a hill, turned a wide circle, and pointed the Cruiser back the way we'd come.

"This is it, guys," I said, shutting down the engine. I stepped out, and the only sound was the hot engine ticking in the cold morning air.

"Before we set up camp, I'm going to walk to the top of the hill and scan with the thermal. Let me give you the okay before you start breaking into the trailer for the tents and other stuff."

It took less than two minutes to make it to the top of the hill. I performed a 360-degree scan and then a slower, more deliberate second scan. Other than a rabbit hopping from bush to bush two hundred yards out, there was nothing out there.

I keyed the comms and told them they were clear to get started. I saw five headlamps glowing brightly in my NVs as I hiked back down the hill. Burt must have slipped them headlamp sets when he took them to the store's camping section.

Kathy was showing the rest of the group how to set up the tents when I walked into our impromptu campsite.

"Every two months like clockwork, my husband and I take a long weekend and backpack the various trails back home. These tents are the same brand and model we have, so I'm super familiar with them," Kathy explained.

"Burt gave each of us our own tent, but we've decided to share a tent since sleeping alone would be a little scary," Melissa said. "So, it will be me and Monica in one, Kathy and Kris in the next, and you and Renee in the third."

"Sounds good, ladies," I replied.

Kathy finished setting up the first tent and watched as the other women set up the second by themselves.

Finished with the second tent, I helped Renee set ours up. Within five minutes, we had the sleeping pads, two-person sleeping bag, and pillows in place.

Renee pointed to the tent, said, "Kathy says that the gear Burt set us up with is top of the line. She went through each item by name and explained the benefits."

I chuckled, said, "You sound like a YouTube backpacking product reviewer."

"Yeah, well, follow me, mister," she said, and taking my hand, she led me outside and pointed to six chairs the women had set up.

"Sit," Monica commanded.

The chairs the girls had set up were small fabric affairs with skinny, tentlike poles acting as a frame and holding it all together.

"That itty-bitty thing won't hold my weight," I said. "I'm six-four and 230 pounds. Well, after Vegas, maybe 240."

"Sit," Renee ordered, pointing to the chair.

"We have the same kind back home," Kathy said. "It's a Helinox and will hold your weight. My husband is six-two, weighs two fifty, and it doesn't even creak when he sits in it."

I sat and sank into the comfort of the small, low-slung camp chair. I wiggled my butt and settled in.

"You're right, this is awesome," I said. "Burt must have had fun setting you up."

"He kept saying 'better you than the assholes' as he walked up and down the aisles grabbing stuff," Monica replied.

"I hope that someday I'll be able to properly thank him for making this trek possible," I said, wiggling further into the comfort of the chair. "Without all of this equipment, I'm not sure we would have attempted this road trip in the first place."

It was now five thirty in the morning, and it would soon be light out. I gathered the group closer together.

"Take a seat," I said.

"Turn off your headlamps, please. We need to start conserving battery power. Turn them on only when safe and necessary. Same thing with your NVs. First things first," I said, "is setting up a watch system. There are six of us, and a normal watch schedule would be four hours on and twenty off. But until we all get used to standing watch, we'll do a twelve-hour schedule, so two hours on. It's still dark, and I'll take the first two-hour watch, followed by Monica, Melissa, Kathy, Kris, and finally Renee. Then me again. This is designed by tent occupants, so when one gets off, she can wake her tentmate without disturbing the others. And if you're on watch and don't feel you can do the full two hours, call me on the comms and tell me. We can't have anyone fall asleep on watch . . . It's the absolute worst thing you can ever do.

"Second, whoever is on watch will keep their comms on, and I will always have mine on. The others should turn them off to conserve power.

"Third, before you zip into your sleeping bags, pack your backpack so, if necessary, you can slip your shoes and chest rigs on and be ready to go. You should only have to pack your pad, sleeping bag, pillow, and tent. In the army, we practiced this until we could be boots on and fully loaded-up and ready to go in under three minutes. Just something to think about if an emergency presents itself and a quick exit is needed."

I saw lots of yawns. I ended the discussion at that and told them to get some shut-eye.

I told Monica I'd wake her in two hours, but if I was still good for an extra hour or two, I'd let her continue sleeping.

"Thanks in advance for that. I am beat, but I'm ready to stand my watch whenever you come down," she replied. "Oh. Wait one."

Monica ducked into her tent and reappeared holding a pair of Nikon binoculars. "Burt asked me to give these to you, but I forgot about them until now."

"Thank you, Burt," I said aloud. Once again Burt had taken care of a need that I had completely overlooked.

"And thank you, Monica."

"You want some coffee?" Kathy asked me. "Burt gave us an entire plastic tote of Franklin's freeze-dried coffee. It will take only a couple of minutes, and I'll kill two birds with one stone by showing the ladies how to work the backpacking stoves."

"We have coffee," I said, not a question but a statement. "I thought I'd have to do without for the rest of my life."

"A little dramatic, boss," Melissa said. "The world would not grind to a halt without coffee."

"Excuse me," I said. "I live in Seattle. I survive on coffee."

"Cream and sugar, right?" Renee asked.

"Yep. Life is good again," I exclaimed, the thought of actually having coffee the way I love it—light and sweet, perked me up.

I stood, and Renee came up and hugged me tight, said, "Go on up. I'll bring it to you when it's ready."

"Thank you."

It was getting lighter out as I grabbed one of the camp chairs and carried it up the hill. Not wanting to stand out on a hilltop ridgeline, I set the chair behind a low boulder and sat. I put my feet up on the boulder, and I was as comfortable here as I was in my chair in front of my television back home . . . all that was missing was warmth from my fireplace.

We were at least a half mile from the road, and from this vantage point I could see a good three miles of the northbound roadway before it dipped down and out of sight. Southbound another mile or so. I glassed the area where we'd gone off-road and could see no tire tracks. I looked behind me and could see our camp and the four women being taught how to set up and use their backpacking stoves.

The road was clear in both directions. The air was still chilly, but my jacket kept me comfortable. I was ready to take off my chest rig, but experience had taught me to keep it on until I fell into bed.

Fifteen minutes later, there was a noise behind me.

"It's just me," Renee said, handing me a large tin cup with a fold-out handle. Steam rose from the cup and disappeared in the chilly air.

"It's hot. Be careful," she warned.

"Thank you," I said, wrapping my left arm around her thighs.

"I have to wait hours for you to crawl into bed."

"Did you happen to notice the watch rotation I put together?" I asked.

"Everyone with half a brain noticed."

"Once I do show up, we'll have several hours of quiet time."

I slid my left hand to her butt and squeezed.

"Promises will get you everywhere, mister," she said, reaching down and pressing her palm against the front of my fatigues. I'd just started to grow hard when she withdrew her hand. "I want some of that later, and I'm not going to waste it on a cold hilltop."

"Now that's what's called a prick tease," I said in mock seriousness.

"See ya, mister," she said, giving me a kiss on my cheek and smiling sweetly. She turned and walked down the hill, all the while with an exaggerated swing of her hips. I watched until she disappeared into our tent. Wow, what a wonderful and beautiful woman . . . and she still chose me.

The night turned into day, and with the help of the coffee, I was able to stand watch for the full four hours. It had been quiet with absolutely nothing moving on the road the entire time.

DAY TWO

CAMPING. SMILEY FACES. BABIES. CONNIE.

THIRTEEN

It was now nine in the morning. I was ready to head down the hill and wake Monica when movement off to the left caught my eye.

Making its way slowly north, from my left to right, was an old Ford Country Squire station wagon. Probably a late fifties model, it was fire-engine red and sported wood paneling along its flanks. Piled on top were suitcases, cardboard boxes, and several five-gallon water and gas cans like the ones stored in our trailer. I counted three red gas jerry cans and two blue water cans. The water cans each sported a yellow Forrest Gump–type smiley face decal, which brought a smile to my own face. What a great movie that was.

It was chugging along at twenty-five or thirty miles an hour—the engine misfiring and leaving a white cloud of smoke in its wake. I watched it make its way north, where it finally disappeared from view.

"Good luck to you and Godspeed," I said aloud.

I made a final 360 sweep with the binoculars, and all was clear. I left the chair where it was and headed down the hill.

Monica was in the process of making herself a cup of coffee and greeted me by raising her cup. "Anything interesting going on out there?" she asked, taking a delicate sip of the steamy hot coffee.

I told her about the old station wagon and that I'd left the chair up there behind the boulder. I handed over the binoculars and explained about not standing out on the ridgeline. "Even though we're a distance from the road, any unusual shape will stand out like a sore thumb," I explained.

"Got it. Go get some rest."

I tried to stifle a yawn but lost the battle. "I will. Thanks. I've got the comms on, so let me know if you think I need to know something. No need to report walkers or cars driving by unless you think they pose a threat. And please pass that along to Melissa."

"You got it."

"See you later."

I turned toward our tent and saw that Renee was there waiting for me, a big grin on her face. She silently helped lift the plate carrier over my head and then kneeled and undid my boot's laces, slipped them off, and deposited everything in the tent's vestibule.

Without a word, Renee backed into the tent. I handed her the M4, which she placed next to hers. I then followed her inside. Renee zipped the entrance flap closed behind us, and we set about removing each other's clothes. Soon we were in the double sleeping bag making quiet love. Thirty minutes later, we were asleep in each other's arms.

I slept soundly until three o'clock when I was woken by Renee opening the tent flap. She stuck her head inside and asked if I was hungry.

Now that I was awake, I felt hunger pangs and answered in the affirmative.

Renee was dressed, chest rig on and rifle attached to the sling. She was wearing a pair of gold-rimmed aviator sunglasses.

I could see myself in the reflective lenses, and it wasn't a pretty sight.

"You look hot in that getup," I said, trying to extricate myself from the sleeping bag. "You remind me of the women in the Norwegian Special Forces that completed a month of special training with us in Afghanistan. They were blond fighting goddesses."

"Well, I'm glad you think so, but my hair is greasy as hell, and I feel yucky and need a hot shower."

I thought it best to avoid that topic, instead asked, "How long have you been up? I didn't hear or feel you moving around the tent."

"Half hour or so. You were sleeping like a baby, so I didn't molest you."

"Next time, molest me."

"Get dressed," she said, smiling and letting the tent flap drop. "I'll get you some coffee."

Five minutes later, I joined Renee and Kathy in the communal area outside the tents. I attached the M4 to the sling as I watched them boil water on two of the small backpacking stoves sitting atop a collapsible camping table. Loud hissing produced hot blue flames, and within four minutes they had plenty of hot water for three pouches of Mountain House meals with enough left over for coffee.

"You want beef stroganoff, turkey dinner, lasagna, or breakfast skillet?" Kathy asked.

"I'll go with the breakfast skillet. Thanks."

While the hot water worked its ten-minute magic in the meal pouches, I brushed my teeth and splashed my face with cold water from one of the jerry cans. Renee handed me my coffee, sugar and cream already stirred in.

Seeing the water cans reminded me that the Cruiser needed to be refueled. I chided myself for not having done this earlier . . . If we had needed to leave quickly, we'd have only gotten fifteen miles or so before running out of gas. Not a good scenario if we were being pursued.

I took three of the eight jerry cans and one by one emptied them into the Cruiser's tank. Using all three cans meant we'd had a gallon of gas left in the tank. Stupid. Stupid. Stupid.

We had five five-gallon gas cans left: my original two and three of Burt's five. The remaining twenty-five gallons would get us three hundred fifty miles. If we babied the Cruiser's gas pedal, we might get close to the Oregon/Idaho border, but certainly no further. We'd have to siphon gas from somewhere.

I put the jerry cans back in the trailer and, with that task finished, went back to Kathy and Renee. Renee handed me the breakfast skillet pouch, which I promptly attacked. Skillet eggs and coffee, the all-American breakfast.

"Anything interesting happen during your watch, Kathy?" I asked between bites.

"Nothing," she answered. "Not one person or vehicle passed through."

"Perhaps most of the walkers from the abandoned cars found someplace to shelter," Renee offered. "At least the ones that found themselves so far out, like here, for instance."

"You could be right," I said. "I think we're going to have pretty smooth sailing from here to Ely. We should make good time tonight and during the early morning hours." I glanced up the hill. "Kris made it up there okay?" I asked the two women.

"She did," Renee answered. "Monica and Melissa are sleeping."

"We should break camp and be on the road by six thirty tonight," I said. "That should give us twelve hours of run time and get us close to the Oregon/Idaho border by early tomorrow morning."

Kathy stood, stretched, said, "Sounds good. I'm going to take a quick catnap. Mind waking me up fifteen minutes before we head out?"

"Sure, but first you might want to use one of these," I said, reaching behind me and holding up a box of combat cleansing wipes. "I found a couple dozen boxes in the trailer, probably another present from Burt. We were issued these when we overnighted in Afghanistan, and they work great. Not saying you need them, just saying you'll feel better after using one. Each box has twelve packages, and there're twelve wipes per package. Share, okay?"

Both ladies lunged for the box. I gave the first box to Kathy, and she practically ran to her tent. Renee stood waiting for her box, which I had behind my back. I slowly brought it out. She reached for it, but I raised it up beyond her reach.

"Give that to me right this instant," she hissed, looking at me with catlike squinted eyes.

"Yes, ma'am. Right away, ma'am," I said, handing the box over.

"Asshole," she said, snatching the box out of my hand. She turned and headed for our tent.

"You need help with those, Renee?" I called after her.

A middle finger aimed my way emerged from the tent.

It was turning into a warm day. I leaned my head back and let the sun beat down on my face. I relaxed in the chair and had almost dozed off when Renee told me to get in the tent.

I poked my head in and was handed a wipe. "You use one of these every day, and we'll continue to share a tent and sleeping bag," she said, smiling. "Now take your clothes off, mister."

———

IT WAS SOON RENEE'S WATCH, and once she'd walked up the hill to replace Kris, I packed up our sleeping bag, pad, and tent. I stowed everything in the trailer.

At six, I woke the women and had them break down camp. At six thirty, I hiked the hill, and Renee glassed the road one last time. Together we made our way back to camp.

Waiting for darkness to overtake daylight, we got our NVs together and replaced batteries as needed. This afternoon I'd charged the thermal scope using the solar charger, and it was now fully charged and ready for another night of use.

Last night, Melissa had fired a full burst on auto over the heads of the four yahoos.

"Melissa, did you replace the rounds in the magazine after last night's excitement?"

"No. Sorry."

"Don't be sorry, but do it now while we're waiting, okay?"

"Okay."

While Melissa did that, I checked each woman's chest rig and rifle.

When Melissa finished loading her magazine, we secured the tarp on the trailer and loaded into the Cruiser. Five minutes later, we were tires on pavement. I stopped and performed a thermal scan in both directions. Clear both north and south, I headed north. I brought the Cruiser up to forty-five and left it there.

"The next town is Sunnyside, and it's about five miles ahead. It's small, and we shouldn't have any problems blowing through," I said, speaking to the group. "We've then got a thirty-mile stretch up to a town called Lund, and again, it's a small one. After Lund, we've got a straight shot up to Highway 6, where we turn right and head twenty miles north to the first larger town we've encountered so far, Ely.

"I drove through Ely during a college spring break. It was large and busy, mainly with semitrucks and travelers traversing the state on Highway 50, which divides the state in half—east and west. I'm hoping we can take surface streets to bypass downtown and hit 50 somewhere west of town.

"Once we're on 50 West, we've got almost 150 miles until we hit Austin, Nevada. That's where we'll connect with Highway 305 north to Battle Mountain. That's another ninety miles."

"Holy cow, Nevada is a tall state," Kris said. "I had no idea."

"You mention Nevada, and only two or three places come to mind: Las Vegas, of course, and if you're not geographically challenged, maybe you think Reno and Lake Tahoe," Kathy said. "And who gives a shit about the rest of the state."

"Well, we're pretty much traveling the entire state from bottom to top," Renee added.

"Fun trip, isn't it? And there's a lot more of Nevada to go," Kathy said.

"Once we're at Battle Mountain, we turn west on Interstate 80, and we've got another fifty miles or so to Winnemucca, Nevada. In one sense, we're very lucky," I said. "The blast happened early in the morning, so the roads were at their emptiest—we're mainly going to encounter semitrucks on the road. I won't sugarcoat this, guys, the stretch of Highway 50 between Ely and Austin and then the stretch of Interstate 80 between Battle Mountain and Winnemucca could be dangerous. Up until now, we've gone out of our way to avoid towns and other people, but there's no other route we can take going west. We're stuck with 50 and 80."

"We'll be all right," Melissa stated matter-of-factly. "We own the night, as my brother says. Once we're on the larger roads, let's turn on the thermal and leave it on."

"We can do that," I said. "I believe the run time on the thermal is something like fourteen hours. I fully charged it earlier today, so we should be good. The range on it is eleven hundred yards . . . That's eleven football fields. We keep our speed at forty-five and under, we'll have plenty of time to stop if we see something ahead."

"Drive-by-thermal," Kathy said with a chuckle. "My Tesla, which has every possible option and can drive itself, doesn't have thermal sights."

"You have a Tesla?" I asked her.

"Yes, bought it last month."

"We pay you too much," Renee said. "Just kidding, everyone," she quickly added. "I shouldn't have said that. Sorry."

"You pay us fair and square," Melissa said, giving Renee two thumbs-up.

"Thank you for that," Renee said.

"Since we're on the car topic," Monica said, "what kind of car do you drive, Renee?"

"A 2023 Porsche 911 4S Cabriolet. Like Kathy's, it's brand-new with less than a thousand miles on it. And it does have thermal—a windshield heads-up display shows people, deer, and other animals ahead and gives like a quarter mile warning."

"My Tesla is now a hunk of useless metal," Kathy said in a sad voice. "It's a computer on wheels, which I'm sure is now dead as a doornail. It was my first new car."

"My Porsche should start right up. It's sitting in an underground garage in Kentucky waiting for me to show up someday," she said, reaching into her backpack and taking out a set of keys, dangling them in front of her.

"Why do you think it survived the blast?" Kris asked.

"If she told you, she'd have to kill you," I said. "Secrets and all . . ."

"Town ahead," Melissa said, the road sign giving us a quarter-mile warning.

I brought us to a stop and thermal scanned ahead. Nothing, no heat signatures other than some still-warm, sun-heated trailers off to the left. Back inside, I got us up to forty-five. We zipped past the town and left it in the rearview mirror.

Kris was not done quizzing Renee about her car. "Why do you think your car survived while no one else's did?" she asked.

"It's parked in a facility we own in Kentucky," Renee answered. "The entire building is buried forty feet underground and is EMP-proof, along with its enormous garage. A software update needed to be installed onsite, and instead of flying to the facility, I decided to make a road trip out of it. I took the Porsche. I had the facility's shuttle bus take me to the Taylor County Airport in Campbellsville, where the company's Gulfstream met me and flew me to Las Vegas. And that's how the Porsche came to be in an EMP-proof building."

"I own a rusted-out '85 Jetta, and it's sitting on a street in Seattle," Melissa said. "With that nice bonus check Jon gave me, I was going to buy a new Honda Accord."

"Good car," Monica said.

The next hour flew by as good-natured banter filled the Cruiser. Before I knew it, we saw the road sign for Lund, and after stopping and scanning the small town, which turned out to be a collection of trailers, we were past it and up to speed again.

Fifteen minutes later, we came to Highway 6 and turned right. A road sign on the right said Ely was twenty-two miles ahead.

We were halfway to Ely when I spotted a car blocking the northbound lane, our lane. I brought us to a quick stop. The trailer thumped the hitch and the passengers in the back slid forward, Kathy saying, "Whoa there."

"Sorry, guys," I said. We were a hundred yards from the stopped car. I turned the motor off, set the parking brake, and stepped out. I scanned the entire area a full 360 degrees with the thermal and saw nothing. I stuck my head in the Cruiser and told them to set a close-in perimeter.

"Turn your comms on, please. I recognize the car, ladies. It's the only car that passed by our camp today."

The women set the perimeter.

"Melissa, walk with me but stay back ten yards. Safety off. Watch our six."

The station wagon's four doors were open, as was the rear tailgate. Suitcases had been opened and their contents spilled out across the road. As I approached the passenger side, I was able to see in the green glow of the NVs a woman in the back seat. She was holding an infant. Both had been shot in their right temple with a small-caliber round, likely a .22. Another step forward and I saw a man half out of the driver's door, his left foot on the pavement. He, too, had been shot in the head.

Stepping back from the carnage, I could see the roof rack was missing the water can with the yellow smiley face decal along with one of the three gas cans.

"Why didn't they take the running car?" I asked aloud.

"Because they already have a working vehicle?" Melissa answered.

"Then why not take the other gas and water cans. Why leave them?"

Melissa was silent and then said, "Because they couldn't. They didn't have room. Maybe a motorcycle or an ATV?"

"You're probably right."

I slowly toured the area surrounding the car and saw that both front tires had been shot out. Standing at the front bumper, I stepped on a dozen or so spent cartridges. Upon closer inspection, I could now see impact spider webs across the front windshield. A cartridge had landed and stayed on the hood. It was a standard NATO 5.56 round.

I stepped back to the woman and removed my glove. I put my palm on her forehead and felt some warmth there. It hadn't happened long ago, maybe three or four hours.

"Melissa, please go back to the Cruiser and bring it down."

I keyed the comms and told the ladies to walk alongside and set a new perimeter when the Cruiser stopped.

I reached up and wiggled one of the gas tanks. Full.

Once the Cruiser was parked behind the station wagon, I had each of the women, one at a time, walk up to see the carnage firsthand. Kris and Kathy threw up right then and there, and Monica and Renee were barely able to suppress doing the same.

"Fuckers," Melissa said, unable to look away from the mother and child in the back seat. "The people that did this don't deserve to live."

"And they won't," I replied, "if we come across them. We didn't pass them, which means there's a good chance they're ahead of us."

I climbed onto the car's hood and handed the gas cans down to Melissa. I opened each and smelled to make sure it was gasoline. It was. Another ten gallons.

"What about the water?" Melissa asked while I was still on the roof.

"Let's leave it for someone else."

I stowed the two cans in the trailer and strode back to the station wagon. I found blankets in the very back and covered the mother, the infant, and then the father.

The comms came to life. "You going to bury them?" Kris asked.

"No."

"Why not?"

"You all need to listen to me," I said. "What you saw here is going to be the new norm. You're going to see this happening everywhere we go—this death by violence. These people didn't deserve to die like this, but there'll be others like them, innocents being killed for what they have. Get used to it."

"And why are we not going to bury them?" Kris persisted.

"Because we can't bury them all," I said.

"Shut the fuck up, Kris," Melissa said. "Enough with your BS. We need to get a move on, people."

"Agreed. Let's load up," I said.

"Jesus, Melissa, I was just asking," Kris said.

I drove around the station wagon and brought the Cruiser up to forty.

"Melissa, get the thermal out and boot it up. Let's keep a sharp eye out."

"How are we going to know who did that?" Renee asked.

"They'll have a five-gallon water can with a yellow smiley face decal on the side. We're not going to go out of our way to hunt them down, but if we come across them on the road, we are going to deal out a hand of justice," I said.

As expected, the only objection came from Kris. "Why not just leave them alone? Why kill them? Killing them makes you as bad as them."

"And let them do it to someone else?" Renee asked. "Because given the chance, you know they will."

I wasn't looking for anyone's approval, but Melissa, Renee, Kathy, and Monica all agreed with me.

"I won't be part of it," Kris stated flatly. "I just won't. I'll stand watch over the Cruiser, but I won't outright kill someone for vengeance."

"That's fine, Kris," I replied.

We continued on in silence, Melissa using the thermal sight and me navigating with the NVs.

"They couldn't have gotten far," I said. "They're carrying a lot of weight with those jerry cans and would have to be very careful."

"We've got to be pretty close to Ely by now," Kathy said.

"There's always a chance we passed their home along the way, though I didn't see a driveway or side road," Melissa said. "And I saw no heat signatures in the thermal."

We continued on, seeing nothing but darkness. I was afraid we might have missed the killers.

"I've got a road sign up on the right," Melissa said. "And now I've got two strong heat signatures up ahead on the left at nine hundred yards.

"They're on horseback!"

FOURTEEN

We were on a gentle downslope, and I put the Cruiser in neutral and let it coast. Melissa read down the distance as we gained on them. "Six hundred yards, five hundred yards."

"Let me know when we're fifty yards out, Melissa."

"Two hundred yards."

"Just let them be," Kris shouted. If even one of the Cruiser's windows had been rolled down, the riders could have heard her.

"One more outburst like that and I'm going to muzzle you," I hissed back at her.

The two riders emerged from the dark into the green glow of my NVs. Each rider appeared to have a bundle that rested on their saddle horn. Both riders rode with their right hand holding the reins and the other holding on to the bundle.

"I've got them, Melissa," I said. "Renee, please hand Melissa my rifle. When we stop, set up a close-in perimeter. Melissa, cover the thermal with a blanket or towel—a sudden bright light might harm the sensors."

When we were fifty feet behind them, I turned off my NVs, then turned the Cruiser's headlights and powerful roof-mounted off-road lights on. Together, both sets of lights were so bright they could probably be seen from the International Space Station.

I brought the Cruiser to a stop, stepped out, and yelled for the two riders to stop. Both riders had semiautomatic handguns in belt holsters and wore fully loaded backpacks.

"Stop where you are. Now!" I shouted. "Don't touch those weapons!"

Both horses were startled, heads bobbing and turning tight circles, straining against the reins. But the riders were doing their best in trying to bring them under control. One horse turned sideways to us, and I could see what the rider was holding . . . the rider was a woman in her early twenties, and she was balancing an infant in a car carrier.

I lowered the M4 and approached the riders.

The other rider was a woman as well, older, and maybe the first rider's mother. She was also holding a baby in a car carrier. Both women were squinting their eyes, trying to lessen the impact of the Cruiser's powerful off-road lights. The older woman brought her horse under control and was now standing still.

"Jesus Christ, mister," the older rider exclaimed. "What the hell do you think you're doing scaring us and the horses like that?"

"Sorry, ladies, we thought you were someone else . . . a case of mistaken identity. I apologize."

I keyed the comms, said, "Melissa, kill the lights, please."

A few seconds later, the lights went out, and I turned the NVs back on.

With darkness back, I could see the older woman reaching for her weapon. I raised the M4, said, "Ma'am, please don't remove that weapon from its holster. We mean you no harm, and I promise there's no need for it."

The woman slowly lowered her hand.

"Mom, come on," the younger woman said. And then to me, "Sir, are you military?" Her horse was still turning circles, and with only one hand holding the reins, she was not having much luck bringing it under control.

"No, ma'am. Ex-military, now civilian."

"How is it your vehicle and electronics are working?" the mother asked. "Ours are dead."

I slowly walked up to the younger woman's horse and took hold of the right-side cheek piece. In a calm voice, I told the animal to quiet down. "Our vehicle is old, pre-computer-chip old. And the electronics were protected in a faraday cage in Las Vegas."

The younger rider's horse stopped the head bobbing and stood still.

"You know your way around horses," the mother said.

"Born and raised on a ranch in Montana, ma'am," I answered. "It's not safe out, ladies. And unless you truly need to be somewhere critical, it's best to hunker down at home . . . at least for a few weeks until things start sorting themselves out."

"My husband is a naval aviator and is currently posted in San Diego, so it's just myself, the babies, and my mom at home. We're taking the girls to my sister's ranch on the other side of Ely. We're going to stay with her for a while," she explained.

"Safety in numbers," the mother added, brushing a strand of hair out of her eyes.

"Our place is beautiful and remote, but as I said, Mom and I are alone out there. While we have plenty of hay and water for the horses, we are very low on human food. My sister and her husband are so-called preppers and have a barn full of food and supplies. Heck, knowing them, they've probably been looking forward to this happening since the day they were married."

"Speaking of which, do you have any information as to why the power is out? And why our cell phones and cars aren't working?" the older woman asked. "Did someone hack our power grid again?"

I repeated what we knew, and they took the news as well as could be expected.

The baby the younger woman was holding started to cry. Crying wasn't the right word to describe it, however. More like wailing. Loud wailing.

"She's hungry, Stacy, and not going to wait until we get to Cindy's," the mother said as the baby continued to cry.

Then the baby the mother was holding started wailing. It was now a high-decibel duet concert—in stereo.

I keyed the comms, said, "Kris, can you come on down and lend these ladies a hand?"

"One of our team members is a mother of two and can help you," I said. "We'll keep a watch out while you take care of whatever it is you need to do."

"Thanks, I'll take you up on that," the daughter replied.

Kris appeared out of the dark, said, "Hi there, I'm Kris. You are?"

"I'm Stacy, and that's my mom, Cathy. My babies are twin girls, Kirsten and Avery. Those are some fancy glasses you have there," Stacy said, pointing to Kris' NVs.

"They're flattering, aren't they?" Kris said, laughing and flipping them up. "You want to dismount and feed your babies?"

"Yes. Can you take her so I can get off this horse?" she replied, shouting to be heard over the baby's high-decibel crying.

Stacy leaned down, and Kris extended her arms up and took hold of the car carrier with the baby still belted in. Stacy dismounted, undid the seat's restraining belts, and took hold of her baby. She then undid a Velcro strap on her shirt and popped out a swollen breast. The baby latched on and started to suckle happily away.

Still holding the reins, I keyed the comms. "Melissa, you scanning with the thermal?"

"Yep. Clear in all directions."

"Monica, Kathy, Renee, everything good?" I asked.

"Affirmative, yes, and yep," came back at me.

"Who are you looking for?" the mother asked, having to shout over the din of a baby crying at ear-shattering levels.

"A few miles back, we came across a car with a family of three inside. They'd been executed," I answered.

"Including an infant not much older than your two," Kris added.

"We were thinking we'd run into the attackers on this highway," I said.

"About a half hour ago, an ATV zipped past us doing fifty or so," Stacy said, holding her daughter's head up to a breast. "Two males sitting in tandem, but they went by so fast I didn't get a good look at them."

"Were they carrying a couple of jerry cans, by chance?"

"I don't think so. It was a small model and didn't look like there would be a way to hold two jerry cans. But like I said, they went by pretty fast."

The baby burped and spit out the nipple.

"Mom, time to make an exchange."

The exchange was made, and Avery attached herself to the other breast. Several minutes later, she'd had enough, and Stacy covered herself back up.

"How far do you have to go?" I asked, watching as Stacy belted Avery in the car carrier, handed the seat to Kris, and mounted her horse.

Kris handed the now sleeping Avery back to her mother.

"Not far, another ten miles or so is all."

"If at all possible, we'd like to avoid Ely," I said. "Do you know a way around town?"

"Yes, and you can follow us," Stacy said, settling the carrier on her lap. "A couple of miles or so up on the left, there's a dirt track that crosses a creek, which then connects to Mill Street. Mill Street is about two miles west of town, and there's nothing out there except a few abandoned trailers and old meth sheds. It leads right to Highway 50. It's the route we always take going to and from my sister's place by horseback."

"The creek crossing isn't a problem for a four-wheel drive?" I asked.

"Gosh no. We're talking six inches deep after heavy rain. Now, maybe an inch or two," she answered, lowering her head and kissing her baby's forehead.

"If you want, we can make sure you get to your sister's," I said.

"Thank you for the offer, but once we pass under Highway 50, the street peters out about a quarter mile further on. We then follow old cow paths on pretty steep hillsides until my sister's place. Your four-wheeler could never follow us."

"You won't see or hear us, but we'll be behind you until Highway 50. We have a thermal scanner that's good out to eleven hundred yards, and if we see something ahead of you, we'll chirp the horn in warning. If and when you hear that, stop and stay put. We'll handle any threats."

And that was what we did. We stayed a hundred yards behind with Melissa constantly scanning ahead with the thermal. It was very slow going, and I let the Cruiser maintain forward momentum with no pressure on the gas pedal, instead letting it idle along. On the downhill inclines I had to ride the brakes in order to not get too close to the horses.

We'd gone about a mile, had crested a hill, and were about ready to start heading down the other side when Kris spotted a headlight appearing on the hill behind us.

"Headlight approaching. It's just now crested the hill behind us and should be on us in a minute or two," she said.

"Speed?" I asked.

"It looks to be moving pretty fast," Renee said. "The headlight just disappeared from view. They've got to be down in the low dip and are probably headed up the hill right behind us."

I sped up and got to within ten yards of the horses. I cut the wheel to the left and blocked the southbound lane with the Cruiser, which left the northbound occupied by the trailer. I chirped the horn.

"Renee and Melissa, take cover ten feet off the roadway. Quick as you can, please. Kathy and Monica, take positions behind the trailer. Kris, stay in the Cruiser." I could see that Stacy and her mother had led the horses off onto the right shoulder. "Kris, better yet, maybe you could help the ladies get the little ones down and off the horses."

"I can do that," she said excitedly as she stepped out of the Cruiser and ran toward the two horses.

I opened and closed my door, then stationed myself next to the Cruiser's left front fender. I put the rifle's sling over my head and rested the rifle in my arms. I released the Velcro closure over the Glock to make sure it was readily available.

I waited.

———

"IT'S A MOTORCYCLE, JON," MELISSA reported. "I can see it in the NVs." Two seconds later, Melissa came on the comms and said it was a three-wheeled trike.

"Roger that. No one fire unless I say so. Renee, set to three-round bursts, and when I say your name, fire behind them—aim for the pavement ten feet behind the bike."

"Okay." She sounded hesitant.

"You want Melissa to handle it?" I asked.

"I've got this. Really."

"Okay then. Fire one or two bursts when I say your name."

The trike crested the hill, the bike's headlight flickering and bouncing every which way. It sounded like an older Harley Davidson. The rider spotted us and jammed on the brakes. The two rear tires locked up, and the rear end started chattering. It looked as if it would flip and do sideways cartwheels, but the rider deftly brought it under control, stopping fifteen feet from where I stood. The headlight was pointing directly at the left shoulder but far enough south not to light up Renee and Melissa.

I could see in the NVs that the driver was a heavyset male and the passenger a female. The driver had a rifle in a scabbard that lay across the trike's handlebars, and the woman a pistol in a belt-held holster.

"Renee," I said.

Two three-round bursts tore up the asphalt behind the trike. The driver reached for the rifle's butt.

"Don't touch that rifle," I shouted.

His hands retreated.

"Turn off the headlight, and both of you dismount. Then lay facedown on the ground with hands on your heads," I said.

"Fuck that, dickhead. I ain't getting off the bike," the driver shouted, but he did turn off the headlight.

"Renee. Again, please."

Another two quick bursts convinced both to get off the bike. "Okay, okay. Stop shooting, for fuck's sake," the man screamed. He cut the engine and helped his passenger off the bike. Both lay on the ground and put hands on heads. The driver turned his face toward me, said, "Why are you doin' this, asshole?"

I closed the distance and slid the rifle out of the scabbard. The woman's pistol was a .40-caliber Glock, identical to ours, and the rifle an AR. I dropped the mag and could see on the magazine's side the raised numbers—5.56. There were five rounds remaining. I threw both weapons off to the side. I patted the man down and found another pistol, a nice Ruger conceal-carry-sized .22-caliber in an ankle holster. He also had an expensive combat knife in a leather sheath attached to his belt. I found no further weapons on the woman. I threw both the knife and Ruger toward the other weapons.

"You got no right to take our weapons, dude," the man said.

"Melissa, come on over and watch these two," I said, taking a step back.

"What the fuck you want with us?" the man asked.

Melissa was now standing next to me.

"Shoot them if they move," I said.

"Roger that, Master Sergeant."

"You two military?" the man asked, sounding surprised.

"Kris, how are our two riders?" I asked, ignoring the man's question.

"Off their horses and babies sleeping."

"Hey, asshole, I asked you a question. Are you military?" the man asked again. "If so, this ain't no way to treat American citizens."

I didn't answer, instead walked to the rear of the trike. On a luggage rack on the rear were two jerry cans: one gas and one water, a yellow smiley face right there on the water can. Both were secured to the rack with bungee cords.

I walked back to the two on the ground.

"Okay, you can sit up. Lean back on the rear tire and keep your hands on your head."

I watched the woman pop right up and sit with her back to the tire, hands on her head. The man struggled to raise himself up off the pavement. A minute later, he was snuggled close to the woman, both leaning on the trike's rear tire.

"Renee, come on over."

"Kathy, take an overwatch position twenty yards down the road. Monica, do the same twenty yards past the horses."

I watched both women, one running up the road and the other down. Both took a knee and were in position less than thirty seconds after me telling them.

Renee approached and stood to my right, five feet from the two riders.

Both riders were bundled up in typical biker wear: hoodies with black knit ski hats, black gloves and boots, jean jackets over the long-sleeve black hoodies. The man was in his mid-forties and very large. He had longish black hair and matching black beard. The woman was in her early thirties, slender, with long blond hair tied in a braided ponytail. She was very attractive.

"Where did you get the two jerry cans on the luggage rack?" I asked, watching their expressions closely. The woman managed to keep all expression off her face, but then tears formed and started flowing. Her lips began to quiver. The man's eyes were blinking a mile a minute. His mouth opened and then shut.

"Those are ours," he finally answered.

"Okay," I said. "Where did you buy them?"

"I've had 'em for years," he answered. "I've forgotten where I bought 'em. Jesus, is this why you shot at us? To steal our gas and water? Hell, just take 'em and we'll be on our way, dude."

"Whichever one tells me where you got the two cans I will let live. The other will die. And before you answer, make sure it's the truth."

"He took them from a family down the road," the woman said.

"Shut up, Connie!" he screamed.

"What kind of vehicle were they in?" Melissa asked.

"It was an old red station wagon. It had wood paneling on the side," the woman answered. "I don't know the make. And just so you know, I had no part in any of that."

"I know," I answered.

"How do you know that, dickhead?" the man asked.

"Because the bullet holes in the baby's and mother's heads were from a small-caliber round . . . from a gun just like your Ruger," I answered. "And you shot the shit out of the car with your AR."

Melissa took two steps toward the man, raised her rifle, and fired a single round into his head. His hands dropped, and his torso slumped against the woman. She lowered her hands and pushed him off. She immediately put her hands back up. A dark stain appeared in her jeans, spreading outward.

Melissa stepped directly in front of the woman and raised her weapon.

I put my hand on Melissa's rifle and gently pushed the muzzle toward the ground. "Easy does it."

"He is, was, my neighbor, ma'am," she said, addressing Melissa. "After the blackout, he offered me a ride to my parents' home in Salt Lake City. I'm single with no husband or boyfriend, and I took him up on his offer. He gave me the gun you took, but I've never fired it. I swear. We came across that poor family, and he killed them for the water and gas."

"Stay there and don't move," I said. "Melissa and Renee, come with me."

Melissa stood there shaking, with the rifle again pointed directly at the woman's forehead.

"Please, ma'am. Please don't," the woman pleaded, shrinking back from Melissa and holding both palms up defensively in front of her.

"Melissa, follow me, please," I said firmly. "Now."

Melissa lowered the rifle, and the woman slumped in relief. Melissa turned and followed as I walked to the other side of the Cruiser. "I believe her," I said. "She had no part in those murders back there."

"She had the gun, Jon, and could have stopped him," Renee said.

"But didn't," Melissa quickly added.

"Hang on, you two," I said, turning.

I made my way over to the couple's discarded weapons. I picked up the woman's Glock, released the magazine, and found it full. The weapon wasn't even charged.

Back with the women, I told them what I'd found. "It hasn't been fired."

"Do you trust me to handle this?" Melissa asked, chest rising and falling after taking a calming deep breath.

I looked at Renee, who nodded.

"I don't want you to harm her," I said, looking her in the eye. "I mean it . . . not a scratch."

"I won't. I promise."

"Okay. Then handle it."

We walked back to the woman. Renee and I stood back, and Melissa approached and stood over the woman.

"Your name is Connie?" Melissa asked.

"Yes, Connie Van Husen. I'm a nurse in the cardiac care unit at UNLV."

"Do you know how to drive this thing, Connie?"

"He showed me how. So yes."

"Take off your boots and socks. Then the jeans, that vest and hoodie. Now."

"What?"

"Take them off."

"What? Why? I told you I had no part in that," Connie said, shaking now, looking from Melissa to Renee, then me.

"Take them off. Do you prefer a bullet in the head?"

"Please don't kill me. I'm a good person."

"Then stand up and take off your clothes. This is the last time I'm going to say it," Melissa said, raising her rifle and aiming at Connie's head.

Connie stood. With shaking hands, she undid her bootlaces, took the boots off, and then the socks. The jean jacket was next, her jeans, and then the hoodie. She had a white T-shirt and black yoga shorts on.

"Hands on your head," Melissa yelled. "And take the T-shirt off."

The woman removed the T-shirt, revealing a black Nike jog bra.

"Melissa, I told you I didn't want her . . ."

"Trust me, Jon."

"Okay. But hurry this up."

"Please don't. Please don't," Connie repeated, putting her hands on her head and shaking uncontrollably.

"You could have prevented those murders, Connie. But didn't. I saw that family. They didn't need to die."

"I'm so sorry for what happened back there. I will never forget them. Ever."

Melissa gathered Connie's clothes and took the key out of the trike's ignition. "You have any more clothes in those luggage compartments?"

"No, they're filled with camping equipment, food, and his books of all things."

"We're taking your clothes and the ignition key and leaving them on the side of the road a mile up. Start walking or running now. Get dressed, then get back here and take off on the bike. We'll leave you the gas and water."

Connie's knees gave out, and she slumped to the ground. A minute later, she was able to stand.

"Thank you. Oh my God, thank you," she said.

She quickly stepped up to Melissa and hugged her. Connie turned and did the same to Renee and me. She then started walking north, hands on her head. She passed the ladies and horses.

"You did well, Melissa," I said, pushing the trike to the shoulder. I left the man's body in the road.

"Thanks. Shall we leave her with her gun and holster? She's going to need it."

"Affirmative," I answered. "Why'd you make her undress?" I asked. "Seems unnecessary."

"What could we have done to her? We didn't want to hurt her, but she needs to suffer. The road will hurt her feet, and it's cold out. Seemed fair to me."

"I agree," Renee said.

"Okay, I get it," I said. "But what made you think of it?"

"Last week I binged-watched the *Game of Thrones*," she answered. "At the end of season five is Cersei's nude walk of shame scene."

"I loved that show," Renee said. "Sad though, at the end."

"My Sunday nights haven't been the same since the series finale," I said. "Although, the prequel, *House of Dragons*, is pretty good." I keyed the comms. "Kris, have them mount up. We're leaving. Monica and Kathy, come on back, please. Renee and Melissa, please gather those weapons and store them in the trailer. Then search the luggage compartments on the trike. Take all the ammo except for any extra .40 cal. Leave that for her."

I searched the man but only found four one-hundred-dollar bills, which I stuffed back in his front pocket. I removed his knife and sheath and placed them on the Harley's seat.

A few minutes later, we were ready to go. But first I walked up to the two women riders.

"We found the killer of the family."

"I figured you had when I heard the gunfire," the mother said.

"What's up with the half-dressed woman?" Stacy asked.

"She was with the man who executed the three family members, but she took no part in it. She's a nurse at UNLV and is a good person who unfortunately ended up with the wrong travel companion."

"But why walking half-dressed?" Stacy asked again.

"She could have prevented it but didn't. Melissa, one of our team members, is the one who doled out the punishment, not me. We didn't want to hurt her but felt she should suffer something. That, and Melissa binge-watched *Game of Thrones* last . . ."

"Ah, Cersei's walk of shame," Stacy said.

"Yep. We're leaving her clothes, the key to the trike, and a weapon a mile up the road."

"I'd say that's more than fair," Stacy said.

"Go ahead and get going. We'll catch up shortly."

Back at the Cruiser, I asked Melissa to open the glove box and hand me a black permanent marker.

I walked over to the dead biker and wrote "Killer of innocents" on what remained of his forehead.

FIFTEEN

A half mile up, we came abreast of Connie, who was making remarkably good time. She turned, saw us, and put her hands back on her head.

I rolled my window down. "We're leaving your gun and holster with your clothes. Some advice: Ride without the headlight on if you can. Hide out during the day and run at night. Stop for no one. And don't be afraid to use that Glock if need be. Good luck to you."

"Thank you, sir. You too, ma'am," she said, speaking to Melissa, who was riding shotgun. "I will never forget that family and all of you."

"You can lower your hands, Connie," Melissa said. "Hop on the running board next to Jon and hang on. We'll give you a ride the rest of the way."

Connie stepped up on the driver's side running board. She reached up and held on to the roof rack with both hands.

"Thank you, again. And thank you for believing me," she said, lowering her head and speaking through the open window.

I followed the horses, and ten minutes later, we watched as the two riders turned left onto a dirt track.

I stopped, and Melissa got out. She handed Connie her clothes and ignition key. Melissa dropped the Glock's magazine and handed the gun over. She threw the magazine down the road.

"Good luck, Connie," Melissa said, watching her dress. "Be smart and be safe. Take Jon's advice and travel only at night. I hope you make it to Salt Lake. And don't forget to pick up that magazine."

"Thank you for sparing me," she said, slipping her socks on. "Safe travels."

We turned off the roadway and followed the two riders. We crossed the creek without any issues and were soon on pavement. A half hour later, we passed under Highway 50.

Stacy and her mom stopped and waited for us to catch up. I got out and approached the waiting riders. The women silently formed a close-in perimeter behind me.

"Thanks for guiding us around town," I said, reaching up to shake hands with both women. "I wish you well and hope that your husband finds his way home soon. If it's any consolation, we met an Air Force pilot who said that his squadron's planes had undergone hardening to protect them against EMP pulses. So maybe your husband can hitch a ride on a still-working plane."

"I pray every night for his safe return, and I miss him something fierce," Stacy replied, her voice filling with emotion. "But if anyone can get home with all this shit happening, it's my Owen."

"Fingers crossed," I said. "Is there an on-ramp here, or do we need to cut some fencing to gain access to the highway?"

"Go left here," Stacy said, pointing to the area next to the highway overpass. "Drive parallel to the highway and in a quarter mile or so, you'll come to a pull-out the Highway Patrol uses to radar unsuspecting speeders coming down the overpass."

"Not something we have to worry about anymore," the mother offered. "And sorry to say, but to my knowledge, and

I've lived here my entire life, there is no way to avoid Highway 50 . . . no parallel highways you could take. You could head south, then west, then finally north, but chances are those roads are closed for the season because they cross mountains at very high elevations. And then you're dealing with snow. You're traveling at night, right? Because you have night vision?"

"That, yes. We also have thermal sights that allow us to see heat signatures up to eleven hundred yards out," I answered, curious as to why she was asking.

"If it was me, I would wait until daylight and travel during the day. At least from here to Winnemucca," she added. "You'll be traveling a road that's called the Loneliest Road in America for a reason . . . There's no one on it, and it's got wide-open vistas. You climb a few mountain ranges, sure, but when you reach the summits, you can see twenty or thirty miles out into the distance. I would think you could make good time and do it safely because you can see the road ahead for miles and miles."

"That's a great idea, ma'am. Thank you," I replied.

And it was a good idea. We'd only been on the road a few hours tonight, but taking another night to rest might not be a bad idea.

"You sure you'll be okay getting to your sister's? It's pretty dark out . . ."

"The horses know the way and that there's treats waiting for them," Stacy said. "We could drop the reins and they'd get us there no problem."

We said our final goodbyes, and Melissa watched with the thermal until they disappeared behind a hill a few minutes later.

"Did you all hear what she suggested?" I asked.

"It's a great idea," Renee said. "So yes." Also voting yes were Melissa and Monica.

"I want to keep going," Kris chimed in.

"Kathy?" I asked.

"Whatever the group decides is fine by me," Kathy said, undoing then retying the scrunchie that was holding her hair in a ponytail.

I truly wanted to eat up the miles while things were still unsettled and people were in denial. If most folks still hoped the power would soon be restored, then those fortunate enough to have a supply of food and water on hand would stay put until forced to venture out when they ran low.

My decision made, I said, "Okay, how about this: let's hit the highway for an hour or so and then find ourselves another hill to hide behind. We'll get started again an hour or two after first light."

The ladies were good with the idea of continuing on for a while longer.

I made a left turn, hopped the curb, and drove parallel to the highway until the turnout appeared ahead. Once on the road, I brought the Cruiser up to forty-five. With Melissa checking ahead with the thermal, we made excellent time.

We soon passed a large road sign that proudly stated that Highway 50 was officially designated as "The Loneliest Highway in America." And soon another sign announced that the road followed the original route of the Pony Express Riders.

There was the occasional abandoned car, hood up, and sometimes with the driver's door still open. But otherwise, we had the road to ourselves. We stopped at an abandoned eighties-model Chevy Malibu and, using Burt's manual pump, siphoned enough gas to fill our three empty jerry cans and top off the Cruiser's tank.

We cruised along for another hour and then gradually started climbing and gaining elevation. My ears popped as I downshifted into third and kept the speed at a steady forty. We passed a road sign that said Robinson Summit, two miles ahead, elevation 7,088 feet.

I rolled my window down and stuck my hand out. I guessed it was in the upper thirties.

"It's cold out there, ladies. We can look for a place to camp for the night up here or continue to a lower elevation and hopefully find someplace warmer."

Warmer was the unanimous decision, and we drove for another half hour, descending until smaller hills once again dotted the landscape. Finding one on our right, we off-roaded for a mile or so and pulled into a small, fifty-yard-wide valley wedged between two hills. Taking a camp chair, I hiked the hill to our west and used the thermal to complete a full 360-degree scan.

We set up the same watch rotation schedule as before, with me taking the first two-hour watch. The women set up their tents and went about boiling some water for dinner. Renee brought up a pouch of Mountain House lasagna and kissed me with promises of a warm sleeping bag waiting for me.

Nothing passed by on the road during my two-hour watch. The night was chilly and the air amazingly clear, with the stars appearing close enough to reach out and touch.

Two hours later, Monica relieved me. I handed over the thermal and made my way downhill to camp. I removed my chest rig and boots and crawled into the tent, where I was met with a welcoming body wipe.

DAY THREE

RV'S. KOALA BEARS. NOOSES. GRETA. WINDMILLS.

SIXTEEN

The night passed without incident, and we were packed and on the road by seven. The sky was clear but cold, the sun barely peeking over the mountain range we'd passed through the night before.

The views ahead were awesome . . . vistas as far as the eye could see with seemingly endless horizons. The road was two lanes, straight as an arrow, and other than a few cracks in the asphalt, was in good shape. After glassing the next forty miles with the binoculars, I brought the Cruiser up to fifty, holding it there for the next hour. There was nothing out here—not ranches, farms, or buildings—nothing man-made other than the road itself that seemed to run on to infinity.

We were steadily climbing and soon crested Little Antelope Summit, which the road sign said was 7,400 ear-popping feet above sea level. Before dropping down into the next valley, we stopped at the summit for a stretch break. I took the opportunity to glass the next twenty miles of the roadway below and spotted a small group of vehicles stopped on the road about three-quarters of the way across the valley, maybe fifteen miles out to the west. Where the vehicles had stopped was at the low point between the mountains to the west and where we were to the east.

There were two sets of vehicles—one set of three facing west and another set of two facing east, toward us. Dividing the two groups of cars and blocking the highway in both directions was a large, late-model diesel-pusher RV with a small white SUV sitting on a dual-axle car carrier behind it. There was very little shoulder where the RV had stopped, and there was no way a car could slip by on either side. The narrow shoulders gave way to a very steep drop-off, maybe twenty to thirty feet straight down to a dry riverbed below.

From this far away, it appeared as if one of the west-facing vehicles was touching the car carrier's left rear wheels, the second touching the first's rear bumper, while the third looked to be stopped a few hundred yards back. A likely scenario might have had the RV driver overcompensating for the sudden loss of power and inadvertently putting the camper in some kind of spin with the rear end skidding out of control. A car following too close, also suddenly without power or fully working brakes, would have plowed right into the left rear of the towed car trailer.

The east-facing cars appeared to be older models and were parked one behind the other in a nice follow-the-leader arrangement.

None of the vehicles appeared to be occupied, but they were a long way off, and I couldn't be sure.

"Ladies, come take a look at this," I said.

Each of the women took turns looking through the binoculars and offered opinions of what might have happened.

Renee offered up the most likely scenario. "The pulse hit, and the RV lost control," she said. "Then the first of the following cars slammed into the car carrier. The next car looks as if they slammed into the first car, and the third avoided the crash but were able to stop a short distance back."

While the ladies took turns glassing the roadway, I went back to the trailer, dug out the Pelican case, and wheeled it next to the Cruiser. Opening the case, I removed the Barrett's upper and lower receivers from their resting place in the Pelican's black cushions, then readied the lower receiver to accept the upper. A few minutes later, I had the Barrett ready to fire if I chose to. But the likely targets were much too far away, and this was strictly a reconnaissance look-see.

I got into the prone position and flipped up the sight's front and rear lens covers. It took a few seconds to acquire and then focus in on the vehicles in the distance, but the Barrett's powerful scope did offer a much better view.

"I have two individuals. Pretty sure one is male, and I can't be sure of the second," I reported. "Certainly not enough people to account for all those cars."

"Some of those drivers could have walked away," Monica said.

"They must have walked west, because we would have seen them had they gone east," Kathy said.

I glassed the car windows and saw nothing that looked like a head or shoulders sitting inside. "Well, if they didn't walk out, then they're in the RV," I said. "And it doesn't appear that any of those west-facing cars touched the car carrier or each other.

"I see a moving car out in the distance," Melissa shouted. "It's just starting down the grade and headed in our direction."

I brought my eye up from the scope just in time to see the sun glinting off of chrome or the windshield.

"Looks like they're moving pretty fast," Kris said.

All the women were watching the road ahead, leaving our six unwatched.

"Someone needs to watch our six," I said. "Please."

"I'll do it," Monica replied, turning and walking back behind the trailer, where she took a knee.

Kathy had the binoculars and was watching the new arrival close in on the cluster of cars and RV.

"Car is slowing down," she said.

I brought my eye back to the scope and watched as the car stopped behind the other two cars. The vehicle was an old sixties-era VW Bug. The driver's door opened, and a man stepped out, reached back inside, and came out with a rifle or shotgun. He walked past the three parked cars and slowly approached the RV.

The person we thought was a man who was hiding behind the RV suddenly stepped out. The new arrival slowly put his rifle on the ground and raised his hands.

"This is not good," Kathy said.

"What's going on?" Renee asked.

"Take a look," Kathy said, handing the binoculars over to Renee.

The new arrival turned and walked behind the RV with the original man walking a safe distance behind. They both disappeared into the area behind the RV we couldn't see. The original man appeared again, and two seconds later, we all heard the crack of a single gunshot.

"What the heck," Renee said. "Did he just shoot the guy?"

I couldn't be sure what had just happened. I then saw the passenger door of the VW open and a woman emerge. She turned and started running in the direction they'd come from.

"It's a woman," I reported. "And she's running away."

"Come on, baby, run!" Renee shouted. "Run, run, run!"

Even though from this distance the running woman looked like a little stick figure to the naked eye, it was plain to see that she was bookin' it for all she was worth.

I maxed out the scope, which really narrowed the field of view, but I could now see that the person we thought was a man was perhaps a larger-sized woman. The woman raised her right arm, and I could see that she was holding a large-caliber handgun. Pointing the gun at the sky, her hand jerked, and a puff of smoke came out of the gun. Three seconds later, the boom of the shot reached us.

"She fired a warning shot," I announced to the group.

The fleeing woman stopped, turned around, and put her hands out defensively.

"Noooooooooooooo!" the women shouted. "Keep running!"

The shooter motioned with her free arm for her companion to come up beside her.

In the scope, I had a better view, and I could tell that the second person appeared to be a young man, but a skinny one with longish hair. The man reached the shooter, paused for a few seconds, then continued walking up to the VW woman.

The man reached VW Woman, grabbed her hair, and started pulling her back toward the RV. The woman tried to swat the man's hands away, but the man stopped and hit her in the face with a handgun.

She fell to the ground, the man grabbing her hair and pulling her toward the RV. The woman was able to stand and stumbled alongside the man. They disappeared behind the RV.

I expected to hear a shot, but the woman shooter followed the man behind the RV, and all was quiet again.

"You know what they're going to do to that poor woman," Kris said. "Can we do anything for her, Jon?"

"Not from here," I replied. "But down there we can."

FIVE MINUTES LATER, I SLOWED to a crawl and parked two hundred feet behind the second car. The Cruiser's driver and passenger windows were rolled down.

On the drive down the hill, we'd reviewed the plan from start to finish, and I went over it again.

"Kathy, as soon as I step out, you crawl up into the driver's seat and then get out and rest your barrel on the window frame. Melissa, you do the same on the passenger side."

Melissa had taken Kris's rifle, as it was capable of firing three-round bursts.

"Melissa, you and Kathy both turn your safeties off, charge them, and make sure the fire selector is set for three-round bursts—the sun is going to be in their eyes, and they won't see you. When both the RV woman and man step out from behind the RV and walk toward me, I'm going to drop to the ground. When you see me drop, open fire. Don't hesitate, just fire. Keep that red dot on their upper torsos and make darn sure you keep the RV out of the line of fire—we don't want to harm the woman we're trying to help.

"Monica, Kris, and Renee, as soon as Kathy and Melissa step out, you do the same in the back and set up a close-in perimeter. Kris, use your Glock."

Before setting off down the hill, I'd taken off my chest rig and comms. I felt naked without them, but I had the Glock tucked into my belt in the small of my back.

"And what happens if only one person shows themselves?" Renee asked.

"Then we go to plan B," I answered.

"And just what is plan B?" Renee asked.

"I'm not sure. Hopefully plan A will work. We ready?" I asked.

"Good to go," was the gist of the replies.

I opened my door and stepped out but left the door open for Kathy. I slowly made my way as far left as possible, leaving as much roadway as I could for a clear fire lane for Kathy and Melissa.

I was fifty feet from the RV when the woman stepped out with a long-barreled pistol aimed at me and told me to stop. I stopped. "Is that your RV?" I asked.

"Don't matter none to you, sweetheart," she said, moving off to my left to walk on the shoulder toward me. Perfect, just as we hoped.

"You out here all by yourself?" I asked.

The woman was on the younger side, maybe early forties, and had greasy unkempt prematurely graying hair. She was heavy, outweighing my 230 by a good thirty pounds. She had severe acne scars on both cheeks, and her forehead was pockmarked with creases and lines.

"You seem to like askin' questions," she said. "How about you just shut the fuck up and walk toward me, real slow like."

"I don't like that plan. How about we trade safe passage for some water," I said, trying my best to ignore the cannon in her hand. "You look like you could use a drink."

"You have water?"

"Lots of it. Almost thirty gallons. And I'll let you have half if you let me through," I said.

"Rory, git your ass out here. Pronto!" she shouted. And to me, she said, "You got yourself a deal, honey. My son will help carry it."

Her son appeared from the side of the RV and followed the same path as his mother. Once the son was on the shoulder behind her, I dropped prone on the ground and waited for the shots.

Seeing me drop, the mother yelled, "The fuck you doin', dumbass . . ." and got no further as several short bursts of automatic gunfire erupted behind me. I watched as neat black holes appeared in both bodies, running from the stomachs to heads. Both mother and son bucked every which way as the bullets found their mark.

The firing stopped. I heard magazines being ejected and hitting the ground, followed by the sound of their replacements being inserted into empty wells, tapped in, and weapons charged.

I stood and walked back to the Cruiser. "You two okay?" I asked. Kathy was shaking and looked pale.

"I'm fine," Melissa shouted. She hadn't put her ear protection on, and her ears must be still ringing from the gunfire.

"I'm going to be sick," Kathy said, putting her hands on her knees and throwing up. Renee came from behind and grabbed Kathy's hair to keep it out of the line of fire.

Once Kathy was done, I said, "You both did well. Wait here while I check it out." I put my chest rig and comms on but left my rifle in the Cruiser. Taking my Glock out and two-handing the weapon chest-high, I approached the camper. I didn't bother checking the two bodies, as I knew they were gone.

I stepped around the front of the camper and walked up to the RV's door. The door was open, and I stuck my Glock in first and took two steps up into the interior. Seeing nothing in the passenger or driver's seats, I turned to my left and glanced down the full length of the camper. A king-size bed was in the very back, and lying on her side facing away from me was the VW woman, fully dressed but bound and gagged.

"You're okay now, miss," I said. I walked up to her and put my hand on her hip, and she did her best to wiggle away from me.

I holstered the Glock and hit the comms, said, "Renee and Monica, can you please come down. Kris, please stay on perimeter."

"Miss, we're here to help you," I said. "I'm going to take your gag out and then release your bindings." She craned her neck and looked up at me with wild eyes as I took out the gag and then set about undoing the elaborate knots.

Finished untying, I helped her up and followed her as she made her way to the front of the RV. Her cheek had an inch-long gash where she'd been hit with the man's pistol, and blood was flowing freely. I found a pile of paper napkins on the sink counter and told her to put it over the cut and to keep pressure on it. "You're going to need to get that stitched up."

"I have large Band-Aids in my V Dub. I'll be fine. Thank you. Where are the two that killed my boyfriend?" she asked, rubbing her wrists where the rope had bound her.

"Both dead," I replied, offering no further information. I helped her down the two steps to the pavement.

"That woman, I guess the boy's mother, was going to teach him how to fuck a woman. And the woman was, like, going to be me. She was actually going to guide him through the process.

They were about ready to start with me when they saw you drive up."

VW girl had black hair and was petite and very cute. For warmth, she wore a blue jean jacket with little glass beads covering the collar. She had on a short black skirt and was wearing black Chuck Taylors with thick white laces.

I hadn't seen her boyfriend's body, and then it hit me. I walked over to the shoulder beside the camper's right rear wheel well, and peeking over, wished I hadn't. Because down on the desert floor, some twenty-five feet below, were at least a dozen bodies.

The bodies were piled on top of each other, with arms, legs, and heads intermixed with one another. It was impossible to count bodies, as the pile was such a tangled mass.

It was clear that the woman and her son had executed these people . . . shot them and probably watched the bodies tumble down the steep incline.

The VW woman had watched me walk over to the edge and look down the embankment.

"Is Cal down there?" she asked, tears rolling down her cheeks.

"He is." He was lying face up on top of the pile.

"Oh my god, why would they kill him?" she asked, sobbing and taking big gulps of air. "He was just a big puppy dog and wouldn't hurt a thing."

"Most likely for your water and food," I answered. "And you."

Monica, Renee, and Kathy showed up, and I told them we needed to unhitch the car carrier from the RV's rear bumper.

"But first, let me show you something," I said, waving for them to follow me. Reaching the edge, I pointed down.

"Ohhhhhh myyyyyy God," Monica said, backing away from the edge, turning around, and throwing up. She straightened, took a swig from a water bottle, rinsed, and spat it out.

Kathy glanced down the incline, turned away, and said nothing.

Renee just stared at the pile, seemingly mesmerized.

"Renee?"

"I'm okay," she answered. "I just can't believe that people can do this to other people. I mean, I know monsters are out there, history has shown it time and time again, with Hitler and the Jews, the mass genocide in Africa, and Putin in Ukraine. But in Nevada?"

"Evil is everywhere, and it's just waiting for an environment that allows it to surface," I said.

VW girl suddenly sagged, and I helped her sit on the RV's retractable metal bottom step. Unprompted, she said, "Cal and I were on vacation in Lake Tahoe when the power went out. People were like, you know, going nuts, and no one's car worked, and when they saw ours, they like, you know, tried to take it from us. Cal is, was, I mean, a gun guy and had his AR in the back seat. Without that rifle, I can't tell you how many times it would have been, like, over for us."

"Where do you live?" Renee asked.

"Salt Lake City," she answered between heaving sobs. "What am I going to do now? Cal is, was, my life. He took care of me and now . . ."

"You're going to help us move this motor home out of the way so we can all drive away from this mess," Renee said. "Then you're going to drive to Salt Lake City and get with family."

"It's all so fucked up, it's like that TV show, *The Walking Dead*, less, like, zombies," VW girl said.

"What's your name, sweetie?" Monica asked.

"Tabatha, but I go by Tabs."

"Tabs, I'm Monica. This big guy is Jon, and the two ladies are Renee and Kathy."

"Nice to meet you, Tabs," Renee said. "I'm sorry about your boyfriend. But we don't have the luxury of having a bunch of time to grieve—that will come later. Right now, we need your help getting this trailer moved. Can you help us?"

"Sure."

I undid the dual towing chains, pulled the hitch pin and wiring harness, and released the trailer's coupler ball hold-down lever. I released the swivel jack, took hold of the handle, and cranked for all I was worth. The black plastic wheel touched pavement, and the trailer tongue lifted itself off the hitch ball.

"Let's push this thing so the trailer's tires are facing the shoulder and then push it over the side," I instructed. "It shouldn't take much of an effort."

The four of us grabbed the trailer coupler and swiveled the carrier to the point where we then simply shoved it, and on its own, it gained speed, disappearing over the embankment.

"That was fun," Renee said as we watched the trailer flip head-over-heels once, land on its tires and scoot thirty or forty feet out into the desert before it stopped, tires bogged down in deep sand. Remarkably, the small SUV was still sitting upright on the trailer.

"Now the hard part," I said. "Moving this beast out of the way."

"How are we going to do that?" Monica asked.

"With the Cruiser's towing strap," I answered. "It's rated up to fifteen tons. Hopefully the RV's transmission is in neutral, and we simply have to release the parking brake and pull it back. If it's in gear, we hook up the winch, put the Cruiser in low range four-wheel, and pull like hell. Either way, we need to move the thing back about ten feet," I said, standing back and mentally judging distances.

"I'll go check," Renee said.

A minute later, the driver's window slid back, and Renee said, "It's in drive, and the parking brake is off."

"Put the parking brake on and . . ."

"Isn't the idea to roll the camper back?" Renee said.

"Yes, but if you're able to put the transmission in neutral, you'll probably roll down the embankment," I explained.

"Oh. Duh, that makes sense. Parking brake set," she said.

"Monica," I said into the comms, "please find something to wedge in front of the RV's driver's side front tire.

"Like what?" she asked.

"Look in there," I replied, pointing to the car next to her.

Monica opened the passenger door and emerged with an older model computer CPU, which she wedged in front of the RV's tire.

I moved the Cruiser so its front end faced the rear of the RV at a forty-five-degree angle, close to the seven o'clock position. Setting the parking brake, I then dropped the tranny into four-wheel drive low range and then ran around and reached up and opened the rooftop Thule cargo box. I grabbed the thirty-foot Rhino tow strap and Rhino Hitch Receiver along with a couple of heavy-duty shackles. This tow strap was rated up to fifteen tons, but I couldn't even begin to guess how much that forty-five-foot monster RV weighed.

I removed the RV's receiver and inserted mine, then slid in the hitch pin, securing it in place. I attached one of the shackles to the receiver's ring and then threaded the three-inch webbing end ring through that. I then attached the strap's other end through the second shackle to a built-in ring welded on to the Cruiser's front bumper.

Concerned with the strap breaking and flying around like a razor blade, I had Monica, Kathy, and Tabatha move over to the other side of the roadway.

Tow strap in place and ready to go, I moved the Cruiser back until the strap was taut.

I keyed the comms, said, "Renee, release the parking brake. Monica, remove the computer."

"Releasing," Renee said.

I immediately felt tension on the strap.

"Renee, when I start pulling and the RV starts moving, turn the wheel counterclockwise."

I slowly released the clutch and gave it gas. The RV moved a foot and then two. I could see the front tire start to turn, and the RV's rear end swung toward me in response. I fully released the clutch, and all four tires started chirping in response to the load. But the RV moved and kept moving until there was plenty of room for cars to drive past. I depressed the clutch, jammed on the brakes, and let the Cruiser idle. There was still tension on the tow strap.

"Monica, wedge the computer back under the front tire. Renee, set the parking brake, please."

That done, I let the Cruiser drift forward, taking tension off the cable.

I undid the tow straps from both vehicles, retrieved the Rhino hitch receiver, and stowed the tow strap equipment back in the Thule.

I keyed the comms and asked Kris how our six was looking.

"All clear," she answered. "Both east and west."

We spent the next fifteen minutes gathering up weapons and all the food and water we could find. We retrieved the mother's and son's handguns along with Cal's AR and gave them all to Tabatha.

"You know how to use this?" I asked Tabs, holding the weapon up for her inspection.

"We go out beyond the Great Salt Lake to BLM land and go through, like, ten thirty-round magazines," she answered. She took the weapon from me, released the magazine, checked the chamber, reinserted the mag, palmed it in, and charged it.

"That answers that," I said. "And the handguns?"

"Same answer."

"Good. Last question: You know how to drive a stick shift?"

"I know how to use a stick. The VW is mine," she answered. "And I'm never stepping foot in an RV again."

"Can't say I blame you," I said.

We'd found six cases of Costco bottled water under the bed in the rear of the RV and loaded the VW with three. We scrounged up enough snacks and candy bars to take her to Salt Lake City and beyond.

We also found an empty five-gallon plastic gas can in the trunk of one of the cars and filled it using Burt's siphon pump and gas from the same car. Using bungee cords from the VW's trunk, I secured the gas can to the Bug's rear bumper and engine lid. We filled the VW and Cruiser's tanks as well.

Ready to go, the women hugged Tabs goodbye. Before she left, I gave her some last-minute advice. "Don't stop for anyone or anything. If someone jumps in front of you and asks you to stop, slow down but don't stop—keep going. Trust me, they'll get out of the way—especially if you show them the handgun," I said, patting the roof of the VW.

We watched her accelerate away, her left hand poking out her window in a final wave goodbye.

"I hope she makes it," Melissa said.

I continued to watch the V Dub climb the steep incline until it faded from view.

"She's stronger than you think. She'll make it," I said, truly believing it.

"Are we going to leave these pieces of shit lying in the roadway," Kris asked.

"Leave them where they are," Kathy answered. "The vultures or coyotes will take care of them."

Not wanting travelers happening upon the scene to wonder what had happened, I said, "Wait one." I went back into the RV and found what I was looking for in one of the kitchen drawers.

Neither the mother nor the son had a forehead left so, pulling the mother's pants down to her ankles, I wrote with permanent marker on her thigh: "Killer of innocents." I repeated the process with the son.

I walked back to the waiting women, said, "I wasn't allowed to do that in Iraq or Afghanistan, but here and now, too damn bad."

On her way back to the Cruiser, Kathy had stopped at the bodies of the two lying in the road. She was staring at the woman.

Concerned, I started to walk down to her, but Renee took hold of my arm and said to give her some alone time.

I nodded in understanding, said, "I'll never forget the first person I killed in combat. It was during my fourth patrol. Later that night, my sergeant joined me in the mess hall and asked how I was. We talked for an hour or more. It helped."

"Give her some time. You'll know if you need to step in and help."

Ten minutes later, Kathy climbed in the Cruiser. We drove by the RV and got up to speed.

SEVENTEEN

e'd traveled sixty miles, gone over two more high-elevation passes, Pancake and Pinto Summits, without any of our usual banter. Silence, no conversation taking place at all, just the constant, confident-sounding drone of the Cruiser's engine purring along.

I was concerned that the women weren't dealing well with the situation we'd left behind, and I had to remind myself that none of them had the combat experience I had. Unfortunately, death was something I'd dealt with on an almost constant basis on each of my overseas deployments, and while I never got used to it, I'd come to grips with it.

"It's awfully quiet in here. How's everyone handling what we just saw?" I finally asked, breaking the silence.

Melissa was the first to answer. "I'm all right. I keep thinking about those people at the bottom of the embankment. I just can't believe they killed them," she said, palms up in question. "And for what? Candy bars and a few bottles of water?"

"I've said it before and I'll say it again, desperate people do desperate things," I answered. "There's just no getting around it."

"Those two weren't desperate," Melissa said. "They had food and water, yet they continued to kill."

"I have no answer. Sometimes the unexplainable remains that way."

"I feel sorry for those people back there, but we no longer have the luxury of allowing ourselves the time to deal with it," Renee said. "It's now, in my mind anyway, time for full survival mode."

"I agree with you, Renee. Anyone gets in our way, we plow right on through," Kathy said. "I mean, it's been three days since the pulse and look at what we've already been through. If it's this bad now, just think what it's going to be like in a week or a month."

"A week? Make that two or three days," I said. "So far we've stuck to the less-traveled roads and have managed to avoid crowds of people, but we're going to be traveling on Interstate 80 later today, and that's going to change things up big-time."

"Like how?" Kathy asked.

I really thought about what to say before answering. "Interstate 80 is the major east-west route in the US," I began, "and is one of the heaviest traveled roads in America. Dead semitrucks will be everywhere, possibly hundreds of them, parked where they died. Hundreds of trucks means hundreds, perhaps thousands, of drivers out of their cars or trucks and now walking.

"Then there's the private vehicles that died along with the semitrucks. So far, we've been lucky and haven't had to deal with hundreds of dead cars because the pulse happened early morning. But this is Interstate 80, and we're not talking middle-of-nowheresville . . . There's going to be a lot of dead vehicles out there, which means a lot more people."

"And people are our enemy," Melissa added.

"I would agree with that but would change the word *enemy* to the word *obstacle*," I said. "People are going to see us and will want what we have: a working vehicle and a trailer full of supplies. They'll become obstacles, which we need to make our way around."

"How are you, Monica?" I asked.

"I'm good," she answered. "It's becoming clear that we can't dwell too much on the past when the here and now is the important thing. Surviving each day so we can do it all over again the next day, and the next, and the next."

Kris remained silent, and we left her alone.

We soon crested a smaller hill, and I could see that we had a long flat road ahead of us. The road ran straight and appeared deserted for the next thirty miles.

"Let's stop here and stretch," I said. "Take ten."

It was now nine thirty, and it was time to get underway. I gathered the group together, said, "We're going to have a driving lesson. Melissa and I are the only two that know how to drive a stick shift, and that has to change. We have a nice flat road ahead of us, and it's the perfect place to learn and practice."

First up was Renee, who took directions well and within fifteen minutes was taking the Cruiser through all four gears and up to speed. Next was Kathy, and after a couple of confusing clutch and gas pedal synchro issues, she had the knack of it. Monica couldn't find second gear and kept dumping the tranny into fourth and lugging it. But she kept at it and, after thirty minutes of trial and error, had it going on.

When Kris finally got behind the wheel, she said, "I know how to drive a stick," and took the Cruiser up through the gears as if she'd been doing it for years. "My dad had a dune buggy with the same shift pattern," she said by way of explanation.

"And you didn't bring up this information until now, because why?" Melissa asked.

"Because I thought you and Jon sharing the driving was enough."

"That's fucked up," Melissa said with a hard edge to it. "If we're going to make it to Seattle, then we need to be a team, and being open and honest with each other is a good starting point."

"I agree with Melissa," Kathy said.

Monica reached over the front seat and touched Kris's right shoulder. "New beginnings starting now?" she asked, playing the role of group counselor.

"I guess so," Kris replied, adjusting the rearview mirror.

"Group?" Monica asked.

Everyone agreed.

I had Kris continue driving.

Wanting to keep the banter going, I asked each woman where they were born, raised, went to college, and where their parents and siblings live. "Monica, why don't you start off," I said.

"I was born and raised in Lancaster, California. I graduated from the University of California, San Diego, with a degree in accounting. I went to work for the city of San Diego and passed the California CPA exam three years later. I took an accounting position with Hewlett Packard at their company headquarters in Palo Alto, California. I did that for fifteen years and then transferred to sales and liked it. I met my ex there. HP transferred me to Seattle, and I worked Washington State for HP before Jon hired me for Securetech. My parents are in their late eighties, but both are still very active. They live in a retirement community outside Laguna Beach, California. I have a younger brother who lives in Austin, Texas."

"Melissa?" I asked.

"I was born in San Clemente, California, which is only twenty miles or so from Laguna Beach," Melissa said. "Monica, do your parents happen to live in Laguna Niguel?"

"Yes, they do. They love it. Especially after living in Lancaster, which is basically desert. They live in Laguna Woods Village."

"That's a beautiful place," Melissa said. "Well, like I said, I was born in San Clemente, which is a beach town about twenty miles south of Laguna and sixty miles north of San Diego. I was raised there too. I surfed full-time for two years after high school and had my hopes of turning pro dashed when I took a bad spill over in Hawaii."

"What happened?" Kathy asked. "If you don't mind me asking."

"No worries, Kathy. It was the last heat of a competition, and I was coming down the face of a sweet-looking twenty-six-foot-plus wave. I had just dug in to turn and head back up when my skeg hit a rock. The board stopped, and I kept going. I was wearing a leash, which is a bungee-type cord that's attached to my ankle and keeps my board from being swept away. The wave broke over me, and I was dragged along the bottom for at least half a minute. Sometime during those thirty seconds, my skeg hit me in the head and I lost consciousness. I was rescued by a wave runner and taken to the hospital. I came to four days later and spent the next two months in the hospital. The surfboard split open my skull on the right side. All kinds of ocean gunk got in there, and it took two months to get rid of it all. They shaved the right side of my head, and I decided to leave it shaved. Well, not completely shaved—I let an inch or so grow to hide the gnarly scar."

"I didn't know any of this," I said.

"I never had the chance to tell you . . . You hired me within five minutes of meeting me."

"And one of the best hires I ever made."

"You told me I was the best hire you ever made," Kris said.

"Funny, he told me that too," Monica threw in.

"He never said anything like that to me," Kathy said.

"You're all the best. Now back to Melissa," I said.

"Well done there, Kristen," Renee said.

"Thank goodness you recovered," Monica said.

"It wasn't fun sitting in a hospital for two months, but my mother flew over and was with me every day. My dad flew over, and they took me home to the mainland.

"I decided to get serious and enrolled in Saddleback College for two years. I was accepted to UC Irvine but spent the summer in Seattle with a high school friend and never went home. I saw the Indeed job posting for Securetech, and the rest is history.

"Oh yeah, my dad is an attorney for the California Coastal Commission. The Coastal Commission is a San Diego-based government agency that protects California's coast . . . mainly from money-hungry developers and tech billionaires. I have two older brothers and one younger sister. My brothers flip houses along the coast, and my sister is in nursing school at UC Irvine. My mother handles the books for my brothers' flipping business."

"Your turn, Kathy," Renee said.

"Oh, okay. I was born in Freemont, California, and raised across the bay in Sausalito. I attended college at San Francisco State and went to grad school at Stanford. I have a master's degree in electrical engineering . . . in other words, I was a computer geek. I worked for Facebook as a programmer and lasted six years before I burned out. I met Bradley at a bar in Menlo Park, married him, quit Facebook, and moved to Seattle when he was offered a position with Amazon in their legal department. Jon hired me even though I had no experience in sales or customer support."

"The best hire I ever made," I said, which brought much needed laughter to the Cruiser's interior.

"My father and mother were attacked in downtown San Francisco during the anti-Asian furor during the early months of the pandemic. They moved from Sausalito across the bay to Walnut Creek after they finished testifying at the asshole's trial."

"Tell me he was convicted," Kris said.

"Oh yeah. The judge slapped him hard with an attempted murder conviction and sentenced him to twenty-five years. The trial was a huge deal in San Francisco."

"I think I remember that trial," Renee said. "It made national news. Weren't your parents attacked by a Black guy who ran across the street and blindsided them? A security camera recorded the attack."

"Yep, that's the one."

"Are your parents okay now?" Melissa asked.

"They are, and are very happy living in the East Bay. I have two older brothers, both doctors, and an older sister who is a professional violinist and plays with the New York Philharmonic."

"Was your mother a—what do they call them . . . a . . ." Monica started to ask.

"A tiger mom?" Kathy answered for her.

"That's it," Monica said.

"Yes, big-time," Kathy said. "She raised two doctors, a professional violinist, and a computer engineer. Your turn, Renee."

"Well, I was born in Tampa, Florida, and raised in Boca Raton. I went to MIT and entered their computer sciences program. I met Ben in my fifth year, started our company with him in my sixth, and received a doctorate three years later."

"I didn't know you had a doctorate," I said. "That's impressive."

"It's just a degree. I don't use it. I am who I am regardless of the title in front of my name."

"I get that, Doc," Kathy said, earning herself a middle finger from Renee.

"I'm an only child. My father is an oral surgeon for the VA, and my mother was an emergency room nurse . . . She retired last month. They still live in Boca."

"Your turn, Kris," I said.

"Compared to the rest of you, my life has been very ordinary," Kris began. "I was born in Portland, Oregon, and raised in Hillsboro, Oregon. I went to the University of Oregon in Eugene and graduated with a useless degree in English Lit. I interned at Microsoft headquarters. They liked me and hired me for their sales department, and I was very successful. I met Evan on an online dating site, and we were married a year later. We have two kids and live in Ballard. My dad was a grocery store district manager, and my mother was an old-fashioned stay-at-home mom. Dad retired a few years ago, and they moved to Oro Valley, Arizona, which is just north of Tucson. I had an older sister, but she passed away at seventeen from a brain aneurism."

"Thank you for sharing, Kris," I said. "And sorry to learn of your sister's passing. And thank you, everyone, for sharing."

WE CONTINUED TO EAT UP the miles. I constantly scanned ahead with the binoculars and except for a couple of dead cars saw nothing that worried me. Black clouds were building to the west, and a half hour later, light rain began falling. A few minutes later, a road sign appeared on the right saying the town of Eureka, elevation 6,481 feet, population 620, was two miles ahead.

"Kris, please pull over and let me drive," I said. "Melissa, come up front with me. Get your Glock out and make sure a round is chambered."

The changeover complete, we headed down a hill into town, passing a Nevada State Bank on our right, then DJ's Diner and Drive-In a block later. Both were closed and boarded up. A large white billboard announced that we were entering, "Eureka, The Friendliest Town on the Loneliest Road in America."

I could see the historic downtown section a half mile ahead. The road narrowed, with buildings on both sides crowding the roadway—only a narrow, two-foot-wide sidewalk provided separation between the buildings and the road. A half block farther, the road took a gradual right, disappearing from view. No way was I going to take us down that choke point.

Not liking what I saw ahead, I turned right at the first opportunity and then took a left a hundred yards up the hill. We were now running parallel with Highway 50, which I could see below us. We were above the town, on Spring Street, and I picked up speed on the wet road. We were flying through a residential street filled with a mixture of rusty trailers and beaten-down, century-old homes with sagging porches and sand and rock front yards. The road ahead gradually took a bend to the left, and we found ourselves back at Highway 50. I ran the stop sign, turned right, and brought us up to speed again.

I hadn't seen a soul in town but had a bad feeling that something might have been waiting for us in the old section of town. Too many times to count, our armored column had gone into Afghani villages and come under fire. With no way of retreating, we'd just had to rely on overwhelming firepower and our friendly neighborhood A-10 Hog to make it through.

We were now on an open plain with nothing in front of us but a straight highway running through a flat valley floor. A road sign said that the next town was Austin, Nevada, seventy miles ahead.

Melissa scanned the road and declared it clear.

I came to a stop and asked who wanted to drive.

"I do. I do," Renee said excitedly, beating out Monica and Kathy.

Renee took over the driver's seat, and I sat shotgun.

"Keep it at fifty," I said. "We get the best gas mileage at that speed."

It was raining harder now, the windshield wipers becoming less effective. A few minutes later, snowflakes replaced the rain.

"I love the snow," Kris said, breaking her silence. "There's something pure and simple about it. Like covering up the bad and letting the good emerge."

"I've always liked it, too," I said, "except in downtown Seattle. Having to drive up and down those steep hills when they're covered in snow is nerve-racking."

I brought the binoculars up and glassed ahead and saw four walkers heading our way about five miles out. "We've got walkers ahead," I announced.

I glassed the walkers again and could now see that it was a woman with three small children. They were dressed for the weather in down parkas, puffy gloves, and wool hats, some sporting animal ears. Vapor was forming in front of each of them with each breath they took.

The woman must have spotted us, for she brought the group to a sudden stop, gathering the children behind her. I could see the little ones, ever curious, stick their heads out from behind her and watch us approach.

"Renee, slow down to twenty-five and stop when we get within twenty yards of them," I said.

A few minutes later, Renee brought us to a stop. I opened my door and stepped out into bitter-cold air. The women spilled out of the Cruiser and set up a close-in perimeter.

Seeing what looked to be five fully outfitted soldiers spilling out of a civilian vehicle must have frightened her, for she and her kids stepped back in alarm.

"Where are you headed?" I shouted.

"We're going to Eureka. We're from there," she yelled back. "We've been walking for two days now. We have energy bars, but we've been out of water since last night. Can you spare any?"

"We can," I said. "I want you to raise your hands and walk toward us and stop ten feet out. Do you have any weapons?"

"I don't, sir," she answered as she walked toward us, hands held high. The children, seeing their mother raise her hands, did the same.

Smiling at the sight, I said, "I'm going to send someone out to search you, miss. Nothing personal, it's for our protection as well as yours."

"I understand."

"Melissa, can you please check? The children, too."

Melissa had them open their coats, and she began patting each one down. The youngest child was jumping up and down in excitement, saying, "Check me next! Check me next!" which Melissa did, to the delight of the youngster.

The woman was in her late twenties and attractive in a cute-girl-next-door way. She had long, jet-black hair, which she wore pulled back in a ponytail. She was tall like Renee. Even though she had a large puffy jacket on, I could see she was slender. Her kids were carbon copies of their mother.

Melissa stepped back, said, "All clear."

"It's okay to lower your hands. Follow me," I said, waving and leading the group to the rear of the trailer. I undid the corner of the tarp and pulled out a full case of the Costco bottled water. "Take as many as you'd like."

"Thank you so much," she said, watching the children grab more bottles than they could possibly drink. "Children, only take what you know you can drink."

"What are your names?" I asked, watching the kids return several bottles of water.

"Barbara Lopez," she replied, opening a bottle for the youngest child. "And these are my children, Marty, Kai, and my youngest, Chloe."

"I'm Jon, and this is Melissa," I said, opening one of the bottles for myself.

"They're adorable," Melissa said.

"Thanks, they've been real troopers these past two days," she said. "We'd been visiting my parents in Austin and were headed home when the car died and my cell phone went dark. We waited for someone to drive by, but we've only seen one car, an older model VW Bug, and the driver must not have seen us on the side of the road—it was dark. After waiting another hour or so, I decided to walk home to Eureka instead of going back to my parents'. How is it that your Land Cruiser is working?"

I filled her in on what we knew and why the Cruiser was still working.

She put her hand over her heart and looked at me in shock. "Why? For what possible reason would they do that? Hatred of America and what we stand for? Maybe just Americans in general? Because we shot down that stupid balloon? And Nancy Pelosi's visit to Taiwan back in August of last year really pissed them off."

"All good points," I said. "But who knows?"

"What kind of future do my kids now have?" she asked, tears starting to flow.

"Mommy, why are you crying?" the children asked in unison.

"I got sad, guys, but I'm better now," she replied, wiping tears away and smiling. Now composed, she said, "An EMP, huh? I've read about them but thought they were caused by sun storms or something like that."

Before I could answer, I felt a tug on my jacket. Looking down, I saw the little girl pointing to her ski hat. "Do you know what animal I have on my head?" she asked.

"It looks like a koala bear," I answered, kneeling down and patting the girl's head.

"Yes, it is. Mommy, he's really smart."

"He is, isn't he, sweetheart?"

"My daddy works in a big dirt hole," the smaller boy said.

"It's called a mine, honey," Barbara answered, showing more patience than any ten people I know put together.

"You okay on food?" I asked, standing.

"We are, thanks. We've only got another ten or eleven miles to go and we'll be home." She then added, "We're Mormon and have a very full pantry that will last us six months or so. My husband's parents live with us, and they have a large network of fellow worshipers that have a community food pantry."

I secured the tarp and was ready to say goodbye when each of the children came up to me and said thank you, accompanied by a big hug.

"You're welcome," I said. I bent down and spoke to the children. "You are very strong and very brave. Listen to your mother and all will be well."

I gathered the women together, and each said their goodbyes and exchanged hugs with the mother.

When it was my turn to say goodbye, we hugged long and hard. I tried to disengage, but she held on tight and whispered in my ear, "I'm scared. Scared to be out here alone without my husband. But I can't be scared in front of the kids. So, thank you for being nice to me and especially to the children. They will remember this encounter, and I can remind them that there are still good people out there."

I stepped back and looked at the mother and her children and thought, *Ten or eleven miles is only a half hour or so, round trip.*

Pointing to a turnaround up ahead, I said, "Melissa, drive up to that turnaround and bring the Cruiser back. We're driving them home."

Renee smiled and put her hand up for a high five. Kris, Monica, and Kathy all did the same.

Renee stood in front of me, hands on hips, trying to look tough, said in the deepest voice she could conjure up, "Absolutely no stopping for anything or anyone, huh?"

"Well, you know . . ." I said, trailing off.

Renee hugged me tightly. "I knew there was a reason I like you other than for your hot bod," she said.

I brushed a snowflake off her nose and kissed her.

Barbara had seen our exchange, smiled knowingly, said, "Thank you. Thank you. Thank you!"

"You're welcome," I replied. "I'll need you in the Cruiser with me so we know where to go. The kids can ride in the trailer. But if you think it will be too—"

"They'll love it," she broke in with. "They'll treat it like the Halloween hayride we do every year."

Melissa brought the Cruiser to a stop next to us.

To the women, I said, "I need a volunteer to ride in the trailer and keep the children company. I—" was as far as I got.

"I'll do it," Renee offered.

"Me too," Kathy and Monica offered in unison.

"All three of you can ride in the back," I said. "Just bundle up because it's going to be cold. And sit on the ammo cans toward the front. You can use the tent stuff sacks as cushions. Keep the children secure on your laps. Okay?"

I lifted the kids up and handed each woman a very happy child.

I opened the rear doors and Kris, who was already in the back, reached out a hand and helped Barbara up and onto one of the Cruiser's rear side-facing bench seats.

"If at all possible, I want to avoid the downtown area," I said, closing the rear doors.

She waited until I was in and we were on our way before answering. "We live on the northeast side of town, and normally we use a street just a block or so from the town center, but I know a shortcut," she said. "We've got about a six-mile straight shot up Highway 50 before we'll turn left."

Melissa brought us up to thirty, as fast as we felt it safe to do with the kids and women in the trailer. I turned in my seat and watched the kids laughing and having a great time in the trailer while the women held them tightly in place.

"I don't think there will be much laughter in our future," Melissa said, seeing the scene playing out in the rearview mirror. "It sucks, big-time."

"Our town is very small, and everyone knows everyone else. There's seven hundred of us in the town proper. Including outlying areas, about double that. If this goes on for long, we'll organize and keep our community together," Barbara said, watching the kids having a grand time in the trailer. "We'll make sure the laughter never stops."

"I have two children of my own, two girls, seven and nine," Kris said. "We live in a community just outside downtown Seattle, and other than some parents of a few of the girls' friends, we know no one, not even the people across the street from us. So, count your blessings."

"I do," Barbara replied. "Every day."

"I'm not sure what I'll find when I finally get home," Kris said. "My husband is a former college professor and is now a stay-at-home dad. He's a wonderful husband and father, but he's not a natural protector and wouldn't know one end of a rifle from the other."

"I knew he was a professor at one time, but what did he teach?" I asked.

"He was a botanist for the agriculture department before turning to teaching. He knows more about plants and how to grow things than just about anyone in the Pacific Northwest."

"If this blackout continues for as long as I think it will, your husband is going to be among *the* group of the most in-demand people in the western US," I stated emphatically.

"Our turn is coming up on the left," Barbara said. "Turn into that new apartment complex. We're going to drive through to the back and take the access road to County Road 101."

We turned into the complex and saw that most of the parking slots were occupied but only saw one person, a young woman, walking between buildings.

"Where is everyone?" Melissa asked.

"This complex was built by the mining company for their employees," Barbara answered. "They shuttle all their workers up to the mine, and my guess is they're still up there or walking home like we were. My husband, Ronny, is the mine's second shift foreman."

Reaching the rear of the complex, we turned onto a short dirt access road, which led to a paved road.

"Turn left here. This is County Road 101, and in three miles or so you'll be turning right onto Fioronza Street. It's a dirt road but in good shape. Our place is at the end of the road about a mile up."

As we climbed the steep hillside, we passed older, well-kept homes set on half-acre lots. Large, old-growth trees surrounded the houses. Bare now, they would provide much-needed shade in the hotter months of the year. Several residents, mostly older, were out in their yards and waved as we drove by.

"Most of the folks up here on the hill are retired miners and are lucky in that they have secured pensions," Barbara said. "The younger miners lost their pensions or 401(k)s in the 2008 recession when the mine closed for almost three years.

"Ronny was hired by the mine's new owners in 2011 and has been there ever since. He helps out on the ranch during weekends."

"Is it a working ranch?" I asked. "I was raised on a ranch in Montana, and my parents still work it."

"It is a working ranch," she answered. "We have a natural spring on the property, and we farm fifteen acres of rotating crops. We also pasture cows and horses. We have 180 acres total. How big is your parents' ranch?" she asked.

I hesitated before answering, as I didn't want to appear to be bragging. But maybe the time for feeling that way was over. I went ahead and answered.

"The ranch is 128,600 acres, but only 35,000 or so are managed," I answered. "We also have another 203,000 acres of public grazing land under long-term lease from the BLM. We're primarily a cattle ranch but also grow wheat, hay, and barley. We have several long-term tenants that farm a hundred acres each, and a couple of them raise hogs."

"My gosh, 128,600 acres. We have a hard time running our 180," she said. "I can't even begin to imagine what it must take to run a ranch that size."

"Well, my folks don't do it themselves—we have a dozen full-time ranch hands, and in the spring, summer, and fall, we have city folks who come out and play ranch hand for a week or two."

"Like a dude ranch?" she asked. "Do you have cabins, chow hall . . ."

"Yes, exactly like a dude ranch," I answered. "For two weeks, guests get to ride horses, wrangle cattle, fly fish, go on trail rides—some overnight, hike, mountain bike, or just float down a river in an innertube. In the fall, we have guided hunting trips that take folks into horseback-only areas bordering national forest lands. At night there are campfires and cookouts.

"And yes, we have ten, one and two-bedroom guest cabins, and a three-story lodge with forty-eight guest rooms. We host weddings, family reunions, and a lot of corporate retreats and meetings. There's a conference center and a guest dining room. We even have a runway on the property that can handle private jets. We also have two hangars that can hold a total of eighteen aircraft.

"My younger sister, Abigale, runs the dude ranch side of things, and my dad runs the commercial ranch operations. My mother helps with both."

"And you grew up on the ranch?" Melissa asked.

"Yes, and born on the ranch, too. Just like my father, and his father, and his. Our family has owned and managed the land for a hundred and forty years."

"And you left, why?" Barbara asked. "Because to me, it sounds pretty awesome."

"It was awesome, and I can't even imagine growing up anywhere else. I initially left for college and then joined the Army after graduating," I answered. "Years later, I saw an online job posting for Securetech, the company we all work for."

"Take the next right," Barbara said, pointing to the intersection ahead.

"Was your dad upset that you didn't come back to the ranch after you finished college?" Barbara asked.

"Yes, at first, but I told him that when he was ready to slow down and start relaxing, I'd come back. He was good with that."

"I didn't know any of that," Melissa said.

"I knew some, but not all of it," Kris added.

A minute later Melissa said, "We have people ahead where the road ends and that driveway begins. All are armed."

"That's our ranch," Barbara said.

"Stop here, Melissa," I said.

The road ended fifty yards ahead. Their driveway wound its way another fifty yards past that to their front porch and then on to a six-car garage on the left. Their house, like the others we'd passed on the way up the hill, had leafless trees surrounding it, but this ranch house was a whole lot nicer than any of their neighbors.

It was a low-slung, single-story white ranchette with a large wraparound porch on three sides. Situated on the top of a higher hill, it had a commanding view of the land behind it. From the road, I could see the house, and beyond that, a good-sized pond with a short dock with a red rowboat tied to it. Past the pond was a newer red barn large enough to stable a dozen horses. Hundreds of hay bales were neatly stacked and covered by an enormous tin roof. I could make out a half dozen sleeping cats snuggled in the bales.

"Those are my in-laws, Stanley and Elinor, and my husband Ronny," Barbara announced, excited. "Let me out so they can see that it's me and the kids."

I opened my door and then the rear of the Cruiser. I helped Barbara out, then helped her lift the three children to the ground.

"Set a close-in perimeter, guys."

That done, I watched Barbara and the kids run up to their waiting family. After hugs, kisses, and excited exchanges, Barbara's husband gave his rifle to his father, and he and Barbara walked toward us.

Ronny Lopez reached us and extended his hand. "Thank you for helping Barbara and the kids, Master Sergeant," Lopez said, shaking my hand. "We've been very worried, and with no working vehicle, we had no way of venturing out to check."

"Your wife is the one who brought them home safe. We just gave them a lift the last few miles," I replied.

Looking over at the women in their close-in perimeter formation, he asked, "Are you current military?" Pointing to my M4, he said, "That weapon and the others are full auto or three rounders and aren't generally available to civilians."

"Ex-Army Special Forces, civilian for six years now," I answered. "The rest are strictly civilian, with a very quick course in weapon use." I didn't answer his weapons question. "Are you ex-military yourself, sir?" I asked.

Ronny Lopez was quite a bit older than his wife, maybe by twenty years. He was very tall, approaching my height, but had me by thirty or forty pounds. His hair was dark with silver wing streaks in front of his ears and cut in a military buzz cut. To my eye, he was clearly ex-military.

"I've been out since 2010. Retired a captain. Put in twenty with the Marine Corps, the second half of those twenty with Forecon," he answered proudly. "Spent most of my time doing battle damage assessment and remote sensor operations."

"Tough assignments for sure," I replied. And they were. Especially BDA, where you needed to put eyes on targets. Forecon did a lot of the same types of mission specs as the Army's Special Forces.

"Sir, we really need to get moving," I said. "We have a long drive ahead of us."

"Understood, Master Sergeant. I don't want to hold you up, but I wanted to let you know that my dad has an old ham radio set, and he's willing to try to contact anyone you may want to reach out to."

Now that was of interest.

"Yes, sir, there is. My name is Jon. Can I call you Ronny?"

"Of course," he answered. "And the old coot up there is my dad, Stanley."

We walked up to his father, and introductions were made.

"Nice to meet you, Mr. Lopez," I said. "And thank you for your offer. I'd very much like to take you up on it."

Mr. Lopez senior was a chiseled-rock of a man. Seventyish, with silver hair cut like his son's, he looked like an older version of the Marlboro Man, even down to the denim jacket with cream-colored fleece collar.

"No problem, son," he replied. "You have any information you can give me, like his call sign?" He took out a mini yellow legal pad and was ready to take down some information.

"His name is Neil Kristen. I don't know his call sign. He's been a licensed operator for as long as I've been alive, and his set is a pre-WW2 model, one he is very proud of. He's tried to get me interested, but I've never taken to it. But there's no doubt in my mind that with what's happened, he'll be monitoring it as much as possible."

"And where does he live?" he asked.

"He lives outside Whitefish, Montana."

"Does he have any type of special antenna?"

"He has several antennas. I know because I helped install them. They're on top of a hill, and he built remote control stations because of the distance between the ham set and the antennas."

"Montana isn't far in ham terms," he said. "Basically, a stone's throw away."

"I do remember something," I said. "He usually likes to go on in the early evening, and I'm not sure if I have this right, but I seem to recall him saying something about 40M to 80M."

"Well, hell, Jon. That'll help a bunch," he said. "That means he monitors North America and usually does so in the early evening."

"Sorry I don't have more information to give you, sir," I said.

"I'll put out a CQ on those frequencies. Can't promise I'll ever connect, but hey, gotta try. Now, what do you want me to tell him if I can connect?"

"Please tell him that his son, Jon, is okay and is making his way to Seattle in the Land Cruiser and will then immediately head to the ranch."

"Anything else?"

"If there's time on your connection, please tell him what caused the blackout—I told Barbara what I know about the pulse."

"She told me. Sons of bitches, all those fuckin' Chinese might make a move on the West Coast."

"It's a big maybe, Mr. Lopez," I cautioned.

"The more I think about it though, it does make some sort of sense. The coronavirus set China back, economically, at least a decade or more. Then of course, there's Nancy Pelosi's visit to Taiwan last year."

"I hear what you're saying, Mr. Lopez."

"If you look back at history, say, the situation the Japanese were in prior to WW2, and their shortage of oil, why . . ."

"Dad, enough of the history lessons, please," Ronny said, cutting the elder Lopez off. "They want to get back on the road."

"You're right, son. Sorry, Jon."

"It's fine, sir. Really."

I keyed the two-way and asked Melissa to turn the Cruiser around and for the rest of the team to load up.

Melissa turned wide and completed the U-turn, bringing the Cruiser to a halt, and waited for us to load up. But the team had a mission to complete first, and that was to run up to say goodbye and offer up a last hug to the little ones.

Watching the group hugathon, Ronny smiled and said, "Good luck to you, Master Sergeant. Watch your six."

"You too, sir. And thanks in advance for your efforts to get ahold of my father, Mr. Lopez," I said.

EIGHTEEN

Twenty minutes later, we passed the spot where we'd first encountered the Lopez family. With Melissa driving, I sat back and tried to relax.

It was snowing harder now, but it was melting as soon as it hit the roadway. I scanned ahead but couldn't see more than a mile through the white curtain of snowflakes.

The Cruiser ate up distance, and the next sixty miles saw us traversing a long, wide-open valley with an occasional dirt ranch road leading away from the main highway. The roads usually led to a ranch house, which more often than not was surrounded by a mass of bare trees, and oddly enough, green pastures. The green pastures were most likely made possible by an underground spring and a ton of fertilizer. Otherwise, it was barren desert, brown and dreary, with undulating, hilly topography. There were thousands of hills, most no more than twenty or thirty feet tall, breaking up the landscape.

Leaving the valley floor, we hit a steep grade, which brought us up to Scott Summit and 7,195 feet elevation according to the obligatory road sign.

"Can we stop here for a few minutes, Jon?" Renee asked from the back.

"Good idea," I replied.

Melissa brought us to a stop.

At this elevation, an inch or two of snow had accumulated on the roadway and even more on bare ground.

We all stretched. Large vapor clouds appeared in front of us as we exhaled into the cold air.

"I'm hungry. Can we eat?" Kathy asked.

I unfolded a map and figured we had another ten or eleven miles to go and we'd be on the north side of Austin.

"Can we wait until we get past Austin?" I answered. "Maybe an hour or so? We may be able to break through some of this snow."

"Sounds good," she replied.

"Melissa, I'm going to drive us beyond Austin. We have one higher summit to traverse, then another ten miles of very twisty, steep road to navigate before we hit Austin. I know it's a little late to be asking this, but does anyone get car sick?" I asked.

"I do," Monica answered. "Especially on twisty roads and if I'm sitting in the back seat."

"Then you're sitting shotgun," I said, "which means you'll be scanning with the binoculars. You'll need to have your firearm ready if needed. Good?"

"All good."

We dropped quickly down Scott Summit, traversed a small valley, and then steadily climbed our way to the 7,200-foot Austin Summit. It was snowing heavily at this elevation, and I hoped it would clear up before we hit the twisty portion of our route.

Once on the downhill side, the road was very steep, with twelve miles of narrow, twisty hairpins. Lucky for us, the snow had stopped falling, but I still had to constantly work the gears through the turns. It became so steep that instead of overheating the brakes, I left it in second gear, which forced our speed down to fifteen. Though the road only wound twelve miles from

Austin Summit to the outskirts of Austin, it was forty-five minutes before the town itself appeared in the distance.

The town of Austin was small and sat in a narrow valley, so narrow that the residents had only a football field worth of level ground before hills on both sides jutted up at forty-five-degree angles. Dozens of old mine tailings littered both hillsides with old shacks and trailers sharing every square foot of available buildable space.

Like the town of Eureka to the east, the roadway narrowed once it hit the small downtown section. Further on, perhaps half a block, the road made a sharp right, disappearing from view.

Thick black smoke rose from the downtown area, and flames were working their way up the steep hillside that comprised the western slope of town. I could see dozens of individuals running down the steep streets that were somehow free of flames. Many were holding infants or small children in their arms as they made their way toward the flat ground that was the town.

"What's with all the fires?" Kathy asked.

"Most likely transformers on power poles. They caught fire during the pulse and with no fire trucks to fight them just spread unabated. Then there's propane tanks that most if not all of these houses have in their yards and use for heating and cooking. Some of those tanks contain hundreds of gallons of gas."

I stopped the Cruiser a quarter mile from downtown. We were on a hill, high above the town, looking down. Ten seconds later, a shock wave rocked the Cruiser, followed by the sound of a huge explosion. We watched in stunned silence as a home on the hill exploded into a million pieces. Chunks of home and who knows what rained down on the town below.

"We're not driving through that town. No way," I said, putting the Cruiser in gear and setting off.

"Stop, Jon," Monica said, putting her left hand on my right arm. "Stop now." Monica had the binoculars up and was focusing in on the area where the small downtown section began. "There looks to be . . . No, it can't be." Monica held out the binoculars. "Look. Do you see what I see?"

I brought the Cruiser to a quick stop. I took the binocs from Monica and focused in on this side of downtown. I glassed the area from left to right, and then I saw it, or I should say *them*. Hanging from the horizontal portion of a light pole were two men and a woman. Black zip ties held their ankles together, and their arms were bound behind them. A cardboard sign was somehow attached to the chest of one of the men, but at this angle I couldn't quite make out what it said. I waited as the wind slowly rotated the body and I could read the message.

"There are two men and a woman who have been hung from a light pole," I said. "A message written on a piece of cardboard has been attached to one of the men. It reads 'louters will be shot.' They spelled looters l-o-u-t-e-r-s."

"Get us out of here," Renee said.

"Asap," Melissa shouted, "before the fire spreads to the other hillside."

"We're not looters," Kathy said. "We don't have anything to worry about."

"Having folks hanging from light poles at the entrance to your town does make a statement, though," I said.

"Yeah. It says, 'Stay the heck away,'" Melissa said.

"There are laws to protect people from that kind of punishment . . . not to mention basic civility," Kathy said.

"There are no more laws. Or civility. It's do whatever you want to whomever you want," Renee said. "And stealing something from someone who probably had little to begin with would, I think, be considered the ultimate crime. Along with murder."

I was studying the scene below with the binoculars. A door to a store opened, and I watched as a dozen men and women exited, only three old guys carrying rifles. They were leading a man and woman by long thick ropes fashioned into nooses and already tightened around the necks of the group's two intended victims. Their hands were zip-tied behind their backs, but their feet had not been bound. The woman and man were in their thirties, well-dressed and clean-cut and didn't exactly fit the profile of your average looter—whatever that was. The woman dropped to the ground in an attempt to stop their forward momentum, but the rope strained on her neck, and she was forced to stand and move with their captors.

"They're doing it again," I said, describing the scene below.

"We need to stop it," Kathy said. "What if they're innocent?"

"Even if they are, it's not our fight," I responded, keeping eyes on the events unfolding below.

"Jon . . . maybe we should help." Renee spoke to me softly as if she were a mother encouraging a reluctant child. "I can see from here that they don't exactly look like looters."

"My job is to get you safely to Seattle. If we intervene in what's happening below, I'm putting the five of you at risk."

The woman had let herself fall to the ground again, but this time the entire procession came to a halt. I could see the woman screaming and shouting at the crowd of onlookers. An older man in his seventies or early eighties approached her, leaned down, and hit her with his fist. Bam! She appeared to be knocked silly. Her head bounced off the pavement, and she damn near went limp.

The onlookers rushed the procession, but the old guy pointed his rifle at them, and they shrank back. The procession started moving again, the slack rope tightened, and the woman was half dragged along the pavement. The man did his best to help her, but both his elbows were being held by too very beefy-looking guys, and he lacked much movement other than forward.

Kris was the last person I thought would want to intervene, but she spoke up for all to hear. "The onlookers are obviously on the side of the two about to be hung. Would a crowd be that upset if they were really looters? If we're going to help those two, we need to do it now," she said. "Right now!"

"Good points, Kris. Group, how vote you?" I asked.

Final tally: five yeses.

"Then we're helping them," I said. "And god help us if we're wrong about those two." I put the Cruiser in neutral and let it coast down the hill. "Okay, listen up. I'm going to stop a hundred yards in front of the crowd. This leaves that one street up on the right as our only exit option. Hopefully it goes up and then north and gets us around town. Melissa, watch my six. Safety off, full auto. No, make that semi. If you need to shoot, do so from a kneeling position and make sure you turn on and use the red dot. Renee, Monica, and Kathy set up a close-in perimeter. Kris, get out but stay at the back of the Cruiser. I am going to get those two and bring them to the Cruiser. You help the two get in the back. Throw them on the floor if you have to. And don't worry about how uncomfortable they might be."

"Roger that," they all replied.

"Make sure your comms are on. I'm going to run right at the group and take down the three that I see holding rifles. I'm pretty sure the remaining group members will turn and scatter without firing back. Melissa, your job is to watch for overwatch positions and loner heroes. Pay attention to windows and rooftops. I'll watch the crowd and deal with the couple."

"Everyone ready?"

I stopped the Cruiser, put it in neutral and set the parking brake, but left the engine running. In the time it took to roll down the hill, the old men had zip-tied their ankles, thrown ropes over another light pole's horizontal support strut, and were in the process of tying the ends of the ropes to a bumper of an old dark blue Chevy Chevelle. I jumped out of the Cruiser and waited two seconds for Melissa to exit the Cruiser's rear doors and form up next to me. I raised the M4, jammed the buttstock into my shoulder, brought the Eotech's red dot to center mass of the first of the three armed old guys, and started running down the road.

Out of the corner of my eye, I saw that Melissa was to my right and two steps behind. We were now fifty yards from the crowd, and I told Melissa to stop where she was and provide overwatch. Several procession members were now pointing in our direction. I stopped, took a knee, and fired a quick burst at target number one. Several rounds hit the guy in the chest and left leg. I brought the red dot to target number two, fired off another quick burst, and saw him slump to the ground. Both procession and onlookers turned and hightailed it. Target number three had taken refuge behind the Chevelle and was using the couple as human shields. I couldn't fire at him for fear of hitting the couple.

I stood and started fast-walking right toward the guy. *Pop your head up, asshole. Please.* Not knowing for sure how many rounds were left in the M4's magazine, I swung the rifle back and to the side and brought the Glock out of its holster.

As if my thoughts had been heard, the guy popped his head up to see what was happening. I fired two quick rounds and saw one enter his left eye and the other miss him by a foot, hitting the car's headlight.

I hadn't heard Melissa fire off any rounds. "Melissa, give me a sitrep."

"All clear."

The couple were gazing at me in puzzlement—probably asking themselves if I was there to kill them or help them.

I first went to the man and cut the zip-ties on his wrists and ankles, then cut the woman's. They hugged and waited for me to tell them what to do.

"Get those nooses off. And stay right here," I instructed, pointing to the ground in front of them. I walked to the front of the Chevelle, stepped over the dead man, and raised the hood. I yanked out the spark plug wires and with my knife cut them in half, hoping that would render them forever useless. Just to make sure it couldn't be driven and used to give chase, I fired a single round into each of the car's four tires, leaving eight rounds left in the magazine.

The man had his noose off and was helping the woman with hers.

"Hurry," I told the two. "Hustle up the road to that Land Cruiser up there."

The woman's noose came off, and the three of us started running up the hill. I swung the rifle up in front of me, ejected the depleted magazine, pocketed it, and slammed in a new one. We had passed Melissa when a shot rang out, pavement breaking apart ten feet to my right. Melissa fired several short bursts in response, and no further shots came our way.

"Let's go, Melissa."

She stood and ran behind the three of us. We had just made it to the Cruiser when a round hit the ground in front and to the right of us.

"Kris, get them in, fast. Melissa, hop in the driver's seat. Renee, watch our two guests and make sure they behave."

I'd seen muzzle flashes from the roof of the building where the couple had been held prior to being led to the impromptu gallows. I flipped up the Eotech's magnifier and focused in on the shooter. The shooter was a girl, no older than fifteen or so. Her weapon was a single-shot bolt-action rifle. Her hands were shaking, and I watched as she fumbled a round and dropped it. She leaned down, disappeared from view, then came back up with head and shoulders in clear view. I changed the rifle's fire selector from auto to semiauto and then moved the red dot from her head to her left shoulder. I fired a single round. Her rifle flew up and dropped to the sidewalk below. The girl sat hard on her ass, brought her right hand up to her shoulder, which was now running red with blood, stood, and ran behind a large commercial HVAC unit.

Not seeing any further threats, I ran to the Cruiser's passenger door.

"Move out, Melissa. Don't forget we have a trailer behind us with a life of its own. Right at the next street."

"Got it," she answered.

"Fires have now spread to the eastern hillside," Kris said, eyes peeled to the area below us.

"Regardless, we need to get around that," Melissa said, turning right on East Street and heading uphill.

I took the Glock out of its holster and kept it at the ready.

We drove past an RV park and church on our right and kept going higher and higher. The road was dirt and gravel, filled with potholes, and very narrow, with houses close-in on both sides—so close to each other that there were no driveways to accommodate cars. Dead cars were parked on both sides of the roadway, which made passing through difficult.

"I hope there's a road we can turn left on that will take us north of town," Melissa said, worry clearly filling her voice as the road became steeper and steeper.

"There is," our male passenger said from the rear of the Cruiser. "Turn left on Water Street. It should be close. It will take you almost to the other side of town. A couple of miles up, you'll hit Bateman Street. Turn left on Bateman and then an immediate right on North Street. Take North to Reese Street. Turn left on Reese, which after a few twists and turns will dump you out on Highway 50."

"Flames are chasing us up the hill," Kris reported, glancing back down the hill.

"I'm going as fast as I can," Melissa shouted back.

"Everyone, settle down," I said.

"What are your names?" Renee asked.

Melissa had to downshift to second and creep along at five miles per hour. Unable to dodge potholes, the ride was bumpy and uncomfortable.

"We're the Tillages—Randy and Isabelle. We're teachers here in town."

"Turning left on Water Street," Melissa said.

"Are you looters?" Kris asked point blank.

Both Randy's and his wife's eyes opened wide in disbelief. "Heavens no," the wife answered for them. I glanced back and saw a bruise had already started forming around her left eye. The old guy packed a punch. The dead old guy.

"Then why were those people going to string you up?" Renee asked.

The couple looked at each other and decided the wife would answer. "Long story short: the town's richest bigshot, Terrance McDaniel, who, by the way, was the man behind the Chevelle . . ."

"He's the guy that hit you with his fist?" I asked.

"Yes. Well, yesterday, his son, Dylan, abducted our teenage daughter, Debra. Took her right from our front yard . . . just drove up in his father's old Chevelle, hopped out, grabbed Debra, and made off with her. We were down the street at a neighborhood meeting, organizing the gathering of food and supplies, when a guard that had been posted outside came in and asked why our daughter would be hanging with someone as old as Dylan. Who is in his early forties, I might add. Can you imagine someone as old as that "hanging" with a fourteen-year-old girl?"

"Happens all the time," Renee answered. "Unfortunately."

"Not in this town," Randy said forcefully.

"Well, to keep the story going, hon . . ."

"Please feel free to condense, Mrs. Tillage," I said.

"Of course. Well anyway, we, along with several neighbor friends of ours, walked down the hill to Dylan's apartment, which is above the Trading Post on South Street. The Trading Post is owned by his father and is one block off Highway . . ."

"If you don't hurry the story up, we'll be in Battle Mountain before you finish," Randy said.

"We have people walking toward us," I said. "A group of six teens. They don't appear armed."

"May we sit up? I may prove useful to you acting as a navigator," Randy said.

"Sure," I answered.

Melissa kept the speed up, and the group of young teens parted to make way for us. They waved as we passed.

"Those kids are in my history class," Randy said. "They're good kids with good parents. We've got a couple of miles to go on this street."

This road was wider but was still crowded with dead cars. We passed by countless older double-wide trailers and houses probably built early in the previous century. But the road was more or less level, and we were making good time.

"Shall I continue the narrative, Randy, or are you going to interrupt me again?"

"Let me help you get to the ending," Monica said. "Did you get your daughter back?"

"Yes," she answered.

"Unharmed?"

"That's a good question. We have . . ."

"Yes or no is what I'm looking for."

"Then yes."

"Did you kill the younger McDaniel?"

"Yes."

"Did the father then take you two?"

"Yes, early this morning."

"Is your daughter safe?"

"She was to run up to the top of Virginia Street and told to wait for us at the trailhead. We hope she's still there."

"The older McDaniel was going to hang them under the guise of being looters," Renee said, "especially since there were already three hanging from the light pole."

"Turn left at the intersection up ahead, which is Bateman," Randy instructed. "Then take an immediate right onto North Street."

Melissa completed the two turns.

I was confident these two weren't looters. "Where can we drop you off?" I asked.

"The corner of Reese and North would be perfect," Randy answered. "Our home is right up the hill from there. I'll take my old minibike with a lawn mower engine on it and pick up Debra. Turn left here and stop."

Melissa stopped at the corner, and Kris opened the rear doors. The couple got out and stretched.

"Continue on this street, and it will dump you right onto northbound Highway 50," Randy said through the two rear doors. "And thank you for rescuing us from that crowd. You are our saviors."

"From the bottom of my heart, thank you," Isabelle said, placing both hands on her chest.

"You two going to be okay?" Renee asked.

"If by that you mean, are we safe from the McDaniels? If so, then yes. You killed not only Terrance McDaniel, but you also killed his two younger brothers, Axle and Anderson. The only McDaniels left are two eighty-something widows."

"Good luck to you, then," I said. "Kris, shut the doors and let's blow this pop stand."

"What are you going to do if the fire spreads this far north?" Kris asked the two.

"You didn't see it, but the original city planners thought ahead and put in a two-hundred-foot firebreak that divides the east side of town in half," Randy answered.

"Our side, the north side, is okay," Isabell added.

The couple shut the doors and waved as we sped away.

Reese Street looked as if it ran parallel to Highway 50. After some twists and turns, it did merge onto the main highway. We quickly resumed travel speed.

"I can't believe they are actually hanging people," Kathy said. "It's as if America has become a third-world country overnight."

"Believe it," I said. "I've been preaching just how bad things are going to get. Well, you just saw proof that it's far worse, far sooner, than even I imagined it could be."

"Do you still think we'll make it to Seattle?" Kris asked, clearly concerned.

"We'll get there. It may take some time, may be a little more difficult than we originally thought, but we'll get there," I answered.

A road sign on the right read "Highway 305 North, one mile ahead."

Two minutes later, we were headed north on 305. Off to the left was a large cemetery, and through the curtain of snow, we saw a large group of people walking away from an open grave. Behind the group and toward the road were a dozen horses tied to a chain-link fence. Left behind were two men with shovels filling the grave using dirt piled beside the gaping hole.

"Do you see the men manually filling that grave?" Melissa asked. "I guess we really have gone back to the way things were done two hundred years ago."

"An apt description, Monica," Renee said.

NINETEEN

We were gradually losing elevation, and a few miles further on we entered a wide-open area which a road sign said was the Reese River Valley. There was the occasional ranch or farm nestled next to a small stream that looked as if it followed the road out into the far distance. Otherwise, the land was inundated with miles and miles of sagebrush and little else.

"When you think about it, hundreds of thousands of people have probably died today alone, from pacemakers that stopped functioning the day the pulse hit," Kathy said. "Pacemakers keep hearts beating, and without a working unit, the heart can only work unaided for so long."

"And opened bottles of insulin must be kept refrigerated and goes bad if left at room temp," Kris said. "There are millions of people that are diabetic who are not going to last long without it."

Twenty miles into the valley I turned left onto an old gravel service road and drove until the road ended at a picnic area at the stream's bank. We were at least a quarter mile from the road and shielded from the highway by tall bushes. I felt this was as safe a place as any to park for an hour or so.

"Let's figure on spending an hour here. I'll walk back a couple of hundred yards toward the highway and keep watch while you guys eat. Keep your comms on, chest rigs on, and your rifles slung. Watch your six at all times."

I helped the women set up the camp table and then poured water from an almost empty jerry can into two camp pots. Camp stoves were ignited and pots set onto hissing, high-pressure blue flames.

I left the group and hiked a couple of hundred yards back down the service road. Clearing a space off to the side of the road, I took a knee and kept watch. It was quiet, and I started to relax.

"Let the rifle hang in the sling, soldier man," a deep voice suddenly commanded. It had come from my right.

"Now!" another voice said, this one from my left. "And raise your hands."

Taken by surprise and outflanked, I took my hands off the M4 and slowly raised them, keying the comms with my left thumb at the same time.

Ten yards out, two men in hunting gear stood from a prone position and walked toward me. Hunter right was decked out in a fully insulated camo hunting jacket and overalls. A red stain on his jacket appeared to be from cleaning a fresh kill. Hunter left had on old blue jeans and a large black sweatshirt with a hood, and over that a camo down vest with a Bass Pro Shop logo over the right breast. Each had on a camo wool knit hat. Long hair spilled out from both men's hats, and each sported a long, ZZ Top–style beard.

Each man had what looked to be a Remington 700 bolt-action hunting rifle pointed at me.

"Well, well, what have we here, brother?" hunter on the right asked, stopping fifteen feet away.

"Looks like after being stuck out here for three days, we finally got ourselves a working vehicle," hunter left responded.

"Our truck just up and died on us three days ago, and we haven't seen a working vehicle since," hunter right said, slowly walking toward me.

"Then we're in our tent just over there," hunter left said, pointing to an area off to our right, "discussing the unpleasant possibility of having to walk home to Austin, and lo and behold, we hear tires crunching on gravel and a beautiful-looking Land Cruiser pulling a trailer load of what has to be something useful drives on by."

Didn't these morons wonder why I'd walked two hundred yards from the Cruiser and taken a knee?

"I'd be happy to give you a ride somewhere, fellas," I said. "I'm all alone and have extra seats in a warm cab."

Thank you, tinted windows. During the Cruiser's restoration process, I'd debated whether to tint the windows and was glad I had, as these two had seen the Cruiser but not its occupants. Nor had they seen all of us exit the Cruiser and set up a quick camp.

"I don't think you understand, dude. We're going to take your Jeep, and if we're nice, we'll leave you here and not kill you," hunter right said, moving toward me, stopping less than ten feet to my right.

"First off, don't ever call a Land Cruiser a Jeep. That's just going too far," I said. "And secondly, you are not taking my Land Cruiser."

Both laughed, and hunter right spat a wad of chew toward me, missing my boot by a foot. "Is that a fact," he said, smiling, showing a mouthful of yellow-stained teeth.

"It is. And I'll tell you what: if you set those rifles on the ground, step back five paces, then lie face down on the ground, I promise to let you live," I said to the two men.

"I've had enough of this bullshitting around, brother," hunter left said. "Let's fuckin' put a bullet in his head and get on home."

"Melissa, the one on the left, please," I said, dropping to the right and hugging the ground.

"What . . ." hunter left said, right before his chest and head exploded from the impact of a single three-round burst of NATO 5.56 rounds.

Hunter right saw his brother go down, raised his rifle to fire, and pulled the trigger. Nothing happened.

From ten feet away I'd seen he'd left the rifle's safety on.

"Sucks when that happens, doesn't it?" I said, now kneeling. Holding the Glock with my hands fully extended, I was looking through the sights at the area between his eyes.

"Fuck, I'm sorr—" was as far as he got. I lowered the sights and sent two rounds, both hitting center chest. He slumped to the ground and lay still.

Hunter left was on the ground, his extremities twitching as signals from his dying brain tried to make sense of what was happening. I'd seen this twitching in Afghanistan and knew it could go on for several minutes. I walked over and put a single round into his forehead. The twitching stopped.

There were six rounds remaining in the Glock's fourteen-round magazine. I dropped the mag and inserted a fresh one.

I heard crunching on gravel, turned, and saw four of the women running toward me. Looking back to the Cruiser, I saw that Monica had remained behind, maintaining overwatch. They were truly learning.

The four women came to a stop and formed a loose perimeter.

I walked over to Melissa and hugged her. Stepping back, I put my hands on her shoulders, said, "That was an awesome show of marksmanship, kiddo. I know career soldiers that couldn't have done better than that. Thank you for saving my sorry ass. You all right?"

"I'm a little shaky. But like Burt said, deep breaths."

"That was a three-round burst. You exchanged rifles, didn't you?" I asked.

"Yeah. I figured if I fired mine on full auto, I most likely would have hit you too," she explained. "That would have been no bueno."

I stepped back and looked at the rest of the crew. "I fucked up, and I put you all at risk. I'm sorry for that and will try my darndest to do better."

The women looked at me and then at the dead men. "All's well that ends well," Kathy said, a smile planted on her face.

"Renee and Kathy, will you please go check out their tent?" I said, pointing to the area the dead men had indicated. "If there's anything worth taking, bring it to the back of the trailer, and we'll take a look. Also, there might be a car or truck somewhere close by. Kris, please cover their sixes."

"Their what?" Kris asked, looking truly clueless.

"Cover the area behind them," Melissa answered for me.

The two walked away with rifles hanging down and not in the ready position. "Rifles pointing at the ground do no good, you two," I shouted after them.

The two raised their rifles into the ready position and scanned 180 degrees as they made their way to the tent. Kris followed twenty feet behind.

Melissa and I gathered up the two hunting rifles, and I searched the dead men's pockets for anything of value. I found a box of .270 Winchester in hunter one's coat pocket and a key with a Dodge logo on it in hunter two's front pant pocket. There was nothing else.

Hunter one had a pair of expensive Danner insulated hunting boots on, and I removed them—size eleven, which unfortunately wouldn't come close to my thirteens. They wouldn't be making these for quite some time, if ever, and I figured they'd be a good barter item. We carried the rifles and boots back to the Cruiser, where Monica was waiting.

She watched us approach. "What happened out there? Everything okay?"

I dropped the boots behind the trailer, and we put the two rifles on top of the trailer's tarp. "It is now," I answered. "Thanks to this one, here," I said, pointing to Melissa.

To Melissa, Monica said, "Fill me in."

While Melissa was replaying the events of a few minutes ago, I checked the two rifles. They were Remington 700s chambered in .270 Winchester and in like-new condition. Both had Nikon scopes on top and bipods from a manufacturer I'd never heard of.

These would make great sniper rifles, and hopefully, the three ladies checking out the tent would come back with more ammo.

"What's on the menu for lunch today?" I asked. "I'm hungry."

"Me too," echoed Melissa.

"How do you do it?" Monica asked us. "Kill someone and then eat? I'm not judging, just curious how you seem to get over it so quickly."

"For me, it's either them or us," Melissa answered first. "They threaten us, then they deserve to die. Once it's done and over with, I don't think about them again. Before all this shit happened, I never would have thought I could kill another human being. But now, things are entirely different."

"Well said, Melissa," I said. "And as for me, throughout my military career, I've killed dozens, maybe even hundreds, of enemy combatants. Dozens that I saw the bullet I sent hit the person I was aiming at. As Melissa said, it's them or us. Simple. And you eat when you can and sleep at every opportunity, because you never know when you'll get another chance."

"Well, okay then," Monica said. "Thank you, both, for talking about it. Water's still hot, and we have pouches of chili mac with beef, beef stroganoff, chicken fajita bowl, or chicken fried rice. Take your pick," Monica offered.

Picking chicken fried rice, I ripped off the top of the mylar pouch, took the oxygen tab out, poured in what I guessed to be one and a half cups of hot water, and stirred the mix around a bit and resealed it.

I took the Glock's depleted magazine and replaced the expended rounds. I asked for the rifle Melissa had used and replaced those three rounds as well.

I keyed the two-way. "Kris, Renee, Kathy, what's going on?"

"We found the tent and truck," Renee answered. "Their camp is downstream from your position about a quarter mile or so. They have a lot of stuff. Most of it looks almost new."

"They have large backpacks we're going to use to haul the stuff back. We'll be there in ten minutes," Kathy added.

"You three hungry?" I asked. "We can start the process of getting a meal ready for you."

Three orders of beef stroganoff followed and were soon being prepared.

I was sitting in a camp chair and eating my chicken fried rice when the three women appeared. They were not alone.

Oh boy, was my first thought.

TWENTY

sn't she cute," Renee said, petting the head of a beautiful dog. "We found the poor thing shivering inside the truck. We put one of the sleeping bags from the tent around her, and she seems much better now. She kind of looks like a German shepherd, but with shorter fur and much longer legs."

"This beauty," I said, putting my hands under her chin and rubbing, "is a Belgian Malinois. They're super smart, agile, and very loyal. And ultra-expensive. We had one with us on almost every patrol and op in both Iraq and Afghanistan. They rode with us in helicopters, rappelled down ropes with us, and tandem-jumped from planes with us. The Secret Service uses this breed to patrol the White House grounds."

I took a step back and the dog followed, walking behind me and sitting on my left.

"Have you heard her bark?" I asked.

"Not yet," Kris answered.

"Interesting." I said, stepping back another ten paces.

"Why is it interesting?" Renee asked, sounding puzzled.

"She won't bark, because she's been trained not to," I said as I watched the fifty-pound brown and rust-colored beauty as it again followed and walked behind me. She sat next to my left leg, looking up at me with those beautiful, sad brown eyes.

"She's obviously been trained. I wonder if she's a current or past military or law enforcement working dog? If she's a US military working dog, I wonder how she came to be with those two?" I asked. "Unless she's retired and they got her that way. But usually, an MWD—military working dog—will retire into their last handler's care. Let's see if she's got some skills," I said, walking away from the dog and then turning around, and with hand signals I'd watched dog handlers use for years on deployment, asked her to come. And she did, up on my right, around my back, and sat down on my left.

The girls clapped, and the dog's ears pulled back in alarm and then relaxed when a bomb didn't go off.

I suddenly walked forward, and the dog stayed right by my side. I turned left, and she hung back for a second, giving me room to complete the turn. I stopped. She stopped. I walked. She walked. I walked and turned right, and she stuck like glue to my side, constantly looking up at me as if wondering when the fun would end.

"Oh, she's good. I don't know how to test if she'll go after someone if I ask her to, but I bet she would. Normally a handler would have her leashed, but this gal is super trained, and if I recall correctly, is referred to as a 'push button.'"

"Can we keep her?" Renee asked. She crossed her fingers and held both up for me to see. "Please."

"Of course," I answered. "We can't leave her out here. Did you find any dog food?"

"In the truck's cab. A small, half-empty bag and a larger, unopened one," Kathy answered, holding up the half-empty bag.

"Well, that's good. We'll have to try and get some more, though. Go ahead and put the sleeping bag on the floor in the rear of the Cruiser and make a travel bed for her. But I still don't like the fact that she was with those two scumbags," I said.

"Trained dogs like this gal here can cost up to twenty-five thousand dollars."

Renee poured dog food into a camp bowl and set it down in front of the dog. The dog sniffed and attacked it. The food was gone in four seconds flat. She looked up at me and then Renee, obviously looking for more.

"A little bit more might be nice, right, darlin'?" I said to the canine beauty. She licked her chops, waiting. Renee gave her more.

I poured water into another bowl and set it down next to the now empty food bowl. She lapped at the water for a good forty-five seconds.

Renee, Kris, and Kathy attacked their beef stroganoff.

"Renee, when you're done eating, I'd like you to show me the truck and tent."

When Renee had finished eating, the two of us, accompanied by the dog at Renee's side, walked the quarter mile to the tent. Some distance beyond the tent was a newer model, light-gray Chevy Silverado pickup.

"That is not the men's truck. Not the right make. I'm going to let her search and see what she comes up with," I said.

I reached down and touched the dog's back, said, "Seek" and put my left hand out in front of her. She left my side and started searching in a left-to-right, right-to-left grid pattern, expanding out with each turn.

"What are you thinking?" Renee asked.

"I think those two killed the dog's caretaker but couldn't bring themselves to do the same to the dog."

We watched the dog work, and within a minute, she suddenly sat down, looked back at us, and whined. She was two hundred feet further downstream and very close to the truck. We walked to the waiting dog, and there were two bodies on the ground, a woman and a man. The man had been shot in the chest with a large-caliber weapon, and the woman appeared to have been strangled, as dark bruises the size of hands stood out against the pale white skin of her neck.

The woman was naked from the waist down, with her panties and blue jeans wrapped around her right ankle. Her shirt, bra, and jacket were pushed up and scrunched around the top of her breasts. Her hands were zip-tied behind her back. Her head was turned toward her companion, and her eyes were open and vacant. I brushed my fingers across her eyes and shut the lids.

"They shot the man from a distance and kept the woman alive and used her," I said.

Renee nodded and stayed silent.

"For some reason, the couple put the dog in the truck, because there is no way she would have allowed the woman to be attacked like that had she been free."

The man had been stripped of all his outer clothing and was wearing only boxers and a bloody T-shirt. I put my fingers on both necks to check for a pulse. The man was cold to the touch and gone. But the woman was still warm and had been alive up to a couple of hours ago.

"She still has some warmth to her. It wasn't long ago that one of them strangled her."

Pointing to a smoothed-out area to the right, I said, "This is where the couple set up their tent, which makes sense because why set a tent up so far away from the truck?"

"And then when the pulse hit, the two scumbags are walking back to town and stumble upon this camping couple," Renee said. "I bet we come across their vehicle further up the road."

"We searched the two hunters and found no wallets or IDs," I said. "Let's search her and see if she can tell us something."

Renee nodded, and I pulled the woman's pants off, checked all the pockets, and came up with a set of keys and a baggie of dog treats. Renee had cut the zip ties with her knife and pulled the woman's bra, T-shirt, and jacket down into place. In a zipped pocket over the right breast, she found a small black leather badge wallet which contained a military ID and badge.

Opening the wallet, she said, "Her name is Katherine Burns Hendriks. She is active-duty military, and her ID indicates she's military police."

"She's probably the dog's handler, who was enjoying a camping road trip with her companion and work dog," I said.

"This is a police dog?" Renee asked, petting the dog behind her ears, who was looking up at her with sad brown eyes.

"I bet she is. They're also referred to as patrol dogs or MWDs, or military working dogs. Or at least that's what we called them in combat areas. Military dogs usually wear a tactical vest that contains the dog's identification. You said you searched the truck. Right?"

"We searched inside the cab, but the rear cargo bed has a cover and it's locked," Renee answered, still petting the dog.

"We now have keys," I said, jiggling the set. "But first, can you help me dress her? I don't want to leave her like this."

Renee gently pushed me aside and completed the grim task while I kept overwatch.

We made our way to the rear of the truck and started trying keys in the cargo cover's lock. The fourth was the charm, and the lock clicked open. I slid the cover toward the cab, and the six-foot truck cover folded itself open.

The first thing I saw was the dog's active-duty working vest. It was made of desert-tan canvas with a large, heavy-duty handle on the top. The dog's ID was in a pouch on the front right side.

Reading from her ID, I said, "Her name is Greta. She was born on July 5, 2019, and trained at Lackland Air Force Base."

The dog's ears came to attention at hearing her name. Her tail thumped the ground twice and then remained still as she watched me with those sad, intelligent eyes.

"Let's put this on her," I said, grabbing the vest and kneeling next to the dog. Greta stood and allowed me to put the vest on, then did the doggy wiggle as if she'd just come out of the water. She danced and jumped around Renee in unabashed doggy joy. Working dogs are happiest when they're working.

I hopped up into the cargo bed and found a four-burner Coleman camp stove, a full, grill-sized propane bottle, pots and pans, two battery-powered lanterns, other miscellaneous camping equipment, and an assortment of freeze-dried packaged food. There were also two blankets and two blue vinyl tarps.

Finished searching and just about ready to jump to the ground, I caught sight of two hinges set into the cargo floor. I pushed on the area in front of the hinges, and a lid popped up, exposing a four-foot-long by twelve-inch-deep cargo bin.

Inside the bin were two high-quality Daniel Defense AR-15s fitted out with Bushnell optics. A dozen loaded thirty-round 5.56 magazines were lying on the bottom of the compartment. There were also two SIG P320 handguns, along with extra magazines, ammo, and inside-the-belt holsters for each handgun.

I keyed the comms and asked Melissa to load the Cruiser and drive as close to our location as possible.

I took one of the two blue tarps and covered the couple. I weighed down the four corners with rocks I found by the streambed.

Melissa and crew arrived a few minutes later, and while they were loading the trailer, I fueled the Cruiser using the contents of two of the seven jerry cans.

"Guys, while we're here, why don't you filter some stream water using that fancy water filter Burt gave you. We should top off the water jerry cans whenever we can. Kathy, you said you've used the same model before, right?"

"Yep, easy-peasy," she answered as she bent down and retrieved the filter.

Melissa grabbed the two jerry cans and handed one each to Monica and Kris.

"Can you show the other ladies how to use it?" I asked her.

"Will do," she replied, already walking toward the stream.

"Make sure someone acts as overwatch," I reminded them.

Greta looked at Renee, then me, and decided to stick with Renee.

Taking my own advice, I scanned the area with the binoculars. All appeared clear. I raised the Cruiser's hood and checked the oil level and the belts. I opened the radiator cap, and the antifreeze was at the max level marker. With the engine check completed, I checked each tire on the Cruiser as well as the trailer's four. All good.

I had one final thing to do.

I keyed the comms, said, "Renee, can you please come back to the Cruiser?"

"On my way," she responded.

She and Greta appeared two minutes later.

"I need to go back to the two scumbags for a minute," I said. "Can you and Greta provide overwatch for the Cruiser?"

"Of course. What's up?"

"I forgot something. I'll be gone ten minutes tops," I said.

"Go, we'll stand watch," she said, petting Greta under her chin.

"How's the filtering?" I asked.

"They've got one can filled and are working on the second. It's a slow process," she replied.

I made my way back to the two bodies and was finished a couple of minutes later. I stood back and viewed my work.

Using the black permanent marker, I'd written "Killer of Innocents" across the thigh of one and the forehead of the other.

I WAS READY TO GO.

I walked to the tent, debated breaking it down and taking it, but decided to leave it be—someone might happen by and put it to good use.

A few minutes later, the women reappeared, and after stowing the two water cans in the trailer, we got underway. Kathy was driving.

Greta seemed happy to be in the back and was soon sleeping, snuggled on top of her makeshift sleeping-bag bed and surrounded by people feet.

The road began to climb, and we soon entered what was, according to the map, the foothills of Ravenswood Mountain. Leveling off, we emerged into a high-elevation valley whose main feature was a meandering, swift-moving stream. Several old ranch ruins, stone foundations and fireplaces intact but with wooden walls and roofs mostly missing, dotted the landscape. In stark contrast to the lower-elevation desert, this valley was green with a variety of grasses and trees, though trees now leafless.

Light snow was falling, and the entire scene was what I would describe as a winter wonderland.

"My God, it's beautiful up here," Renee said behind me.

"It's like something you'd see on a postcard," Kris said. "Almost makes you think all's well with the world."

Rounding a bend, we spotted a rusted out, eighties-model Dodge pickup parked on the shoulder of the southbound lane.

"I bet that's the dead men's truck," Renee said.

"Kathy, please stop beside it. Let's see if there's any gas left in the thing," I said.

"Why didn't we siphon gas from the truck we just left?" Kris asked.

"Because newer-model cars and trucks have anti-roll-over valves which act as an anti-siphon system," Melissa answered.

"How in the world do you know that?" Monica asked her, obviously impressed that she knew the answer.

"Simple. I have brothers," she answered.

"I could have crawled underneath the couple's truck, drilled a hole as high up the side of the tank as I could, then fed a hose in it, but I kind of figured we'd run into the scumbags' truck . . . and here it is," I said. "Actually, Renee is the one who figured we might run into it."

The truck's tank was almost full, and I felt fairly confident that it was fresh fuel. We topped off the Cruiser's tank, then filled both of our empty five-gallon gas jerry cans. Renee let Greta out, and like the good four-legged soldier she was, she dutifully pooped and peed.

On the road again, we soon left the higher valley and started descending the hills, entering a long flat desert valley. The road stretched out before us as far as the eye could see and stayed perfectly straight with only a slight bend every five to ten miles. We hadn't passed one dead vehicle other than the two men's truck.

The snow turned to light rain, and forty miles further on we came up on a deserted highway rest stop. At the end of the rest stop's off-ramp was a road sign that announced the next town, Battle Mountain, forty miles.

We passed two working mines, each several miles off the highway and high up on hillsides. We could see dozens of people standing out in front of the mines' front entrances.

"Why haven't they started walking home?" Melissa asked.

"Maybe too far to walk, especially in this weather," Kris said. "I mean, it's like what to Austin, sixty miles? Would you walk that? Not me."

"Maybe they think this is temporary," Monica said. "If I lived in Battle Mountain, I'd walk the thirty miles—especially if I had a family depending on me."

"Thirty miles in this weather? I don't know, guys," I said. "I doubt any of them has backpacking gear with them. To set out without a tent, sleeping bag, and the big necessities—water, food, and shelter—would be suicide."

"Barbara Lopez and her three young children did it," Kathy pointed out.

"Very true. Little troopers, those three," I said, smiling at the thought of the three youngsters and their mother.

As we neared Battle Mountain, we could see ranches on both sides of the highway. There must be a good water source out there somewhere.

And thirty minutes later, we saw another road sign saying we'd just entered the city limits of Battle Mountain, Nevada. Elevation 4,511 feet. Population 3,635.

"Kathy, pull over please," I said after having glassed the area a quarter mile out, front and to the sides.

Turning in my seat and addressing the group, I said, "Listen up, ladies. We're just a few miles outside of Battle Mountain. Compared to the towns we've been through, it's a metropolis whose population has likely been augmented by hundreds, maybe even thousands, of stranded motorists whose cars died on Interstate 80. There's going to be lots of thirsty, hungry folks who are willing to do whatever it takes to provide for themselves and their families.

"We'll be a target of opportunity. We could be shot at, run at, and most likely, they will try to stop us. I won't sugarcoat this: it could be brutal at times . . ." I said, trailing off.

"It'll be fifty-five miles of Interstate 80 obstacles," I added. "There's a good chance you'll be shooting your weapons at people. Kris, are you ready for that?" I asked, she being the one person I was most concerned with.

"If it comes down to them or me, I think I can do it," she answered.

"That's not the answer I was hoping for, but still better than what I was expecting," I said. "But that's okay."

"Melissa, I think I know your answer, but I want to hear it anyway."

"I'm ready and will fire on anyone who threatens us," she answered.

"Kathy?"

"Yes, I know I can do it."

"Renee?"

"Whatever I have to do to keep us safe, I'll do. Just tell me what to do, and I'll do it," she answered, squeezing my shoulder as she said it.

"Monica?"

"I'm ready, Jon. Point the way, and I'll be right there with you."

"We could find a place to hide close by and venture out once it's dark," I said.

"Pros and cons, please," Renee said.

"In the daylight, we can see further out, like twenty times further out, and spot any danger that might be ahead of us," I said. "We can react sooner and take evasive measures if needed."

"Like call in an airstrike from an A-10?" Melissa said, deadpan.

Puzzled, I looked at her, then smiled, remembering our motorcycle couple outside Vegas, Brandon and Ruth.

I laughed, and the others joined in, getting it about the same time I did. Sensing the mood change, Greta sat up and wagged her tail.

"Wouldn't that be wonderful," I said, once the laughter had died down.

"The con is a big one: if we can see them, then they can see us," I said. "But we are six heavily armed assholes who will under no circumstance allow anyone to take from us what's ours. If we see armed individuals or groups ahead, we stop, set up an attack line, and if need be, fire on them. Though I bet with a single burst of automatic fire they're going to reevaluate their bravado."

I stayed silent and let it sink in.

"Are we good to go, or are we going to hide and wait for darkness?" I asked the group.

Five "Let's go now" was the final tally.

"Okay, we're agreed. We go now," I said. "In that case, I want you all to go back to the trailer and grab as many loaded rifle magazines that will fit in your pants' cargo pockets. Also, grab a couple of extra Glock mags."

We piled out, and I kept overwatch while the women raided the ammo cans that contained the loaded magazines. Once they were done filling their pockets, I asked Melissa to stand overwatch. I went back to the trailer and took out the Pelican case and the Barrett it held. I laid the case on the pavement and assembled the rifle, finally slamming in a ten-round magazine. I put two .50-cal mags in one of my cargo pants pockets.

Renee wandered over and asked if I thought we'd need the Barrett.

Greta came up to me and nuzzled my hand, looking for doggy rubs. Obliging her, I rubbed under her chin and answered Renee.

"The Barrett is not an anti-personnel weapon, it's an anti-material weapon," I explained. "Its main purpose is disabling vehicles and heavy trucks, although I've used it on exterior walls and doors before. I've shot through foot-thick brick walls and hit the sniper hiding behind it. In the here and now, I'll use it on a vehicle we think might pose a danger. It takes a few minutes to assemble, minutes we won't have in an engagement."

"Makes sense," Renee said, watching as I put the case back in the trailer.

I gathered the women together. "Okay, likely scenario: we're driving along, and we see cars or armed people blocking our path. We stop, and I ask for an offensive line. That means you spill out of the Cruiser as fast as humanly possible and spread out ten feet apart. You go into a prone position on the ground or pavement. Like this," I said, dropping and lying down on the pavement with my rifle butted against my shoulder, my stomach flat on the ground, and my feet splayed out and apart behind me.

"This prone position offers the most stability when firing, and you don't present much of a vertical target. You turn your safety off, and once I tell you to fire, you shoot at targets in the area in front of you. You fire three-round bursts. With the Eotech scope and magnifier, anything that red dot lands on, you'll likely hit. So shoot smart—acquire a target, get that red dot on center mass, and slowly pull the trigger."

I stood, said, "Now drop in the prone position and show me you paid attention."

The ladies were paying attention, and all assumed the proper position.

"The important thing is, you do not fire until I tell you to," I said, walking behind the five women and with my boot spreading feet further apart. "Six heavily armed individuals forming a sixty-foot firing line will be an imposing sight, and trust me when I say this, will scare the shit out of most everyone we're likely to encounter.

"We want to avoid firefights if at all possible. Let me talk our way through or let me fire above them before you guys get involved. Understood?"

Four yeses and a nod.

"Okay, let's load up and get going," I said. "Kathy, I'll drive."

Once the women were situated, with Melissa sitting shotgun, I had her take hold of the Barrett's barrel and pass it back to the women in the back. Once the buttstock and monopod cleared the door, I had the women in back place the muzzle on the floor by their feet and very close to Greta's bed. The buttstock rested on the padded elbow rest between the front seats.

"Wow, how much does this thing weigh?" Kris asked, helping lift the rifle to the rear.

"About thirty pounds, and it's fifty-seven inches long," I answered, closing Melissa's door. "And about a foot longer than that with the suppressor attached."

"Is it loaded?" Monica asked.

"It is, but the safety is on, and I haven't charged it, so no round in the chamber."

Walking back behind the trailer and up to the driver's door, I realized that it would be far easier to load the Barrett from the rear ambulance doors.

"When I need to use the Barrett, let's unload it from the rear," I said, stepping up and settling into the driver's seat.

It suddenly hit me what we were about to undertake—run a fifty-five-mile gauntlet of unknown obstacles on a major interstate in broad daylight. I'd been involved in more dangerous road trips in Iraq and Afghanistan, but hell, we had drones watching over us every inch of the way, on-call A-10 gunships ready to spit death to anyone I wished obliterated, and if in the vicinity, Apache Longbow helicopters that would gladly clear a Taliban roadblock or rooftop of combatants for us.

But we were on our own here—no gunships, drones, or helicopters—and these women were counting on me to get them home. I wasn't going to follow the script of a "go get 'em" John Wayne movie.

Decision made.

"Stand down, ladies," I announced. "We're going to find a place to hide and wait for dark before we take on Interstate 80. We own the night and might as well take advantage of it."

"Thank God," Kris said, letting out a deep breath. "I've really gotta pee."

TWENTY-ONE

Thinking we were too close to Battle Mountain for comfort, I turned the Cruiser around and headed back south.

I was now looking for an area that was hilly and devoid of any inhabitants or structures. We needed to hide behind a hill, but there were ranches and farms out here, and I wondered just how far south we'd have to backtrack before finding a suitable location.

The rain had stopped, the clouds parting, letting rays of sunlight stream through and lighting up the land beneath. We'd gone about five miles and were now headed down a steep grade which would soon give way to a wide, long, flat valley floor. Hills and dry riverbeds were the predominant features to the east, and the roadway hugged the hillsides. We had an unobstructed view ahead and could see several farms and ranches out in the distance.

Melissa was glassing the area ahead with the binoculars. "You're not going to believe this, but there's an elderly man in a walker waving us down," she said. "He's a couple of miles ahead and is standing at the end of a ranch access road where it intersects the highway."

I stopped and glassed the area with the binoculars, and sure enough, there he was, waving his arms like a windmill, obviously trying to get our attention. I flashed the high beams, and he stopped the arm-waving. He put his hands down and rested them on an aluminum walker with black plastic wheels in front and what looked to be bright-orange tennis balls on the two rear struts.

He stood there waiting for us, right hand over his eyes in an attempt to block some of the midday glare.

"He certainly doesn't look threatening, does he?" Melissa said, more of an observation than a question.

"Let's see what he wants," I said.

"What happened to 'we will not stop for unarmed individuals or groups?" Kris said with a nasty, sarcastic edge to it.

"You think we should ignore him," I said. "Just drive on by? This isn't Interstate 80. This is middle of nowhere, and an old guy with a walker is waving us down. And I think I said *armed* individuals or groups."

"You tell her, Jon," Monica added, giving Kris a dirty look.

"Enough with the dirty looks and comments, people," Kris said.

"Then quit being an asshole." This from Kathy.

"Can we drop her off somewhere?" Monica asked. "Please!"

"Fuck you, bitch," Kris said.

"Nice language. You talk that way with our customers?" Renee asked.

Kris didn't answer, mustering up enough sense to remain silent.

"God, I hope not," Renee said.

"Okay, enough already," I said. "As my mother says, 'If you don't have something nice to say then . . .'"

"Don't say anything," Kris finished. "Yeah. Yeah. I know. SORRY."

We slowly made our way down the hill. The access road the old guy was standing by was paved and led downhill to a large, well-kept ranch house a half mile away. The ranch house, barns, stables, and corrals were surrounded by acres of green wheat-like plants growing in large irrigated circles. Flying cross-country, I'd often seen the green circles from the air, and here were six of them. If I had to guess, I would estimate close to two hundred acres' worth.

Far out in the distance, I could see more than a dozen old-fashioned, tin-bladed windmills sitting atop newer-looking four-post steel towers. The blades weren't spinning. Grazing cattle dotted the landscape, which was mostly pastureland as far as the eye could see. Horses grazed in a fifteen- or twenty-acre pasture next to the stables.

I stopped, and the women formed a close-in perimeter. Melissa hopped in the driver's seat, ready to head out if necessary. Greta was glued to Renee's side.

I glassed the area carefully, remembering the hard-learned lesson of earlier this morning. It appeared safe. I handed Melissa the binoculars.

Keeping the M4 in the resting position, I slowly approached the elderly man.

"I didn't know I was waving down the military," the man said, his voice strong for such a frail-looking guy.

"We're civilian, sir. You armed?"

"Oh, heavens no. Don't trust myself with a steak knife anymore, let alone a weapon of any kind. Doesn't mean I don't have any, but not sure I could even lift one out of its rack nowadays."

He was bent over and appeared very frail, but forty years ago, he would have stood over six feet tall and packed a hard punch. What was left of his hair was brilliant white, and tufts were blowing uncontrolled in the light breeze. His skin was tanned from decades of long days working under a hot sun. Liver spots covered both hands. He was dressed in faded

245

farmer's overalls and well-worn brown work boots. He had an expensive, dark blue North Face puffy down jacket on.

"Excuse my manners. My name is Sig Alderson. My wife, Molly, and I own this place," he said, pointing behind him. "What's your name, son?"

"Jon. Nice to meet you, Mr. Alderson," I said, extending my hand. "It's quite a hike up here from the house."

He accepted my hand. His grip was strong, the skin calloused, but the hand bony.

"Likewise, Jon," he replied. "Please call me Sig." He turned and looked back down the drive, said, "It is a distance, isn't it? Especially with the walker. But I felt I had to come out to the highway in the hopes someone else came al—"

He started coughing and dug into one of his overall's pockets. He came up with a dark gray inhaler and, after giving it a couple of good shakes, pushed the top button down and inhaled a puff of medicine.

He took a couple of deep breaths and was able to continue.

"I was sitting on my porch earlier today and saw you drive by. You were only the second vehicle I've seen in three days."

Walking a half mile in his condition was a major feat, and I wondered what had prompted him to undertake it.

"You and your wife okay, Sig?"

"Well, that's the thing," he replied. "Molly and I are doing just fine, but the ranch hasn't been tended to since the power went out. Our ranch hands, all five of them, haven't returned since leaving four days ago. They usually stay out here during the week and take turns remaining on weekends to watch things, but there was a birthday party for Miguel's daughter in Battle Mountain. She turned two. They're all cousins and such, and they all attended the party."

"How many acres do you have here, Sig?"

"Forty-one hundred," he answered, pride filling his voice. "We've got roughly eight hundred of that irrigated and are growing winter rye now. The other thirty-three hundred are used for grazing almost nine hundred head of cattle."

I sensed something was wrong other than his workers hadn't returned to the ranch. "You need help with something, Sig?"

"The cattle have been without water for three days now," he began. "Miguel, my ranch foreman, convinced me to convert all of our windmill pumps to solar, but I managed to walk out to the first pump over there, and the trough is dry. I think the computer and sensors that run the things were fried when the power went out. Not sure about the other sixteen, but I bet they're out of commission as well."

"I see the windmills out there. Are they able to function?" I asked.

"They should. When we converted to solar pumps, we simply braked the blades," he explained. "So, yes, they should start pumping once they're freed."

"Anyone else down there?" I asked. "Besides your wife?"

"No, we're alone."

"We'll help you, Sig," I said, "but before we do, we're going to search your place and make sure you're alone. Nothing personal, just being safe."

"Understood. Search away. We sincerely appreciate any help you offer us."

I keyed the comms, asked Melissa to bring the Cruiser to us and for the others to walk overwatch alongside.

A minute later, the Cruiser was idling next to us.

Introductions were made, and Greta came over and nuzzled her hello.

"Let's get you loaded up, Sig. No sense in having you walk when we've got a perfectly good vehicle."

We got him loaded up into the front passenger seat and his walker folded up and stowed in back. Melissa drove, and I stepped onto the passenger-side running board and hung on. As we made our way down toward the ranch house, the women followed alongside.

Before the Cruiser came to a stop, the front porch screen door swung open on squeaky hinges, and a woman came out waving. She was younger than Sig, but not by much, and had on an apron with wildflowers printed on it. She had white hair like Sig's, wore it long and corralled into a ponytail. She was tiny and short, not much more than five-two, and was so skinny, a strong desert breeze could have knocked her over.

She was a striking woman, and if you told me she was Miss America 1960, I'd believe you.

"Thanks for bringing the old coot back," she said, stepping down off the porch and approaching the Cruiser. "He's been standing up there on the highway for a couple of hours."

The women had fanned out around the Cruiser and had taken a knee. Greta approached the woman and sniffed her offered hand. Satisfied, Greta returned to Renee's side.

I helped Sig out of the passenger seat, and he was standing waiting for me to retrieve his walker. "Everyone, this here is the boss of the place and my wife of sixty-six years, Molly," he announced. "Molly, this here is Jon." He pointed to the others and recited the ladies' names, apparently nothing wrong with his short-term memory.

"Jon has agreed to help us get the windmills working again," Sig said as she hugged him. "But first he wants to search the place and make sure we're not hiding anyone."

"It's just a safety precaution," I explained.

"If it means getting the water flowing to the cattle, then do whatever you need to do, young man," she replied. Molly reached in one of the apron's deep pockets and came out with a black knit winter beanie hat. "How many times have I told you to wear a hat, old man." She put it over his head and pulled it down over his ears.

"Thanks, hon bunch."

"Renee, can you take Greta and search the house and then the two barns? You remember how I had her search earlier today?"

"I remember," she answered, already heading up the porch stairs.

"Melissa, can you watch her six, please?"

"Of course," she said, standing and following Renee up the porch. The screen door squeaked open, and they disappeared into the house.

"Let's get you up on the porch, old man, so you can sit and rest a bit," Molly said.

I followed Sig up the steps and watched as Molly helped him sit in one of the half dozen porch chairs. It was one of those rocking jobs that not only rocked but swiveled. Sig gave a contented sigh as he sank into the chair's thick cushions.

"Please, Jon, have a seat," Molly offered. "You too, ladies," she said, indicating Kris, Kathy, and Monica, who looked at me for permission. I nodded assent.

"I was about ready to make some hot chocolate," she said, turning around and heading back inside. "I'll make a big batch. It'll only take a few minutes."

The screen door squeaked, and Renee and Melissa appeared with Greta close behind.

"All clear, Jon," Renee reported, already headed down the porch stairs in the direction of the barns.

"Be careful in those barns, ladies," Sig shouted after them. "We've got half a dozen barn cats that are just plain mean and would love nothing more than snacking on fresh canine."

"Thanks for the heads-up. We'll be careful, Mr. Alderson," Renee said.

Sig settled in the cushions, and Molly retreated into the house. She came back out a few seconds later with a brown wool throw, which she draped across Sig's knees.

"Sig, would you mind if we drove the rig behind one of the barns?"

If Sig was at all curious as to why I wanted to hide the Cruiser, he gave no indication.

"Of course, there's a concrete equipment staging pad behind the furthest barn. But an even better idea is to put both your four-by-four and the trailer inside the far drive-through barn. It's full of farm equipment, but there's plenty of room for that itty-bitty thing."

"Kathy, will you move the Cruiser, please? Kris, go with her," I said.

"You open the rear barn doors and drive in. When you leave, open the front doors and simply drive straight out—none of the usual hassles of trying to back up with a trailer on the back," Sig said.

We watched the two women drive the Cruiser toward the barns, turn right, and disappear from view.

I keyed the comms and asked Renee how the search was progressing.

"Greta cleared the first barn, and she's now in the second," she answered. "Kathy and Kris just showed up with the Cruiser."

"Kris?"

"Yeah?" she answered.

"Please stay with the Cruiser."

"Why do I have to stay with it? Why can't someone else stay with it?"

"Can I please hit her?" Monica said.

"No, Monica, you can't. Kris, stay with the Cruiser until I get back there."

Silence.

"Kris?"

"Fine."

"Sounds like you've got yourself an unhappy camper," Sig said with a grin that silently but clearly said, "been there."

"Yes, and getting worse. But we've been through quite a bit these past few days, Sig, and I'm trying to give her some slack," I explained.

A sudden breeze hit the porch and with it came the sound of a high-revving engine. "You have a working generator?" I asked.

"Yes, behind the house," he answered. "It's an old water-cooled Generac we've had since the late sixties. It pumps out forty-five thousand kilowatts and runs on propane. We've got two one-thousand-gallon in-ground tanks out back—one for the ranch house and the other for the new ranch hand bunkhouse.

"Miguel wanted to replace it with a new model, but it's been good all these years, and I saw no need. In a power-out situation, it powers both the house and the old and new ranch bunkhouses. We've been running it for two hours in the morning, an hour at noon, and two hours at night. Keeps the freezers and fridges cold and gives us some heat and light at night."

The squeaky screen door announced Molly's return. She was carrying a large serving tray with a stainless-steel pitcher like the kind restaurants use to refill your water glass. Steam rose from the pitcher, and I counted seven ceramic mugs with Christmas wreaths printed on them. I stood and took the tray from her.

"Thank you, young man. Put it on the table over there, and everyone can help themselves," she said, filling a cup and handing it to Sig.

"Thanks, hon," he said. He wrapped his hands around the warm mug, said, "Speaking of the past few days, any idea what's happened? I may be old and all that implies, but I'm not dumb—cell phones and cars don't quit working in a power outage."

The comms came to life. "The second barn is clear, Jon," Renee reported.

"Excuse me a second, Sig," I said.

"Okay, come on back to the porch and enjoy some hot chocolate," I said. "Kris, stay with the Cruiser, please. We'll bring you a mug."

"You do know that there are four other people here that are perfectly capable of standing watch. Right?" Kris pointed out.

"Roger that, Kris," I replied. "Good to know my head-count is correct."

"What an asshole," Kris said.

"Kris, your comms is keyed, moron," Monica said.

"Oh . . ." Kris trailed off.

Sig chuckled and looked at me with a smile planted on his face.

Molly laughed and said, "Sorry, I shouldn't laugh . . . but, hey, it's kind of funny."

We sat there and sipped our hot chocolate.

"You're right, Sig, power outages are the least of our worries," I said. I then went through the story as I knew it. I watched Sig's and Molly's reactions go from "golly gee" to "oh my gosh" in the time it took me to tell the story. Molly sat down and covered her mouth in disbelief.

Sig shook his head, said, "It was only a matter of time. Things have just gotten so nasty, what with democrats and republicans at each other—this investigating committee investigating this and their committee investigating the investigators of the first committee, it doesn't seem to ever end, this seesaw partisan political rhetoric which eventually finds its way into foreign policy."

Renee, Melissa, and Greta returned and sat down with a steamy cup of cocoa. Greta stretched out next to Renee and promptly fell asleep.

"That's a beautiful bunkhouse you've built, Mr. Alderson," Renee said, petting Greta behind her ears.

"Thank you, young lady. We completed it a few weeks ago. Miguel and his crew work hard, and it's because of that hard work we're successful as we are."

"They deserve a nice place to sleep," Molly added, patting Sig's knee. "You're welcome to stay there as long as you'd like, or at least until Miguel shows up. It's got electricity, hot showers, and two sets of brand-new Kenmore washers and dryers," she said, offering them up like can't-refuse prizes. "They're very basic models with no fancy computer settings in them, so they're working just fine. The freezer and fridge are stocked with food and drinks. We've got satellite television, though we haven't been able to get any channels since the power went out—I really miss my nightly news with Lester Holt."

"All electronics are fried, Mrs. Alderson," Melissa said.

"Did I hear the words *hot showers*?" Kathy asked, climbing the porch steps.

"If you're serious, Mr. and Mrs. Alderson, I think we'd like to take you up on that offer," I said.

"Wouldn't have said it if I didn't mean it, son," Molly said.

"Well, what do you say, ladies?"

"Yippie!" Kathy shouted while trying not to spill her hot chocolate. "And thank you, Mrs. Alderson."

"Mrs. Alderson was my mother-in-law. Call me Molly, please."

"Molly it is," Melissa said.

"Renee, can you organize the bunkhouse arrangements?" I asked. "I've got to get out to the windmills and get them working again."

"Be happy to," she replied. Then added, "What about Kris? Bring her in or leave her out there?"

"Bring her a cup of hot chocolate and let her shower and rest. But keep an eye on the Cruiser. In fact, please lock it up and keep the keys in a safe place."

"Melissa, can you tag along with me and watch my six?" I asked. "I hate to take you away from a hot shower and a bed, but I need someone to watch my back while I'm climbing towers."

"Of course. No problem," she answered.

"Thank you."

The girls left for the bunkhouse, and it was just Sig, Molly, Melissa, and me on the porch.

I wanted to get to all the windmills during daylight but wasn't sure how far out they were. On Kristen Ranch, we had dozens of windmills pumping water for thousands of cattle over tens of thousands of acres. They were separated by miles of rough ATV tracks, and if you wanted to visit each one, you'd be camping out for two nights. I know, because it was my first job on the ranch—every four weeks like clockwork.

"How long will it take me to hike out to the furthest windmill, Sig?" I asked.

He thought for a moment, then said, "If you were a crow, it would be about four miles. But the road winds its way between and around hills, gullies, and streams, which probably adds another two miles to your trek."

"Sig, they could take a couple of the horses," Molly suggested.

"Why, you betcha," he said. "Good idea, Molls."

"Uh, not gonna happen," Melissa said. "Don't like 'em, and they don't like me. Uh-uh, no way, no how."

I looked at Melissa in question, and she just shook her head at me, eyes wide open and daring me to change her mind.

"I think we're good, Sig. We'll unhitch the trailer and drive our vehicle out there," I said. "Cool, Melissa?"

"Much better. Thank you," she answered, relief plain in her voice.

"Sig, I just follow the dirt track, and it takes me by all the windmills on the property?" I asked.

"Yep, they're all next to the road. Most fill watering troughs, but there are three ponds they fill and aerate. You'll need to climb the tower to the platform," he said. "Once up there, you'll see a foot-long metal handle that's in the down position and held in place by a metal swivel clamp. Undo the clamp, and the handle will pop up and release the brake. If there's any wind at all, the blades will start turning."

"Am I going to have to prime or grease anything?"

"They were all serviced when we did the conversion to solar. They should be fine."

"Sounds good, Sig. Let's go, Melissa."

I keyed the comms and told Renee what the plan was. She was stepping into the shower. "I put our stuff in the foreman's room. I hope that's okay with Mrs. Alderson," she said.

Molly, hearing the exchange, nodded and gave a thumbs-up.

"Molly says fine. See you in a few hours," I said.

"We'll put some steaks and potatoes on the grill when you get back, Jon," Molly said.

"Can't wait, Molly," I answered. "Thank you."

We made our way to the Cruiser and unhooked the trailer. Melissa handed Kris a mug of hot chocolate, who took it and without a word turned and headed toward the bunkhouse.

"What's up Miss America's butt?" Melissa asked.

"I can only imagine," I answered.

I noticed the horses crowding the near pasture fence in what appeared more than usual horse curiosity. I checked their water, and all was well, so they were probably hungry.

We found the haystack under a high, long tin roof on the other side of the second, furthest barn. We made two trips, tandem-carrying bales to the fence line. We cut the two strings and threw hand-sized bunches of hay over the fence to the waiting horses. The horses were on the piles of hay before the last bit of hay had landed.

I retrieved the hide-a-key, loaded in the Cruiser, and followed the service track six and a half miles to the end of the road. We passed many windmills and the three ponds. The cattle in pond-fed pastures were fine, but pastures with watering troughs had cattle bunched around the bottom of the still windmills, waiting for water that hadn't come for three days.

With Melissa standing watch, I climbed the first tower and released the brake. The blades gave a few squeaks of protest, then started spinning like crazy. By the time I'd climbed down, the water was flowing into the galvanized-steel troughs. The troughs were deep, and the cattle were waiting for the water level to rise to a drinkable level.

We reversed direction and parked near the next windmill. I hopped the fence that separated pastures and waded through the bunched-up cattle. I climbed the tower and got the blades spinning. I could already see water dropping into the trough down below and the cattle fighting for position. From this height, I had a direct sightline to the ranch house. I keyed the comms.

"Renee?"

"Yes, Jon," Renee replied a minute later, sounding out of breath. "Sorry, I was drying off in the shower."

"Everything okay?"

"Better than okay, actually," she said, "Now that I've just enjoyed a hot shower."

"Glad you liked it. Do you have eyes on the trailer?"

"Yes, the barn door is open, and I'm looking at it now. It's sitting pretty. How's it going with the windmills?"

"We're making progress," I said, blowing hot air on my fingers and wishing I'd brought gloves. "Two down and fifteen to go. It's cold and windy, and from the looks of the dark clouds moving in, I'd say it might start raining. Listen, I'm sorry to ask you, but can you and Greta stand watch on the front porch of the main house?" I asked. "We've got to have eyes on the highway as long as we're here."

"Sure, let me get dressed and feed Greta. I'll be over there in ten minutes."

"Thanks," I said, then added, "Ladies, Molly is grilling some steaks and baked potatoes for dinner, so no freeze-dried for us tonight."

I climbed down as the comms were filled with "awesome" and "can't wait."

We made good time and had fifteen of the seventeen windmills running three hours later. The fifteenth had a frozen brake, and I had to climb down, get the crowbar out of the Cruiser, climb back up, and whack the lever ten times before it popped up and released the blades. Melissa volunteered to climb sixteen and seventeen while I provided overwatch.

Finished with the seventeenth, we drove to the equipment barn a couple of hundred yards away. Melissa slid open the barn door, and I drove in and around the trailer. With Melissa giving me directions, I backed up to the hitch. We connected hitch to trailer, and the two were once again mated.

It was now five thirty. Melissa left to take a shower, and I walked to the main house's front porch and Renee.

Renee gave me a hug, and Greta thumped her tail in greeting. Renee leaned back and ran her hand over my face and its stubble of unshaved four-day growth. "Don't get me wrong," she said, smiling, "I like the unkempt look, but I'm not looking forward to the beard rash."

"I use an electric shaver and not sure the thing even works."

"If it doesn't, I've got a couple of spare razors I'll give you," she said, then kissed me. "Better put to use on your smooth face than my hairy legs. I even have shaving cream."

"A girlfriend in college let the hair on her legs grow out one winter," I said, returning the kiss. "It was scratchy for the first couple of weeks, then turned soft. She was blond like you and the hair on her legs grew out blond . . . not sure how I would have liked it had they grown out dark."

"Well, you'll get smooth legs tonight because I shaved them in the shower earlier."

I smiled and kissed her. We sat on the top step of the porch, holding hands and gazing out at the beautiful scenery before us. Greta butted her head in between us and wiggled her way in. We laughed, and right then, things didn't seem so bad.

TWENTY-TWO

It started to rain, light droplets at first, then a few minutes later turned into to a steady downpour. Torrents of rain would roll through, and for ten or fifteen minutes, the rain hitting the house's tin roof sounded as if heaven were conducting target practice by dropping millions of stone pebbles, our roof serving as the target's bullseye.

We sat and watched night replace day. Thick black clouds, heavy with rain, rolled in from the west, dumped their moisture on us, and then moved on east, disappearing behind the hills that flanked the highway in front of the ranch house.

Molly came out shortly after dark and told us she was going to start getting dinner ready. She asked me to start the propane grill on the back porch. She brought out eight large potatoes wrapped in aluminum foil, and we cooked those, and then Sig and I tended to the steaks. Renee and Greta stayed on the porch providing overwatch.

"I can't thank you enough for feeding the horses and getting the windmills going again," Sig said, standing in front of the grill, one hand on his walker and the other holding a long grilling fork.

"Happy to help, Sig. And thank you for your hospitality. I speak for the women when I say thank you for the hot showers."

"You're welcome. I'm going to keep the generator going until eleven tonight. I figure that's enough time for you to shower and do some laundry."

Sig went silent for a minute and looked as if he was thinking about what he wanted to say. He broke the silence, asked, "Do you think you and your group could stay another day or two, or at least until Miguel shows up?"

"I'd be happy to stay, Sig, but there are six of us, and we'd have to discuss it and then decide," I answered. "I'll bring it up later tonight and let you know. Good enough?"

"Absolutely. And I understand if you decide to leave tomorrow."

"I meant to ask earlier; do you have any children that might be on their way home?"

"We had a son, Kevin, but he died in Vietnam . . . The helicopter he was piloting was hit, and he crashed his second week in-country," he said, flipping the steaks. "Our second child, a daughter, June Allison, lives in New York City and is an attorney with a big-ten law firm. She and her husband have a fun-farm in upstate New York, and I'm sure they'll try and get out there. We have no grandchildren, but both Molls and I have cousins, nieces and nephews that we'd be happy to take in, but the nearest lives in South Dakota so probably won't even attempt the journey."

When the steaks were cooked and dinner ready, Molly rang a metal triangle on the front porch. The ladies streamed over to the house, and we had a very nice steak dinner in the main dining room.

A ranch house with lights on during a blackout could be seen for miles and would attract attention. I retrieved the thermal scope from the Cruiser and, every ten minutes, would excuse myself from the table and stand on the front porch, scan the highway and access road. During my latest scan, snow was falling.

"It's snowing," I announced, resuming my seat at the dining room table.

"Are the cattle okay in the snow?" Renee asked.

"And what about the horses?" Kathy added.

"Horses handle the snow fine," Sig answered. "Horses that spend time outside of barns and stables grow long winter coats, which insulates them and keeps them warm and dry to the skin. Rain is a bigger concern to them, and that's why we have shelter sheds in the horse pastures."

"Cattle are fine in the cold and snow, and actually prefer it over warm and hot weather," I said. "In winter, a cow's thick skin and hair is a natural insulator. When it snows, the hair catches it and forms a layer over the cow. This creates an air pocket between the snow and the cow's skin, which is then warmed by the cow's natural body temperature of 102 degrees."

"Well, well, someone knows their cattle anatomy," Sig said.

"I grew up on a cattle ranch outside Whitefish, Montana," I said by way of explanation. "Youth was no excuse for not working. My folks still work and run the ranch."

"What ranch?"

"Kristen Double T Ranch."

"Your dad's Neil Kristen?" Sig asked, obviously surprised.

"He is."

"Heck, I've known your dad for years," he said. "We served together on the boards of a couple of cattlemen associations over the years."

"And I know your mother, Andrea," Molly said. "How are they?"

"They're both doing well. Still working the ranch."

"Your mother can kick up her heels on a dance floor," Sig said, smiling at the memory. "I certainly couldn't keep up with her, though the last time I saw them, she was probably forty and I was on the other side of seventy-five. She was an imposing sight, as tall as she is."

"You still got it going on, Sig," Molly said. "Did I say that right, ladies?"

"Perfectly," Monica answered, and we all laughed.

"Don't suppose you've spoken to them since the blackout happened?" Sig asked.

"No, although someone from Eureka said he'd try to contact my dad on his ham radio. If he gets through to him, he said he'd pass along a message from me."

"Well, I hope he gets through."

Sig was fading, and Molly suggested he get to bed.

"Okay, Molls. I'll go. Jon, the generator is on a timer and will go off at eleven tonight and come back on at seven tomorrow morning."

"Thank you, Sig. See you in the morning," I said.

Sig got to the screen door, turned, and said, "And thank you, Melissa, for helping Jon get the windmills going."

"You're welcome, Mr. Alderson."

Molly helped Sig to bed, and the ladies and I took care of cleanup. Finished, the six of us retreated to the front porch.

"Time for a quick meeting," I said, and told them about Sig's request that we stay another day or two.

"I could stand another day or two sleeping in a soft bed and taking hot showers," Melissa said.

"I'm in," Kathy said. "Especially if there's more steak and potatoes on the menu."

"In," Monica said, raising her hand.

"Me too," Renee said. "These are good folks who need our help."

"I agree," I said. "We should stay."

We all looked to Kris.

"Well gee, what a surprise, I'm last again," she said with a sneer.

"What's your problem, Kris?" Monica asked.

"Oh, let me see," she replied, sticking a finger up. "First, we were supposed to travel only at night. Second, we were never going to stop for anyone. Third, we were never going to stop for anything. Fourth, we would drive until we couldn't—meaning we should be in Oregon and approaching Washington by now.

But here we are, still in Nevada. So, I say fuck no. Let's load up now and head out. You say they need our help. Well, what about my babies? They need help, too."

"You have a husband at home," Monica said. "I'm sure he's taking good care of them."

"You don't know that."

"That's true. Is there a reason you think he's not?"

"Well, no."

"I seem to remember you telling me that your parents live in the guesthouse over your garage," Melissa said. "So, they're there, right?"

"I hope so," Kris answered.

I'd heard enough to know that Kris's kids were likely being taken care of.

"Kris, we all want to get home," I said. "But we can't just hop on the road and go full tilt—we'd never get there. But I do agree with you that we need to make progress. We're behind where we should be. But I can't leave the Aldersons out here alone. I just couldn't do it, and I doubt you would either. Learn and adapt."

Kris remained silent, and I knew I wouldn't get anything more from her. She was going to have to go along to get along.

"We're going to stay until we know the Aldersons will be taken care of," I said, the decision made. "Let's break up now and get back to the bunkhouse. We'll go back to the watch schedule starting now. That means Monica is on until eleven p.m., and then Melissa, Kathy, Kris, Renee, then me. Then the cycle starts again.

"You wear your vest and carry your rifle with you on watch. The thermal scope is fully charged and ready to go. Make sure your two-way is fully charged and working. Mine will be on and ready to receive at all times."

We broke up, and each made their way to the bunkhouse. Monica gathered her equipment and took up her post on the front porch of the main house.

Renee took my hand and led me to our room. It was the first time I'd seen it, and it was nicer than most of the off-base apartments I'd lived in. I took off my clothes, and Renee took both hers and mine to an empty washing machine and got them started.

Our room had its own bathroom with a large, walk-in, tiled shower. I stepped into the hot water and quickly rinsed and soaped up. I was washing my hair with my eyes closed when I heard the shower door open and felt a naked body meld with mine, large natural breasts pressing against my back.

"Will we be able to do this in Montana?" Renee asked, helping me rinse off.

"Absolutely. We'll take one of the larger guest cabins for our own," I answered. "Hey, didn't you already shower today?"

"Yep, never know when I'll get another, though," she said, reaching around and stroking me the way she knows I like.

Wanting to return the favor, I reached behind, and after a quick search, found her favorite spot.

We took turns drying each other off and then fell into bed. We were asleep in each other arms thirty minutes later.

Before shutting my eyes for good, I saw Greta awake and on guard at the end of the bed. She was vestless and looked pretty comfortable. She saw me looking, lifted her head in acknowledgment, and thumped and swished her tail.

DAY FOUR

RETRIEVAL. DEPUTY SUSAN. DOC BERNIE.
THREE TRUCKS. A BIG GUN. KRIS.

TWENTY-THREE

My watch was to begin at seven, and my internal alarm woke me at six forty-five. I searched for my camos and remembered that Renee had put them in the washing machine. We'd heard the end-of-cycle buzzer last night, but neither of us was about to stop what we were doing to load wet clothes into a dryer.

Unlike the women, who had two sets of camos, I only had the one. I emptied my backpack and slipped into blue jeans, an old black T-shirt, and an equally old, red University of Utah hoodie.

Barefoot, I tiptoed through the open floorplan and made my way past the sleeping women. I loaded the clothes in the dryer and would get them started when the power came on at seven. Back in our room, I put socks and boots on and then slipped on the plate carrier. I zipped up my camo field jacket, conducted a quick weapons check, and attached the rifle to the sling.

I relieved Renee a few minutes early. Greta nose-bumped my hand, looking for a chin rub. Renee said there had been no activity on the highway during the night.

I would come off watch at nine. It had snowed in fits and starts for most of the night and had melted soon after hitting the ground. The sky was filled with heavy black clouds and looked as if snow or sleet could return at any time.

Renee joined me for the last half hour of my watch. "Your camos are on the bed," she said, handing me a mug of hot coffee.

"Thanks," I said, grateful for the warm wake-me-up and company.

Monica spelled me, and after a short briefing, we left her to it.

Molly had made a hearty ranch-style breakfast and had it set up buffet style in the dining room. I scooped up scrambled eggs, bacon, and toast. Renee and I ate together at one end of the empty table.

Sig soon joined us but only wanted coffee. Drying her hands on a dish towel, Molly sat down next to Sig. "Good morning, you two," she said.

"And good morning to you," I replied, wiping bacon grease off my lips. "Thank you for the awesome breakfast."

"My pleasure," Molly answered. "It's a lot more fun cooking for a large crowd."

"Our group met last night to discuss your request that we stay on until your ranch hands return," Renee said. "And we're going to do that."

"Thank goodness," Molly exclaimed, her tiny body sinking back in the chair. "Thank you."

Sig smiled and nodded in acknowledgment.

"But there's no way of knowing when they might return. If ever," I said.

"And we have homes of our own to get back to and can't stay long," Renee added.

"If we can get to Miguel and the other men, would you be okay with them bringing their families out to the ranch and living here until things settle down?" I asked.

Sig and Molly made eye contact, and I could see they were good with the idea. They both eagerly nodded agreement.

"Good. To help speed up Miguel's return, I propose we unhitch our trailer and hook up the six-horse trailer I saw in the equipment barn." Normally the Cruiser couldn't pull the weight of a fully loaded trailer with six horses. But loaded with three or four families and some of their belongings? It shouldn't be an issue.

"We'll then drive into town, let them load some belongings, and bring them back to the ranch. Do you know where Miguel lives?" I asked the two.

"Yes, it's been a while, but I know Battle Mountain like the back of my hand," Sig said. "I can find it."

"One of you will accompany us into town and show us the way. Just as important, you can help defuse any local problems we may encounter."

"I'm ready to go anytime you are," Sig offered.

"Then let's go now," I said. "No sense in waiting. "Renee, do you mind staying here and watching over the ranch? We'll leave Kris here with you."

"Sure," she answered after an initial hesitation.

"I don't trust Kris enough to leave her alone to watch over things . . . especially the trailer," I explained.

"Got it. I'll keep an eye on it. Just be careful and come back, please."

"I will," I said, hugging and kissing her. "I promise."

Before leaving, I gave Renee some last-minute instructions. "Position yourself on the porch. If you see someone driving or walking down from the highway, get Molly and ask if she knows them." I looked at Molly, and she nodded. "If she doesn't know them, tell them to stop and turn around. If they continue toward you, fire a warning shot. If that doesn't turn them around, start firing three-round bursts. And at that point, you aim to hit, not scare.

"Before we leave, get as many magazines as you can fit in your cargo pockets. Be precise with your firing . . . Don't just pull the trigger and keep firing—watch where the bullets hit and adjust the next burst. If there are many of them, look for the leader and then fire at him or her and don't let up on them until you know you've hit them. Then start working on the others. Fire three or four bursts from one position and then move and fire the next few from a new position. Keep moving. Hopefully Kris will jump in and help, but don't count on it," I said before kissing her again and walking away.

I ran to the bunkhouse and changed into my clean camos. Next stop was the equipment barn.

On the way, I keyed the comms and told Melissa, Monica, and Kathy to get dressed and patrol-ready with full gear and weapons.

"Meet me in the equipment barn asap," I said. "Bring any full magazines you may have."

I unhooked the trailer from the Cruiser, then backed up in front of Sig's horse trailer. The trailer's hitch was lower than the Cruiser's ball, and I spent a minute cranking the trailer jack to get the hitch high enough to fit over the Cruiser's ball. I got back in the Cruiser and backed up until I felt the ball hit the trailer's coupler.

I lowered the coupler onto the ball and watched the Cruiser dip in the rear with the trailer's added weight. But not too bad—the trailer was riding level, and I'd have to have the weight loaded toward the front of the trailer and hitch.

It took another minute to set the safety chains and receiver lock into place. I then checked the trailer's four tires, and they were all in good shape and full of air.

The Barrett and several fully loaded magazines were still in the Cruiser, and rather than wrestling them out and storing them in our trailer, I decided to leave them be. I grabbed a full case of 5.56 rounds from our trailer, a thousand rounds, and deposited it alongside the Barrett.

The three ladies arrived, and we loaded in. We pulled up to the ranch house porch steps, where we helped Sig into the front passenger seat, putting his folded-up walker in back.

Molly watched as we helped her husband climb in. "Don't you dare play soldier, Sig Alderson," she said. "Those days are long gone, old man." She shut the door, leaned in the open window, and planted a big kiss on his cheek. "I love you, Siggy."

"Right back at ya, Molls," he replied, putting his hand on her cheek and smiling.

We retraced the route we'd taken yesterday morning, and drove past the spot we'd stopped and made the U-turn.

The Cruiser had no problems towing the large horse trailer and only noticeably strained on the steeper grades.

The road was empty and the landscape snow-covered at the higher elevations. The sky was clearing with just a few white puffy clouds here and there.

Sig knew all the ranches we passed and provided a running commentary on their past and current ownership. And like it or not, the women learned about cattle breeding.

FORTY MINUTES LATER, WE STARTED seeing warehouses, car and truck repair shops, and heavy farm and ranch equipment dealerships. There were a few dead cars on both sides of the highway. Had the pulse happened later in the day, there would have been dozens, perhaps even hundreds of abandoned cars. But we had no issues with any of them blocking our way, and we saw no one out and about.

Power lines hung from burned-out poles. On-pole transformers were burned with molten, lavalike mounds on the ground underneath them. There were a few plumes of black smoke but not nearly to the extent that Austin had experienced. Perhaps last night's heavy rain put them out.

Up on the left was a Nevada Highway Patrol building and a U-Haul rental business directly behind it. There were six or seven uniformed officers in the parking lot. They started waving and yelling for us to stop, with two running toward the highway.

I drove on, ignoring the running officers.

"The runner on the left is Dan Isaacson's son, Ken," Sig said. "Kenny worked summers on the ranch when he was in high school. You're not going to stop?"

"No, I'm not," I answered. "Chances are they'd try to confiscate the Cruiser, and I'd rather avoid having to refuse their demands."

"I'm surprised they're still working," Kathy said. "I would have thought they'd have made their way home and to their families by now."

"This is a big office and has a large contingent of officers, a couple dozen at least," Sig said. "They cover all of Interstate 80 from here, east to the Utah border. Those are probably the last of them."

"Hard to patrol and do your job without a patrol car," Melissa said.

Up ahead I could see the Interstate 80 overpass. We drove underneath and passed Battle Mountain High School on the right. Its parking lot was full of people milling about, trash cans with flames and smoke pouring out. There were dozens of bicycles nearby.

"Students maybe," Melissa ventured. "With nothing better to do than hang out in the parking lot."

"Yeah, party on, dude," Kathy said in her best teenage-deepened voice.

All heads turned toward us, and hands pointed as we drove by.

We were still on Nevada 305 North, but the city had assigned it a name—South Broad Street.

"Stay on South Broad until you get to West Fifth, where you'll turn left," Sig said. "Miguel lives a half mile or so up Fifth on the right-hand side. Don't know the address, but I'll know it when I see it."

There was a steak house on the right, and all its windows were broken and open to the elements. The front door was shattered and had been torn off its hinges. It was lying in the parking lot, sunlight glimmering on thousands of pieces of broken glass.

A Burger King was next door, and it too had been looted, its front door shattered.

"I've never seen anything like this," Sig said, taking in the damage. "Except maybe in Germany at the end of World War II."

Most power poles had burnt tops from exploded transformers and looked like giant used matchsticks. Downed power lines draped along the roadway.

"You see that building on the left? That's the library," Sig said. "Or what's left of it."

It had burned to the ground and was still smoldering. A lone brick wall and a bare, tall metal flagpole were all that remained.

"Why on earth would anyone want to burn a library?" Melissa asked.

"I doubt if anyone set the place on fire. A power surge most likely started a fire in an interior wall," I answered. "Just guessing though."

"There's no longer a fire department," Monica said. "Unless they're using fire trucks from the 1960s."

"I built that building as a gift to the city. They named it after my son, Kevin," Sig announced, a tinge of sadness in his voice.

"I'm sorry, Sig," I said.

"Things happen for a reason, I guess. Turn left up there," Sig said, pointing to the next intersection.

I turned left onto West Fifth Street, and a half mile further on, Sig had me stop directly across from Battle Mountain Hospital. Miguel's house was a neat, single-story ranch. A lawn, now winter brown, was ringed by a hedge of neatly trimmed junipers and rose bushes. A new gunmetal-gray Ford diesel-powered F-250 Super Duty was parked in the driveway. The dealer's paper plate was still on the truck. A $75,000 truck now just a hunk of metal and plastic.

"We bought that truck two weeks ago," Sig said.

The front door opened, and a short, stocky, middle-aged man with a large Pancho Villa-style mustache stood in the doorway. A small child dressed in Little Mermaid pajamas hugged his legs. Both looked out at the street.

The women formed a close-in perimeter, and I got out and walked around to the passenger front door.

"That is our horse trailer," the man said, stepping off the porch and approaching the Cruiser. He picked up the child and carried her in his arms.

"Hi, Miguel. It's Sig."

"Mr. Sig, I have been worried about you. How is Mrs. Alderson?"

"We're fine, Miguel. We'd like to offer you and your family refuge out at the ranch. It will be much safer out there, and of course there's plenty of food and water. And these folks are travelers helping me out. This is Jon, Melissa, Monica, and Kathy."

Several neighbors were now standing out at the street, staring at not only a working vehicle but the battle-dressed individuals with assault rifles protecting it.

"Molly and I are hoping you'll bring your family out to the ranch and live permanently with us. We plan on getting Lucas, then Mateo and Izan and their families. Trust me when I say that the power isn't going to be coming back for years, maybe even a decade or more," Sig said. "We don't have time to explain what's happened, but gather up everything you want to bring to the ranch and get it loaded in the trailer."

"Just a second, Mr. Sig," he said. "Let me tell Maria what you are proposing." He disappeared into the house and two minutes later reappeared with his wife.

"Thank you, Mr. Sig," Maria said. "We're almost out of food, and the water stopped running two days ago. We've been gathering and drinking rainwater."

"Sorry to rush you, but we've got to get going," I said. "You've got thirty minutes to load up. Think clothes, shoes, papers, medicines, sheets, blankets, and towels. And don't forget any weapons and ammunition you may have."

They both nodded and ran back inside the house to pack.

"Jon, we've got nosy neighbors approaching," Monica shouted, not bothering with the comms.

I strode back to the driver's side and saw a group of ten men and women crossing the street and walking toward us. Two had hunting rifles, and one young teenage boy held a black semiauto handgun in a Gangsta-style sideways one-handed grip. I could see hospital scrubs under the coats of several.

"Guys, safeties off and set for three-round bursts," I said. "Follow my lead. Melissa, keep your head on a swivel and watch our six."

The group was now forty feet away. Time to put a stop to this foolish march.

"Stop right there. Do not approach any closer," I shouted, raising the barrel of the M4 and aiming for the kid with the handgun. "You, the kid with the handgun, drop it."

The kid stopped and looked back at the group following behind him. A man in a long black wool overcoat with light blue scrubs underneath raised a hand and pointed to the ground in front of the kid. The kid appeared confused but placed the gun on the pavement.

"Thank you," I said. "Now back away from the weapon. You two with the rifles, keep those barrels pointed down."

The man with the overcoat stepped forward and walked up to me. "My name is Dr. Bernard Williams. I'm chief of surgery at the hospital. What military branch are you with?" he asked.

Williams was in his late forties to early fifties and carried himself with an air of authority. He was on the shorter side, coming in at perhaps five foot eight or nine. He was lean and athletic with longish gray hair. He sported a fading vacation tan.

"Is that Doc Bernie?" Sig shouted from the front seat of the Cruiser, the horse trailer blocking his view of the group. "It sure sounds like the arrogant little shit."

Williams smiled, said, "That certainly sounds like Sig 'the Asshole' Alderson."

I motioned to Williams to approach the Cruiser. I stepped back and let him pass.

Spotting Sig in the front seat, Williams said, "What the hell you doing, Sig? You should be home in bed. Or did Molly finally kick your withered-up ass out of the house?"

"Jon, shoot this guy, please," Sig said.

"Enough of the miss you, love yous," Williams said. "Seriously, what are you doing out here, Sig?"

"We're collecting our foreman and ranch hands and bringing them back to the ranch."

"That's good. We're going to need to keep the ranches and farms operating. But you're sitting in one of only two working vehicles we've seen in four days. Don't suppose we could borrow it for a few hours, Sig?"

"Not mine to lend, Bernie. Sorry."

"We've got patients we need to get to Winnemucca for care we can't give 'em here," Williams said. "One of them is Lilian Calibrese."

"Oh no . . . I'm sorry to hear that, Bernie. We received your wedding invite and planned to attend. You know how Molls and I feel about Lilian, but it's not my vehicle. These folks aren't military. They want to get on home to Seattle."

"It's mine, Doctor," I said. "And as soon as we collect the ranch hands and get them back to Sig's, we're heading out."

"If you're headed to Seattle, you're going to drive right by the hospital in Winnemucca," he said. "It's less than a mile from the junction of Interstate 80 and Highway 95."

"There are six of us, sir, and there is no room for another passenger," I explained. "I'm truly sorry. I wish I could help you, but we simply can't."

"If we bundled them up and laid them out in the trailer, maybe under the tarp . . ." Monica said, trailing off. Seeing the look of dismay on my face, she mouthed a quiet, "Sorry."

"How many do you have, Doctor?" I asked.

"Four."

"We could handle four in the trailer laying crosswise," I said. "But I want something in return."

"What might that be?"

"Two things. One, we need a medical kit, a good one—professional. One that only a hospital could put together, and not like one you could buy at Costco or your local Walgreens. Two, twenty-four courses of antibiotics—six each of the four most important ones."

"Deal. When can you pick the four up? Sorry, there's five," Williams said, pointing to one of the men with a rifle. The man stepped forward, and Williams put his hand on his shoulder. "This is Terry, and he's a registered nurse. He's going to accompany the patients. Terry's parents and sister live in Winnemucca, and he'll be staying there during this blackout."

"It's not a simple blackout, Bernie," Sig said.

"Tell me," Williams said, and Sig started relaying what we knew.

Miguel had opened the trailer's ramp and was running boxes and suitcases into the trailer. Maria was last out of the house and locked the door behind her. With tears in her eyes, she turned and faced the house. She and little Sophie then waved goodbye.

Miguel helped them into the trailer and got them settled. He then ran down the ramp and up to the detached garage's side door and disappeared inside. He emerged two minutes later with both hands manhandling a large black duffel bag, which he then deposited in the trailer. He ran back to the garage and a minute later came out carrying a desert-brown AR and a camo backpack.

Two shots rang out in rapid succession. We all ducked and waited. Three more shots followed the first two.

"They came from the hospital," Miguel said. "And from two different guns."

"A long gun and a handgun," I said. "The handgun is a large caliber, possibly a forty. Miguel, can you watch Sig and the others while I check it out?"

"Of course. Anything."

"Melissa, follow me. Monica and Kathy, please stay and watch the Cruiser and trailer."

Williams came up from a crouch and started running toward the hospital.

"Doc, stay here," I shouted after him. "Let me deal with this—it's something I've done many times. I'll let you know when it's safe to return."

"Most likely someone's going for the pharmacy," he said, stopping and turning around. "Yesterday we had an individual come in and try to rob us. Luckily, we had a couple of policemen in place, and they arrested him."

"Pick that handgun up, Doc, and don't give it back to the kid—he's way too young and has no idea how to handle it properly."

MELISSA AND I RAN toward the front entrance portico of the hospital. We came to a stop at the roundabout where patients are dropped off and picked up.

A uniformed police officer was lying on his back outside the broken front doors, blood running from his head down the sidewalk and into the gutter. His gold-colored nameplate read Russel Gibson. His service weapon had been taken. I reached down and felt for a pulse. Finding none, we continued through the opened sliding doors.

"Stay behind me and watch our six, Melissa," I instructed. "Keep your hand on my vest so I know you're there. Let me run offense and you defense. Safeties off, and both rifle and handgun chambered and ready to fire."

"You got it, boss," she said. "I'm ready, and my finger is off the trigger."

"Let's go."

I let the rifle hang on the sling and moved it to the side where I could keep it quiet and better control the bouncing. I took out and charged the Glock. We entered the hospital.

We emerged into a large, airy two-story lobby/reception area. Straight ahead was an information desk that would normally be manned by a couple of elderly volunteers. Over the desk, a silver mylar balloon with Snoopy wishing you a speedy recovery was still airborne and affixed to a glass vase with wilted flowers. Dark corridors led off at nine, twelve, and three o'clock. Signs and arrows on the wall told us the hospital pharmacy was to the right and down the three o'clock hallway.

I heard shouting and screams up ahead, and two shots rang out. We came to an intersection with another corridor and after clearing it made our way forward. Up on the left was an indoor patio with an abandoned coffee cart and a dozen tables and chairs. The area was thick with the scent of gunpowder. A policewoman lay on her side beside an overturned table.

I entered the café while Melissa took a knee next to the wall and covered the corridor.

The officer's chest rose and fell in an attempt to get air. I crouched down beside her and sat her up. The name tag over her left breast said her name was Susan Foster. Her shoulder was bleeding from an entrance wound, and her blond ponytail and the left side of her face were slick with blood. I checked front and back, and it looked as if another round had hit her vest front dead center—she'd had the breath knocked out of her.

She stared at me with impossibly large blue eyes. She was taking huge gulps of air, and I figured she was going into shock.

"Susan, you've been hit in the shoulder. Your vest stopped another round, but the impact has knocked the breath out of you. You're panic breathing. Slow your breathing down," I said in a calm voice.

She nodded in understanding, and I could see her attempt to relax her breathing.

"I'm going to drag you over to the coffee cart's wheel so you can remain sitting upright. You ready?"

She nodded. I grabbed the drag handle on the back of her vest, pulled her ten feet to the wheel, and helped her rest in an upright position.

"Where's your weapon?" I asked. "And how many shooters are there?"

She pointed to another overturned table. Melissa retrieved the weapon, a Glock 17, handed it to me, and resumed her position at the corridor. I dropped the mag and cleared the chamber. One bullet missing. I put the chambered bullet back in the mag and rammed the magazine into place. I charged it and put it in her hand.

Her breathing was slowing down, and between breaths, she managed to tell me. "Three males. All armed. All white. All late twenties. Two in black hoodies and one in a red UNLV sweatshirt."

I stood and looked for something to stuff her wound. I settled on a handful of napkins I found on the cart.

"This is going to hurt. You ready?"

"No," she said, managing a smile. She was a smart-ass. I liked that.

"Too bad," I said, smiling back. I loosened her tie and ripped open the collar of her uniform shirt. I slipped my fingers down between skin and vest and pulled the vest away from her, at the same time jamming a wad of napkins over her wound.

She closed her eyes and moaned.

I took her free hand and placed it over the wound. "Keep pressure on it. A doctor will be here soon. Okay?"

"Have you seen my partner?" she asked.

Not knowing how to soften the news, I said, "I'm sorry, he didn't make it."

"Oh," she said, looking me in the eye. "Okay then, two with handguns and one with an AR. Go get 'em. Put 'em down. Please."

I nodded, said, "I promise. Let's go, Melissa."

We left the wounded officer and started down the hallway.

Screams rang out ahead. "Get the fuck out of the way," a man shouted.

"Open the fucking door, bitch," another male voice yelled.

"I told you I can't. I don't have the key code," a female voice shouted back.

"Brian, grab the fat one and kill her if they don't open the door by the time I reach five." The voice started counting. "One. Two. Three . . ."

"Please," she pleaded, "I don't have the code . . ."

I rounded the corner with the Glock in a two-handed shooting grip. Two men were facing away from us and were standing in front of a closed door, which presumably led to the pharmacy. The man on the right, standing five feet behind his buddy, had his arm around a young woman's neck and was holding a gun to her head.

I came up behind him, took hold of his gun arm, and shoved it up and away from the woman. Wanting to make sure the bullet would miss her, I put the Glock's muzzle in the nape of his neck and, aiming straight up, fired a single round, the bullet exiting the top of his head and knocking out one of the ceiling tiles. Not watching him fall, I turned and immediately put two rounds into the other man's chest, blood splattering the pharmacy door and wall.

There was a loud boom behind me. Turning, I saw a man in a red hoodie fall into a heap ten feet away, the contents of a carton of medical supplies scattering across the polished floor. He must have rounded the corner and run right into Melissa's gun sight. The AR he'd been holding skidded across the waiting room floor and ended up at her feet.

I keyed the comms, said, "Kathy. Monica, let the doc know it's clear to return."

Nothing but static—too many walls between us and the two women.

"Good shooting, Melissa," I said, giving her a quick shoulder bump. "Go let the doctor know it's okay to come in. You good?"

"I'm good," she answered, looking down at her victim, then turning and running toward the hospital's entrance.

I went over to the man Melissa had shot. He was on his back and had both hands over his stomach attempting to staunch the flow of blood.

"Hurts, doesn't it?" I asked, looking down at him.

"Yes," he managed to say between clenched teeth. "Get me a doctor."

"Don't think so," I replied.

"I need a fuckin' doctor, dude. Please."

"I do that, and he'll try to save your life—that oath they take and all that."

"That's what they do."

A female nurse wove her way through the waiting room chairs toward the man on the floor. I put my hand up and shook my head. I pointed in the direction she'd come from. She got my drift, for she nodded, turned, and headed back.

I turned my attention back to the man on the floor. "He'd be using needed drugs and supplies on you. I don't think that's fair. Do you?"

He started to answer, but before he formed a word, I put a round in his forehead.

Several women who'd witnessed the exchange screamed and ran away.

Three rounds used here—eleven left. I holstered the Glock, picked up the AR and handguns, and walked back to the coffee cart and the wounded deputy.

I came to the corner of the coffee shop, stopped, shouted, "Deputy, it's the man who moved you. Don't shoot."

I turned the corner, and the deputy had her weapon up and aimed in my direction. Her hand was shaking, and when she saw it was me, she let her hand drop to her lap.

"How are you holding up?" I asked, sitting down next to her. Her breathing had slowed and appeared close to normal.

"It hurts like you can't believe," she said. "I heard shots. You put the fuckers down?"

"Like I promised, Deputy."

"Thank you."

"The doc is on his way. I've seen lots of wounds like yours, and while you're never going to serve like Serena Williams, chances are you'll have full use of your arm in a few months."

"I hate tennis. Chasing fuzzy balls around a court is stupid. I'm a runner—long-distance endurance runs."

"You have a place to recuperate?" I asked. "And someone to take care of you?"

"My apartment. And I live alone."

"Family, boyfriend, or significant other?"

"Girlfriend, but we broke up, and she moved her ass back to Los Angeles," she said.

"Ah, sorry."

"Me too. It was a nice ass, magnificent even," she said, smiling and then grimacing.

"Well, you've got a place to rest and recover now," I said. "The doc is going to get you fixed up. Then we're going to stop back, pick you up, and take you out to the Alderson Ranch."

"Molly and Sig's place? Cool. They're good people."

"I suggest you stay out there, maybe offer to provide security in exchange for a place to live."

"I have a job, ah, I'm ashamed to say I don't know your name," she said.

"Jon," I replied.

"I've got a job, Jon, and have to get back to it."

"Your job is already gone, Deputy."

"Why do you say that?"

I told her what we knew about the pulse.

"I've heard of EMPs and have read a couple of novels about trying to survive one," she said. "But the Chinese angle is scary. Do you think they sent the missiles because of what's happening in Taiwan, Russia, and the South China Sea?"

"Could be. But who knows? The politics of it all are beyond me. But you need to think about yourself, Deputy," I said. "The bad guys will prevail, at least initially, and you won't be able to stop them."

Melissa, followed closely by Doc Williams, arrived and took a quick survey of the deputy's wounds. He left and came back with two nurses and a wheelchair. I took her handgun and put it in her holster. "Never let that leave your side, Susan."

I filled the doctor in on my plan to take the deputy to the Aldersons'.

"Depending on the damage I find, it shouldn't take much more than a couple of hours," he said, helping the two nurses settle the deputy into the wheelchair.

I stowed the Glock in its holster and moved the rifle from my side to a resting cradle position, said, "We'll stop by on our way back to the ranch and pick up the deputy."

"Our deal still stands, right?" Williams asked.

"Yes, sir. We'll see you in a couple of hours, if not sooner. We'll take the deputy back to the Aldersons' and then stop back here on our way north and pick up your patients."

"Thank you so much," he said, watching the two nurses wheel the deputy to the ER. "I'll see you in a couple of hours."

Melissa and I hustled back across the street to the waiting group.

"We heard more gunfire," Kathy said.

"That was us. Situation resolved," Melissa said. "Three assholes trying to take what wasn't theirs. They killed a deputy sheriff and wounded another."

"And the three?" Kathy asked.

"Dead."

"Good," Monica said.

I spotted Miguel at the rear of the horse trailer. "You finished loading, Miguel?"

"Yes, sir. I'm going to ride in the trailer with Maria and Sophia." He took hold of a rope and raised the ramp from the inside.

"Then let's move out. Melissa, Monica, Kathy, load up."

I started the Cruiser. Not wanting to jar our trailer guests, I took off slowly.

"Where to now, Sig?"

"Turn right up here onto South Humboldt Street. Then three blocks up, turn left onto West Second Street."

I told him about Deputy Foster, and he said he'd be glad to take her in. "She can stay in the main house with us. Molly will like having someone to take care of besides me," he said with a chuckle.

"The doctor seems like a good man," I said. "You two friends?"

"I paid for his college and medical school," he said. "Once he graduated and finished his residency at the University of Arizona in Tucson, he came back to work in the hospital here and joined our weekly poker game. I accuse him of cheating, and he accuses me of being senile."

"Seems like you're the town benefactor, Sig," I said. "You built the library and pay for medical school. That's nice."

"I've been very fortunate in life, Jon, and want to pass it along."

"All from ranching?"

"Oh gosh no, ranching is my passion. The money comes from my grandad and father. They were gold miners and owned and operated the largest gold mine in Nevada. It's still in operation right outside town . . . and the largest employer in northern Nevada."

"Impressive. You no longer own it?"

"No, Dad sold it to a South African mining conglomerate while I was still in college."

We passed several groups of people standing in front yards. Some simply waved while others yelled for us to stop and ran after the Cruiser. One teenager managed to stay with us for a block before finally giving up.

"That kid was fast," Kathy said. "If he's not on the track team, he should try out . . . would be a star."

"See that church up on the left? Lucas lives two buildings down," Sig said.

The street was full of dead cars and pickup trucks. I double-parked in front of the apartment building, and several residents sitting on the front steps got up and started walking toward us. The women quickly formed a close-in perimeter, and the curious crowd shrank back.

I walked to the rear of the trailer. Miguel had already dropped the ramp and was waiting for me at the curb. "I'll go get him," he said. "I know which apartment is his."

"If he's home and wants to leave with us, tell him he's got thirty minutes to pack up," I said.

He nodded, gripped his AR, and ran into the apartment building, the residents sitting on the steps clearing a path for him.

"Stay back," Melissa yelled, followed by a single gunshot. I turned and saw a sizable group of people streaming out of the church and headed our way.

The group stopped a good fifty feet away.

"That was a warning shot. The next will be in your ass if you come any closer," she shouted, addressing the crowd.

"We only wanted to ask if you had any water or food you could spare," an elderly woman shouted, her palms out and facing Melissa. "We've been out of food since yesterday, and the water stopped running two days ago."

"We have no water or food with us, ma'am," Melissa said. "I wish we did, but we don't."

"Tell them to check Battle Mountain Food Co-op on Front Street," Sig shouted out his window.

"The co-op has been cleaned out, and travelers from the interstate are living in it. It isn't safe to venture out anymore," one of the men answered.

"Have you seen any government response out there?" the woman asked.

"Nothing at all," I answered.

"No FEMA or National Guard?"

"No."

"Tell them what's happened, Jon. They should know," Sig yelled from the front seat.

"Tell us what?" the woman asked.

I approached the group and stopped ten feet in front of them. I told them what we knew.

Several people dropped to their knees and made the sign of the cross. Most started to cry and asked God why he would have allowed this to happen.

"Jon, we have Lucas and his girlfriend, Samantha," Miguel shouted from behind the trailer. "We're ready to go."

I turned and ran back to the Cruiser. "Load up, everyone!" I shouted.

The church group watched us retreat and started shouting for us to give them a ride.

Several men broke ranks with the crowd and ran toward us. I heard the Cruiser's rear doors close and was ready to put it in gear and take off but realized the men would reach us before I could get going.

I removed the Glock from its holster, stuck it out the window, and fired a single round over the approaching men. Which stopped them in their tracks. I was able to get the Cruiser in gear and take off. Ten rounds left.

"Where to now?" I asked Sig.

"We stay on this street. Mateo and Izan live in a trailer park three blocks up on the left. They're brothers and live next door to each other."

We passed a burned-out liquor store, still smoldering, smoke rising into the blackened sky. On the next block, we drove past the Little Indian Motel. Its parking lot was full of cars, with only a handful of folks out. Most were sitting on old-fashioned metal rocking patio chairs outside their rooms.

"Turn left here," Sig said.

The Lander County Mobile Park was shaped like a horseshoe, with single- and double-wides occupying the outer edges of the shoe. Inside the shoe was at least an acre of brown grass with a drained swimming pool, a closed clubhouse, and an open but most likely nonfunctioning laundry room. In the spring, summer, and fall, it was probably quite nice.

The brothers' trailers were located on the horseshoe's left-hand side. I slowly drove through the narrow lane, and Sig had me stop at a nice-looking double-wide. It had a driveway and carport with a newer-looking Toyota Corolla parked underneath. Covering the entire left side of the trailer was a large stained redwood deck.

The women set up the usual close-in perimeter watch.

The trailer's door opened, and two men stepped out onto the deck. Both had handguns with the barrels pointed down. The curtains on the windows on either side of the front door were pushed aside, and four little faces peered out. Standing behind the children were women I guessed were the mothers.

"Hello, Mateo, Izan. It's Sig. Miguel is in the trailer and will explain why we're here."

I walked back to the rear of the trailer. I helped Miguel lower the ramp, and he introduced me to Lucas and his girlfriend, Samantha. Lucas was young, probably no older than twenty-five. He was tall and rail-thin, with short red hair and a full red beard. His girlfriend, Samantha, was his age, short, probably five-one or two, and was a dark-haired Mexican beauty.

Mateo and Izan were standing at the bottom of the mobile home's stairs. "Hello, Mr. Sig," the two said in greeting.

"Miguel, what's going on? Who are these soldiers, and why are they with you?" Mateo asked.

"Protection," he answered. "It is terrible out there, bros. Buildings on fire. People killing cops and other people. And these folks are not soldiers." Miguel made the introductions, said, "We have some news about the blackout to share with you." He then went through the story. He finished by asking them if they wanted to move out to the ranch.

"Hell yes," Mateo answered without hesitation.

"Thank you, Mr. Sig," Izan said, extending his hand through the passenger window and shaking Sig's.

They both went back inside the first trailer. Two minutes later, Izan and his wife and two children came out and walked to the trailer next door.

Several neighbors approached the Cruiser, asking Miguel questions. Miguel answered the big question, and the group dispersed after absorbing the news.

Mateo and Izan made two dozen trips from their mobile homes to the horse trailer, bearing armloads of clothes, sheets, towels, pillows, blankets, even mattresses.

"Miguel, I haven't seen any toys come out of the trailers," Melissa said. "Kids need toys, regardless of what's happening in the world."

Nodding, Miguel ran to both trailers, relaying the message. Soon the children started ferrying their favorite toys out to the trailer. I watched them scurry back and forth from trailer to Cruiser, little legs moving in fast-forward determination. I dropped the Glock mag and reloaded while watching the show.

Finished loading, doors were locked and goodbyes said.

"There's one more ranch hand, right?" I asked Miguel.

"That would be Edgar, but a friend got his old truck running, and two days ago they drove to Elko to stay with his friend's mother and father."

"So, we're good to go?" I asked.

All the ranch hands looked to me and shrugged.

"What?"

It was Izan who spoke. "We know of a storage locker loaded with rice, beans, and other survival food," he said. "It's a ten-foot by ten-foot space loaded to the ceiling with supplies."

"Is it yours?" I asked.

"Doesn't matter," Sig cut in. "We have all the food we need in the cold storage barn next to the old bunkhouse. You know that because you all loaded it for me."

"Excuse me, Mr. Sig, I do not mean to overstep," Miguel said, "but the owner is a friend of ours and flew to Honduras last week. He will never be back, and I know he would want us to take it."

"I'll go along with it," I said, "on one condition."

"Which is?" Miguel asked.

"On our way back, we stop by the church across from Stan's apartment, and you give them enough rice and beans to last a few weeks."

"Agreed."

"Where is the storage facility?" I asked, resigned to making the stop.

"It's on Front Street, right around the corner from the church," Izan answered.

One nice thing about small towns is that they are small towns, and you don't have to drive long distances to get from one place to another.

"Do you have the key to the lock? Or do you have bolt cutters to cut it?" I asked.

Izan held up a four-foot-long, red-handled bolt cutter that was almost as tall as him. "These will do the trick."

"I would hope so. Let's load up. Izan, please hop in the Cruiser and guide us there."

TWENTY-FOUR

We exited the trailer park and turned right onto Second Street. Izan had us take the first left and then right onto Front Street. The storage facility was a hundred yards up on the left and sat behind a double set of raised railroad tracks.

The facility was huge, with row after row of roll-up doors. "Where's the locker?" I asked.

"Right there. The one on the end," he said, pointing to a roll-up door on the other side of the chain-link fence. "Park here, and we'll cut the fence and carry the buckets from the locker across the tracks to the trailer. It's only fifty feet."

"There's not a rental office on the property?" Sig asked, his head swiveling right and left, checking out the facility.

"No, sir," Miguel answered.

"Ladies, let's set the perimeter and keep watch," I said. "We don't want to be mistaken for looters."

The men made quick work on the chain-link fence and had the unit's roll-up door's lock cut in under thirty seconds. They raised the door, and inside were neat stacks of orange plastic buckets. Each five-gallon bucket was sealed with a white

Gamma lid and labeled with the contents and preparation directions.

"There's got to be two hundred buckets in there, guys," I said. "If they're filled with rice and beans, then they're heavy. Move the lighter stuff to the trailer's rear and put those buckets on the hitch side of the axles."

All the adults helped move the buckets while the children sat on the ground under Melissa's watchful eye.

I watched them load buckets of rice, black beans, quick oats, pancake mix, freeze-dried meats, vegetables, and powdered milk. There were even twenty, five-gallon, stackable blue water storage containers.

They transferred the entire contents of the storage unit and had the ramp raised and in place in less than thirty minutes.

My initial estimate of two hundred buckets was off by 150—there were 370, and I could really feel the added weight in the trailer. The Cruiser strained through the gears, and five minutes later we were parked outside the church. The same group we'd spoken with earlier were still milling around outside.

I told the elderly woman and man who'd spoken out earlier to approach.

"We secured some food and water and are going to share it with you. We'll leave it on the pavement behind the trailer. Stay right there and do not approach us," I said, not trusting them one bit.

I went to the rear of the trailer and lowered the ramp. The men carried five buckets of rice and five buckets of black beans down the ramp and off the trailer, depositing them on the pavement.

"They need water, Miguel," Sig said. "There's an endless supply at the ranch."

"Si, you are right, of course," he said, taking ten of the five-gallon containers and setting them next to the rice and beans.

"There's enough food and water there to last two or three months if you are careful," Miguel said. "Good luck to you."

"God bless you all," the woman said, making the sign of the cross on her chest.

We loaded up and drove to the hospital, parking across the street from Miguel's house.

Leaving Monica and Kathy to watch the Cruiser and trailer, Melissa and I set out for the hospital and Deputy Susan.

Officer Gibson's body had been removed, but the officer's blood remained, pools and rivulets still wet and pooled on the sidewalk and in the gutter. There were now two saddled horses tied to a bike rack next to the hospital's front door. Inside, we found Deputy Foster sitting in the lobby surrounded by two police officers, one older and the other so young he had to be a rookie, Doctor Williams, and the same two nurses. The deputy's left arm was in a black sling.

The older of the two officers was tall, matching my six-four. He was thin, but still powerful-looking, gray hair sticking out from underneath a black cowboy hat. He was wearing a light-tan summer uniform. Black pointy cowboy boots polished to a military-grade shine complemented the cowboy appearance.

The younger officer was short, heavy, bald, with a belly that was held up by a tight duty belt. He had a double chin, and both pale white cheeks were red with heavy veins running every which way. Old acne scars dominated the surface of his forehead and chin.

The older officer eyed our weapons, abruptly stood, and put his hand on his service revolver. Melissa raised her rifle into a shoulder-high firing position and released her safety.

"Whoa, everyone!" Deputy Foster said. "Captain, chill, these are the two civilians that saved my butt and put down the three assholes. This is who we've been waiting for."

The older officer took his hand off his weapon and visibly relaxed. Melissa lowered her rifle but kept it at the ready, safety still off.

"Cap, this is Jon and Melissa. Guys, this is Dan O'Brien, my captain. This young officer is George Carter."

I closed the distance and extended my hand to the older of the two, said, "Nice to meet you, Captain. Officer Carter. I'm sorry about Officer Gibson."

"Thank you. And thanks for helping," O'Brien said, shaking my hand.

I nodded and offered a quick smile. "Those your horses out front?"

"Yes, no other way to get around."

"You came back," Williams said, speaking up and looking surprised.

"One's only as good as their word," I said. "And we'll be back tonight to pick up your patients."

"No need," he said.

"What's changed?" I asked, secretly relieved we weren't going to have to transport five people in our trailer.

"One of the dead men had car keys in his pocket," Deputy Foster answered. "The hospital staff searched the parking lots and found they fit an old, still-running cargo van. It was parked in the very back of the rear lot, which is why no one heard them drive up."

"The four patients and Ted are already on their way to Winnemucca," Williams added.

"I hope you armed someone and sent them along," Melissa said.

"We did," the deputy answered. "We set him up with the dead guy's AR. They're going to return here after dropping them off."

"We'll keep the van here in Battle Mountain and use it for local transport," Doc Williams said. Captain O'Brien shot a look at the doctor. "And, of course, we'll share it with the police department."

"Good idea. And in another week or two, you're going to see more working vehicles out on the road," I said. "People with pre-seventies cars, and there are still a good number of them out there, are eventually going to have to venture out for food and water."

"Speaking of which, there are some community members that are meeting in the hospital's employee lounge as we speak," Williams said. "They're talking about setting up armed citizen watches, forming groups that will search for food and water, and agricultural committees that will coordinate with local farms and ranches for food production."

"Sounds like the community is getting proactive," I said. "That's what's going to be needed to stay viable and alive going forward."

Williams stood, and we shook hands. "The news you shared with us on the blackout hit home with the community leaders," he said. "Without it, I'm pretty sure they'd be twiddling their thumbs waiting for the power to come back on. And thanks again for your help in putting those assholes down for us."

Williams had been holding a large Ziplock bag filled with plastic prescription bottles. He handed it to me, said, "These are for Deputy Foster. There's a full course of antibiotics, which should take care of any infection that may pop up. There are also some pain management meds.

"She got lucky—the bullet stopped in a muscle and missed bones altogether. We got the bullet out intact and closed her up. She's got full range of motion in her arm and hand, so she's okay nerve-wise. She's very lucky. All she needs to do now is rest and keep her arm immobile. I'll need to see her in fourteen days to remove stitches and instruct her on some physical therapy exercises."

"We'll get her to the Aldersons'," I said. "She'll be safe and well taken care of out there. Where's her duty vest?"

"We threw it in the trash. It's bloody and yucky," the younger of the two female nurses answered.

"Please get it," I said. "She's going to need it."

The nurse looked at Williams, who nodded. The nurse stood and walked toward the emergency room.

"I know our deal was an emergency medical kit and twenty-four courses of antibiotics in exchange for transporting the patients," Williams said, reaching behind him and sliding out a large red duffel bag. "That's not happening now, but we put together a medical kit for you anyway. One that would be the envy of any EMT team in the country. And we're giving you the twenty-four courses of antibiotics, too—they're in the duffel bag. We owe you and the young lady standing next to you quite a bit, and this is our way of saying thank you."

"Just glad we were close by and could help," Melissa replied, both of us watching the young nurse run up and hand the bloody duty vest to the deputy.

"Thank you for the kit and meds. Doctor, we need to get going," I said, helping the deputy stand. "Best of luck to you." I stuck my hand out and shook his.

"Safe travels, Jon," the doctor said. "And we'll see you, Miss Foster, in two weeks." He waved goodbye to the captain and young officer, turned, and headed back toward the emergency room, the two nurses tight on his heels.

Captain O'Brien had been silently observing my conversation with Williams. "Deputy Foster tells me you and your group have skills. Skills that we could really use around here," he said.

I shook my head. "Sorry, I understand your predicament, but we need to get home. We're probably leaving tonight."

"You're now in the company of half the Battle Mountain police force," the captain said, desperation filling his voice. "As you know, we lost Gibson. And Officer Foster here is out of action for who knows how long. Three others—Sebastian, Cooper, and Simon—haven't shown up for work since the blackout, and we assume they're with their families. I understand wanting to be with family, especially young families, and I'm not going after them. The other three are at the station house with no way of getting around or communicating. We're sleeping in the holding cells."

"We passed a Nevada Highway Patrol office this morning and saw a few officers out in the parking lot. Have you spoken with them?"

"The office commander rode his bicycle to our offices yesterday. They're in the same shit pile we are: no working vehicles, no communication, three-quarters of his officers haven't shown up for work, people streaming into the station asking for help and they're not able to give it. It's bad out there. Again, we could use your help."

"Sorry, sir. But we're going to take Deputy Foster to the Aldersons' and then head out after dark. We do have some food we can leave with you," I offered.

"Well, that's good news," he said. "We'll take it. Can you drop it off at the station?"

"We can."

"Thanks. Susan can guide you there."

"Good luck to you, Captain."

"You too, Master Sergeant."

———

WITH THE MEDICAL KIT, THE deputy's service vest, her service belt, and her Ziplock bag of meds in my right hand, I took hold of the deputy's elbow with my left. "We're parked across the street. You think you can walk two hundred yards?"

"One thing I have is strong legs," she said, smiling.

"Melissa?"

"Right behind you."

"Safety your weapon, please. And take your finger off the trigger."

"Right," she said, pushing the safety lever up into the safe zone.

"How is it that you have a working vehicle?" the deputy asked. Strong legs or not, she was shuffling along, a grimace showing on her face with every step.

"It's a pre-computer-chip four-by-four, a 1972 Toyota Land Cruiser—there's nothing in it that the pulse could fry. Well, that's not true—the new radio is toast."

We rounded the corner of the hospital, and I could see the Cruiser. Monica and Kathy were still set in a perimeter position. Miguel, Mateo, and Izan were manhandling a large mattress out the front door of Miguel's house—not a bad idea considering there likely wouldn't be another one mass-produced for years.

Melissa and I helped Deputy Foster into the back of the Cruiser.

Foster sat on the bench seat and let out a soft whistle. "I have a Barrett .50-cal between my legs," she said, running her free hand along the scope and buttstock. "It's beautiful." Noticing Sig in the front seat, she said, "Oh, hello Mr. Alderson. I'm Susan Foster. We met last month at the police department's fundraiser dance."

"How could I forget, Miss Foster. You are one heck of a dancer."

"Well, thank you, sir. It was a fun night."

"And how is that beautiful woman you were with?"

"Bethenny? She moved back to Los Angeles."

"I'm sorry to hear that. You two made quite the couple," he said. "We'll be taking good care of you, Deputy. No need to worry about a thing."

"Thank you, sir. I'll forever be in your debt. Jon, any chance we can stop by my apartment so I can retrieve some of my things? I need some clothes and personal items. I also have a few weapons and some ammo in my gun safe."

"Sure. Where is it?"

"Behind the high school on Wilson Street. Keep going straight on this street for about two miles and turn right onto Wilson. My complex will be on the left-hand side. It faces the interstate."

"Where's your station house?"

"It's a mile up this street. Easy-peasy."

"Let me tell the others what we're doing."

At the back of the trailer, I removed the comms unit from my vest and handed it to Miguel. I explained how to use it and then told them where we were headed next.

"Two more stops and then to the ranch, guys. Everyone okay?"

"The children are enjoying the ride. For us older folk, not so much, señor."

"Call me Jon, please. We'll be back at the ranch soon," I said. "Use the comms if you need to talk to us."

We were on our way a minute later.

"How does your gun safe lock? With an old-fashioned combination dial or an electronic keypad?" I asked the deputy.

"Old-fashioned spinning dial."

"Good, we'll be able to get it opened." Newer safes with electronic keypads were locked forever, their electronics fried in the pulse and the safe's contents hidden away for all time. I had a gun safe in my Seattle home, and it did use an electronic keypad, but it could also be opened with a key.

Rain clouds had moved in from the west, their shadows moving across the desert floor, encompassing houses, streets, and entire city blocks before quickly moving on. The rain was falling, and street gutters were starting to fill.

We reached the police station a few minutes later, and I pulled over to the red zone curb in front. A dozen people were milling about the parking lot, and a Black female deputy was guarding the station's entrance door. She was telling the crowd to disperse, that there were no food or water handouts available.

"That's Sheila. She's tough as nails and doesn't put up with crap from anyone," Foster said.

Sheila was tall and shaped like a hot air balloon: wide on top and narrow and skinny on the bottom. She had an enormous chest, and I wondered how she managed to get her service vest on. Her black hair was piled high in a ponytail, and streaks of crimson-red ran through its length.

The crowd wasn't listening to the deputy and started to surge toward her. The deputy took out her service weapon and fired a warning shot over the crowd. They took the hint and ran off, leaving the parking lot empty.

"Let's set up a close-in perimeter, guys," I said. Melissa, Kathy, and Monica hopped out and took a knee at various positions around the Cruiser.

Seeing soldiers hopping out of a working vehicle and sporting weapons, Sheila ran surprisingly fast back inside and reemerged with two deputies in tow.

"What the fuck you think you're doin'?" she shouted at us, stepping back and drawing her weapon.

"Your fellow deputy, Susan Foster, was shot and wounded at the hospital. We have her in the back seat and have been asked by Captain O'Brien to drop something off," I replied.

"Oh. Well, good enough," she said, holstering her service weapon. "I'm going to approach you, so don't be shooting my ass. I like my ass. Some folks may think it might be a tad too large, but I like it all the same."

Once she was close enough to not have to yell to be heard, I told her the situation and what we were dropping off.

"Food? Tell me you gotcha a dozen Big Macs or Whoppers with cheese in the back of that thing. Maybe some fries too."

"No, Sheila, just me and some rice and beans," Deputy Foster shouted.

"Is that you, Susan?"

"True it is, Sheila."

"Miguel, please take off five of each pail," I shouted. "And some water."

The ramp came down. The pails and two water containers were left on the curb, and the ramp went back up.

"What's all that?" Sheila asked, eying the orange buckets.

"That's twenty-five gallons of rice and twenty-five gallons of black beans. Get them inside before the crowd comes back and takes them."

"Yo, lazy butts. Get your skinny behinds out here and move those things inside."

The two deputies made five trips each and quickly had the pails inside.

"I got a camping stove at home we can cook that on," she said. "Thanks."

Deputy Sheila walked up to the passenger window and saw Sig. "Well, hi there, Mr. Alderson. Nice to see you."

"Right back at you, Deputy Crawford."

Sheila stuck her head in Sig's window and spied Deputy Foster in back.

"You don' look nothin' like your usual pretty self, girl."

"Being shot will have that effect on a person, Sheila."

"Where's that partner of yours?"

"You haven't heard?"

"I ain't heard nothin'. Uh-oh, what is it?"

"Russel was shot and killed earlier today."

Sheila's face dropped, and tears ran down her cheeks. "Oh boy oh boy. What has the world come to? Fuckin' A. Who shot him?"

"Three piece-of-shit druggies. Killed Russel and got me, then tried to get to the hospital pharmacy. Jon and Melissa here put them down for us. They're out in the field behind the dump waiting for the coyotes and buzzards."

"I'm sorry, Deputies, but we need to get a move on," I said. "Guys, load up."

Sheila and Susan said their goodbyes, and we were on our way. I turned right on Fifth Street. The deputy pointed to a large apartment complex on the left and had me turn in and drive to the very back.

There were dozens of folks standing in groups. All eyes were on us as we slowly drove through the complex. Individuals broke off from their groups and formed a larger group, which followed us.

"Kathy, when we stop, exit and run behind the trailer. Get those folks to back off and stay back fifty feet. Answer any questions they may have."

Parking, I said to Deputy Foster, "You stay put. Melissa and I will get your stuff. Monica, set up a frontal perimeter, please." The rain was really coming down, and the ladies would get soaked. "It's okay to set up watch under the stairways—keep drier anyway."

"Anything special you want us to grab?" Melissa asked the deputy.

"Nope. Just the usual stuff. I've got an empty duffel bag and backpack in the bedroom closet you can throw stuff into. Don't worry about folding or any of that nonsense. Empty all the dresser's drawers into the duffel bag. As for my bathroom stuff, just drop it all in the backpack.

"Oh. Oh. Under the bathroom sink are six boxes of tampons. They're big boxes, with 120 in each. Gonna need those. And if you can grab the pillows on my bed, I'd appreciate it—they're special down pillows."

"Which is your apartment?" I asked. There were dozens of doors, sidewalks, and stairways leading up to more doors and stair landings.

"My apartment is at the top of that set of stairs," she answered, pointing ahead and to the right. "It's unit number 202. Here are the keys. It's kind of messy, so no judging."

"Least of our worries. What's the safe's combination?" I asked, digging for a pen in the center console.

"Twelve, twenty-four, ten. Right, left, right."

I wrote the numbers on my palm.

"Stay back fifty feet," Kathy shouted at the approaching crowd. "I will fire if you get any closer." Kathy fired off two rounds. "I have some news for you, but I'll only share what we know if you stop advancing. Thank you." Kathy started telling the crowd the news.

Sig opened his door and was attempting to exit the Cruiser.

"Whoa, Sig," I said, watching him turn sideways and attempt to slide off the seat to the ground. "Where you going?"

"I need to stretch my legs. Needed to for the last hour," he responded as large raindrops plastered the white hair to his scalp.

Monica rushed over to help, but he waved her off. She backed off but retrieved his walker and set it up for him.

"Thank you, young lady. Please leave me to it."

"Have at it, then," I said, making my way to the back of the trailer. Kathy was at the point of the news where she was explaining why the power grid would be down for a decade.

"Miguel, we're going up to the deputy's apartment to load up some of her things. Get the ramp down, please, and help Monica keep watch."

"That's all we know," Kathy told the crowd, who slowly dispersed after she'd answered a few of their questions.

Miguel's wife, Maria, offered to help. I waved her out of the trailer and had her follow us up the stairs. I unlocked the front door, and we stepped into a bright, cheerful, modern space. With kitchen off to the left, living and small dining room to the right, the bedroom and bathroom straight ahead, it was a well thought out floorplan.

Up against the living room wall was a large, forty-eight-gun Field and Stream gun safe. I wouldn't have wanted to be one of the several men it must have taken to get the thing up the stairs and placed inside the apartment. In all honesty, I was shocked that the safe hadn't crashed through the floor and into the apartment below.

I headed to the safe while Melissa and Maria made a beeline for the bedroom and bathroom.

I spun the dial, hit the numbers, and after spinning the steel-spoked wheel, the doors opened on smooth, well-balanced hinges.

"I have a few weapons" was an understatement. Inside the safe were five AR-15s—four Colts, one of them fully automatic, and a Daniel Defense—four semiautomatic handguns, a black Remington 870 pump shotgun, and of all things, a Fostech Origin 12-gauge semiautomatic shotgun with a thirty-round drum magazine. I'd heard about this destruction-producing weapon but had never seen one.

Inside the safe, stacked alongside the rifles, were hundreds of boxes of ammunition. And packed in every nook and cranny were magazines for the various weapons.

Moving all this to the Cruiser was going to take some time.

"Melissa, please radio Miguel to send up Lucas and the two brothers."

It took the four of us several trips to transfer the safe's contents to the trailer. Melissa and Maria had finished gathering clothes and personal items and were already waiting in the trailer and Cruiser. I took a last look around the apartment. On top of a bookcase in the dining room was an eight-by-ten silver picture frame with a picture of a beautiful black-haired woman—the deputy's ex-girlfriend? I took the frame and locked the door.

The crowd was gone.

"Kathy, in the Cruiser, please," I said as I hustled down the stairs.

I handed the last of the ammo boxes to Miguel as he raised the trailer's ramp behind him. "Everyone good to go back here?" I asked. The children were playing together on one of the mattresses and appeared to be having a grand time. The parents not so much. The mothers looked apprehensive and the fathers concerned.

"We're now headed to the ranch," I said. "We had a clear path on the way to town, and there's no reason to think it should be any different going back. Miguel, you have my two-way. You see something behind us, say something."

"Will do."

"Mateo, Izan, Lucas, each of you take one of the deputy's rifles and use it if necessary. You know how to load magazines?"

All three nodded. "We all do," Lucas answered.

"Good. Then dig through those ammo boxes and get the 5.56 out and start loading those mags. The women can help.

Miguel, I know you know how to operate an AR. Will you make sure the three men know as well?"

"Yes, of course."

"Two of those rifles have red dot scopes and are going to be hard to aim, so use the three with hard sights. Miguel, do you know how to load and operate a shotgun?" I asked him.

"Yes," he replied, already digging through the pile of ammo boxes.

"If a vehicle is close enough to take out our tires on the trailer or Cruiser, then use the shotgun. Aim for the windows and keep pumping out rounds until the weapon is empty."

"Si, I will do that," he answered.

I patted the side of the trailer and walked up to Sig's window. "We're all set to head on back to the ranch. You ready?" I asked.

"I am, and so are my legs," he said. "My legs start cramping if I don't move every so often."

I stuck my head in the window and asked Melissa, Monica, Kathy, and Deputy Foster if they were good to go.

"Yep," the ladies replied in unison.

"Melissa, will you do a comms check with Miguel? Let's make sure he's got it on and knows how to use it," I said.

"Miguel, Miguel, comms check," she said.

"I hear you loud and clear," Miguel answered.

I handed the picture frame to the deputy. "Not sure if this is a picture of your ex-girlfriend, but in any case, I figured you might want it."

"Thank you. It's Bethenny on her twenty-ninth birthday," she answered, staring down at the framed picture. "Taken last month."

"By the way, Deputy, that's one hell of a gun collection you have," I said. "The full auto Colt is a model even a member of law enforcement can't own. Then you've got that very special twelve gauge, and I'm not talking about the 870."

"Ah, the Fostech. Yep, she's one sweet hunk of metal. A girl can't have enough firepower."

I started the Cruiser and headed toward the front of the complex. At the street, I had a choice to make—we could go right or left. Left looked to take us by the rear of the high school. Right, into residential areas and backtracking from where we wanted to go.

"Which way, Deputy?"

"Left is quicker and is a straight shot to South Broad Street," she answered. "At Broad, we turn left, and we head south all the way on 305 to the ranch. Turn right, and we backtrack through residential streets."

"Left it is." I turned and could see the high school straight ahead. Fifty yards up, the road curved right almost ninety degrees. The oval running track and baseball diamonds were back here along with a large gravel storage lot for a dozen or so yellow Battle Mountain School District buses. The road then curved back another ninety degrees to the left, and a block ahead another sharp turn to the right. I took the turns slowly, not forgetting our passengers trailing behind us.

We hit Broad and turned left. It would now be a forty-five-minute drive back to the ranch.

TWENTY-FIVE

The high school parking lot was to the left. It was still packed with dozens of teenagers and their bicycles, but they'd abandoned the burn barrels and were now huddled under the building's eaves, trying to stay out of the rain.

I'd shifted into second gear when an old, dull-red GMC pickup with four men standing in the bed shot out of a Super 8 Motel parking lot on our right side and slightly ahead of us. It was pretty obvious he was trying to bring us to a stop, but he overshot and skidded right on by on the wet pavement, missing our front bumper by mere inches. They came to a stop twenty feet to our left.

I gunned the Cruiser, and we slowly gained speed, shooting past the truck. The four men in the truck's cargo bed were pounding on the roof and yelling for the driver to give chase.

"That's Brett Matthews and his brother Dave in the cab," the deputy said. "They're dirtbags, street-level drug dealers. I don't know the four standing in the bed."

Two more trucks exited the motel lot and followed the first truck.

One of the men in the lead truck's cargo bed brought up a rifle and let loose with a salvo. I wasn't sure if any rounds had hit the trailer, but their intentions were now pretty clear.

I was ready to ask Melissa to have Miguel aim for the windshield when he started firing the shotgun. The windshield shattered, and the truck violently swerved. It rolled onto its left side, throwing all four men out of the bed and onto the roadway. The truck rolled several times, crushing the four ejected men before I lost sight of it in the passenger side-view mirror.

"Miguel, what's your status back there?" Melissa asked.

"If you are asking if we are okay, then we are good," he answered. "The children are very scared and crying."

"The other two trucks have stopped and are checking on their buddies," Kathy reported.

We had miles of straight road ahead. I brought the Cruiser up to speed and leveled off at fifty; any faster and trailer sway could become a dangerous possibility.

The rain stopped as we passed the Highway Patrol office we'd seen earlier. The lot was now empty, and I saw no activity behind the station's large plate glass windows.

Some minutes later, we were cresting a long high butte when in my side-view mirror I saw sun reflect off two specks. Looking closer, I could make out two vehicles in the far distance. They were now cresting the butte, which led down to the valley we'd just crossed. They were ten miles behind and closing.

Melissa's comms came to life. "There are two trucks behind us," Miguel reported. "They are eight to ten miles back and getting closer. I think they are the other two trucks from town."

The next downslope was a half mile ahead, and we would soon lose sight of the approaching vehicles. I brought us to a stop with the Cruiser facing the left shoulder and the trailer blocking most of the right lane.

"Enough running," I said. "If we keep going, we'll lead them right to the ranch."

"What's your plan?" Sig asked.

"It's time for some heavy deterrence."

I ran to the rear of the Cruiser and swung open both doors. "Melissa, Monica, hand me the Barrett. Deputy, can you scoot your legs out of the way, please."

"Going to reach out and touch someone?" the deputy asked, tucking her feet up high enough for the Barrett to pass beneath.

"Oh yeah," I answered.

Monica grabbed the barrel and Melissa the buttstock, and they half carried, half scooted the rifle toward me. "Now the magazines. Four should be enough."

I stepped over the hitch and carried the rifle past Sig's window and unfolded the Harris bipod. I rested the bipod's legs on the Cruiser's hood and flipped up the Nightforce's two plastic lens covers. I'd used the hood of a Humvee as a firing platform in Afghanistan, but the Cruiser's hood was nowhere near as wide as a Hummer's, and I was supporting a lot of weight with my right shoulder. I wouldn't have full confidence in my shot, which was a big no-no.

I took a step back from the Cruiser, leaned down, and rested the bipod on the pavement. I released the monopod, and the rifle was now in a fully supported resting position.

Melissa, Monica, and Kathy were standing next to me. Melissa handed me the four loaded magazines—forty rounds. Plenty. *Better be*, I thought.

"Kathy, as a precaution, have the ladies take the children out of the trailer and into the ditch past the shoulder. Tell Miguel what I plan to do."

"What are you planning on doing?" Monica asked.

"He's going to take out those approaching trucks!" Deputy Foster answered. She had crept up behind us and was watching me get the rifle ready. "I am not going to miss the fun."

"Monica, will you get my earplugs out of the glove box? Melissa, grab the binoculars and spot for me. They're not going to be perfect, but it's all we have."

I watched the trailer ramp hit the ground, followed by the four women steering the children down the ramp and into the ditch.

The two trucks were now about four miles out.

Monica handed me my custom-made silicone earplugs. I inserted each plug into the proper ear.

"Deputy, do you have ear protection?"

"Yes, in the trailer somewhere. Buried."

"Monica, Melissa, Kathy, did you bring the ear protection Burt gave you?"

No from Monica and yes from Melissa and Kathy.

"You three have to stand behind me—you can't be next to the barrel. I'll yell 'firing' a second or two before I pull the trigger. Monica, if you're going to stay here, you've got to put your fingers in your ears," I instructed. "Melissa and Kathy, go get your ears and put them on. Deputy, you've got no ear protection and only have one hand to use, so you're going to have to step behind the trailer."

I lay prone behind the Barrett and scooted into a firing position, the buttstock tight against my right shoulder. There was already a magazine in place, and I pulled the charging handle back, released it, and heard the satisfying sound of the first bullet seating itself in the chamber.

I put my eye to the lens and focused out. Working the focus, I picked up the two trucks. One truck had three men in the rear cargo bed along with the driver and passenger, the other a driver and single passenger.

"Two trucks. Seven men," I said.

"How far out will they be when you fire?" the deputy asked from the rear of the trailer.

"I'll send the second round when the lead truck is about fifteen hundred yards out—a little under a mile. I'm sending the first round as a test—see where it hits. I don't have a spotter, so I don't know wind or drop and don't have time for calculations. And the thermal would take too long to get ready. I'm going to fire off one practice round. Melissa, I'm aiming for the signpost out on the right. You see it?"

"Yes."

I released the safety and brought the signpost into focus. "This is about fifteen hundred yards out."

There was no wind or rain. There was quite a drop from our current position atop the butte to the valley floor below, maybe one hundred to one hundred fifty feet in elevation change. If I remembered correctly, at a thousand yards, a .50-caliber round drops about twenty-two feet. I put the crosshairs six mills above the target. I didn't adjust right or left, as there was no discernable wind. I put my left hand on the monopod and my finger on the trigger. I told the group I was ready to fire.

"Firing!" I shouted.

I slowed my breathing and then held it. I pulled the trigger, and the Barret recoiled and then quickly settled back into place. I brought my eye up to the scope in time to see bits of pavement flying into the air. The bullet had hit twenty yards in front of the sign. I'd have to adjust slightly higher, perhaps another two mils.

"You're too low," Melissa said. "About fifty feet too low."

"Monica, make sure you've got extra magazines for your rifle, then form a perimeter line behind the trailer. You're the backup in case I can't stop their advance. Kathy, watch my six, please."

The two trucks were coming fast. At the rate they were moving, they'd hit my signpost marker in another thirty seconds.

I brought the scope into focus on the signpost and then moved it slightly left. The round would take one and a half seconds to reach the target. I was going to have to lead the first truck by fifty feet.

The first truck came into my field of view. I slowed my breathing and waited for the truck's front grill to fill the lower third of the scope.

"Firing," I shouted.

I made sure the reticle was placed correctly and pulled the trigger. The Barrett slid back in recoil and then settled. I watched through the scope and saw pavement break apart thirty feet behind both trucks.

Get it together, Jon.

"Too high," Melissa said.

Still watching the lead truck, I lowered the scope two mils. "Firing."

I sent the next round and watched as it hit the left-front headlight of the lead truck. The entire fender flew off the truck, exposing the front tire, shock absorber, and left-front suspension. The engine hood, lacking the support of the missing fender, was now flapping in the wind. Released from its entire left side restraint, it flew straight up and over the cab and cargo bed and landed in front of the following truck.

"You hit it," Melissa yelled out.

"Thanks. I've got this now."

The lead truck slowed to a controlled stop. The following truck was unable to stop in time and plowed into the engine hood, the right front tire bursting upon impact.

I watched as drivers and passengers emptied out of the disabled trucks, no doubt trying to figure out what had just happened.

It was time to permanently disable both trucks.

"Firing!" I sent the remaining seven rounds into the front half of the lead truck. Six of the seven rounds hit the mark. After the last round hit, the front bumper was sitting on the pavement in pieces and with both front tires flat. Steam was rising from the exposed engine bay.

I released the empty magazine and inserted a full one. I charged it and turned my attention to the second truck.

All seven men seemed to realize that the remaining truck might become the next target of opportunity and started running for the roadside ditch—no dummies in that group.

"Firing!" I brought the truck into focus and sent a round out, hitting the truck's front grill. The truck rose on its suspension and settled back down, steam erupting from under the hood.

I sent another nine rounds into the second truck, and it was now on fire, black smoke rising high into the late morning sky.

Seven heads popped up over the ditch's rim, watching as both trucks were systematically destroyed.

"Wow, that thing's a cannon!" Monica shouted, her ears no doubt still ringing. "Those trucks will never run again."

"Perfect for a scrap heap . . . not that they're able to come pick up the pieces," Melissa said.

That was kind of fun.

The two trucks' occupants were still hiding in the roadside ditch. I didn't want to worry about these men walking toward the ranch. I dropped the empty magazine and slammed in a third. I focused on the area to the left of the men.

"Firing!" I sent a round ten feet to their left. It hit the roadway, bits of asphalt flying up and raining down on the cowering men. I watched in the scope as they left the cover of the ditch and ran down the road back toward Battle Mountain. I sent one last round toward their rear and watched as the bullet hit asphalt twenty feet behind the last man. I followed the men's progress for the next five minutes. Satisfied that they were indeed headed back to Battle Mountain, I stood and brushed the road grime off my camos.

"Melissa, radio Miguel and have him load the women and children back into the trailer," I said, carrying the Barrett to the rear of the Cruiser. "Melissa, Monica, Kathy, hop on in and help load this beast. Careful of the barrel. It's hot, and it'll take some time to cool down."

The deputy followed the Barrett up and into the Cruiser, and I shut both doors behind her. Miguel herded the last of the children into the trailer, and I helped raise and secure the ramp. I took the next couple of minutes gathering up the spent cartridges for reloading back at the ranch in Montana.

Sig watched me as I brought the Cruiser up to speed. I looked over at him, said, "That was fun. You good?"

"I haven't heard a .50-caliber since World War II," he replied, smiling. "Of course, they were automatic machine guns and mounted in armored vehicles. Didn't have .50-caliber rifles back then. I would imagine they are very accurate when used as you just used yours. In my day, it was point and shoot and overwhelm the enemy—precision wasn't a must."

"They certainly have proven useful in the war zones I've been in," I said. "Its long reach has saved my butt more times than I can count. Between the Barrett and the A-10's we sometimes had on call, the odds of being involved in close-in engagements were dramatically reduced."

"I watched a PBS television show on the A-10, and my goodness, what an aircraft that is. Its nickname is Hogwarts, right?"

"Hogwarts is Harry Potter's School of Witchcraft and Wizardry," Kathy corrected him. "The A-10's nickname is Warthog."

"We just called it the Hog," I added.

"There is a School of Witchcraft and Wizardry?" Sig asked. "Where is it located?"

"There is no school, Mr. Alderson," the deputy said. "There is a series of best-selling fictional books about a young boy named Harry Potter who attends the school."

"I've never read the books, so I wonder how I could have heard the name?"

"There have been several Harry Potter movies made. Maybe that's why," Monica said.

"Now I remember. It was on HBO or Showtime. I liked it, especially the three dragons."

"The dragons are from a television show called *Game of Thrones*," Kathy said.

"There's the ranch," I said, pointing ahead, but more importantly changing subjects. We'd been climbing the north side of a high butte, and the road had just leveled out, offering a view into the far distance. Sig's ranch was on the valley floor ahead, maybe eight to ten miles out.

"Monica, try and raise Renee on the two-way. Let her know we're ten minutes out."

"Renee, Renee," Monica said into her mic.

"Renee here," came the immediate response.

"We're ten minutes out. Just descending the butte now."

"I see you, Monica."

Ten minutes later, we turned off the highway and onto the access road leading down to the ranch.

"Go ahead and park in front of the ranch house and let the deputy and me out," Sig instructed, placing his hand in front of his mouth and trying unsuccessfully to suppress a yawn.

"Call me Susan," the deputy said. "Please."

"Susan it is," Sig answered. "Jon, once the two of us unload, go ahead and pull into the equipment barn. Miguel can unhitch the trailer and help you get your trailer hooked up. Your group can continue staying in the new bunkhouse, and Miguel and his group can use the old bunkhouse—it's much larger anyway. Stay as long as you'd like. Sound like a plan?"

"Works for me. We're thinking of leaving after dark tonight and get past Winnemucca and then into Oregon before daylight tomorrow morning. If the plan changes, we'll let you know. Melissa, let Miguel know we're dropping Sig and Susan off and then heading for the equipment building."

I pulled into the circle in front of the ranch house. Renee and Greta greeted us with a wave and a tail thump. I gave Renee a thumbs-up and brought the Cruiser to a stop next to the porch steps. Molly greeted the ranch hands and their families and then helped Sig out of the Cruiser.

I opened the Cruiser's rear doors. Molly spotted Susan as she stepped out of the Cruiser. "I believe I know you, young lady, but can't say from where."

"Hello, Mrs. Alderson. We met at the policeman's dance last month. My name is Susan Foster."

"Quite right, young lady. I remember now. You were with an astonishingly beautiful woman as I recall. Where is—"

"Molls, time for twenty questions later," Sig cut in with. "The deputy . . . sorry, Susan, was shot and wounded during an incident at the hospital. She has no one to care for her, and I invited her here to recover."

"Let's get her inside then," Molly said, setting up Sig's walker. "Monica, Kathy, will you help the deputy up the steps and put her in a rocker—I need a few minutes to get one of the guest rooms ready."

Monica and Kathy brought Susan onto the porch and helped lower her into one of the rockers. Susan settled into the rocker and let out an "ahhhh" as she sank into the chair's deep cushion. "I think I'd like to sit here for the rest of the day," she said, pointing with her good hand to the expansive view. "It's beautiful here."

They helped Molly half carry Sig up the steps and into another rocker, where he closed his eyes and promptly fell asleep.

"He'll sleep in that chair until well after sundown," Molly said, smiling down at her husband. She took Sig's wrist and counted out his pulse and murmured, "Looks good."

"Let us help you make up a room for Susan," Kathy said.

Molly opened the screen door, smiled, looked back, said, "Thank you, hon, but I know where the sheets and towels are. It'll only take me a sec. You two take a rest break." She disappeared inside, holding the door until it closed quietly behind her.

"Melissa, can you stand watch here while I get this trailer moved into the equipment barn and ours sorted out?" I asked.

Melissa nodded and sat on the top step, holding her rifle with the butt resting two steps below her.

I reached in the Cruiser and grabbed Susan's bag of antibiotics. I handed the bag to Melissa and told her it was probably time for the deputy to take another round of pills.

"Kathy, Monica, Renee, take a break. Renee, I'll see you in the bunkhouse in an hour or so," I said. "Susan, you rest up. I'll take a look at that wound as soon as I get this trailer put away."

The three ladies and Greta were halfway to the bunkhouse when I passed them. I drove around back, then through the barn's two rear sliding doors. I backed the horse trailer into its original parking spot, hopped out, and helped lower the ramp. The kids piled out, followed by the fathers and mothers.

"Miguel, we're planning on leaving tonight, although I need to meet with our group for a final decision. We slept in the new bunkhouse last night, and some of our things are still there. If it's all right with you, we'd like to rest up there and then leave tonight."

"Mr. Sig, he informed me," he replied, taking off the borrowed comms set and returning it to me. "Regardless of when you depart the ranch, we will sleep in the old bunkhouse until you do. We will unload today only the most necessary things from the horse trailer. I will bring in the old tractor and tow the trailer to the new bunkhouse after you leave. Mr. Sig told me to make sure we filled your gas tank and extra cans."

"Thank you, we'll take you up on it," I said, unhitching the horse trailer as Miguel wound down the trailer stand and wheel. "Does your old tractor run on diesel or gas?"

"Gasoline. We have two almost new—less than 1,500 hours, anyway—John Deere 7130s that run on diesel. But the old tractor is a 1970 Deere model 5020 and runs on gasoline. Mr. Sig, he wants to always have fresh gasoline on hand, and if it sits in the main tank for longer than eight months, he has the gasoline company drain the tank and put new in. This gasoline is now two months old. We have a 750-gallon aboveground gasoline tank. And for diesel, we have a 2,500-gallon underground tank."

"Does the ranch have any older, say 1970 or earlier, diesel or gasoline-powered pickup trucks?"

"Yes. Cinco—five. All older diesel models. Lucas is our ranch mechanic, and he says he can probably get at least three running again. He is working on one as we speak."

"I hope so, because the deputy needs to return to the hospital for a follow-up visit with Doc Williams and have her stitches removed."

"We will make sure she is taken care of," he said. "I promise."

TWENTY-SIX

For the next hour, I replenished the Barrett, AR, and Glock magazines, helped Miguel fill the Cruiser's gas tank, and then topped off the gasoline and water jerry cans. I checked the Cruiser's fluids and tire pressure, and cleaned the windows, inside and out. I had a "thing" about clean windows.

I moved the Cruiser and hooked it up to our trailer. I double-checked the tarp tie-downs and left a corner open for last-minute items.

The Cruiser and trailer were ready to roll.

Our group was meeting at seven tonight on the Aldersons' front porch. It was now four, and I found Renee in our bunkhouse room organizing our packs. Greta was lying on the foot of the bed, but seeing me, she sat up, waiting no doubt for a chin rub. Getting one, she closed her eyes and emitted a quiet groan. Her tail started thumping in rhythm to my chin rubs. Renee had removed her working dog vest, and Greta was as relaxed as I'd seen her.

"All clean clothes, yours and mine," she said, folding the last T-shirt and placing it in her pack. "We have clean towels to use with our showers tonight. We leaving or staying?"

"Thank you for the clean clothes," I said, nodding in the direction of the door. She grabbed her rifle and turned on her comms. I took her hand and guided her out of the bunkhouse. Once outside, she adjusted her vest and sling and brought her rifle to a cradled resting position. We made our way to the horse corral, where we leaned on the fence and watched the horses as they munched their way among scattered piles of hay. Greta sat beside us.

The rain had stopped, and the sky was clearing, but heavy black clouds were just creeping above the mountain range to the west. I could see rain falling twenty miles out and headed our way.

"I wanted to speak with you without the others hearing," I said, squinting at her through bright sunshine. I dug out my Ray-Bans and slipped them on. "Do you think we should head out tonight?"

"If it was up to me, I'd stay another night, rest up, and then leave tomorrow night," she answered. A tall, black-on-white Appaloosa, perhaps fifteen hands tall, wandered over and put her head down, and she and Greta touched noses through the lower fence rails. Satisfied, the horse put her head up and forward, looking for treats or at least forehead scratches.

"I'm with you," I said as we both scratched away. "One more night is not going to make a huge difference. But if we stay, we're going to have to deal with Kris. By the way, did she relieve you and stand a watch today?"

"Never saw her."

"All day?"

"Not once."

"You talk to her?" I asked.

Renee shook her head. "I called her on the comms several times but never raised her. I didn't want to leave the porch unguarded, or bother Molly with Kris's bullshit, so I never tried to find her."

"Let's go check on her," I said, concerned.

We hit the bunkhouse first and found her bed empty but did find her rifle and comms set under the bed. Her service vest and night vision goggles were missing.

"She's supposed to have her weapon with her at all times," Renee said. "Why is it under the bed . . . with her comms set?"

Monica and Kathy were sleeping, and I woke them both.

"Sorry to wake you. We're trying to find Kris. Have you seen her?"

"She was here when we got back, but I fell asleep right away," Monica answered. "Why, what's going on?"

I looked over at Kathy.

"Ditto here," she said.

"Nothing . . . I hope," I answered.

I keyed my mic, said, "Melissa?"

"Yes, Jon," she answered.

"Have you seen Kris?"

"Nope. Though an old truck left the ranch five minutes ago, but I couldn't see the driver. It turned left at the highway."

"Which means it's headed north toward Battle Mountain," Kathy said.

"And on toward Seattle," Renee added.

"Thank you, Melissa. I'll be up there in a few minutes to relieve you."

"Sorry for waking you," I told the two. "Go back to sleep. We'll see you later at the meeting."

Renee and I turned to leave. But I stopped and turned back so quickly Renee bumped into me.

"Whoops, sorry, Renee. Gals, would you like to stay another night and leave tomorrow night, or leave tonight after dark?" I asked.

"Stay," Kathy answered.

"Same answer," Monica replied.

"Okay, thanks. Go back to sleep. And sleep in, we're staying another night."

"Please wake me if Molly is making dinner," Kathy said.

I looked at Monica, who nodded eagerly.

We walked out of the bunkhouse, Greta, as usual, glued to Renee's left side.

"Let's go see Miguel and Lucas. Lucas is the ranch mechanic. I bet he'll know if Kris took off in the truck."

We found both men in the old bunkhouse. They were moving the mattresses inside from the horse trailer.

"Yes, she asked if she could drive the old Ford around the equipment yard," Lucas answered. "I'd just finished doing a quick, mini tune-up and had filled both the main and auxiliary fuel tanks. I had it warming up. It has a three-speed on the steering column, and she said she wanted to practice shifting. She drove it around the yard and then up the access road and onto the highway. I figured she wanted to go through all the gears and needed to be on the highway for that."

"Did she have a backpack with her?" Renee asked.

"Yes, she had to take it off to get in the truck."

"What is going on?" Miguel asked, clearly concerned.

"We don't think she'll be coming back," I said. "She's anxious to get to Seattle and thinks we're taking too long. You've most likely lost a truck."

"Shit, I'm sorry, Miguel. I didn't know," Lucas said, appearing genuinely upset.

"Not your fault, Lucas," Renee said, her hand on his arm. "How far can she get with full tanks?"

"Each tank holds twenty-two gallons of diesel," he answered, his mouth silently moving and brow furrowed as he figured it out. "She can go roughly six hundred miles. But she doesn't know how to switch tanks. It's not automatic. You have to manually shut off the main tank and open a valve on the auxiliary tank. That second valve is not marked, and it's under the dash."

"There are two more trucks," Miguel said. "Can you get another one running?"

"Oh yeah. They'll need more work for sure, but no problem."

"Okay, then. Why don't you get started on that and let me finish up with moving these things?"

Lucas nodded and headed off to the equipment barn.

"I'm sorry, Miguel," I said, grabbing hold of one end of the mattress and helping him carry it into the bunkhouse. "We're headed to the ranch house now, and I'll let Sig know what's happened."

Done with moving the mattresses, Renee and I walked to the ranch house.

"Why would Kris leave the one weapon that could save her life?" I asked, watching Greta take point.

"She was never comfortable with it," Renee said. "She pretty much told us she would never fire it at anyone."

"At least she has the Glock. Though I have doubts about her will to use it."

"What do you think her chances are of reaching the Seattle area?"

"Zero," I answered. "Never in a million years. Even though she has her night vision, she has no way of recharging it. She'll travel during the day and attract all kinds of attention. And of course, there's the fact that she's a woman traveling alone. And an attractive woman at that. There are people out there that will do anything to take her."

"I have a hard time wrapping my head around the fact that women have suddenly become slaves or barter items," she said, grabbing my hand and holding on a little tighter than necessary. "I mean, really. Slavery ended after the civil war."

"With no law enforcement out there, it's become a free-for-all," I said. "People abruptly find themselves not having to answer to anyone for the things they do."

"Poor Kris. She just wouldn't listen to reason. At least she knows the route you planned on taking. She'll follow that. Maybe we'll catch up to her, or the truck anyway."

"She's got enough gas in the truck's main tank to get her well into Oregon. She'll follow 95 North into Oregon until she hits Burns Junction, which is where she'll need to take Highway

78 toward the town of Burns. Depending on how fast she drives, the truck is going to run dry a few miles before or after Burns."

"Are you thinking about going after her?"

With no hesitation, I answered, "No."

"Well, that was a quick answer."

"She's on her own. She made the decision to leave, and I'm not going to put myself or any of you four in danger chasing after someone who doesn't want anything to do with us. I feel for her and understand her desire to get home to her kids and husband. But there is a support group in place at her home in Seattle, and I'm sure they'd prefer she shows up alive and well rather than die trying to get home a few days or a week sooner."

We reached the ranch house front porch. Sig had woken up, and he, Melissa, and Susan were chatting away, all three sitting in porch rockers. Greta hustled up the front steps and stuck her head between Melissa's knees, looking for ear rubs.

Receiving exactly what she wanted, Greta's tail wagged away.

"I think Greta is adapting to civilian life a little too quickly," Renee observed.

"She seems to enjoy the attention," I said.

"I think she'll do her job when the need arises," Renee said.

"Hi, guys. Can we join you?" I asked.

"Of course. Pull up a chair," Sig said.

I grabbed a chair for Renee and moved it near the others. I sat down on the top step, leaned back against one of the front porch roof columns, and faced the group.

"Sorry to interrupt your conversation, guys, but we have some news to share," I said.

"Bad news, actually," Renee added.

Better to just say it right out, I thought.

"Kris has stolen the truck that Lucas got running and has taken off. We believe she's headed to Seattle."

"By herself?" Sig asked, sounding surprised.

"Yes," Renee answered.

"She'll never make it," Sig said. "After going through what we went through earlier today? Nope. And she's going to encounter those men whose trucks you destroyed—they're most likely still walking back to Battle Mountain and will be for several hours. Are you going after her?"

"No. She's on her own. And I am so sorry about the truck."

"Nonsense, Jon. It's just a truck. We have others. And for what you and your team have done for us, we owe you much more than a truck."

"Well, thank you for that, Sig. Though I still feel awful about it."

Greta made her way over to me and lay down with her head in my lap. She looked up at me with those sad eyes and then closed them once the ear rubs started up.

"You mind if we spend another night? We'll leave tomorrow once it's dark."

"Well, of course you can," Molly answered, joining us on the porch, wiping her hands on her ever-present apron. "Why don't we barbecue some ribs tonight, Sig? I'll whip together some potato salad, and I'll make those baked beans you like so much."

"Hot damn, Molly. I am one lucky fella to have you as my woman."

"What's gotten into you, Sig Alderson?" Molly said, smiling.

"It's a changed world, Molls. I saw that today and thought I should tell you how I feel."

Sig put his head back and closed his eyes. A snort soon followed, then slow easy breaths. He was asleep.

"He does that when he's content," Molly said, rubbing his head. "Or had too much Jack Daniels."

We all laughed at that. It felt good to laugh.

"Let me get started on that dinner," Molly said. "Let's plan on eating at eight?"

"Sounds terrific," we all said.

Molly disappeared inside, and I addressed Melissa. "You okay with staying another night?"

"Yep."

Kathy strode up to the porch and sat down across from me on the top step.

"Couldn't sleep?" Renee asked her.

"Nope. I kept thinking about that pile of people at the bottom of that highway embankment."

"Give it some time, Kathy," I said. "Time will slowly erase the image."

"I hope so."

"You still okay with staying another night?" I asked her.

"Yes, of course. Nothing is waiting for me in Seattle. Bradley flew to Spain two days before the pulse and won't be home anytime soon."

"I'm sorry about Bradley," Renee said. "There's always a chance he'll get home."

"He knows how to sail, so I wouldn't be surprised if he's already headed across the Atlantic. And now is the best time of year to make the voyage—the winds and currents work in favor of an east to west crossing."

"He's a sailor?" Renee asked.

"He is. And he's sailed across the Atlantic once before. There's a sailboat rally held every November that goes from Las Palmas in the Canaries to the island of St. Lucia in the Caribbean. It's called the ARC, which stands for Atlantic Rally for Cruisers."

"How cool would that be?" Susan said.

"I'd like to try that someday—sail long distance and cross an ocean. But for now, back to terra firma and land-based reality. Susan, let's take a look at that wound," I said. "You take another pill?"

"Yes, and a pain pill. I now understand the wide appeal of oxycodone."

I smiled and gently pulled the sling over her head and lowered her arm. I tried to undo the buttons on her shirt but fumbled at the attempt.

"Let me do that," Renee said, pushing me aside. "You're usually much better at unbuttoning women's clothing." She realized what she'd just said and turned beet red. "Well, you all know what I mean. Right?"

"Let's just say I'm more accustomed to having a woman undress me," Susan said.

"You're gay?" Melissa asked, sounding surprised.

"Bi, but I've been with a woman for the past two years. She left me a few weeks ago."

"Wow, the pulse must have knocked my gaydar out of whack," Renee said. "What happened? Or is that too personal of a question?"

"Time for twenty questions later," I said, quoting Sig. "Can we get serious, folks?"

Renee got Susan's shirt off and unwrapped the dressing. The wound was looking good. I'd seen quite a few gunshot wounds in my day, and this was a good stitch job. It was swollen, which was to be expected, and puckered, as it should be.

"It looks good," I said. She had quite a bit of dried blood in her hair and on her neck and shoulders. "You should have someone wash your hair and give you a sponge bath. You'll feel much better with that blood off you."

"You offering?" she asked with a seductive edge.

"He's not," Renee answered for me. "I will, though. Right here with you in that chair."

Renee went inside to heat a large pot of water and borrow shampoo from Molly.

She came back a few minutes later with the pot, shampoo, an oversized sponge that looked like it would be used on a semitruck, and a large bath towel.

"Jon, why don't you take off . . . go check and make sure our little thief didn't take anything from our trailer," Renee said.

"Isn't it a little cold to be giving her a bath out here?" I asked.

"No, it's fine," Susan answered. "Now go."

"What about Sig over there?"

Renee gave me that look, more of a stare really, that silently conveyed the universal message women send out telepathically to us mere males—quit being an idiot, you moron.

I went. Melissa walked with me and then veered off and headed toward the new bunkhouse.

Behind the equipment barn, the children had set up a makeshift soccer field using two red buckets at each end of the field as goals. They were laughing and seemed happy and acting like kids should act. I knew then that they'd be okay.

I checked our trailer, and all seemed intact with nothing missing.

I found Miguel feeding the horses and asked if he could have one of his men stand guard on the ranch house front porch for a few hours.

"No problem, Mr. Jon."

"Thank you. If you would, please have him start in an hour or so."

"Of course."

I left the barn and walked back to the new bunkhouse. I took off my vest and boots and fell into bed.

TWENTY-SEVEN

I was awakened by Renee gently pushing down on the tip of my nose.

I came awake and made a grab for her. She deftly eluded my efforts, said, "Dinner is in five minutes."

"It's eight?" I asked, incredulous. I attempted to get hold of her, but she swatted my hands away.

"You've been sleeping soundly, baby."

"Did you just call me baby?"

"That kind of slipped out. Well, you are rather cute-looking. Childlike, but with man abs. You could have graced the cover of *Men's Health* magazine with those."

"Glad you like 'em," I said, making another grab for her, which she dodged.

"Stay still," I said.

"No. We'll get to that later, mister. Now, it's time to get up. We're all waiting on you."

"Did you get the others up?"

"Yes, they're already at the ranch house."

She slipped off the bed and walked out of the room. "You're going to want to hurry up . . . We can only hold off for so long," she said over her shoulder.

I slipped on boots and vest, grabbed my rifle and thermal scope, and was sitting at the dining room table three minutes later. The table had been expanded to hold sixteen adults. The kids' table was off to the side, and they were already eating. In the middle of our table were plates of still-steaming ribs, side dishes of potato salad, coleslaw, mac and cheese, and Molly's famous baked beans.

"Glad you could join us, Jon," Sig said.

"Wouldn't miss this for the world," I answered, releasing my rifle from the sling and leaning it against the wall in the kitchen next to Renee's. "Have the rifles been made safe?" I was thinking of the children and their curiosity.

"Yes," from the adults in the room.

"Miguel, is anyone on watch?" I asked.

"Izan was up until a few minutes ago. Nobody now."

I slid my chair back and excused myself as I booted up the thermal. "I'm going to do a quick scan," I said. "I'll be right back."

I was back in my chair forty-five seconds later.

Sig clinked a spoon on his water glass. The tables fell silent.

"I'm not usually one for saying words before eating, but tonight I'm making an exception," he said. "These are exceptional times, and I never would have believed it possible to see it happen in our country. Today I saw how bad it really is: hungry and thirsty people, desperate people, kind and then mean people, heroes—he pointed to Susan—and criminal types.

"We're going to have to adapt to this new reality and must be strong and resilient. I thank God that you're here with us and ask that He watch over Jon, Renee, Melissa, Monica, and Kathy during their long journey home. Also, please watch over their friend, Kris, who is alone out there in such a dangerous world. Thank you for having Miguel, Lucas, Mateo, and Izan and their

330

families join us at the ranch. And lastly, please look after our ranch hand, Edgar, and our guest, Deputy Susan Foster, who we wish a speedy recovery. Amen."

"Well said, darling," Molly said, standing and passing one of the plates of ribs to Kathy. "Everyone, dig in before it gets cold. And take seconds and thirds. We have a lot more ribs staying warm in the oven."

It took an hour for us to finish off the ribs. Every ten minutes, I went out to the front porch and scanned the road and horizon with the thermal. The black clouds from earlier had made their way over the ranch, and intermittent rain had started to fall, although not nearly as hard as the night before.

I gazed out at the highway and thought about Kris. If she'd been driving nonstop since leaving the ranch, she should be rolling into Burns about now. *What on earth were you thinking, Kris?*

Renee and I helped clear the table and then rinsed off the plates in the kitchen sink. Greta was chomping on a meaty rib Molly had given her, but never took her eyes off Renee. Molly opened the oven and brought out three pies: apple, cherry, and Dutch apple. She asked me to go in the pantry and retrieve vanilla ice cream from one of the freezers. She then carried the pies into the dining room. Renee followed me into the pantry and grabbed paper plates for the pies. We had just turned to leave the pantry when we heard screams and shouts coming from the dining room. Greta dropped the rib and was at Renee's side within a matter of seconds, looking up at Renee and me for instructions.

"Is there anyone else here?" a male voice shouted in question.

"No, it's just us here," Melissa said. "What do the three of you want?"

Good thinking. There were three bad guys.

"What do we want? Easy. First off, I want you and you and you to take out those handguns and place them on the floor. Good, thank you. Are there any other weapons? If you say no and we search you—and we are going to search you—and find one, I will shoot one of the children for each weapon we find."

I heard three other weapons hit the floor. One of the mothers started crying.

"Thank you. Now put both hands on your head. If you all do as you're told, no one gets hurt. We're here for food. And we'll start with those three pies."

"You might have tried asking," Sig said.

"Right, and my father is the pope," the voice said.

"Not everyone is filled with malicious intent such as yourself," Molly added.

I put my finger across my lips and motioned for Renee to follow me. We crept out of the pantry, grabbed our rifles, and opened the rear door, closing it softly after Greta passed through. We stepped down into the backyard and then sprinted the thirty feet to the rear of the generator shed.

"Turn your radio to channel 28," I said, loud enough for her to hear me over the din of the running genset. We both turned our comms to 28, and I said, "Test," and she gave me a thumbs-up. "Set it on the lowest volume. Now give me a test."

"Test."

"Good."

"The one guy I heard sounded like he might be ex-military—the procedure and phrases are straight out of an armed forces textbook. They're going to search the house. They'll send one man to search upstairs and one to search the back of the house. The third will stay in place and watch his hostages.

"When the man who searches the back of the house opens the rear kitchen door, I am going to put him down. You and Greta then go inside the house and walk into the kitchen and stay there until you hear me fire. As soon as I fire, you step into the dining room, yell for everyone to get down, and locate the third shooter. If I haven't already neutralized him, you shoot. Two hands, Renee. Take your Glock out now. Finger off the trigger until you're ready to fire. Is it charged?"

"Yes," came her shaky answer.

"After I take this guy down, I'll go to the front of the house and wait for the upstairs searcher to walk back downstairs. I'll shoot through the screen door as soon as he steps off the last riser. You ready for this?" I asked.

"No."

"Good, had you said yes, I know you'd be lying. Follow me and take hold of the back of my vest so I know you're there. We have to hurry. Let's leave our rifles here."

I removed the Glock from its vest-mounted holster. We left the shelter of the generator shed, crossed the yard, and pressed against the house next to the back screen door. It would open on our side, and the plan was I would grab his weapon and pull him down . . . as quietly as possible.

I put the Glock back in its vest holster—I would need both hands in order to disable him. If this guy was any good, he would push open the screen door with his weapon's barrel and extend his arms out in a two-handed shooting grip.

I was counting on him being good.

We waited. Renee had her hand on my shoulder. I felt it shaking, and I took hold of her hand, whispered, "Easy, Renee. Breathe."

Greta, perhaps sensing Renee's unease, hugged herself tighter against Renee's left side.

Thirty seconds later, we were rewarded by the sound of heavy boots hitting the kitchen's wooden floor. The screen door slowly opened, followed by the black barrel of an automatic handgun. The gun was held in a two-handed, right-hand dominant grip. I grabbed his right wrist with my right hand and with my left twisted counterclockwise, breaking several of the carpal bones. His hand and trigger finger released the gun, which dropped to the grass. I quickly wrapped my left arm around his neck, put my right knee up on the concrete porch step, and pulled him down onto my knee, hard, knocking the wind out of him. I then flung him to the ground, flat on his back, straddling his midsection. Greta was right there with her mouth next to the guy's neck but was holding off waiting for my instructions. I wished I knew her commands. I put my left hand over his mouth and with my right slipped my Ontario Navy Knife out of its vest-mounted sheath and plunged the tip into the side of his neck, severing the carotid artery. Blood pumped out into the grass as I watched the life leave his eyes. He was in combat dress and had a desert camo service vest on. He was young, maybe twenty-five. The patch over his vest said his last name was Smith. *I'm sorry it came to this, Mr. Smith, though I doubt that is who you really are.*

"Okay, Renee," I whispered, standing. "You go in there and make some noise with your boots—the man watching our people will think it's this guy. You remember what to do?"

She was staring at the man on the ground.

"Renee?"

She took her eyes away from the dead man and looked at me. "I'm good."

I nodded, said, "Then go. And make some noise like you're searching for something." I held the door open for her, and she entered followed by Greta.

I ran along the side of the house, ducking under windows as I came upon them.

Once in front, I glanced in the brightly lit windows and saw the man on overwatch was perhaps my age and three or four inches shorter. He had a crew cut and was wearing combat fatigues. He had a service vest on like mine, with three extra thirty-round magazines for an AR, which was hanging from a two-point sling, and the handgun he was holding. He was standing with his back to the front wall. How the hell did these guys get here without me seeing them?

The children were crying, and the mothers were doing their best to settle them down. Good, the intruder wouldn't hear me. I climbed the front porch steps and pressed against the front of the house next to the window to the left of the open front door. The man was standing six inches from me—on the other side of the outside wall. I considered firing through the wall but dismissed the idea as dangerous to the others in the room. From here I didn't have a view into the dining room, but I could see the stairs through the window. I raised the Glock in a two-handed, chest-high position and waited for the upstairs searcher to come back downstairs.

"Jesus, can't you women keep those kids quiet?" the man asked.

"They are just children, sir. Please excuse them," Miguel said.

I heard upstairs man hitting the steps as he made his way downstairs. He was also wearing a plated vest carrier and had four steps to go before hitting the ranch house's main floor. I stepped in front of the screen door and, aiming for his head, fired off two rounds. At least one hit its mark, for he dropped like a sack of cement.

"Everyone, get down. Now!" Renee shouted a half second later.

The rounds going off inside the enclosed space was deafening. I shouldered my way through the screen door and into the house. For insurance, I put one more round into stair man's head before turning toward the dining room. Twisting left, I brought the Glock to bear on the third man. I watched him raise his weapon toward the seated diners and Renee. He fired off two rounds. Renee's rounds were hitting the wall all around the guy, bits and pieces of plaster flying every which way. Then his right kneecap exploded as one of Renee's rounds found its mark.

I was able to get off two rounds, the first hitting his vest and the second the exposed area on his right side where the vest's front and rear plates didn't cover. He staggered but was able to twist toward me as he was falling, letting loose several rounds in my direction. Luckily, all went high.

Greta flew through the air and latched onto his right forearm and brought him to the ground. He fell on his left side, his gun skidding across the wood floor.

"Greta, come here, girl," Renee yelled. Greta let go of the man's arm and retreated to Renee's side.

Melissa retrieved her Glock from the floor. Bringing it up into a two-handed grip, she stood, walked toward the man, and stood over him. He had one hand up waving it in front of him and was scooting back with his one good leg, saying, "Please don't. Please don't. Please don't."

Melissa looked at me, and I shook my head no. "Not in front of the children," I said.

She nodded, then lowered the gun to her side and turned back to the group, asked, "Everyone okay?"

"Melissa, check him for weapons," I said.

Too late.

The man on the floor slid his good leg up, reached down, and removed a small concealed pistol out of an ankle holster. He was raising the muzzle toward Melissa when the top of his head exploded.

I searched the room for the shooter and rested on Miguel. He stood there with his Glock. "Pendejo," he said.

"That means asshole for you non-Spanish speaking folks," Molly said, seemingly unfazed by what had just transpired in her dining room.

We all remained silent for a full minute. Smoke and the smell of gunpowder filled the air. I opened the two front windows and watched as some of the smoke was sucked out of the room. The children were crying.

"Miguel, it might be a good idea to have the children pull the collars of their T-shirts up high enough to cover their eyes and then carry or lead them out of here," Sig said, pushing back his chair and grabbing hold of his walker. "They shouldn't see the bodies."

Miguel nodded and holstered the Glock. He turned toward the children. "Quiet down now. It is all over," he said. He repeated it in Spanish. They continued crying, with their mothers doing their best to calm them down.

I hustled through the dining room into the kitchen. Renee was sitting on the floor with her back to the oven door, the empty Glock on the floor beside her. She was shaking from the adrenaline high. Greta was at her side, snuggling Renee as tight as she could.

"Are you hit?" I asked, leaning her forward and running my hands along the back of her head, vest, and legs. All clear.

"No, I'm not shot. Just scared," she said, her chest rising and falling as she took in huge gulps of air. "You should be proud of me . . . I didn't pee my pants. That was some scary shit, Master Sergeant."

"You did good, Renee. You did exactly what I asked you to do. Now take a few calming breaths."

"I emptied the Glock like you told me to. Fourteen rounds. I don't think I hit him with any of them."

"You did. In the right knee. Saved my bacon, honey."

"You called me honey," she said, looking into my eyes, doing her best to form a smile. Her breathing was slowing, and she was no longer shaking.

"Just kind of slipped out," I said, smiling back. I took her Glock, released the expended magazine, took a full one out of her vest pocket, rammed it in, and then charged it. I put the reloaded and fire-ready weapon back in her vest holster and stowed the empty magazine in the vacant slot on her vest. I gave her my hand and pulled her to a standing position.

The children had been cleared out and were on their way to the old bunkhouse.

Wasting no time, Miguel came up to me and said he was going to get the old tractor and load the three bodies into the front scoop. He would then drive them across the highway and bury them a half mile from the roadway. "There is a place I know that is very remote, and they will never be found."

We stripped the bodies of everything useful: boots, socks, pants, belts, shirts, and jackets, along with the service vests, slings, and weapons. They were soon left with nothing on but underwear. The dining room man's uniform indicated he was a first lieutenant. There were no wallets or other forms of identification, including dog tags.

Miguel brought the tractor to the ranch house back door, and we loaded back door man first, then the dining room man followed by stair man. We watched as Miguel, Mateo, and the tractor crossed the highway and disappeared into the night. It was raining, and I hoped the tractor didn't get stuck in deep mud.

Molly, Kathy, and Monica set to work picking up spent cartridges and cleaning the blood off the hardwood floors. The remaining men got down on all fours and helped finish the job.

Twenty minutes later, Sig, Molly, Izan, Lucas, Susan, and the five of us were sitting on the front porch. Lucas was using the thermal scope, which was mounted on my AR, and would stand guard until the ranch hands could organize a 24/7 watch schedule.

"Renee, why don't you go back to the bunkhouse and take it easy," I said.

"Why, what are you going to do?"

"These three were wearing clean camos, and their boots had hardly any dirt on them," I said.

"Which means they have a vehicle close by," Melissa added. "We need to find it."

"I'm going with you," Renee said, her tone leaving no question she intended on accompanying the search party. "You want to go, Greta?"

Greta thumped her tail in the affirmative.

"Okay, then. We'll all go—we need two teams anyway," I said. "We'll head up to the highway and then split into two groups: one goes north and the other south. Their vehicle has to be close by. It's probably hidden behind a hill or in a low-lying riverbed. The thermal didn't pick the vehicle up, nor the three men. But it has to be hiding out there somewhere."

"Damn, I wish I could go with you," Susan said, her voice laced with frustration.

"Why don't you stay on the porch and keep Lucas company?" I suggested. Reaching down, I took one of the recovered M4s and handed it to her. "Take this. It's fully automatic and has a full magazine."

"I can do that," she said, and with one hand, dropped the magazine, pulled the charging handle back, and visually checked the chamber. She reinserted the mag and slapped it home. "Sweet."

"Sweet?" Sig asked.

"It means nice, cool," Molly answered.

"How in the world do you know this stuff, Molls?"

"MTV," she answered, producing a chuckle from the rest of us.

"Okay, kit up, you four," I said. "Comms, weapons, and night vision. Muster here on the porch in ten. Go. Hustle."

"Renee, Greta needs to have her working vest back on."

Three women left to get ready. The fourth, Melissa, went over to the deputy, checked her bandages, and asked if she could get her anything.

"I'm good. Thanks."

Melissa put her hand on Susan's good shoulder and gave a slight squeeze. "Let me know if you need anything. Okay?"

"Yep, will do," Susan answered, putting her good hand on top of Melissa's.

Melissa nodded, turned, and bounded down the porch steps.

The women were back in seven, and we were making our way up the ranch access road a minute later. We hit the highway and split into two teams. Monica, Kathy, and Melissa went south. Renee, Greta, and I went north.

"Look for tire tracks leading off the highway. If you find it and can't get us on your comms, then one of you come find us. Don't approach on your own—there could be someone guarding it."

We'd hiked at least a mile south when Melissa's voice came over the comms. "Found it, Jon."

"Guarded?" I asked as thunder rumbled a few miles away.

"Nope. It's a super cool-looking Humvee with a funny-looking gun on the top of the roof. At least I think it's a gun."

We were there twenty minutes later. It had been driven down into a riverbed and couldn't be seen from the ranch house.

I took one look at it and was speechless.

Once I recovered, I said, "It's an up-armored Humvee, ladies. See all the additional armor over the four doors and the extra thick windows? It's basically been bulletproofed and provides extra protection if it encounters IEDs. It's also built to carry a bunch of additional weight. It's painted in desert camo, so it most likely saw action overseas. And see those two whip antennas? That means that the communication and electronics are probably still inside and might be operational." *How did this thing survive the pulse?*

"That, however, is not what makes this baby truly special," I said, climbing onto the engine hood. I reached up and unzipped the weather tarp covering the weapon. "This, ladies, is what's special. This is a General Electric M134 six-barreled Minigun. Its six barrels can spit out up to six thousand rounds a minute. And the rounds are 7.62x51 NATO, which means it can reach out and touch someone at a thousand yards out. This single weapon can easily change the course of a battle."

The women looked at me with blank stares.

"I can see this is an exciting development for you," Kathy said. "For me? Not so much."

Monica shrugged.

"I'm happy for you, Jon," Renee added. "You have a new toy to play with."

"I just want to go back to the ranch and fall asleep," Melissa said, opening the driver's door and climbing up into the seat.

"Uh-oh, where's the key?" Melissa asked. "I don't see a key. I don't even see a place to put a key."

"Military Humvees don't have a key," I said. "Any of you bring a headlamp?"

"I did," Monica said, reaching into her right-front cargo pants pocket and bringing out the light. She turned it on and set it on night-vision red.

"Shine it to the left of the steering wheel," I said. Which she did. "See this three-position switch here? You turn the switch to the start position, and a yellow light above that says "wait" will light up. That light means the glow plugs are warming up. Once the light goes out, you move the switch to "run," and the engine will start. Don't move the switch to run until that wait light goes out. Go ahead, Melissa, start it up."

She followed my instructions, and the engine started right up.

"Wow, it's really noisy," Monica shouted.

"Once the engine warms up, it will quiet down a bit. It will be somewhat quieter inside the cab," I said.

I put the weather tarp back on the Minigun and jumped to the ground.

"Fuel level?" I asked.

"Full," Melissa answered after searching the dashboard's gauges.

I walked to the Humvee's sloping rear end. This Humvee had the later-model, two-level jerry can rack that held an extra eight five-gallon cans hiding behind thick armored plates. I stood on the rear bumper and banged the Glock's butt on each tank—all full but one. I opened the rear passenger door, slid back the weather cover, and climbed up onto the turret platform and swiveled a full 360 degrees. The Minigun was loaded with a long belt feeding from an open ammo can.

I slid open the partition door, which allowed access to the storage area behind the two back seats. There were at least forty more cans of feed belts sitting in brackets welded onto the cargo area's floor. This thing was loaded for bear. Maybe we'd take it.

"Just for kicks, try the radio," I said.

Melissa turned the radio on. It powered up, but the air was full of white noise on all the channels she tried. She turned it off, grabbed hold of a microphone, pushed the transmit button, and said, "Anyone out there?"

The night was full of her voice coming from a hailing device.

"Whoops," she said.

"Melissa . . . shut it down," I said.

"Sorry. I didn't know it was a hailer. Really."

"Let's load up, guys," I said, shaking my head. "Time to head back to the ranch before it starts raining again."

Monica and Kathy sat in the rear while Melissa sat on Renee's lap in the front passenger seat. Greta sat on top of the comms center console. She seemed happy, her tail thumping, and was actively scanning the area ahead of the Humvee. It was obvious she'd done this before.

"There are racks ahead of each seat," I said. "These racks securely hold your rifle vertically and in place. Put the butt stock in the lower portion, red dot scope toward you, and then push the barrel into the top bracket." I watched as each secured their rifle.

"What's with all the electronics in here?" Renee asked. "This thing has more glowing monitors and dials and stuff than our research and development lab in Atlanta."

"Besides the radio, I know the laptop was used to communicate images and video feed from drones. It also could send and receive text messages. I'm clueless as to the other stuff in here."

It had been many years since I'd driven a Humvee, but as they say, you never forget. This baby was a newer Humvee and had power steering and power brakes. It was in all-wheel-drive high-range mode and easily traversed the riverbed. The rain had started coming down hard, and an inch or so of water was already running with us in the stream's river bottom.

I found a traversable exit point, and we effortlessly climbed the riverbank. We emerged onto the highway, and two minutes later drove down the ranch's access road. I flicked the high beams on and off in the hope that Lucas and Susan wouldn't shoot at us. They held off, and we drove to the rear of the equipment barn. Melissa slid off Renee's lap and opened the rear barn doors. I drove in and shut it down in the middle of the barn floor.

It was now a few minutes past eleven o'clock. The lights were still on, and I was guessing that Sig had left the generator on for us.

The girls and Greta headed for the bunkhouse. I made my way to the ranch house front porch, where I found Susan and Molly on watch.

"I relieved Lucas," Molly said. "Susan volunteered to fill in until Miguel comes on at midnight. Sig reset the generator timer to midnight for you."

"Please thank him for us."

"I will. Miguel and Mateo took care of that business. They've been back for a half hour or so."

"You going to be able to stay awake for another hour?" I asked, addressing my question to the deputy. "It's been a hell of a day."

"I'm doing fine. I have the thermal right here. And this puppy," she said, holding up her M4 with her good arm.

"Good enough."

"How are you holding up, Molly?" I asked. "It's not every day three men invade your home and meet their demise."

"Remarkably well, young man," she answered. "As Sig said during his speech, it's a new reality. I'm fully on board."

"Well, it appears things are in good hands."

"Best be on your way to that gal of yours," Molly said.

"You're a mind reader."

"Go get her, tiger," Susan said with a wide smile. "Lucky duck."

Renee was waiting for me in the bunkhouse.

"We have thirty minutes before the power shuts off," I said, leading her to the shower. We undressed in a hurry and were under the hot water a few seconds later. I shampooed and rinsed Renee's hair, then watched as she shaved her legs. She handed me the razor and reached behind me for a can of shaving cream. She lathered me up, hung a small mirror on the shower caddy, and then watched me shave. We were just getting in bed when the power went off.

I was on my back with Renee snuggled next to me with her head on my shoulder and her leg draped over my thighs. Greta had moved to the foot of the bed. Even though Renee had removed her working vest, she was still on guard, her eyes open and ears up, listening for threatening sounds. I patted the bed to my right, and Greta repositioned herself next to me. She closed her eyes and was instantly asleep.

"You want to talk about today?" I asked.

"I'm good. I did what had to be done. No need for further discussion."

"Okay. I'm here to listen whenever you want to talk."

"Thanks." Her body relaxed, and she was soon asleep in my arms.

I moved to get my arm free, but she gripped me tighter, and I gave up trying to extricate myself.

I fell asleep soon after.

DAY FIVE

TEST FIRE. SEATTLE?
GOLD. WARRIOR TWINS & FASHION MODELS.

TWENTY-EIGHT

Jon. Wake up. Hello, Jon," Renee whispered in my ear.

I came awake and realized there was a heavy weight on me.

"I knew that once that organ down there came awake, the rest of you would soon follow," Renee whispered in my ear, her body rising and falling on me.

"What a way to wake up," I said, running my hands over her back and butt. "You've been very horny this past week."

"Complaining?"

"Ah, that would be no."

Renee scooted up a bit and dangled her right breast over my mouth. "Quiet down, mister," she whispered. "The girls are right on the other side of the door."

We both then fully engaged in the current activity and were up and dressed thirty minutes later.

Molly had another breakfast buffet set up, and once again we overindulged. The three untouched pies from last night had been reheated and were available. I taste-tested all three. Mateo was currently on watch, and they had come up with a watch schedule that would work well.

After breakfast, Renee and the ladies headed back to the bunkhouse. I was sitting with Sig, Molly, Susan, and Miguel on the front porch. We were enjoying a cup of Molly's freshly brewed coffee. I heard children playing in the background somewhere but couldn't see them.

"Jon, Miguel tells me there is a new vehicle in our equipment barn," Sig said.

"There is. It's a Humvee. A special high-end model that was probably stolen or highjacked from a recon crew from the Hawthorne Army Depot in western Nevada."

Hawthorne was the world's largest equipment and ammunition depot. It was also where some of the more specialized weapon systems were sent for repair or decommissioning. It would make sense that this particular Humvee would be there.

"I'd like to keep it, if I may, Sig," I said. "I'm very familiar with the weapon system it's carrying, and I've fired it many times in engagements in Afghanistan."

"Please, it's yours," Sig replied. "I would think having it accompany you on your trip home would be invaluable."

"True. If it's okay with you, I'd like to drive a mile or so away from the ranch house and fire off a two- or three-second burst. I want to make sure it works. And I think the ladies might want to see exactly what it does."

"Sure, as long as I can tag along," he said. "How about you, Molls?"

"You betcha," she answered. "Sounds like fun."

I stood, said, "No time like the present, I always say. Bring ear protection, please."

"Let's roll, then," Miguel said. "Let me get one of the trucks Lucas has ready. I will take Mr. and Mrs. Sig and Miss Susan. Get the Humvee and follow me. There is a field two miles or so from the ranch house that has an old rickety shack sitting in a field. It would make a good target."

I gathered the ladies, and they once again squeezed into the tight interior of the Humvee, Greta joining us and sitting on the center comms console. Twenty minutes later, we were on a small hill overlooking Miguel's field. The shack sat in the far back, almost seven hundred yards away.

Renee was squinting in an obvious effort to bring the shack into focus. "I can hardly see it," she said. "That's seven football fields away."

"Or one long par five on top of a long par four," Monica added.

"Just fire the thing already," Melissa said.

"You sure you're okay with using that as a target, Sig?" I asked.

"Absolutely."

"Okay then. We found it ready to fire, and it's got a five-hundred-round belt in the feed chute," I explained to the assembled group of spectators. "It's already fed into the delinker, and I've checked the clutch, chambers, and barrels. It's good to go. I'll fire quick bursts, one to two seconds each. I'll let the barrels completely stop before firing off another burst. You'll soon understand why short bursts are effective."

The weapon was electrically operated, and I turned the Humvee's engine on to produce the electrical juice necessary to run the gun.

"Everyone put your ear protection on," I instructed, and watched to make sure they'd all complied. "Firing in five seconds."

I flipped the red safety cover open and toggled the power switch to the on position, which produced a green light. I grabbed a firing handle with each hand and sighted in the wooden shack.

"Firing!" I shouted.

I lowered the barrels and with my right thumb depressed the rubber-tipped trigger button. The gun fired and sounded like a buzzsaw as almost one hundred rounds fired off in less than one second. Tracer rounds were bright and helped me direct my aim. Spent casings dropped to the gun's left, bounced off the Humvee's roof, and formed a messy pile on the ground.

I immediately released the trigger, though the barrels continued to rotate as they slowed to a stop. Once the barrels had fully stopped, I depressed the trigger again, and the buzzing noise was back and then ceased a second later once I released the trigger. I fired once more, this time letting the gun fire until it was empty.

We all watched as the front porch roof collapsed onto the porch deck. A few seconds later, the entire shack started to tilt to the right and then toppled over. Some of the tracer bullets must have hit metal inside the structure, for smoke was soon pouring out of the collapsed ruins.

The deputy was the first to speak. "Wow, fuckin' A!" she yelled out. "I've seen YouTube videos of a Minigun firing, but in person? Un-fucking-believable!"

We all stared at her, and she soon realized that her language might have been a tad bit enthusiastic for some of the assembled audience. "Ah, sorry, about the four-letter words, Mr. and Mrs. Alderson."

"Well, shit, sweetheart, you're talking to a ranch wife," Molly said. "Fuck, shit, damn, and asshole are pretty much common everyday words on this ranch."

"Well, Molls might be overstating the spoken frequency of those words somewhat," Sig added with a chuckle. "Miguel, can you take us back to the ranch house? I need to rest a bit."

"You want us to put out that fire?" I asked.

"No need. The rain will take care of that," Miguel said.

"I now understand why you were so excited to see this last night," Renee said as we watched the other spectators return to the ranch house.

"I have some news to share with you. We're taking this vehicle with us," I announced. "We'll need to split up, but we'll stick close together on the road. We'll disconnect brake lights and whatnot, but that shouldn't be an issue. This can also tow our trailer and not even know it's connected."

Blank stares and shrugs greeted my news.

By now I could tell when something was ready to hit me. "What is it?"

"The four of us were talking this morning, and we'd like to discuss something with you," Kathy said, her demeanor becoming serious.

I was reloading a fresh belt into the Minigun's feed chute. I pushed up on the belt until it was able to stay in place on its own accord.

"Sure, what's up?" I said, physically rotating the barrels and listening for the loud clicks as the first few rounds filled the chambers. I pulled the pin, and the clutch engaged. The weapon was now ready to fire with a flick of the switch.

"We, the four of us, feel that with Kris no longer with us, we really don't need to head to Seattle," Monica answered.

That statement got my attention. I locked the barrels, spit on them, which produced no spit dance, indicating they weren't hot. I threw the weather cover on the gun and jumped to the ground. "Really?"

"Really," Melissa repeated. "I don't need to go back. I have no one waiting for me—human, cat, or dog—that will miss me. Other than a high school girlfriend I was staying with in Seattle, I have no real friends there—and she flew to Hawaii the day before the pulse hit. So I have no one there I could hang with— survive with. So, if you and your family will have me, I'd like to go with you to your ranch in Montana. I could be a valuable—"

"Say no more, Melissa," I said, interrupting her. "You don't need to convince me of anything. You're more than welcome. Monica and Kathy, you're sure about this?"

"Bradley is in Spain," Kathy replied. "My husband is very resourceful, but there's no way he's getting across the Atlantic Ocean, then across the country to Seattle, anytime soon. Like Melissa, we have no pets or family in Seattle. There are families in the neighborhood I could band together with, but honestly, I would prefer to stick with you guys. I just need to figure out how to let him know where I end up."

"We'll find a way, Kathy. Monica?" I asked.

"My loser ex-husband is shacking up with his twenty-two-year-old assistant. He even absconded with our dog. My closest family are cousins in Portland that I haven't seen in fifteen years. So, I really would like to stay with you. You sure your parents will be okay with us showing up?"

"Absolutely," I said. "One hundred percent sure. My mother is going to love having you all there."

All four ladies were looking at me as if there was something else to discuss.

"There's more, isn't there? What is it?"

The women were looking at each other as if deciding who would begin.

"Just spit it out," I said.

"Susan would like to join us," Renee said.

"Really?"

"Yes. Really," Renee said. "And please don't answer with 'really?' again."

"But she's recovering from a serious wound and surgery," I said, ignoring Renee's dig. "How is she going to get better if we're constantly on the road?"

"What's the difference between sitting in a porch rocker and sitting in a car seat?" Melissa said. "Huh?"

"I can make sure she gets her meds, and I can remove her stitches when the time comes," Kathy added.

"I'll think about it. But don't hold your breath."

"Come on, Jon. Now that you're bringing your new toy along with us, we're going to need another person." This from Renee, who was beginning to sound bossy.

"She can't move that well, and in a firefight, she'll be vulnerable. I'll be worrying about her during the entire confrontation, and I can't worry about her and what we're dealing with at the same time."

"Then we'll put her in the Humvee," Renee said. "According to you, bullets can't penetrate it. You said that, right?"

Shit! Renee was light-years ahead of me in the "makes sense" department.

"I did, but . . ."

"But what? She'll be encased in armor. What are you going to come up with next, mister?" Renee said, hands on her hips and daring me with a death-ray stare.

"I want her to come! I like her, and she likes me," Melissa blurted out, her face and ears turning beet red.

And once again I was caught off guard.

"Like . . . as in *like* like?" I asked her.

"Yes. Like in we care for each other, *like* like."

"When did this happen? This morning? I didn't know you were gay."

"Since yesterday. And I'm bi."

"Really?" I said, staring at Renee.

"Jesus, Jon. Just say yes already," Renee said forcefully, leaving no doubt about how I was to answer.

This was not something I should have to consider. She was wounded, weak, and . . . Well, I couldn't come up with anything else. So, when in doubt, shut up.

I said nothing.

"Well?" Renee asked, after letting the silence go on long enough.

"I don't like it. But in the interest of maintaining group harmony . . . okay."

"Thank you," Melissa said, letting out a big breath. "Make sure she's ready to go tonight," I said. "We leave after dark."

We crammed into the Humvee and headed back to the bunkhouse. I had Melissa drive for a mile, and then Kathy brought us back to the ranch house. Neither had issues and would have no problem driving either the Humvee or the Cruiser.

THE REST OF THE DAY was filled with preparations for our after-dark departure. The electronics were charged, gas and water tanks checked and filled, clothes washed, and weapons cleaned and checked.

Susan was excited to be joining us. She and Melissa had spent most of the day getting Susan's belongings together and organized. Condensing her stuff into her backpack was no easy feat, but by the end of the day, it was task accomplished.

Except for her own personal M4, Glock, and the specialized shotgun, the rest of her weapons and their respective ammo and magazines were staying at the ranch. I conducted a shooting class for the adults, including Molly, who swore she would never be without one of Susan's donated Glocks. Sig even sat in on the class and shot off several AR, shotgun, and Glock rounds. "Like riding a bike, you never forget," he said.

Miguel and the men had come up with a 24/7 watch schedule that would work well—they had decided to post a man up on the hill on the other side of the highway opposite the ranch. From that vantage point, they'd be able to see the highway, both north and south, for miles in each direction, but also the ranch and the area surrounding it. If they saw something fishy, they'd fire off three rounds.

I unhitched our trailer from the Cruiser and hooked it to the rear of the newly acquired vehicle. I would be the lead-off driver in the Humvee. Renee and Susan would ride with me, while Melissa would be at the wheel of the Cruiser, with Monica and Kathy as passengers.

By four o'clock, we had the equipment checked and loaded. The weapons were ready, the comms and night vision charged and in the vehicles. Molly had announced that we would enjoy another steak and potatoes dinner that would be served at seven o'clock. "Promptly, please," she'd added.

I'd informed Sig that Deputy Susan had asked to join us on our journey. He said he understood, and even more so once he learned of the budding relationship between the two women.

"It's hard enough in good times to find someone special, so when times are bad, you've got to grasp it and hold it tight," he said. Sig, the new Dear Abby of the apocalypse.

There was one last issue that needed to be settled, and I gathered the women around the bunkhouse dining table.

"We need to figure out a route," I began. "Originally, we were going to Battle Mountain, west on Interstate 80 to Winnemucca, then north on Highway 95 into Oregon. From there straight up 95 through Idaho and into Washington, where we'd hit 90 West into Seattle.

"Now that we're not headed to Seattle, we could go east on 80 to Elko, then head north on 93 into Idaho and through Sun Valley. Then continue north on 93 up to Missoula, Montana. From there, we're pretty much home."

"What's to discuss?" Kathy said. "We go the alternate route, of course."

"Well, we could, but—"

"No buts, that's the route we should take," Monica said, interrupting me.

"But," I repeated, looking at each of the women to see if they'd butt in again, "we would not be following the route that Kris likely took. Or at least part of the route."

That last statement was met with only silence.

"Who gives a shit what route the stinker took," Monica said, breaking the uneasy silence.

"I do," I said. "The route is basically the same distance as the alternate, but going the original route, we run into far fewer population centers. So, it's much safer."

Melissa held her hand up, said, "I vote for the original route. You had me at safer. And as much as I detest the bitch, she was part of us and deserves us at least keeping a look out for her along the way."

"I know I'm a new member of the gang," Susan said, "but I'm all for safer, too."

"Kathy?"

"Okay, you convinced me. Original route."

"Renee?"

"Original route."

"Monica?"

"Same distance—good. Safer—even better. I'll go along. Although I couldn't care less if we come across Kris."

"Good, it's settled, then," I said, standing and heading out the door to do one last check on our two vehicles in the equipment barn.

Checks complete, I headed back to the bunkhouse intending to take a quick nap.

I opened the door to our room and stepped inside. Renee was standing naked holding up the top sheet to the bed. Greta, vest off, was sleeping on a blanket in the corner of the room.

"What's up?" I said, admiring the view.

"You're really asking me that?"

"Well, I . . ."

"Seriously? I'm standing here naked, trying to look seductive and making my boobs bounce around the way I know you like. Hello?"

"Oh," I managed to say.

"You good now?"

"You know something?" I said, releasing my rifle and then my vest. I took my boots and socks off and then my shirt and T-shirt until I was standing naked in front of her. "I think you're only interested in me as a tool for your own sexual gratification."

"Well duh," she said, patting the bed with her free hand.

"That and the fact that this could be the last bed that cushions the pushin' for quite some time," Monica said through the door, laughing. "Thin walls, guys."

TWENTY-NINE

I helped Sig and Miguel get the grill going and the potatoes wrapped in tinfoil. Once that was done, Sig motioned for me to follow him as he made his way to a room in the very rear of the home. Opening the door, he waved me through and then closed the door behind us.

This looked to be the ranch office. A large, dark wooden desk sat in the middle of the room. It had a thick glass top and was lit by one of those old-fashioned brass lamps with a green glass shade that the old-time movies always used in a scene that had a dude with a visor hitting a telegraph key or making entries in old-fashioned ledger books. Dark mahogany bookshelves lined three of the walls. A floor-to-ceiling window with a sliding door leading to an outdoor wooden deck comprised the fourth. A freestanding safe with a spinning dial was against the wall on our left and sat in a space outlined by bookshelves.

Sig spun the dial combination and opened the safe. Glancing inside, I could see a couple dozen smaller-sized ammo cans neatly stacked. He pointed to the top can in the front row and asked me to remove it from the safe. I grabbed hold of both handles and lifted. Or at least tried to.

"This is heavier than any ammo can I've ever carried, Sig. It's got to weigh at least eighty pounds." I adjusted my stance, and with some difficulty, managed to place it on the desk. Sig had a smile on his face as he watched me struggle with it.

"Grab another one, please," Sig said.

Once I had the second ammo can on the desk, he said, "Those are for you. For all the help you've so generously given us. Go ahead, open them."

I released the snap-down levers and opened the lids. Inside each were four brick-sized gold bars. Each bar was imprinted with the letters BMG.

"The BMG stands for Battle Mountain Gold," Sid explained. "Each bar weighs roughly twenty-seven pounds, for a total of one hundred and eight pounds in each can."

"Sig, this isn't necessary. We were happy to help."

"Nonsense. Without your help, this ranch would have died. Without your help, we would most likely be dead at the hands of those three men. This is the least we can do. Molly and I are just so grateful."

"Sig, this is much too much . . ." I began to say.

"Look in the safe and tell me how many ammo cans like the ones I gave you remain."

I looked and counted. "Twenty-eight."

"Plus, two more safes just like this one in our secure food room next to the equipment barn. Both full."

"That's a lot of gold, Sig. That mine must be a very productive one."

"My father insisted that the mine owners pay their royalties in gold bars. The purchase price was in currency, as it should be, but the quarterly royalty has always been paid in gold."

"I don't know what to say other than thank you. It's incredibly kind of you."

He shut and locked the safe, said, "Best put that in the Humvee where it will be safe. That much gold could someday fund a large army. And from what you've told me about the Chinese, you're probably going to need it.

"As of last week, with the price of gold at a post-pandemic high of thirty-two hundred dollars an ounce, those eight bars were worth a little more than eleven million dollars. In six months, it will be worth a thousand times that much, maybe more. And if you need more, let us know and it's yours."

I didn't know what to say. I was stunned into silence.

"Does your father have a blacksmith on staff at the ranch?" he asked.

"Not on staff, but there is a blacksmith who lives down the road from us. He has a full shop on his property. Why?"

"You'll probably want to break down those large bars into smaller bars, like one ounce or so."

"Like this?" I said, taking one of the one-ounce American Eagles out of my pocket.

"Yes, just like that."

"Does Miguel know about the gold?"

"Yes, Miguel picks it up from the mine office and brings it to the ranch."

"Can I ask him to help me carry them to the Humvee?"

"Of course."

"Before I do that, is there anything you need help with before we leave tonight?"

He remained silent.

"There is, isn't there? Sig, what is it?"

Before he could answer, there was a soft knock on the door, and Molly stuck her head in. Sig waved her in. She closed the door behind her and sat in the chair next to mine.

"I see Sig gave you our thank-you gift," she said, pointing to the ammo cans.

"Yes, and like I told Sig, it's totally unnecessary. But thank you. We'll put it to good use. I promise."

Molly stood and leaned down and gave me a hug. "From the bottom of our hearts, thank you, Jon."

"Molls . . ." Sig started to say.

"Have you asked him yet, Sig?" Molly asked.

"Getting to it, Molls."

"He finds it difficult to impossible to ask for help," Molly explained. "He is usually the one being asked to help."

"Molls, they really need to be on their—" Sig again started to say but was cut off by Molly.

"We wondered if after dinner you could drive Sig to the next ranch over and check and make sure they're okay," she said. "Erik and Carleigh Ericson are our very dear friends and closest neighbors. They live nine miles south of here, and we haven't seen or heard from them since the blackout."

"Molls, really . . ."

"No problem at all," I answered. "We'll take the Humvee."

Sig must have been holding his breath, for he let out a lungful of air. "Thanks. We've been worried. They have horses, and I know they would have come to check on us . . . but haven't."

"Thank you, Jon," Molly said, standing up and giving me another motherly hug. "Let me get the steaks ready for the grill. You still up for grilling them, hon?"

"You bet, Molls."

She nodded, turned, and left the room.

"Can you ask Miguel to help me carry these?" I asked.

WITH MIGUEL'S HELP, WE LOADED the ammo cans into the Humvee. We put them under the front passenger seat, securing them in place with bungee cords we found in the barn. We unhooked the trailer and left it in place to be hooked up later.

Finished freeing the trailer, we hoofed it back to the ranch house.

"Sig and Molly have asked us to check on their neighbors before we leave," I said. "Do you know the Ericsons?"

"I do. They are the same age as the Aldersons. They do not have ranch hands; instead, two sons and a daughter work the ranch. They are farmers more than ranchers, as most of the land is devoted to raising crops and is irrigated. They work closely with the NDA, the Nevada Department of Agriculture. They are a very modern operation, and all their equipment is new and state of the art. There is talk in town that their business is only still going because of the NDA funding they receive for conducting experimental growing tests."

"Does Lucas have another pickup working?"

"Yes, he now has two running."

"Would you mind if you and someone else follow us out to the Ericsons?" I asked. "I'd feel better with some backup."

"Of course. And I am sure Mr. Sig will give permission for us to accompany you."

"Please bring weapons. An AR and handgun for each of you."

"Si, señor. We will do that."

We enjoyed a wonderful dinner of steak and baked potatoes. It was a quiet affair, as the children were eating hot dogs in the bunkhouse dining room, supervised by Lucas' girlfriend, Samantha. Lucas was on overwatch on the hill across the highway from the ranch. Having someone on overwatch with the ability to see for miles in every direction was a great idea and created a much safer environment where we felt we could relax with our guard down.

Greta, smart dog that she was, sat at Renee's side after a futile attempt at receiving scraps from me. She was rewarded by a steady stream of fatty steak that Renee refused to eat.

"You'll regret that later, Renee, when she starts farting that fat."

Renee looked at me, then at Greta munching away on a piece of fat, said, "Damn. No more fat for you, young lady."

Greta's tail stopped its wagging, and her ears flattened. She whined, looked at me with her sad eyes, flicked her tail once, then lay down and stared at me.

"I think Greta is unhappy with me," I said, determined to win the staring contest.

"Seriously, you're having a staring contest with a dog?" Renee asked.

Giving up the contest, I grabbed a nice chunk of fat off my plate and held it out to Greta as a peace offering.

Greta sat up, looked at Renee, who nodded, then gently took the piece of fat from my fingers and woofed it down in one piece. She looked at me for more, but I shook my head.

I told the team that we had one more task to complete before heading out. Melissa would accompany Sig and me in the Humvee, while the three others would wait for us in the equipment barn, ready to help hook up the trailer to the Humvee as soon as we drove in the door. We'd head out soon after.

After dinner, Miguel and Mateo left to weapon up and bring one of the working pickups to the ranch house. Melissa and I walked to the equipment barn, and with Melissa driving, brought the Humvee to the ranch house front steps. We loaded Sig up, stowed his walker in back, and waited for Miguel and Mateo to fall in behind us.

They showed up a couple of minutes later. With lights out and Miguel hugging our rear bumper, we drove up the drive and turned right on the highway. It was a clear moonless night, and the NVs easily reached their maximum range.

We were there ten minutes later. Like Sig's place, the ranch house was situated a half mile west of the highway and accessed via a long, downward-sloping asphalt drive.

We drove down the drive and stopped twenty yards from the darkened house. I helped Sig out of the rear passenger seat and set up his walker. He started shuffling his way toward the house with me following close behind. As we got closer, I could see flickering candlelight through the windows.

We were fifteen feet from the porch when the front door opened and four people stepped out.

"Four people on the porch, Sig," I said, leaning in and whispering in his ear. "Three women and one man."

"Stacey. Frank. Is that you?" Sig yelled.

"Yes. It's Stacey and my husband, Carter, along with Jim's wife, Elinore, and Frank's wife, Carla. Frank and Jim Jr. are in the equipment barn trying to get one of the old tractors working. Is that by chance Mr. Alderson?"

"It is. I'm here with Miguel and Mateo, along with some friends of ours. I'm here to check on your parents. Is everything okay, Stacey?"

Stacey and her husband stepped off the porch and walked up to Sig. I still had the NVs on, and I could see that Stacey was in her midforties, had thinning shoulder-length hair, was about five-six or seven, and very overweight. She was wearing farmer overalls, and the front strained with her bulk. She had two chins, and the loose, hanging skin shook and wiggled with every step she took. Her husband, Carter, also in his midforties, was tall, rail thin, and bald. Sig extended his hand to Carter, and they shook. Sig then moved the walker aside and hugged Stacey.

Stacey had tears in her eyes. "Dad passed last night, Mr. Alderson," she said. "His pacemaker stopped working the day the power went out. He struggled without it until his heart just could no longer work on its own."

"I'm so sorry, Stacey. I had a feeling something was wrong when he didn't show up at our place. Where's your mother?"

"She's inside laying down. We had six armed visitors during the third day of the blackout, and she was pistol-whipped when she tried to stop them from stealing our horses and tack. We think she may have suffered a concussion."

"Ah jeez, I'm sorry to hear that. Let's get her loaded into the pickup, and we'll take her to the hospital. There's still staff working."

"Thank you. Thank you."

"We'll bring her out," Elinore said. "Give us a few minutes." She and Carla turned and disappeared into the house.

"I know Erik has plenty of weapons. You weren't able to fight them off?" Sig asked. "I'm not judging, Stacey, just curious."

"The gun safe has an electronic keypad, and like everything else electronic, fried in the blackout. We're unable to open it," she explained. "All those rifles and handguns . . . useless."

"Did you recognize any of the intruders?"

"Jim Jr. thinks one of them might be a hand at the Fitzhugh's place."

"Horses branded?"

"Yes."

"We'll keep a lookout. We plan on visiting all the local ranches sometime this week. Your generator not working?" Sig asked.

"Dad replaced it a couple of years ago with a fancy computer-controlled unit, and of course, it's fried. Jim Jr. found the old one and is trying to get it hooked up and working again. Lucky for us, it runs on propane, and we have plenty of that. We're farmers and have some mechanical skills, but fixing a sixty-year-old tractor and generator is clearly beyond our ability."

"Lucas, one of our ranch hands, is a mechanic and has gotten three of our old trucks running again. I'll send him over later tonight. If anyone can get the tractor and generator going again, it's him. In fact, I bet he'll be able to get that safe open. He had me buy a fancy-dancy welder that also cuts through steel. It just might do the trick."

"That would be awesome," she replied. "We have plenty of food if you need any. You know Dad and Mom were always stockpiling food and supplies. The smaller barn is filled to the rafters, literally, with rice, beans, flour, freeze-dried food, and every other thing one needs to not only survive but live well, as Father always said."

"We're good. But thanks for the offer," Sig said. "I don't see any of your children, Stacey," he continued. "I know you kids all had kids of your own."

"All five were on a school field trip to the Hoover Dam. They left the night before the blackout. A bunch of kids from Battle Mountain went."

"Oh boy. But I'm sure they'll make it home—they're ranch kids and are smart and tough."

"Your friends military?" Carter asked. His question, while innocent enough, carried with it a little something more than idle curiosity.

"Ex-military," Sig answered.

"That Humvee and the weapon sitting on top is not civilian."

"No, it's not, and I'll be happy to tell you all about it later. But not now."

"Whatever, Carter," Stacey said, clearly irritated with him. "You have any idea what's happened with the power, Mr. Alderson?"

"I'll fill you in on what we know, but why don't we have Jim Jr. and Frank hear the news too."

"Miguel, can you please honk the horn a couple of times?" Stacey asked. "They'll hear it and will be up in just a minute or two."

Miguel honked the pickup's horn, and sure enough, the two men came around the ranch house two minutes later. Through the NVs I could see that one was carrying a metal baseball bat and the other an extra-long crowbar.

The two men came up and stood next to Stacey. "You won't be needing those, guys," Stacey said. "Sig Alderson is here, along with Miguel and Mateo and a couple of others. Mr. Alderson is going to take Mom to the hospital and has offered to have his mechanic come over and help you guys get the tractor and generator running."

Jim Jr. was a stocky guy, five-ten, two hundred pounds, arms bulging out of a dirty T-shirt—the guy could probably lift a hay bale over his head with each hand. Frank was shorter but just as stocky and powerful-looking, with short-cropped hair cut in a military-style crew cut. He wore a well-worn pair of combat fatigues and a long-sleeved T-shirt sporting the Grateful Dead logo.

"Boys," Sig said in greeting.

"Mr. Alderson," Jim Jr. replied. "Nice to see you, sir. How is Mrs. Alderson?"

"She is doing remarkably well. Thank you. Sorry to learn the news of your parents," Sig said. "It's a terrible time, and only to get worse, I'm afraid."

Sig told them what he knew, and I watched as they digested the news.

"Mom will be stressed knowing all that, and I think we'll keep that news from her a bit longer," Jim Jr. said. "Dad, on the other hand, would have been curious and prepared for what could come."

Just then, my comms came alive. "Jon?"

"Go ahead, Renee."

"Susan's doctor is here."

"Bernard?" I asked, surprised.

"I believe that's the name he gave. He'd like to see you."

"On our way. ETA fifteen minutes," I said. "Don't let him leave. We're bringing Mrs. Ericson over for him to check out."

"What's wrong with her?" the doctor asked, speaking right into Renee's mic.

"She was pistol-whipped, and the family thinks she may have suffered a concussion."

"Bring her on over. Now, please," he said.

"Roger that."

"The doctor says to tell the Ericsons that he and some other folks will be out to see them tomorrow afternoon," Renee said.

"You hear that, ma'am?" I asked Stacey.

"Yes, thanks."

"Sig," I said. "Let's get her loaded into the back seat of the pickup. Otherwise, it appears things are settled here, and our presence isn't needed. I'd like to get going."

"Stacey, I apologize," Sig said, pointing to me. "This is Jon Kristen, and the lady sitting in the Humvee is Melissa. Jon comes from a well-known ranching family up in Montana. I've known his parents for many years."

Jim Jr., Frank, and Carter disappeared into the house and reappeared with Carleigh Ericson a minute later. They carried her across the porch, down the steps, and gently laid her across the rear seat of the crew cab. They then climbed up into the truck bed, waiting on Miguel and Mateo.

"I would suggest that perhaps Stacey might accompany Carleigh," Sig said. "Someone should stay and watch the property."

"Get your butt down here, Carter," Stacey said, pointing to the ground. "Stay here and watch the place." She opened the passenger rear door and gently lifted her mother's head, slid in herself, and rested her mother's head in her lap. She watched her husband jump to the ground. "And try and stay awake."

"I'm ready to go now, Jon. Thank you." Sig made his way toward the Humvee. He opened the rear door, turned to the ranch truck, said, "Stacey, I'll talk to Lucas, and if he's willing, he'll come tonight. He's been on watch since midafternoon, and he may be tired. If he doesn't show up tonight, he'll be here in the morning."

"Thank you, sir. God bless you."

"THE DEPUTY'S WOUND IS HEALING nicely, but she should remain here at the ranch a few more days," Bernard said. "Riding in a vehicle and camping out in the desert or mountains isn't the same as resting in a front porch rocker."

"Not gonna happen, Doc," Susan replied, addressing the doctor but also the rest of us. "We're leaving in a few minutes."

We'd been back at Sig's place for the better part of an hour, and we were anxious to get going. It was now quarter to nine, and our goal was to leave at nine. We'd topped off the Humvee's gas tank and hooked up the trailer. We'd checked comms, weapons, night vision, and the thermal scope. We were just waiting on Susan.

Doc Williams had been driven to the ranch by two armed escorts in the panel van found at the hospital.

Mrs. Ericson had been checked out by Doc Williams and judged well enough to recover at home.

"I cleaned and sutured the laceration on her head with ten dissolving sutures. She didn't suffer a concussion, which is very good news."

Seeing the look of dismay on his audience's faces, he said, "I can tell you're all thinking she appears to be in pretty bad shape, but she's eighty-five, for fuck's sake. She's going to recover a lot slower than someone half her age. However, she's going to be just fine, I assure you."

Miguel had then driven the Ericsons back to their ranch. Lucas followed a few minutes later in the second truck with his tools and welding machine. We'd hugged and said our goodbyes to Miguel and Lucas before they left.

We were now on the front porch, listening to Bernard report the latest news from town.

"Battle Mountain has formed a council that will devote itself to two topics: food production and security. There will be committees under the council that will plan and put into effect those plans," Bernard explained. "They'll start small, securing the town boundaries and gathering and protecting the existing food stores. Then work out from there to the ranches, like Sig and Molly's here, the Ericsons' farm, and others even further out."

"Are you securing the roadways into town with barricades?" I asked, scratching behind Greta's ears.

"Already done. They've got all lanes of Interstate 80 blocked a quarter mile out of town on both west and east sides. Each has ten armed men manning them 24/7 and led by someone with military experience."

"Which committee are you heading?" Sig asked. "Animal control?"

"That's very funny, you senile degenerate," Bernard replied, a wide grin on his face.

"Thank you, Bernie. I have full confidence that you'll do a fine job as the town's dog catcher."

"I'm heading a committee tasked with keepin' the hospital organized and running," he said.

"Let me know how we can help, Bernard. Anything you need, just ask," Molly said, giving Sig a disapproving look.

"Thank you, Molly, we'll keep that in mind."

"Oh my gosh," Molly said, bringing her hand to the side of her head. "Bernard, I forgot to ask after Lilian. How did her surgery go in Winnemucca?"

"It went well. Thanks for asking. She's resting back at our hospital."

"I saw hundreds of stranded travelers in town yesterday. What are you going to do with them?" Melissa asked. "How can you feed them?"

"They're going to be given some food and water and told to leave by noon tomorrow. Battle Mountain will be taking care of its own. Non-residents will no longer be welcome."

"Harsh but understandable," I said. "Can I make one suggestion?"

"Of course."

"Question those folks you plan on sending on their way. There may be physicians, nurses, or other medical professionals among them that would be a valuable addition to your community. Others may be teachers, engineers, current or ex-military . . . you get the picture. Life may be better here than where they're from. Ask the same question to those that approach your barricades."

"Great idea. I'll pass that along and make sure your idea is implemented."

"You said you wanted to see me, Bernard?" I asked.

"The town tasked me with the job of asking you for a favor," he said. "Our security committee has set up ten two-man teams patrolling the town boundary on horseback. Two men have family in Winnemucca and would like to go and help organize the same type of patrol there."

"And?" I said, waving my hands in an effort to get him to hurry up.

"I'm getting there, buddy. Don't go waving your hands at me like you're swatting away a hovering bug."

"Sorry, go ahead."

"The town of Battle Mountain would be most appreciative if you could tow a two-horse trailer to a ranch outside Winnemucca. The ranch is north of town right on the route you'll most likely be taking."

"Okay, we can do that. As long as we don't have to go into the town itself. And I don't want to venture too far off the highway."

"They tell me the ranch is less than a mile off Highway 95."

"And where in Battle Mountain are the horses and trailer located?" I asked.

"Just a mile or so north of West Second Street."

"That's up by Mateo and Izan's trailer park," Sig pointed out.

"Sig, you told us that there was a way back to the ranch from there that wouldn't require having to drive through town. If that's the case, then we'll pull your horses for you."

"The route will require driving west on Interstate 80 to the first exit, then backtracking a few miles on surface streets, but there's nothing out there," Sig said.

"What about the barricades the town has put up?" Renee asked. "Are those going to be an issue for us?"

"Those are in place less than a quarter mile from the interchange by the high school and won't come into play, as they're only interested in those coming into town, not going out," Bernard answered her. "I'll go with you and show the way. The panel van will follow and pick me up."

"The panel van doesn't have a trailer hitch?" I asked.

"Nope," he answered. "They tried to jerry-rig one on, but the bumper and frame is not set up to securely tow anything."

We spent a few minutes going over the route, and it was soon time to head out.

I gave Sig and Molly hugs, thanked them and wished them well. Molly handed Renee a grocery bag full of turkey and ham sandwiches, along with a full bag of potato chips. "For the road. Please take care of yourselves and give a big hug to your parents for us, Jon."

"Will do, Molly. I hope to someday make my way back here and say hello."

With formal goodbyes made, I gathered the ladies in front of the Humvee for a last-minute briefing.

"Lights out. NVs on. Comms on. See something, say something. We stop, and you get out and form a perimeter watch. Keep your weapons on your body, charged but with safeties on. Melissa, stay a hundred feet behind the Humvee. That should give you plenty of time to react to me slowing down. Susan, you don't have an NV set, but you're not moving from that vehicle unless we stop for a break. You keep your rifle in the rack and the Glock handy. But we don't expect you to join in any kind of action."

"Shucks, you're treating me like Deputy Bernie Fife, Sheriff Taylor. You going to take the bullets out of my weapons for my own safety?"

"I'd laugh, but I'm trying to be serious here," I responded. "Besides, it's Barney Fife, not Bernie."

"Gotcha, sorry. Golly gee, sir, are you sure it's Barney?"

"It's Barney, Gomer," Renee said, settling the matter. "Gomer, as in Gomer Pyle USMC?"

"Never heard of it," Susan said.

"She's too young to know that show, Renee," Monica pointed out.

"I know the show. And it's not worth remembering. You ready to go?" I asked Susan.

"Yes," she answered, standing and hugging Molly and then Sig. "Thank you for everything. I hope all goes well for you here on the ranch. Stay safe."

Melissa, Kathy, and Monica piled into the Cruiser. Renee and Susan crammed in the rear passenger seats in the Humvee with Bernard riding shotgun.

"You two stay well back from the Land Cruiser," I said to the two escorts, who said they would. "You see anything, hit your headlights twice, and we'll stop."

I opened the driver's door, patted the seat, and watched Greta jump up and sit herself on the comms center console as if she'd done it a thousand times before—and maybe she had.

The mothers and children had gathered on the front lawn and waved goodbye as our small convoy moved out. Sig had even walked out to the turnaround under his own power. He stood there and waved as each vehicle drove by.

"I'm going to miss him," Renee said.

"Me too," I said, giving the assembled folks a quick toot of the horn.

"Not me. Miss him, I mean," Bernard said. "Nah, I don't mean that. I love him like a son would his father . . . although I'll deny I ever said it."

We reached the highway, and before turning left and heading toward Battle Mountain, I flashed the headlights up toward the hilltop lookout. I was rewarded with two quick flashlight beams from Izan.

I kept our speed at forty. Our convoy was spread out over a quarter mile, which was the spatial distance we tried to maintain in Afghanistan while on motorized patrol.

We passed by the two burned-out hulks the Barrett had destroyed. Smoke was still rising from both vehicles. Seeing the damage up close really hit home just how powerful a weapon the Barrett could be.

"That your handiwork?" Bernard asked as we passed the still-smoldering wrecks.

"Yes."

"How about the three dead bodies and one barely alive, all from a truck rollover two days ago?"

"Indirectly. But yes."

"I was there, and in both cases, they had it coming," Susan said, defending me.

"I can't argue with you on that, Deputy," he said, "but I had to deal with the lone survivor, and it wasn't pretty."

"Next time don't treat a scumbag," Renee said. "Why waste valuable meds and supplies on a useless piece of shit?"

She had a good point, and there was nothing more to be said on the subject. Or so I thought.

"I can't do that," Bernard said some minutes later. "Hippocratic Oath and all that. Besides, after tomorrow, there won't be a scumbag to be found in Battle Mountain."

"True that," Susan said.

Twenty-five minutes later, we drove past the Nevada Highway Patrol office. It was dark, and I saw no one in the building or parking lot. Three minutes later, we passed under the Interstate 80 overpass and turned left onto the west-bound on-ramp. I glanced at the high school parking lot and could see dozens of people still milling about.

"They do know that Highway 305 is going to be very active in the next few days, right?" I asked.

"What do you mean?" Bernard asked, sounding truly puzzled.

"Folks streaming up from Vegas will hit here soon. You need to block the highway, perhaps even as far back as the Alderson or Ericson ranch. But for now, they can just walk into town," I explained.

"I don't know what the security committee has planned, although that is one large issue that I'm sure someone must have raised. Regardless, I'll bring it up in our next meeting."

Once on the freeway, I saw the barricades ahead and stopped twenty yards back. Bernard got out and walked toward the tractor trailers that had been pulled into place by an old John Deere farm tractor. The NVs showed ten armed men: six manning the barricade itself and two positioned ten yards forward on the left side and two twenty yards up on the right side . . . both forming a chute of sorts to corral any walkers or still-working vehicles. Someone knew what they were doing, as this was how we set up checkpoints overseas. They obviously hadn't heard or seen us approach, because the man that Bernard spoke to jumped a foot off the ground in surprise and put both his hands on his chest and mouthed what could only be "You scared the crap out of me."

After a brief discussion, the tractor started up, and sixty seconds later our convoy was passing through the gap created for us. Bernard pointed to the Allen Road off-ramp a mile up. We exited onto Allen Road, then backtracked slowly east on deserted surface streets. We passed a boarded-up Shell gas station and a looted Westward Ho restaurant. He had us turn left toward a ranch house that was lit up like a Christmas tree. We pulled around the house to the rear equipment yard, where a two-horse trailer was waiting. The horses were tied to the trailer's rear bumper with saddles and tack already loaded into the trailer's storage locker. At least two dozen large bags of alfalfa and orchard grass pellets were waiting to be loaded.

I stepped out of the Humvee and could hear a small gasoline-powered generator straining to keep power flowing to the house. There was also a vintage portable record player playing Led Zeppelin's "Stairway to Heaven" on the highest volume level.

The ladies formed a defensive perimeter around the two vehicles. Bernard strode over to the record player and after several attempts at turning the volume down finally unplugged the thing.

"I didn't know that I missed music until I heard that playing," Melissa said. "I wish we had music to listen to."

"Ask me tomorrow," I said, raising an eyebrow.

"What's with the eyebrow raise?"

I just smiled at her. I had a small portable Bluetooth speaker and an old iPhone in the faraday bag up in the Thule cargo carrier. The phone served as backup for all my music.

Melissa backed the Cruiser up to the horse trailer, and two men got it connected to the Cruiser's hitch. Twin brothers, Tom and Brent Carlisle, both in full battle gear and with AK-47s over their shoulders, loaded up the horses and put several camo duffel bags alongside the saddles in the storage locker.

The brothers turned out to be identical twins. They were in their late twenties, tall, thin, almost emaciated thin, but had the hardened good-looking work-related toughness that no gym workout could provide. They both had crew cuts that any US Marine would have been proud to sport. They looked like active-duty soldiers except for their beards, which extended at least ten inches below their chin lines. Brent had braided his beard, and it sported red and yellow beads every few inches. They were both kitted out in desert camos, chest rigs, but non-armored models, and both had black semiautomatics in thigh holsters.

They worked silently as an efficient team.

Lightning showed itself off to the west, and during the next strike, the sky lit up like day. For just a second, we could see black storm clouds on the horizon.

"That don't look good," one of the brothers said.

"We'll be headin' right into that shit, dude," the other pointed out. "Gonna scare the horses somethin' fierce."

"Looks to be right over 80," Bernard said. "Maybe ten or twenty miles from here. It's cold enough that you might hit some snow or sleet."

"Fine by me," I said. "It means less people on the road."

"I'll ride with the horses," Tom said. "It should help greatly."

"As long as one of you rides up front with us," Renee said. "To show the way to the drop-off point in Winnemucca."

They took one look at Renee and me, and Tom whistled. "Holy shit, Brent, will you look at how they're set up?"

"Indeed. Impressive it is," Brent answered, speaking like Yoda from Star Wars.

"Is that a Minigun on top there?" Tom asked, pointing to the Humvee.

"It is," I answered.

"Holy shit. Active-duty military, you folks?" Brent asked.

"Former. Army Special Forces."

"Then how did you come in possession of this Humvee and its weapon system?" Tom asked as he helped his brother load the feed bags into the right-side storage locker. "I know military Humvees can be purchased at surplus auctions, but I know for a fact that Miniguns are not on the program."

"Three scumbags staged a home invasion of Sig and Molly Alderson's place a couple of days ago," Susan said, looking directly at Bernard. Getting no response from Williams, she continued on. "They picked the wrong house and are now providing much needed fertilizer to a small patch of desert."

"Would've liked to have helped in the dispatching part of things," Tom said.

"We believe the three 'dispatched' somehow took the Humvee from the original crew," I explained. "Or perhaps stole it from the Hawthorne Army Depot in western Nevada."

"I've driven by that place. It's huge . . . goes on for miles," Tom said.

"I understand how your Cruiser escaped the effects of the blast, but what about the Humvee? Why do you think it's still running?"

"Best guess is it was in a protected shelter," I answered, "like a giant faraday cage or building."

"Hawthorne would certainly have one on base . . . protect the more sensitive and expensive pieces of hardware," Tom said.

"Okay, guys, get a move on," Bernard said. "These fine folks need to get going. Finish your loading."

"We have two armed riders on horseback approaching from the road," Monica announced over the comms. "Looks like rifles lying across their laps."

"That's gotta be our neighbors, Toni and Paulette Johnson," Tom said, closing the trailer storage locker door and securing it shut. "They're part of the boundary patrol."

"They're cool," Bernard said. "Nice girls. Daddy's the second-richest man in northern Nevada . . . after Sig, of course. From mining and ranching. Owns most of the commercial buildings in town."

"Those two are nice but can turn nasty and mean as a tick on an old dog if you rile 'em up," Tom pointed out. "That's why they're on boundary patrol—they'll shoot your ass and not think twice about it." He said it with a certain amount of respect.

"Okay, good references. Let them continue on through," I said into the comm's mic.

"Do you have a bathroom in the house I could use?" Renee asked the twins.

"Yes, ma'am. Straight in and to your right. The toilet's tank is fed by the well, and you can flush it and everythin'," Tom said.

"Greta, come with me," Renee commanded. She held open the porch screen door and with hand signals indicated she wanted Greta to search the house. Which she did, coming back a minute later and sitting next to Renee, indicating all clear with two tail thumps.

"Guard, Greta," Renee said, shutting the screen door and disappearing into the house. Greta sat in front of the door, facing out, and you'd have to be a fool to try to pass her.

"One smart animal, she is," Brent pointed out.

"That she is," I answered.

"Former military, too?" Tom asked.

I nodded. "By chance, you guys happen to have any spare dog food?"

"We do," Tom answered. "In the garage. We had to put our dog down a couple of months back. Cancer of the intestines.

377

Only four years old. Stupid cancer. Let me get it for you. A couple of big bags we got at Costco in Reno."

"Hello, girls," Bernard said as the riders came to a stop next to the Humvee.

"Evening, all," they said in unison.

The two were in their late teens or early twenties. Both had long blond hair cascading from under Stetson hats—one black and the other a darker tan with a red feather sticking out of the side. Both were slender and wore worn black leather chaps over blue jeans. Both had black North Face puffy jackets on. Well-worn cowboy boots completed the outfits. They were strikingly beautiful and could have been models from any New York or Paris fashion house . . . runway models loaded for bear. Both women had belt holsters holding what looked to be black semiauto handguns.

Tom came out of the garage with a large bag of dog food under each arm. "Hello, Paulette, Toni," he shyly stuttered out, obviously smitten with the two.

"Tommy, how are you?" Toni asked, flipping her hair from one side of her head to the other. After living with two sisters, I'd learned that hair flipping is often used by females to subconsciously inform the male of a certain amount of interest from said female.

"Doing well. Leaving for Mucca," he said, slipping the bags of dog food under the trailer's tarp. He grabbed the record player and stuffed it in the horse trailer's left-side storage locker.

"I heard. You take care of yourselves over there and come home in one piece."

"I will. I'm sorry all this happened before you two could return to UNLV," Tommy said.

"Oh well," Paulette answered with a shrug. "Shit happens and you make the best of it."

"It's going to be storming soon," Toni said, pointing over her shoulder. "Don't think we can make it back to our place before it opens up. Mind if we take shelter in your stable until it passes?"

"Of course. Let me get the door opened for you."

"Thank you, Tommy," they answered in unison, both dismounting and guiding their horses to the stables. They'd slung their rifles over their shoulders, and if a photographer took a picture just then, it could have been used as an ad for Colt firearms.

"You have enough ammo?" Tommy asked as he slid open the stable door.

"We do," Paulette answered, patting her saddlebag. "You know how our dad is with guns and such. He loaded up with tens of thousands of rounds while Trump was president. He says he's lived through too many anti-gun administrations and couldn't count on a steady ammo supply."

"Speaking of your dad," Bernard said, "how's the new asthma drug working for him?"

"Really well, Doc," Toni answered. "I haven't heard him wheeze or cough in weeks."

"That's wonderful news. Please tell him I've got a two-year supply I'm saving for him. Have him stop by and pick it up. Got it in my office at the hospital."

A loud thunderclap sounded right overhead, and sure enough, raindrops started falling.

The horses whinnied and snorted but didn't pull on their leads.

I keyed the comms, said, "Let's go. Load up. Tom, do you have stable blankets for the horses? It's only going to be getting colder."

"Good idea. We have several," he answered, turning off the generator. The house and grounds turned dark. Tom produced a flashlight and used it to grab the blankets from the tack room.

Tom gave the two girls a hug, and I could see him turn red in the face after Toni gave him an extra-long, full-body hug. *Good for him*, I thought. Brent simply waved and then jammed himself into the Humvee's driver's side rear seat.

"You're not locking the house?" I asked.

"Nah, Dad will be home shortly. He's on patrol and due back soon," Tom replied, securing the blankets over the two horses. "Everyone knows not to fool around or otherwise touch this place."

Tom slowly walked up the ramp, and I closed it behind him. I watched as he made his way to the front of the trailer, sat on a bale of hay, and started soothing the two horses with soft whispers. I latched the ramp in place and then turned and gave Bernard a quick hug.

"Thanks for everything, Bernard. If things get bad here in Battle Mountain, you've got a place to escape to up in Montana. Sig and Molly have directions to our ranch. There's plenty of room for you and Lilian."

"Well, you never know, I just may take you up on that offer someday." He opened the Humvee's driver's door and spoke to Susan in the back seat. "Listen here, young lady, you do a lot of sittin' and sleepin', not a lot of movin', shootin', or rock n' rollin'. Understand me? That is one serious wound, and I've done my magic to it, so don't go fucking it up. Hear me, Deputy?"

"I do, Doc. Thank you."

"Okay, then," he said, backing up so I could hop in.

I moved the switch to start and waited for the wait button to go out. The light went out, and I started the engine. I keyed the comms and asked for a comms check. One by one the women checked in. All except the deputy. "Susan?" I asked, turning in my seat to look at her in the back seat.

"Oh yeah, sorry. I hear you. Ten-four and over and out." She then gave me the finger but delivered it with a smile.

"No smart-asses allowed in this vehicle," I said in as serious a voice as I was able to muster while at the same time laughing.

I watched as Bernard and his two escorts drove down the ranch's access road and turned left toward town. Toni and Paulette waved as we drove by the stable. Toni stepped out into the rain and slapped the side of the horse trailer. "You come back in one piece, Tommy Carlisle," she yelled. "I'll be waiting."

THIRTY

It was raining cats and dogs as we navigated our way along surface streets headed toward Interstate 80 West. Sleet replaced rain as the Humvee merged onto the interstate's slow lane. I brought the Humvee up to thirty and left it there, giving Melissa a chance to get used to driving the Cruiser in less-than-ideal conditions.

After covering fifteen miles, I saw no stragglers walking the highway and figured we wouldn't need to be scanning ahead with the thermal. It was bitterly cold, and if there were survivors out here, they'd be sheltering in abandoned semitrucks or cars, not exposing themselves to freezing rain. We were now depending solely on our NVs.

Interstate 80 was the major east-west highway in the country, and one would expect to see heavy traffic at all hours of the day. And true it was . . . we encountered dozens and dozens, perhaps even hundreds, of dead semitrucks and passenger cars, mile after mile of them. On the steeper descents, most had managed to pull over to the shoulder, but on uphill sections, they'd probably tried to get over, but their forward momentum had waned quickly, and they'd stopped in the lane they'd occupied when the pulse hit.

We wove our way from lane to lane, dodging semitrucks and passenger cars alike. None of the semitrucks' trailers had been opened, and I could only imagine the supplies each held.

"Brent, you've got to get a group organized soon, like tomorrow morning soon, and get these trailers opened and, if useful items are found, emptied," I said. "You wait for any period of time, and someone is going to beat you to it."

"Put together scouting group we will," he replied.

"You have a way of communicating with Battle Mountain?" I asked him.

"There is a vehicle that does a daily round trip. I'll make sure the word gets back to Battle Mountain to start opening trailers for look-sees."

"And suggest to the city leaders that they roundup as many running vehicles as they can find," Susan said. "They're going to need capacity in order to empty those trailers."

We soon passed the small town of Valmy, which looked to consist of only a motel, a café, a closed-up gas station, and a large trailer park. The town was dark, but I did see a few folks huddled under the roof covering the gas station's single pump island.

Five miles up, I spotted an eastbound rest area. The NVs clearly showed three or four dozen folks taking shelter under the eaves of the restroom building's roof. There were more folks crowding the entrance to both the men's and women's bathrooms, and I could only imagine how many stranded motorists were in the restrooms themselves. I knew they couldn't see us through the darkness and falling sleet, but they must have heard us, for most turned and looked toward the interstate.

I keyed the comms. "Melissa, how are you doing back there?" I asked.

"So far, so good," she responded. "There are more vehicles than I thought there'd be."

"Just take it easy with the weaving. You've got that horse trailer behind you, and if you turn too fast, it's going to whip around on you."

"Roger that. Smooth is the word."

"Gosh, I like that woman," Susan said after hearing Melissa's answer. "She's the smooth one." She must have realized she'd said it aloud, for she said, "Sorry, it slipped out."

"Why are you sorry? Statement of truth is all it is," Renee said, putting her at ease.

"You like girls?" Brent asked, sounding surprised.

"I do. But I also like men," she answered. "A lot."

"Cool, I think it is," he responded.

"Why do you talk like a character out of Star Wars?" Susan asked.

"When I concentrate on it, I can avoid doing it. But it's hard sometimes. When we were kids, my parents watched all the Star Wars movies, like, constantly—were huge fans. Day after day, month after month, year after year, it was Star Wars this and Star Wars that.

"They went to conventions. With us in tow, of course. They even dressed us up as Ewoks. I mean, how cruel is that? I put up with that shit until I moved out of the house at seventeen. Tommy managed for another month or two and then moved in with me. We finished high school and then both enlisted in the Air Force and ended up as PJs. We did two tours in Afghanistan together."

PJs, or Pararescuemen, was an elite Air Force unit tasked with recovery and medical treatment of personnel in both combat and humanitarian environments. If you were a pilot and your plane was downed, you were going to be rescued and brought home by these guys. They were the Air Force's equivalent of the Army's Special Forces or the Navy's SEALs.

"I'm impressed," I said, and meant it. "I met some of you guys at Bagram in Afghanistan. Way before your time, of course. But heck, they were a bunch of true tough guys."

"We were. Tommy and I were the ones they sent into caves and small, narrow canyons. We liked the canyons but hated the caves. Sometimes they wouldn't even send dogs into the caves," he said, pointing to Greta.

He didn't say anything else, and the two women wisely remained silent.

We continued northwest at a fairly decent clip. I lost count of how many abandoned trucks and cars we passed, but it had to be in the hundreds. The weather had turned even nastier, snow now mixed with sleet. But we couldn't have been graced with better conditions, as there was no one out and about—my biggest fear running into large bands of stranded motorists blocking our way.

We were on an interstate, and as such, the roadway was as level as the best civil and highway engineers could construct it. Uphill ascents were gradual with dedicated truck lanes on most of the steeper sections.

A road sign indicated that the Golconda Summit was six miles ahead. We soon started a gradual climb up to 5,100 feet. As we gained elevation, the snow started to really fall, and I reduced speed to twenty. Then to ten. I was now driving in the middle of the roadway, as there were no longer any lane markers visible due to accumulated snow.

The NVs were becoming useless, as the snowflakes were magnified as they flew toward us. I found that if I kept my gaze at about forty-five degrees, somewhere between the middle of the roadway and the shoulder, I was able to see the snowplow guideposts and keep driving in the middle of the roadway.

"Jon, we're starting to lose traction," Melissa said over the comms. "We need to drop it into four-wheel drive."

"Okay. Slowing." I let off the gas, and the Humvee quickly lost forward momentum on the uphill slope. We came to a stop a few seconds later.

I keyed the comms, asked, "You remember how to do it?"

"Yep, give me a minute."

"Roger that," I answered, stepping out into the cold. "Anyone need a break?" I asked. "I'll stand overwatch if you do. That way we don't have to set up a perimeter watch. We have Molly's sandwiches if anyone's hungry."

There were no takers.

"Too cold out there to pee," Renee stated, rubbing behind Greta's right ear.

"What about you, girl?" I asked, speaking to Greta. She looked at me, thumped her tail once, and turned her attention back to Renee and her ear rubbing.

I walked to the back of the horse trailer. Tom was sitting on a hay bale between the two horses and was stroking them under their chins. "You okay back here?" I asked.

"Fine. No problems. Why are we stopped?"

"Dropping it in four-wheel drive."

"Ah, thought I felt us losing traction. It's snowing hard," he said, glancing behind me at the snow falling. "Looks like we might have the makings of a good-sized blizzard."

"Could be. Get you anything? We have sandwiches." He shook his head and gave me a thumbs-up.

"Okay, let's roll," I announced in the comms.

We got back up to speed, and Melissa was able to stick with us. There wasn't another four-by-four that could match the Land Cruiser when it was in four-wheel drive.

The snow was falling hard, and it soon became more like a blizzard than a simple snowstorm. If we didn't have the NVs, which allowed us to see the orange snowplow guide markers sticking out of the snow and outlining the shoulder, we would have had to stop.

"It's like something out of a psychedelic acid trip," Renee said, watching the huge snowflakes flying at us from out of the dark. "Or what I'm guessing it would be like."

"It's pretty trippy, that's for sure," Susan added.

The roadway leveled out, and I figured we ware passing over the summit.

385

"Melissa, we're now headed downhill, and it could get dicey," I said. "You have experience driving in the snow?"

"No, I'm a Southern California surfer chick . . . not a Colorado snow bunny."

"Okay, quick lesson. Keep it in third gear—you're in high range, and you're not going to accidentally gain speed. Once you're up to speed, slowly ease up the pressure on the accelerator pedal and leave it alone. With four-wheel drive, you'll be fine. I won't be applying brakes, so you won't be needing yours. Hard braking is a bad thing in the snow."

"Okay. Got it."

"I'm going to stay at twenty, regardless if we're running up, down, or on level ground."

We made good progress, though at one point, near an approach to a bridge, semitrucks blocked all three lanes. We had to crawl onto the median and make our way around them. The Humvee pulled itself through two-foot drifts without issue, but the Cruiser, with the added weight of the fully loaded horse trailer, had a harder time of it, finally breaking through and back onto the pavement. We were quickly up to speed again and encountered no more obstacles.

We were now driving through the Humboldt River Valley. The snow was still falling but nothing like it had been up on the summit. I brought us up to twenty-five. A few minutes later, we passed another rest stop, this one on our side of the interstate. Through the NVs I could see unnatural-looking lumps in the rest stop's parking lot. Lots of lumps.

"Slowing and stopping, Melissa," I said. "Form a close-in perimeter, please. Safeties off and weapons chambered. Set to three-round bursts. I see something I don't like the looks of."

We came to a stop. The ladies formed a perimeter around both vehicles. Brent joined in and took a knee as well.

I strode back to the horse trailer and told Tom what was up. He offered to help, and I nodded. I helped him over the ramp, and he shouldered his AK as we made our way from the freeway to the rest stop some one hundred yards away.

"I don't like this, Master Sergeant," he said.

"The NVs don't show anything."

"Don't mean nothin'," he said. "Might be waitin' behind the building there."

"Then let's keep away from the building."

"Spoken like a true master sergeant."

Keeping an eye on the building, I stopped at the first of many lumps in the snow. Keeping the M4 to my shoulder and pointed at the building, I took a knee and with my free hand dusted snow off the lump. And as I expected, it was a body. This one was a young girl. She had one bullet hole in her right ear, blond hair plastered with frozen blood. Her hair had been braided with peace symbols and snoopy hairpins. Executed, from the look of it. I didn't want to know if she'd been sexually assaulted. I stood and told Tom what I'd found.

"Same here," Tom said quietly, kneeling over another body. "This is a woman, maybe in her midthirties. Stripped of all outer clothing. Bullet in the head."

There were at least another seven or eight bodies lying under a foot of freshly fallen snow.

I didn't want to just walk away from this without checking the rest of the rest area's grounds first. "Watch my six, Tom."

"Roger that," he replied, following me as I walked up to the bathroom building. I opened the men's room door and glanced inside. Nothing. Next was the ladies' room, and it, too, was empty. At the rear of the rest stop property, I spotted a sixties-era Dodge Ram four-by-four pickup with a newish-looking Northern Lite slide-in camper sitting on the bed. It was parked by itself at the farthest reaches of the lot. Plastered over the rear of the camper were dozens of peace signs and national park decals, which told the tale of a well-traveled family.

A faint light flickered through the curtains. It was a candle.

I held up my fist, and Tom stopped with his hand on my shoulder, letting me know he was right there with me.

"There's a candle burning in the camper," I whispered.

"I see it. You think they might be the ones who did all this?"

"Probably. And I have a certain history with bad guys and recreational vehicles."

"You should let me and Brent handle this. This is what we did for several years, and we're very good at it, Master Sergeant."

"Wouldn't send someone to do something I wouldn't do myself."

Tom nodded, and we had just started walking toward the camper when a shot rang out, muffled somewhat by the falling snow. Then came a burst of what was unmistakably an AK firing as fast as a finger could pull the trigger—Brent.

"Shooter down," Monica reported.

I keyed the comms, said, "Stay where you are, everyone. We'll be there soon."

"If there's anyone in that camper, then they'll be poppin' out of that door any second," Tom said.

We quickly separated and both took a knee. We brought our weapons up and waited for the camper's rear door to open. Which it did, five seconds later.

Three people—two men, one older, the other much younger, and a woman—all armed, piled out of the camper. All three were running toward the rest stop's front parking lot.

"Freeze," I shouted.

Caught by surprise, the two men dropped to the ground. One of the men managed to fire off one errant round before both were silenced with several rounds to the head and shoulders. Seeing both men hit with such deadly accuracy, the woman ran directly at us, screaming just about every obscenity I'd ever heard. She was waving a large handgun but not firing.

"Should I shoo—" Tom began to ask.

I fired a single burst to her chest, and she dropped face down in the snow.

"Shoot her? Question answered. She must have been high on some kind of drug to run toward us like that," Tom said, standing and then walking over to the woman. He leaned down and felt for a pulse. "She's gone."

I keyed the comms, asked, "Everyone okay?"

"We're okay," Melissa replied a few seconds later.

"We need to clear that camper," Tom pointed out.

I opened the door and stepped aside as Tom stuck his rifle in the door. "Clear," he said.

The interior was illuminated by a single burning white candle. The candle was one of those short, thick jobs that usually has a Christmas wreath wrapped around it. A propane space heater was cranking away, and it was warm and cozy inside the small space. Both the heater and candle were sitting on a small, L-shaped dining table.

"This is a sweet setup," Tom said, taking in the dinette table, queen-sized bed over the truck cab, stove/oven combination, mini-fridge, and kitchen sink. He opened a door, and there was a toilet and shower stall. "All the comforts of home."

"You want to take it?" I asked. "You guys need a ride, and here it is. Even comes with a place to live. There's a chrome decal by the door that says it's a 4-Season model."

"Keys are in the ignition," he said, glancing through the slide-through window into the truck's cab. "See if it starts."

I walked around to the driver's door and climbed behind the wheel. I put the stick shift into neutral and turned the key. The engine caught, and a deep rumble came from the diesel engine. "The gas gauge reads almost full."

"And it's a diesel," he added. "Can pull an Abrams with this thing."

I glanced up and wished I hadn't, for there was a photo of the young girl in the parking lot taped to the sun visor. I don't know why, but I reached up and took the photo and stuck it in my jacket pocket. I said nothing to Tom about the truck's occupant.

I shut the engine off and walked back to the rear of the camper. Tom blew out the candle, then turned off the heater. "Bonus. It has a trailer hitch," he said, pointing to the rear bumper.

We walked back to the group waiting for us on the interstate. The snow was coming down harder, and at least an inch had accumulated on the Cruiser's roof since we stopped.

There was a bright red trail of blood from where Brent had dragged a young man from the interstate median. He was sitting upright against the Cruiser's driver's side front tire. He had been hit in the chest and arm and was barely conscious. Red bubbles were forming on his lips.

"What are we going to do with him?" Monica asked.

"You know what has to be done," I said. "He's not going to last long, and we're not bringing him with us."

I took out my Glock and told the women to get back in their respective overwatch positions if they didn't want to watch. Monica, Renee, and Kathy left, leaving Susan and Melissa. Tom and Brent were watching with interest.

I squatted in front of the dying kid. "Why did you kill them?" I wasn't a hundred percent sure he'd been part of killing those people, but the chances were good he was.

"For their stuff," he said.

"And the young girl?"

"Mom said she would take up too much space in the camper."

I nodded and stood up.

"I'm really cold. Am I dying?" he asked, his eyes watching me stand.

I didn't want the bullet to go through him and hit the Cruiser's tire, so I put my foot on his shoulder and pushed him over onto his right side. I put a single round into his exposed temple. He slowly melted into the snowy slush on the roadway.

"Couldn't do that in Afghanistan," Brent said, changing his magazine with a fully loaded one.

"Disgusting fucking asshole," Susan said.

"Seems like there are lots of assholes out in the world now," Melissa said, stripping the puffy down jacket off the body. "I'm sure we'll come across someone that could use this."

"There was never a shortage of assholes to begin with," Tom said. "They just never had a free pass before. Let me show you what we found, brother," Tom said, waving for Brent to follow him across the highway and onto the rest stop property.

"What did you find?" Melissa asked me.

"A working pickup with a nice camper on the back," I answered.

"They taking it?" Susan asked.

"They should. If they don't, we will."

I grabbed the kid's shirt and pulled him off the roadway and back onto the center median.

"And there it is," I said a few minutes later, watching the truck appear out of the darkness and park behind the horse trailer.

Leaving the engine running, Tom hopped out of the driver's door. "We're keepin' it. No sense in leavin' it just sittin' there," he said. "Brent will follow us in the Ram, and I'll ride with you. The horses are fine on their own. And we gathered up their weapons and jackets. Here are their coats. Can we keep the weapons?"

"Sure. Let's get a move on," I said. "It'll take too long to disconnect the trailer from the Cruiser and then hook it up to the Ram. Let's just get to Winnemucca." I'd forgotten something important. "Sorry. Give me five minutes, everyone." I hustled over to the young man we'd shot. I wrote on his forehead "Killer of Innocents" in permanent marker. I crossed the freeway and did the same thing with the woman. I had to write on the two men's thighs, as their foreheads were pretty much missing.

I stood, turned, and bumped into Brent.

"Jeez, Brent! How'd you sneak up behind me without me hearing you? Transporter or something?"

"Years of practice, I've had."

He looked behind me and nodded in understanding. "Tommy asked me to watch your six."

"Well, thank you."

"No problem. Happy to help. And I agree with what you're doing to the corpses . . . writing on them, I mean."

"I feel it's the right thing to do," I said.

"If you'd done that in Afghanistan, you'd be in the brig so fast your head would have spun."

"Well, good thing we're not in Afghanistan. No West Point kiss-ass ordering us to do what the books tell him to do."

"Hooah," he said, thumping his chest once with his fist.

"Let's go," I said, fist-bumping him.

We loaded up and got a move on. The snow let up as we got closer to Winnemucca. The NVs became useful again, and I brought the Humvee up to thirty-five. We still had to weave our way through stalled semitrucks and passenger cars, but they were further apart, and there was no need to slow down. Greta kept watch from the center console, then managed to wiggle her way onto Renee's lap.

"I will never get over seeing what one human being is capable of doing to another," Renee said, rubbing behind Greta's ears. "I mean, why kill all those people?"

"Simple, really," Tom replied. "Just like the kid said, 'For their stuff.' I've done a lot of readin' up on EMPs and their likely aftermath, and we're just experiencin' the very beginnings of what is goin' to be years of terrible times. You think this is bad, wait three months—hundreds of thousands, maybe even millions, dead from starvation, disease, or at the hands of other humans. Then think a year out. Those that survive that long are goin' to be the ruthless, cunning, loner killer types."

"Or part of a larger group that has banded together to survive," Susan said. "We're headed up to a ranch in Montana, and we'll be part of an existing family group that will work as a unit for the good of the ranch and community."

"That almost sounds like you read that from a pamphlet or somethin'," Tom said. "Meanin' no disrespect."

"None taken," she replied, laughing. "It did sound a little stiff," Renee said.

"A community you're both welcome to join," I said. "Bernard will have directions to the ranch. It's outside of Whitefish, Montana. Just show up and use my name. We could use a couple of experienced warriors such as yourselves. Though promise you'll ask Bernard if he wants to come with you, and if he says yes, then give him a ride. And I promise you no caves."

"We can do that. Thank you. If we fail at keepin' Mucca and Battle Mountain safe, we'll head on up there."

The snow had lightened, and the NVs were now working at their full potential. I could see warehouse buildings on both sides of the freeway. There were more dead cars and trucks, and we had to slow to fifteen to safely make our way between them.

We passed under a freeway overpass that had a sign reading Next Exit Nevada Highway 289—Humboldt County Fairgrounds.

"You're going to turn off at the next exit," Tom said. "And go right at the intersection."

"Will do," I said, moving over to the right lane. I watched in the side-view mirrors as the two vehicles behind followed suit. "I'm surprised the town hasn't set up roadblocks on the interstate yet."

"They're settin' 'em up tomorrow. The first one is goin' to be at the next exit up at West Winnemucca Blvd. There's a Walmart Supercenter, Costco, and a bunch of motels and such up there that they want to protect."

I exited the freeway at the next off-ramp and turned right at the intersection.

"This is Highway 289," Tom said, leaning up from the back seat. "We'll take this about three miles up and turn left on Reinhart, which is Highway 795."

Three miles later, I turned left on 795, and we followed the road with ranchettes on both sides of the highway. It may have been below freezing outside, with sleet and snow still falling, but I saw several homeowners out walking their property. Two who were walking their dog close to the road turned toward the sound our small convoy was making and waved as we drove by. Melissa returned the wave with a quick toot of the Cruiser's horn.

"It's nice to know that there are still good people out there," Renee said.

"You mean folks that would rather shake your hand and say howdy than stick a knife in your eye?" Susan asked.

"Yeah, like that."

"Folks who work the land, I think, tend to be more tolerant of others," Tom said.

"I'm tolerant of everyone as long as they don't point a gun at me," Susan said.

Five miles further on, Tom had me take a left on East National Avenue, and then a half mile up another left onto a gravel drive. From behind a tree, two men stepped out and signaled us to slow and stop. One man walked by the Humvee, stopped at the camper and had words with Brent at the Dodge's driver's window. The guard then reversed his directions and waved the procession forward.

The road ended a half mile further on at a large, solid-looking ranch house. "Does it sit on a river?" Renee asked.

"It does," Tom answered. "That's the Humboldt River. This place is my grandfather's. He bought it right after World War II. He started with a thousand acres, and it now has a bit more than four thousand. It used to be even larger, but he sold off most of the riverfront property on the east bank to help pay the fuckin' taxes. Guess we don't have to worry about that anymore."

"The one good thing from all this, I suppose," I said.

"Go ahead and drive 'round back, and we'll unhook the trailer," Tom instructed.

I did as I was told and pulled far enough forward so that Melissa would have room to maneuver. I cut the engine and climbed out. I keyed the comms and told everyone we wouldn't be here long and to just hang tight inside the two vehicles.

Greta looked at me and gave me a quiet whine, which I knew meant she needed a bathroom break. "Okay, girl. Go for it," I said.

She bounded across the driver's seat, to the floorboard, and then to the ground. She circled the Humvee, came back to the original landing spot, circled in place, squatted, and finally peed. Finished, she jumped back up and took her spot on the center console.

A high-revving engine started from somewhere next to the house, and a floodlight came on, illuminating the entire equipment yard. An elderly man walked out of the house and onto the raised rear porch. He was dressed in flannel pajama bottoms and a long-sleeve T-shirt with a picture of Elvis in his famous sequined white jumper on the front. He had fleece slippers on his feet and in his left hand carried a very large revolver, maybe a .44 Magnum Dirty Harry model. With his right, he shielded his eyes from the glare of the overhead spotlight.

"Boys, I cleared out two stalls for you," he said. "There's feed and water already in the stalls, so just unload and stable them. I'll keep the generator on for another half hour, which should be enough time for you to take care of things."

"Thanks, Gramps," Tom said.

"You're welcome. Whose camper is that?"

"We came across it at the westbound rest stop in Humboldt Valley. The owners had been killed by four fellow travelers. We righted the wrong and couldn't see a reason to leave a perfectly running vehicle just sitting there for the taking."

"I don't see anything wrong with what you did, son. And the world has four less assholes in it. A win-win any way you look at it."

Brent unhitched the horse trailer from the Cruiser while Tommy lowered the ramp. "Grandpa. This here is Jon Kristen. He towed the trailer from Battle Mountain for us. Jon, this is our grandfather, Charles Carlisle."

"Call me Charley, and nice to meet you, son."

Charles Carlisle was in his late eighties to early nineties. He was tall, maybe even a bit taller than me. And thin like his grandsons, but unlike them, he was clean-shaven. He had a full head of silver hair and appeared to be a dead ringer for the actor Dick Van Dyke.

"Likewise, sir," I replied, walking to the rear of the Cruiser and checking to make sure the hitch was sorted out. "Beautiful place you have, Charley. At least the parts I can see."

"Thank you. It's been a labor of love. Where you headed?"

"Montana."

"Your last name is Kristen? Any relation to Neil Kristen of Whitefish?"

"He's my father, sir."

"Well, I'll be damned. I've known your dad since the eighties. We served together on a couple of cattlemen association boards. How is your mother . . . Andrea, right?"

"Yep, that's her name. She was fine the last time I saw her, which was a few days before the power went out."

"You want to talk to your parents? I have an old ham radio that works. Does your dad still have his set?"

"He does. And it's a pre–World War II model, so it should work. And the ranch has power."

"Well, heck, invite your fellow travelers in for some hot cocoa, and we'll try and contact him."

I keyed the comms, said, "We're taking a short break here, ladies. Mr. Carlisle has offered to try and reach my father via ham radio. He's invited you all up for hot chocolate. One of you needs to provide overwatch—you decide who."

"No need for that, Jon. You saw the two ranch hands up on the main road. They'll keep an eye out and let us know if we need to tend to something."

"We always have an overwatch when we travel, Charley. Okay if the dog comes in? She's a military dog and a member of our team."

"You betcha. I love dogs. Had one up until right after my wife Margaret passed four years ago. Your dad and I used to be in touch regularly in the past. His call sign shouldn't have changed," he said, leading us into the house.

Monica volunteered for overwatch. Charley greeted the ladies and lavished extra attention on Greta. He set a large pot of water and another for warm milk on the stove and lit the burners.

"That's going to take a few minutes," he said. "I'm going to the back room and turn my set on and let it warm up."

He left us alone in the large family room. There was a fire going in the stone fireplace, and it was warm and cozy. We sat on large, dark-brown leather sofas that faced the fire. Being nobody's fool, Greta lay down as close as she dared to the hearth and soaked up the warmth.

Tom and Brent came into the house, took off their weapons and battle vests, and deposited their boots by the front door. "You all met Gramps, I take it?" Tom asked, switching off the equipment yard light.

I heard water boiling on the stove, but Renee beat me to it. She turned both burners down and stirred the milk. She spooned heaps of cocoa mix into the milk and then added the water. She found eight mugs and filled each one. Carrying four at a time, she distributed the mugs to the waiting group and took the last outside to Monica.

I took the mug intended for Charley and walked toward the back of the house.

I found him in one of the rear rooms, playing with the dials on a large ham set. I set the mug down in front of him and sat in the only vacant chair.

"Ah, thanks. I forgot about the hot chocolate. I'm getting absent-minded in my old age."

Squeals and squawking sounds came and went as he adjusted the dials. After a few minutes of fiddling, he depressed a button on the microphone sitting in front of him, announced his call sign, then said, "CQ calling Kristen Ranch in Whitefish, Montana."

He released the transmit button, and we waited twenty seconds before trying again.

"In normal times, you wouldn't want to broadcast in CQ for too long, as you'd likely piss off a bunch of pinheads. But these aren't normal times, are they?"

"No, sir. They are most definitely not."

"You'd usually hear a lot of chatter and garbled conversation, but now there's nothing. It's very eerie. This could take some time. I'm going set it to a two-minute recorded auto-broadcast and let it do its thing while we enjoy some fire time. I'll set the volume up, and if he does connect, we'll hear it. But it all depends on your dad being on his set."

"I know. And I appreciate you attempting the connection."

We left the set to its own devices and joined the others in the family room. We listened as the two brothers filled their grandfather in on all the happenings in Battle Mountain and then relayed what they'd learned from us on the blackout.

"I should have known the Chinese were responsible for this," Charley said. "They've been on a tear ever since Trump and Xi Jinping started up their trade war bullshit. That bit of brinkmanship cost us and our fellow ranchers and farmers millions of dollars in lost income these last few years alone when China stopped buying cattle from us. And then Pelosi flies to Taiwan and then we follow that up by shooting down their balloon."

"International politics flows both ways, Gramps," Tommy pointed out. "China is goin' through economic hard times, and of course the pandemic didn't help things. Then they went and sent Putin weapons to use in Ukraine, for which we answered with economic sanctions, which isn't helping them financially."

"Charley? Is that Charley Carlisle?" my father asked, his voice booming through the speakers in the back bedroom.

Considering his age, Charley hopped up out of his lounger pretty quick. "Come on, Jon. With this lousy weather, we probably won't have him for long."

He was at the transmit button five seconds later.

"Neil, good to hear you. You're clear," he said, waving me over. He stood and indicated I should sit in his chair.

"I'm handing this over to someone you're going to want to speak with. If there's time later, we'll talk."

"Okay."

"Dad, it's Jon. We're in Winnemucca, Nevada," I said, talking as fast as I could but trying to speak so he could understand me over the air. "There are six of us in two vehicles. We have the Cruiser and a military Humvee. We're fine and are headed for the ranch. We're traveling at night using night vision that Burt Casey gave us."

I realized I was burning airtime and switched to asking questions.

"How are you and Mom? Over."

There was dead air for several seconds. I looked up at Charley.

"Normal. Just wait," he said.

"Good to hear your voice, son. Your mom and I are well. She's right here with me."

"Hi, Jon," my mother, Andrea, said. "Thank goodness you're okay. We love you and can't wait for you to get home, son."

"Jon, this is Abs. Get home soon . . ." More silence.

"Just wait," Charley said again.

". . . be okay until you get here."

"You can stay away forever for all I care," my sister Asta said with a short laugh. "You know I love ya, brother."

"And I miss you too, Asta. You living back at the ranch?"

"Half time. The other at the hospital," she replied.

"You driving Lola?" Lola was a Highland Green 1968 Mustang GT, better known as the Bullitt car. Asta and I had restored it to its original condition over a period of several years.

"Every day, little brother. And the only thing I watch out for now are deer—no more cops with their radar guns."

"You starting to see violence up there?"

"Starting? It started the second day. Lots of gunshot wounds. People have gone nuts, though it's mostly out-of-towners doing the shooting. We're now seeing diabetics and the pacemaker patients having problems, with dozens already dead."

"Sorry to hear that. We've encountered some pretty horrific things down here too. One member of our group was shot in her shoulder and is recovering."

"And she's traveling with you?" Asta asked.

"Don't start with me on this," I said. "I got it from her doctor down here."

"And yet—" was as far as she got before I cut her off.

"You can beat me up later. Listen, I have news to share with you. But first I'm going to share our route. Or at least a tentative route. The weather is nasty here, and we may have to make adjustments."

"Move aside, Asta. Copy that. Go ahead," my father said.

"Headed up 95 into Oregon. Then 395 North to 26 East to 7 East to 84 North. From there it depends on the weather . . . Getting across the mountains could be an issue. Or we just might stay on 95 the entire way."

"Your first route keeps you away from population centers," Dad said. "Much safer than staying on 95. But 95 is a whole lot quicker. Not to mention easier to navigate in the snow. If it was me, I'd go 95."

"We'll play that by ear, Dad. Mom, I have five women with me who will make great additions to the ranch."

"More the merrier, I always say," my mother said. "We need more women here. I can't wait to meet them. How many guest rooms will you need?"

"Four, for now, Mom. There are two couples and two singles."

"And where do you fit in the scheme of things?" Which was mother speak for: Are you part of a couple?

"He has a girlfriend? Unbelievable," Asta exclaimed.

"In the lodge or cabins?" Mom asked.

"If possible, the Roosevelt for myself and Renee," I answered. The cabin was named in honor of Teddy Roosevelt, who visited the ranch during his first term in office. "Lodge works for the others."

"Who's Renee?" Asta asked.

Charley pointed to a signal meter, which was fluctuating wildly. "Not much time left," he warned.

"Listen. You need to know this," I said. "The cause of the blackout is . . ."

Suddenly the airwaves were filled with operators asking for permission to listen in. Call signs came at us for twenty seconds or more. They were from San Diego; Vancouver, Canada; Boulder, Colorado . . . even one from Vietnam of all places.

Charley reached over me and punched the transmit button. He gave his call sign and gave his permission. Dad then gave his call sign and said it was okay with him as well.

"You've got quite a crowd listening in, son," Charley said. "Be careful with what you say, as others could be listening in without you knowing. Like China," he whispered, even though we weren't transmitting.

"The blackout is the result of two nuclear detonations," I said. "Four missiles were sent from North Korea, two of which we took down. The third and fourth got through and exploded in the upper atmosphere over Colorado and Ohio. The explosions created an EMP."

"A what?" my sister Abs asked.

"An EMP is an electromagnetic pulse," my father answered. "I'll fill you in after we sign off. Go on, Jon."

"Other countries were hit as well . . . Russia being one of them. North Korea has been obliterated along with South

Korea. Even though the missiles originated in North Korea, the US government believes that China is responsible. Regardless of who's responsible, we will be without power for years, maybe even a decade or more."

"I knew it wasn't a simple power outage," Dad said, sounding vindicated. "But how do you know all this?"

"Trust me. I heard it from someone who would know. I'm not going to say more over the air."

"Understood. I look forward to hearing the rest of the story."

"I hope the folks in Whitefish are banding together to form action committees. The things we've seen on our road trip have been awful . . . rape, murder, and looting. Even lynching. The list goes on and on. A town down here in northern Nevada has formed security and supply committees. They've barricaded the major highways leading through their town. They're going to start to scavenge the abandoned semitrucks on the interstate. Are they doing any of that up there?"

"They are," Abs said. "Whitefish and Kalispell have joined forces. There are barricades across north and southbound lanes of 93 just north of Whitefish and south of Kalispell. They're working on Highway 2 coming into Kalispell from the west and east. And I heard today that Ted Mitchell down in Missoula has cleared out the problems they initially had, and it's safe from Whitefish all the way down to Lolo."

"Who's leading the effort up our way?"

"Eddy Taylor." Eddy was a close family friend and ex-military.

"Please let Eddy and Ted know we'll be coming through."

I could barely hear Abs, and then she was gone. Others actively started asking questions.

"I'm done, Charley. Thanks."

Charley told those still listening that he was shutting down.

"They're doing well," I reported once we were back in the family room. "Mom is looking forward to having you ladies at the ranch."

"Charley, Brent, and Tom," I said, standing, "we've got to hit the road."

I shook hands with each. "It was nice getting to know you, and I wish you all the best. Charley, thank you for the hot chocolate and for allowing me to speak with my family."

"Safe journey, Jon," Charley said, giving me a strong handshake.

"Just an FYI, Tom," Renee said, after hugging him, "that girl back in Battle Mountain likes you. Don't be shy with her."

"Which sister?" he asked, sounding truly mystified.

"Toni."

"Truly?" he asked, a huge smile planted on his face.

Renee nodded. "Now you know."

Greta was still in front of the fire, not moving. But her eyes were watching every move Renee made.

"Time to go, Greta," Renee said, patting her thigh.

Greta bounded up and ran out the door that Charley was holding open.

THIRTY-ONE

I topped the tanks of both vehicles, and we were on the road ten minutes later. We'd made our way to Highway 95 and were now headed north at fifty miles an hour. There were very few abandoned trucks and cars, and the ones we did encounter were pulled off onto the shoulder. The snow was falling, but lightly, and didn't hinder our progress.

It was now one in the morning. We'd been on the road for an hour and a half, and the first signs of the McDermitt city limits started appearing in our NVs. We passed a Chevron station on the right and then the McDermitt junior high school. I spotted a group of people standing around a burn barrel, flames licking over the rim. They must have heard us, for several of them pointed in our direction as we passed by.

"Any following?" I asked a minute later, remembering what had happened in Battle Mountain as we passed the high school there.

"Negative," Kathy answered. "I still have eyes on them."

"We've got a casino up on the left with a bunch of cars in the parking lot," Renee said.

We passed a looted market and post office on the right. Then a large sign announced that we were in Oregon.

"Why would anyone want to loot a post office?" Susan asked.

"Maybe for drugs," Kathy said. "Lots of people get their prescriptions in the mail nowadays. Or did before the former president and his puppet postmaster general deliberately slowed the mail in order to mess with the 2020 election."

"Biden has been president for almost three years now, and he's still correcting all the harm that the ex-president did to the country," Monica said. "And just an FYI: I happen to be a life-long Republican."

"We're all entitled to a mistake or two in life," Melissa said.

"No more politics, please," I said. "Let's just agree to disagree."

Up on our right was a large sign saying that the highway was also known as Veterans Memorial Highway and nicknamed the ION Highway—Idaho, Oregon, and Nevada. A mile further on was another sign telling travelers that the next services and gas were fifty-five miles ahead at Burns Junction.

Almost immediately we started a long gradual climb, and it wasn't long before my ears popped with the change in altitude. The road was two lanes with no median between them. I worried about the possibility of abandoned semitrucks obstructing both lanes with no way to get around them, but we didn't encounter any problems.

This was truly a high desert, and as we climbed, the snowfall became heavy, with three or four inches already on the roadway. And again, I drove down the middle of the highway, relying on the snowplow indicators on the shoulders to keep us on pavement.

We were approaching the crest of Blue Mountain Pass when out of the darkness, my NVs picked up a vehicle barreling toward us, headlights off but with a rack of amber-colored fog lights on the front bumper blazing bright.

I flipped up the NVs to avoid light damage.

"Truck heading toward us!" Renee yelled, grabbing the dashboard handle with her right hand and Greta's service vest with her left.

The driver was hugging the middle of the road, as were we. I moved over as far right as I could, hoping for the best. I didn't have time to warn Melissa, but I needn't have worried, for a quick glance in my side-view mirror showed she had moved behind us. I flashed the Humvee's headlights, and the driver moved over at the last second, though not quite fast enough, as their driver's side mirror collided with the Hummer's front fender. It was an older-model Ford Bronco towing a small single-axle trailer.

I slowed and came to a stop, but the Bronco kept on going, disappearing into the heavy blanket of falling snow.

"That was close," Renee said, sitting back and releasing her hold on Greta.

"No shit," I said. "Two trucks passing in the night, probably the only two on the highway in all of northern Nevada, and we almost crash into each other. What are the odds?"

"Apparently pretty high," Susan said, laughing.

"That was a close call," Melissa said over the comms. "While we're stopped, we're going to have a driver change back here. Monica is taking over. My eyes are burning up from straining to see with the NVs in this snow."

With the driver change made, we got back up to speed. We were enjoying a gradual descent, and as we lost altitude, the snow started letting up. Burns Junction was roughly twenty-five miles ahead, and at this rate, we'd be there in thirty minutes. It was desolate country out here, and the only topography the NVs picked up was the occasional arroyo and small hill. There was nothing out here—no houses, trailers, or buildings. Just desert and more desert.

We soon passed a sign that said we were entering Mountain Time Zone. Ten minutes later, a road sign said that Burns Junction, the junction of Highway 95 and Oregon 78, was three miles ahead.

I keyed the comms, said, "We have a decision to make ahead: Do we continue north on 95, which is the most direct route to Montana, or do we take Highway 78 northwest toward Burns? Burns is where Miguel and Lucas figure Kris would run out of gas in her main tank."

"We said we'd take this route to see if we ran into Kris," Kathy said. "You all know I can't stand the woman, but we decided to at least make a minimal effort."

"Seems to me that decision was made when we went west instead of east from Battle Mountain," Renee replied.

And then the actual junction appeared in my NVs. I came to a stop twenty feet off the roadway and stepped out into the cold early morning. The snow was falling, and it was eerily quiet. I glanced to our right. At about two o'clock, off in the distance at the outer reaches of the NV's effective range, was a building. It was more of a shack, with windows on all sides and now-dark security floodlights mounted above each window. A traffic light hung from a wire strung between two telephone poles. Concrete lane dividers were set in such a way as to corral trucks onto the scale that must be there but was now buried underneath four inches of snow.

"It looks like a truck weigh station," Melissa said, who along with the rest of the women had formed a close-in security perimeter around the two vehicles.

"Do you guys see what I see?" Monica said excitedly.

"What?" I asked.

"Walk over behind me."

Which I did.

"Now look at the parking lot beyond the building," she said, pointing with her left hand.

I saw six or seven semitrucks parked in the back reaches of the lot—probably drivers who had been getting some of their DOT-mandated rest time when the pulse hit.

But then I saw it.

"It's a white Ford Crew Cab pickup all right," I said. "Good eyes, Monica."

It was parked off to the right of and behind the larger semitrucks. It was covered with a foot of snow and was almost invisible against the white snowy background of the hills behind it.

"I'm going to check it out," I said. "Melissa, cover my six?"

"Right behind you."

"Renee, can I borrow Greta?"

"Greta, go," she said, then put her hand up toward me. I patted my thigh, and Greta ran up and sat down on my left side. I released the rifle's safety, shouldered it, and made my way across the roadway and onto the access drive which led to the parking lot.

As we got closer to the pickup, I could make out the faded Alderson ranch logo on the front driver's door. "Bingo, it's Sig's," I said over the comms.

There were no tire tracks in the snow behind the truck, so it must have been here for a while. I searched for footprints but didn't spot any.

I opened the driver's door, and there were Kris's vest and night-vision goggles on the passenger side floorboard. The key was in the ignition, and her Glock was under the driver's seat. I took the Glock and released the mag, checked it—full—and then reseated it. I took a step back and opened the driver's side rear door. Her backpack, sleeping bag, and two of the ranch's bunkhouse wool blankets were on the back seat. Power bar wrappers littered the floorboards.

"Looks like she was sleeping in the back seat," I said into the open comms. "I'm going to check the semitrucks now. Sending Greta."

At the mention of her name, Greta's body tensed as if she knew what she was going to be asked to do. She whined and looked at me with those brown eyes.

"Greta, search," I said. She took off and ran to the cab of the first semi in a line of six. She put her two front paws on the driver's side cab step and sniffed, then repeated the exercise for the passenger door.

She got to the third semi, sniffed, and immediately sat down. Greta looked back at me and thumped her tail.

I patted my thigh, and Greta ran back. She sat on my left and waited for me to tell her what to do.

"Greta has found something in the red Peterbilt—the third in line," I reported over the comms. "Let's take a look."

I kept Greta by my side and made my way to the Peterbilt. I hit the side of the sleeper with my fist and stepped back ten feet from the driver's door. "We know you're in there," I shouted. "Exit the cab now. Hands up and fingers laced behind your head. You've got to the count of ten. Otherwise, we'll use your cab as target practice."

No response.

I raised the rifle and fired a single round over the cab.

The cab started rocking on its springs, and I could hear swearing from inside. I also heard loud thumping on the side of the sleeper unit.

"You have three seconds. Three, two . . ."

"Hold your horses. I'm comin' out," a man shouted from inside the cab. A second later, the driver's door opened, and a man dropped to the ground. He was in his late thirties with black, thinning, greasy hair. He sported five-day-old salt-and-pepper stubble on his face. His pot belly strained his dirty once-white T-shirt. I could smell his foul body odor from ten feet away.

The thumping noise from the cab started up again, more urgently now.

"What's up there?" Melissa asked.

The man looked at me and then at Melissa, then turned and ran toward the highway.

Melissa watched him run away. She looked at me, said, "Really?"

The man was holding his pants up with one hand but lost the battle. His pants dropped to his knees, and he fell face first in the snow. He stood, hitched his pants up, and started running again. I looked at Greta, who was whining. I pointed to the running man and said, "Go."

She caught up to him in seconds, launching herself the last ten feet through the air. She grabbed his left forearm and brought him to the ground.

"Help me. Call it off. Please," the runner shouted.

I ignored him and left Greta to deal with her captive. I climbed into the cab. The smell was horrendous—urine and body odor mixing to create a retch-inducing smell. A red velvet curtain was drawn across the opening to the sleeper bed. I pulled it aside, and there was Kris. She was on the bed, on her back, with her hands behind her head and secured with handcuffs to an eyebolt that had been screwed into the fiberglass shell of the sleeper unit. Her legs, spread wide open, were being held in place with thick black zip ties on each foot and looped through another two eyebolts set some distance apart. She was naked and had bruises over most of her body but mainly on her buttocks and inner thighs. A washcloth had been stuffed in her mouth, which I removed. Kris took in a deep breath, and tears started flowing down her face.

"Oh god. Oh my god. Thank you," she said, repeating it over and over.

"It's okay now, Kris. We've got you."

I keyed the comms. "Renee, drive the Humvee over here, please. We have Kris."

"He raped me, Jon. He's been raping and sodomizing me since the night I left the ranch. The ranch truck started to buck and hesitate, and I pulled off in here. I was sleeping in the back seat when all of a sudden the door opened, and I was dragged out and thrown in the back of this truck."

She started to sob uncontrollably and could no longer talk.

I took my knife and cut the zip ties that held her feet. "I've got to find the key to these handcuffs."

"In his front pocket," she said between sobs. It was then that I noticed cut marks on her breasts—lots of them. I needed to get Melissa up here. I found a blanket and covered her.

"Melissa, can you come up into the cab?"

I met her at the bottom of the steps. "She's in bad shape. She's still handcuffed, and I need to get the key from Mr. Runner there. She's been raped and sodomized continually since the night she left the ranch. She has bruises over most of her body, and he's cut her breasts. She needs to be cleaned up. Will you hop up there and keep her company while I get the medical kit?"

"Will do," she said, climbing the steps up to the driver's seat.

The Humvee pulled up next to the Peterbilt. I gathered the women and told them what we'd found.

"Renee, can you find the body wipes and help Melissa get Kris cleaned up. Bring Bernard's medical kit too. She's got some bad cuts to her breasts that should be sutured, but we'll have to clean and tape them shut for now. Any of you know what a Steri-Strip is?"

No one did.

"Renee, please call me when you get the med kit up there."

"Kathy, can you stand overwatch?"

"You bet."

"Monica, follow me."

We walked over to the man, who was cowering next to Greta. Greta had released his arm but sat nearby watching him. I had no doubt that had the man tried to run again, Greta would have been on him in a heartbeat.

"What's your name?"

"Clint," he answered, massaging his arm.

"Clint, I need the key to the cuffs."

"It's in my front pocket," he answered.

"Take it out and hand it to me. And don't even think about throwing it in the snow."

He reached in his pocket and handed me the key.

"Turn your pockets inside out so I'm sure you're not armed."

"I'm not," he said, doing as I asked.

411

"Monica, take Greta and have her check the remaining trucks. Please."

Monica and Greta left to start the search.

"What are you going to do with me?" Clint asked.

"I won't do anything to you as long as you sit there and don't try to run."

"Promise you won't do nothin'?"

"I promise."

"Thank you. I appreciate that."

I watched Renee search the trailer for the wipes and medical kit. Finding them, she replaced the tarp and made her way to the Peterbilt.

"Renee, here's the key to the handcuffs." Renee detoured over to us. Smelling Clint, she cinched her nose with her fingers, said, "OMG, I had no idea a human could smell so foul."

"Ain't my fault, lady," Clint said.

"Of course not," Renee said, giving him a look of disgust, turned, and walked over to the truck.

"What the fuck she mean by that?" he asked. "Ain't my fault everythin' gone and died. Hey, it's cold out here. Can I have a jacket or somethin'."

"Not going to happen."

"Come on, dude. Please."

I ignored his plea. "Why did you rape her?"

He said nothing for several seconds. "I wouldn't call it rape," he finally said. "I offered to take care of her in exchange for sex. But hey, look at me and look at her. You think I could ever even get within twenty feet of someone that beautiful? Dude, I mean, come on. She looks like a movie star."

"Why did you cut her breasts?"

He sat there and again said nothing.

"Why?" I shouted at him, my face less than a foot from his.

"She wouldn't blow me," he finally answered. He looked at the ground and then up at me. "I told her I'd cut her every time I asked for a blow job and she said no. She never did blow me."

"You are a disgusting piece of shit. Stay right here," I said.

I walked over and stood at the Peterbilt's door. Monica and Greta had finished the search and joined me. "Nothing. All clear," she said.

"Thank you for checking." I kneeled and said to Greta, "Guard." I pointed to the runner, and Greta ran over and sat five feet from him. She never took her eyes off her captive.

"Come on, dude. It's going to bite me. Call it off."

"Shut up, fucktard," Monica said.

I looked at Monica. "Fucktard?" I asked.

"I heard a kid use that once when I gave him the finger. I like it."

"Can you help Kathy stand overwatch?" I asked.

"Of course."

"Thanks."

The cab rocked, and Renee climbed to the ground. "We cleaned her up the best we could. But those cuts on her breasts are bad. Neither Melissa nor I know how to deal with them."

"I do," I said. First aid and field dressing were skills the military demanded we learn. I keyed the comms, said, "Melissa, seems I'm the only one who knows how to treat those cuts. Please ask Kris if I have permission to treat her."

"She says yes," Melissa answered a few seconds later.

I climbed into the cab and kneeled next to Kris. Melissa helped sit her up. The blanket fell to the floor, and I could see that even after being cleaned with the wipes, she was still a mess—hair dirty and matted, face and body so dirty that only soap and warm water could fully clean. There was no way I was going to clean and work on the wounds with the rest of her body being one big germ factory.

"Kris, there's no way I can treat those cuts with you being this dirty. We have to get you clean."

I got on the comms, said, "Renee, we've got to get her cleaned up. Please set the stoves up and get a couple of large pots of water boiling. Then we'll let them cool down a bit. I'll need a clean towel—an unused hotel towel will work—and some unscented hand soap if we have any."

"Why don't we use the Coleman shower system Burt gave us?" Renee asked.

"That's a great idea," I said. "Anyone remember how to set it up?"

"I do," Kathy said.

"Great. Set it up next to the truck's driver's door. It has a long hose, and the spray nozzle should reach up and into the sleeper area."

Renee got the stoves set up and burners turned up to maximum. Ten minutes later, the water was boiling. We'd use the water for coffee and Mountain House meals.

It was so cold, I was afraid the water might freeze. While waiting for Kathy and the Coleman, I took five jerry cans out of our trailer and put two in the Cruiser's back seat area and three in the rear storage area behind the Humvee's back seats. Twenty-five gallons should last us until Montana. And just for insurance, I grabbed two cases of water bottles and put one in the Humvee and the other in the Cruiser.

"Water is ready," Renee announced. "Who wants Mountain House and coffee?"

"Don't forget we have the sandwiches and chips that Molly gave us," I added.

"Melissa, please ask Kris if she wants something to eat," I said.

"She'd like some stroganoff."

"Can I have some, too?" Clint shouted from across the lot.

"Don't you dare feed that fucking asshole," Kris shouted from the cab.

Everyone else answered in the affirmative. We ate, and a half hour later I made my way to the Peterbilt to see how Kathy was coming along with the hot water shower.

"It's ready to go," Kathy said. "For water, I'm using one of the five-gallon water cans. You've got five gallons to work with."

"Thank you. That's more than enough."

"Can someone relieve Monica on overwatch so she can have a bite to eat?"

"I'll do it," Susan offered.

"Negative on that," I said.

"Come on. Let me be of use," she said.

"Once again, negative."

"I'll eat while I stand overwatch," Monica said. "Not a problem."

"Thanks."

"Melissa, the shower is ready. Susan?" I said into the comms.

"Yes."

"You can be of help. Please bring us a couple of bottles of the hotel body wash and shampoo. Also, a clean washcloth and towel. Asap, please."

"Roger that," she replied.

"I'm gettin' frostbite out here. Can I have a jacket?" Clint shouted.

I ignored him.

"Did he cut you anywhere else?"

"No."

Susan knocked on the driver's door and handed the items up.

"Thanks."

"You need anything else?" she asked.

"Maybe another towel."

"You got it."

I passed the items and shower hose to Melissa.

"Before I can treat those wounds, she needs to be thoroughly cleaned," I said. "You've got five gallons of warm water. Please wash her hair and rinse it well—lean her head back as far as possible and try to keep the water and dirt from running down her chest. Then clean the rest of her, especially her breasts and rear end with water using the body wash on the washcloth—her back and legs too. Clean her chest carefully. Rinse really well. I'm going to get her backpack and see if there is a change of clothes in it."

"There is," Kris said.

"Melissa, you don't need me to help clean her. And don't worry about water getting on the floor or bed."

I jumped to the ground and retrieved the backpack from the ranch truck. I placed it on the Peterbilt's driver's seat. "Please dress her after you get her cleaned up, Melissa. Minus anything on top. Throw that blanket away—we'll find you a clean one. You need any help? I can get someone up there if you need it."

"Nope, I'm good," Melissa answered.

"Okay then, I'll leave you to it."

———

RENEE MADE COFFEE FOR THOSE who wanted it. I ate another Mountain House and topped it off with a fresh cup of coffee. Greta continued to watch Clint.

Melissa was ready twenty-five minutes later.

"Jon, Kris is dressed," Melissa announced.

I found an unused, clean hotel towel and climbed into the cab. I saw that Kris had her camo pants and hiking shoes on. She had the towel wrapped around her upper body, and with clean hair and skin, she looked a hundred percent better.

"You certainly look better," I said. "How are you feeling?"

"I won't say a hundred percent, but maybe as high as seventy," she answered with a weak half smile.

I searched the medical kit and found a bottle of saline wound flush. I washed my hands, dried them, and put blue surgical gloves on. Melissa did the same.

"Are you ready?" I asked Kris.

She nodded.

"Take the towel and wrap it around your waist. I've got to flush those wounds, and the towel will help keep the water off your lower body.

416

"Melissa, I need you to spread the wounds open while I flush."

There were nine cuts on her left breast and fourteen on her right. All but five were small linear cuts, less than one inch long—probably made with the tip of a knife.

Finished with the flushing, I said, "Melissa, pat her down and get her dried off the best you can."

I started working on the smaller cuts first, applying Steri-Strips to all eighteen. I used three Steri-Strips on each cut and further secured the ends to her skin with tape. On the remaining larger, deeper cuts, I applied antiseptic cream, covered them with gauze, and then put a large adhesive bandage over all that.

Forty-five minutes later, I was finished.

"These longer cuts will have to be looked at by a doctor as soon as possible. We'll have to change the bandages twice a day. You have a clean T-shirt to put on?"

"Right here," Melissa said, holding up a nicely folded T-shirt and sports bra.

"No bra. Just the T-shirt. It's cold out, so put a jacket on. We need to get you started on some antibiotics." I keyed the comms and asked Susan to bring up the second medical bag containing the antibiotics that Bernard had given us. I peeled the gloves off and dropped them to the floor. I closed the medical kit and climbed to the ground. Susan was there waiting for me with the medical bag. I rummaged through the various bottles and packages and found amoxicillin, the same drug Susan was taking. I handed Kris the bottle and told her to take three a day.

Melissa was next down, followed by Kris. Kris had her jacket on and was holding her backpack. She hugged me and then Melissa. "Thanks, both of you."

Renee handed Kris her package of beef stroganoff. Kris had it finished off in less than five minutes. "God those are good," she said, wiping her mouth off on her jacket.

I pointed to Clint. "What do you want to do with him?" I asked, putting my NVs back on. "It's your call. I'll go along with whatever you decide."

Kris was silent, but I could tell she was mulling it over.

"I want to handcuff him to the outside of his truck," she finally answered.

Not so bad, I thought. Though, he'd eventually die of hypothermia.

"Then I want to cut his penis off and put it in the snow where he can see it but can't reach it."

"That will be a death sentence. You know that, right?" I looked at the other women, and they returned my look but said nothing.

"I know that," Kris said.

"I get that we can't let him loose to go on his merry way," I said, "but why not a bullet to his head? What you're proposing is more akin to torture."

"What has Kris been through up in that truck? I'd call it torture," Renee said, answering her own question.

And once again, Renee had made sense of it all.

"Okay. I'll get him ready for you," I said. I could have overridden Kris and come up with some type of punishment that wouldn't kill him, but this guy would keep finding victims and get away with it. No, his days of terrorizing women were over as of today.

"Greta, come, girl," I said. Greta came to my side and hugged my left knee as I walked over to the man.

"Get up."

He stood, said, "You lettin' me go, right?"

"Walk to the truck."

He did.

"Sit on the ground in front of the bumper. Put your right hand above the bumper and the other below it and then grasp your hands together."

Which he did. I placed the cuffs on him.

"Not too tight?"

"It's okay, though I could really use a jacket."

"We'll get you one soon."

"Thanks, dude."

"Okay, Kris. Your turn. It's not too late to change your mind."

"I'm good. Thanks."

"I'm going to leave you to it, then."

Sensing something bad was about to happen, Clint said, "Dude, you said you wouldn't hurt me."

"And I'm not. But I never said anything about anyone else."

"You fuckin' tricked me, man," he screamed as he fought to release himself from the handcuffs.

I stood back and watched the women attempt to wrestle his legs together. Renee and Kathy each took a foot and put their full weight into it, but he kicked both women off. The two ladies stood and backed off to reassess.

"Not so easy, is it, bitches," the guy said. "Stupid cunts."

The use of the C-word must have touched a nerve, for Monica slid her Glock out of its vest holster, and after quickly placing the barrel on the top of his left knee, pulled the trigger.

"My ex called me that word almost nightly," she explained.

Clint screamed in pain and thrashed about for a long minute before lying still. Monica touched his neck and checked for a pulse. "He's alive."

Kris straddled the inert body, undid his belt, then pulled his jeans and boxers down around his knees. As if it knew what was about to happen, his penis had fully retreated from view.

"I didn't know they could do that," Kathy said, surprise filling her voice. "My husband's has never done that. How are you going to get it out?"

"An old boyfriend's penis did that after we skinny-dipped in a cold lake. If it gets cold enough, it'll retreat like a turtle's head," Melissa said. "It shocked him as much as me. Took some time to get it out of hiding, even with a collaborative effort."

419

"Reminds me of an episode on Seinfeld," Renee said. "One of the characters swam in the ocean and while changing out of his bathing suit was interrupted by one of the women in his group. She saw it shriveled up and gasped. Thinking she thought he was naturally that small, he then loudly claimed shrinkage. I laughed so hard it hurt."

"Enough of the chitchat. I need a knife," Kris said.

No one came forward. Then they looked at me.

"Seriously. You want to use my knife?" I asked. "No. And that's final."

Kathy retrieved her backpack from the Cruiser, rummaged inside, and dug out a folding Swiss Army knife. "From Burt," she said, smiling at me.

Kathy handed it to Renee, who opened it, exposing the longest blade. Renee then handed it to Kris, handle first. Kris leaned down and after some prodding and pulling got an inch or two of Clint's penis out of hiding. She gripped the head, pulled hard, and then with one clean swipe cut the penis in half. Which brought Clint wide awake.

Kris stepped to the side and held Clint's severed penis in front of his face. Clint's eyes grew huge as he watched Kris toss the appendage into the snow some six feet away. She wiped the knife on Clint's T-shirt, folded the blade back, and handed it to Kathy.

Clint was wild-eyed, crying, and sobbing. I figured between the two bleeding wounds and the extreme cold, he'd be dead in two hours. I took out the permanent marker and wrote on his thigh, Rapist of Innocents. I didn't want to see or listen to him anymore, and I walked far enough away to where his cries and pleas were muted. The women followed.

"Out of curiosity, what's he hauling?" I asked Kris.

"Hershey Kisses. Forty-five thousand pounds of them. He says he's an independent driver under contract with a food distribution company out of Reno."

420

"Let's find the key to the trailer's rear door lock. I like Kisses. I mean, who doesn't? Right? At the same time, let's find the key to his truck's fuel tank cap."

We found the two keys in the semi's ashtray. We unlocked and swung open the trailer's two rear doors. The wonderful smell of chocolate filled the air and was a welcome change from the putrid smell of Clint and his cab. I climbed up and handed down twenty cardboard master cartons. Each carton contained 144 bags of Kisses. And major score: these weren't the normal supermarket-sized packages but the Costco and Sam's Club, club-size bags.

After rearranging the current contents of our trailer, we loaded the twenty cartons. The added weight of twenty cartons would be a feather as far as the Humvee was concerned.

Finished securing the tarp, Renee took me aside. "What are we going to do with Kris?" she asked.

I'd been thinking about it and had come up with a solution that might work.

"What if we were to show her the reserve tank switch on the ranch truck. She could then make a decision: continue on her way to Seattle alone or follow us. If she sticks with us, then under no circumstance will she be allowed to have a weapon. We'll share our food and water with her, but that's it. She'll siphon her own gas from abandoned vehicles with no help from us."

"What happens to her once we're at the ranch?"

"I don't want her with us. She's proven herself unworthy of our trust, and we can't have someone living with us that we don't trust. Long answer? She goes."

"If those are her choices, what's the difference between the two? Both result in her having to make her way to Seattle. Why go all the way to Montana in the first place? Why not just continue to Seattle from here?"

"Good points." Leave it to Renee to tear down my arguments. Thank goodness she can . . . and does. "Ah hell, Renee, I don't know."

"How about this: she comes with us to Montana," she said. "Then we get her to Seattle somehow. Once there, she either stays in Seattle, or she grabs her kids and husband and the whole family comes back to the ranch in Montana. Don't forget, her husband is a famous botanist who worked for the agriculture department of whatever. I'm sure we could use him."

"The final decision on whether Kris can stay at the ranch rests with my parents. My mother is pretty soft-hearted. But my father is another story. He does not tolerate dishonesty . . . especially theft. I'll be honest, hon. Chances are he won't allow her to stay."

Renee was quiet while she thought about what I'd said. "I get it, Jon. We'll have to let her know what could happen."

The noise from the front of the semi had stopped. "That was brutal, what Kris did to Clint," I said.

"No less brutal than what he brought onto her," she countered.

"True that. Let's top off the Humvee's and ranch truck's tanks from the semi's tank. I'll go ahead and use one of the gasoline jerry cans and top off the Cruiser's tank."

I keyed the comms and told Monica, who was still on overwatch, to come on back for a quick meeting. With that done, I gathered the women together, including Kris.

"First off, Kris, this is Deputy Susan Foster," I said, pointing to Susan. "Susan, this is Kris." Both women nodded in acknowledgment, but no words were exchanged. "Susan is with us because she was wounded, and Sig took her in so she could recover at the ranch. She then, ah . . . How to explain this?"

"Jesus, Jon, just spit it out," Melissa said, lightly punching my arm. "You can be such a pussy at times. What he couldn't manage to say is that Susan and I hooked up and are now a couple. Thanks to you, and lucky for us, there was an empty seat, and she took it. If it—"

"Okay, introductions made," I said, interrupting Melissa. "This is going to be an awkward conversation but a necessary one," I began. "We need to discuss Kris and what to do with her.

I guess the best way to begin is to ask you, Kris, what would you like to do?"

"I want to get to Seattle and my babies," she said without hesitation. "But I now know that I'd never get there on my own. So, I'd like to stick with you if you'll allow it."

"Renee, why don't you tell the group the plan that you've come up with."

"It's a simple one," Renee said. "Kris accompanies us to Montana. We try our best to get her to Seattle, where she asks her husband, the semi-famous botanist, to move, with the children, of course, to Montana and the ranch. In Montana, in exchange for food and protection, he works with us and other ranches to increase crop production. However, Kris's acceptance at the ranch is subject to Jon's parents, who have the final say-so. See . . . simple."

"Simple in theory, not so much in reality," I said. "But we need to get to Seattle anyway, for Kathy to leave word of her location for her husband, Bradley."

"Thank you so much," Kathy said, giving me a hug and kiss on the cheek before stepping back.

"Kris, if we decide to allow you to travel with us to Montana, there will be conditions. They are: you'll have no weapons, but we will allow you comms and night vision. You'll siphon your own gas as we find it. We'll share our food and water with you. You are free to leave us at any time—without the ranch truck. And finally, your acceptance back into our group will be put to a vote. Are the conditions acceptable to you?"

"Yes."

"Group? Show of hands for allowing Kris back in."

Five hands were raised: mine, Renee, Kathy, Melissa, Susan.

"Monica?"

"No. I don't want her with us." Monica turned to Kris and said, "I'm sorry about what happened to you here, but you've shown us you aren't trustworthy or honest. To be frank, you are a bitch and an asshole. So, no."

"Monica, I'm sorry, but you've been outvoted," I said. "She's coming with us."

I turned toward the front of Clint's truck. "Who has the handcuff keys?"

Renee dug in her front pocket and handed me the key. I handed the key to Kris. "Take the cuffs off Clint and bring them to me—key too, please."

Kris left to get the handcuffs. "Let's find out what some of these other trucks are carrying," I said. "Look inside the cabs for packing lists or bills of lading. That way we can see what's inside the trailers without having to search through—"

A single gunshot rang out. It had come from the front of the truck. We found Kris standing over Clint, who now sported a hole in his forehead. She was holding a snub-nosed .38 revolver.

Kris handed the gun to me. "He was still alive," she stated. "If it helps, I could tell you he was suffering."

"No. And the gun?" I asked.

"Clint's. He kept it under the driver's seat."

Clint was still cuffed.

"The handcuffs, Kris," I said, holding my hand out.

Kris bent down and undid the cuffs. Released from the front bumper, Clint's upper torso slid to the ground. Kris handed over the cuffs and key.

"Let's check on the other trucks' cargo. I'll stand overwatch. Kris, you up for helping them find out what's in the other trucks?"

"Yes."

"Then pair up with Renee, please. But no lifting. You need to be careful of your wounds."

Kris turned and walked over to Renee and Greta.

"Kris," I said.

Kris stopped and looked back.

SETTING OUT

"We'll get you to Montana as fast as we can. My sister is an emergency room physician and will take care of those cuts."

"Thank you."

Thank you for reading

DARK HIGHWAY HOME
BOOK ONE – SETTING OUT

The story continues in

DARK HIGHWAY HOME
BOOK TWO – REACHING HOME

Available Now.

Read on for an excerpt from

DARK HIGHWAY HOME
BOOK TWO – REACHING HOME

ONE

Susan and I stood overwatch while the remaining five women were out searching the abandoned semi-trucks' cabs for bills of lading, shipment packing lists, and other identifying paperwork. Finding paperwork listing the trailer's contents would be a huge timesaver, allowing them to avoid having to open and physically search each trailer.

It was snowing again, much heavier now, with our tire tracks, footprints, and events of the past hour already covered. I glanced toward Clint, and saw he was now just an odd snow-covered shape in an otherwise flat parking lot. I felt a tinge of regret for what had befallen him, but knew in my heart that given the opportunity, he would have gone on and harmed other women.

"It's really piling up. Gonna need a snowplow to clear a path for us," Susan said, concern in her voice. "Like that's going to happen. Not."

She was trying to tighten her black service plate carrier which wasn't quite sitting comfortably yet after it had been cleaned and dried by Molly Alderson at the Alderson's ranch outside Battle Mountain. With her other arm in a sling, she was struggling one-handed with the adjustment straps. I stepped in and took over for her.

And she was right. Even with all three of our vehicles being four-wheel drive, it was still going to be slow going.

I cinched the last strap and stepped back.

"Thanks." She donned Kris's NVs and cycled them up. "Wow," she exclaimed, swiveling her head from right to left as she took in the inky black darkness which had magically turned into day. "These night vision goggles are amazing. Battle Mountain PD never had the funds for these."

"They are amazing. They've allowed us to make it this far." I scanned the road in both directions with the thermal, and all was clear. The thermal's effectiveness waned markedly in the heavy snow but the scope's screen indicated a reliable reading out to a range of just over 400 yards, far less than its optimum range of 1,100 yards, but good enough.

"Maybe we should shelter in the trucks' sleeping compartments for the night," she said, her NVs pointing in the general direction of the dead semi-trucks. "Hide our trucks behind the semi-trailers."

"That's not a bad idea. Though we'd be more exposed than I'd like."

"If we can't drive in this snow, then most likely, no one else can," she countered.

"True. Though if we did head out, chances are we'd have the highway to ourselves. Which is ideal."

The NVs picked up the five women making their way back to where we were waiting behind the Cruiser. Like the professional she was, Greta was hugging Renee's left side. Each of the ladies had put on boonie hats and tucked their hair up underneath. NVs were down over eyes, and with weapons carried in a cradled resting position, they looked like a typical nighttime recon patrol in Afghanistan.

"Find anything?" I asked the group.

"Five of the six cabs are locked," Melissa answered.

"But we found this," Monica said, handing me an official-looking document. "It was in the one open cab. It's a bill of lading and packing list. And you'd be all set if you were building a new housing tract of eighty-two houses and needed HVAC units for each."

"HVAC? As in air conditioning units?"

"Yep. Totally useless now, of course."

"Can't win 'em all," I said. "Listen, ladies. Susan has suggested that maybe we should take shelter in the cabs' sleeping compartments for the night. We can rest up and get going again at first light. Or we can keep going and use the darkness and heavy snowfall to our advantage. What do you think?"

"Keep going," Kathy answered without hesitation. "We can take turns driving. Let's burn up some distance. Besides, as you say, we own the night. Not the day."

"There's snowplow markers along the side of the road," Renee said. "The top six inches or so are coated with some kind of reflective material. If you turn your running lights on, I bet they'll glow like crazy in our night vision and the going will be a whole lot easier."

"Good idea, Renee," Melissa said. "I say we keep on going."

"I'm with you guys. Let's keep moving," Monica said. "I just want to get to Montana and feel safe and secure again. I've had enough of living with constant danger."

"Ditto that," Kris said.

"Susan, resting in the semis' sleeper cabs was a good idea, but I agree with the others. We should keep going. But first, let's search the other cabs and see if we can find anything useful," I said, opening the Cruiser's driver's door and grabbing the crowbar from underneath the driver's seat.

Susan had been standing by, watching the other women being busy with the search. Maybe it would be a good idea to have her chip in.

"Susan, will you provide overwatch for us?" I asked, handing her the thermal.

"You betcha," she replied, walking fifteen yards toward the road and taking up a kneeling firing position. With her arm immobilized in a black sling, she was unable to carry a rifle and only had her Glock for protection.

"No heroics, please. See something, say something."

"Roger that."

I made my way to the first locked truck. The ladies followed and stood back as I stepped up onto the cab's entry steps and, with one good whack of the heavy crowbar, shattered the driver's door window.

I reached into the cab and unlocked the door. I found the bill of lading in the center console under the truck's Qualcomm messaging unit.

I flipped the NVs up and, using one of Burt's headlamps, read through the multi-page document.

"Another bust, ladies—it's a trailer-load of auto parts."

The second locked truck contained twenty-two pallets of bagged landscape mulch destined for a national home-improvement center in Bakersfield, California. The next was full of Yamaha outboard motors—from small four horsepower four-stroke babies up to eight-cylinder, 400 horsepower behemoths. The fourth locked cab was from Vancouver, Canada, carrying a full load of linens and towels destined for a dozen Vegas hotels and resorts. Now that, at least, was of some interest.

I found the trailer's door key in the spare-change cubby. "According to the bills of lading, this trailer was headed to classy Las Vegas resorts with a full load of bed sheets, towels, bathmats, and other linens," I said, making my way to the back of the trailer. "I'm sure my mother and sister would be most appreciative if we were to bring them a lifetime supply of high-end sheets and towels."

I inserted the key, and the lock sprang open. I swung open the trailer's two rear-facing doors, and my headlamp illuminated pallet after pallet of cardboard cartons. Each pallet was tightly shrink-wrapped, but lo and behold, each was clearly labeled with their respective contents. The first pallet, closest to the door and ordered by the Mirage Hotel, held queen and king sheet sets, along with duvets, bath towels, face towels, washcloths, bathmats, and shower curtains.

"Looks as if each pallet is packed with an assortment of linens," Melissa said. "There are probably a couple hundred sets of each size on each pallet."

"We have room in our trailer for a couple of pallets worth of stuff," Renee said.

"Let's keep some free space in the trailer, so one pallet should do," I said. "Melissa, will you move the Humvee over here and park the trailer so it's below the trailer's doors? No sense in lugging these boxes a hundred yards through the snow."

"Will do," she replied, already headed toward the vehicles.

"Monica and Kathy, hop up here and throw down this pallet's cartons," I said, patting the Mirage's pallet, then removing my knife from its vest-mounted sheath, and slicing the shrink wrap from the top of the pallet down to the wood base. "There's nothing breakable, so just toss them down into the back of the trailer once Melissa has brought it over. We'll straighten and stack them later."

"Does this mean we're looters?" Monica asked.

"Hell, no," Kathy answered.

"It means we got to it before anyone else," I said. "Besides, what good does any of this do just sitting here?"

"I get what you're saying. It's just that it feels weird taking something that isn't ours," Monica answered.

I helped the two ladies climb up into the trailer, and then jumped to the ground, joining Renee who was waiting for me below. We made our way over to the last truck, broke the glass, and opened the cab's driver's door. We found several bills of lading listing toys and puzzles, cabinet door pulls and hinges, and six pallets of USPS Approved, roadside mailboxes.

There was one last shipment listed on the master manifest, and I knew we couldn't leave without first loading it into our trailer. Shipped by Kingman Pharmaceutical Distributors of Spokane, Washington, and bound for Sunset Pharmacy in Henderson, Nevada, the bill of lading stated, *Must arrive by Monday December 18th—New store initial stock*. We'd have to find the shipment's packing list to know exactly what the pallet contained.

I found a loaded key ring under the passenger seat, and after several attempts with various keys, found the one that opened the lock for the trailer's two rear-facing swing doors. I heaved them open, and the Kingman Pharmaceutical pallet was right there, sitting pretty, first in line. It was a standard-sized wood pallet, but was loaded high with locked, dark-blue, plastic security totes, towering to within an inch of the trailer's eight-foot ceiling. The packing list was taped to a tote which was held in place behind several layers of tightly wound shrink wrap. I ripped away the wrap until I had the packing list in hand. The list was thirty-eight pages long with forty items on each page. Listed were drugs of every sort, some I recognized, but most of them strange to me. There was page after page of every kind of drug and item a full-fledged drugstore would need to stock behind a pharmacy counter.

"Well?" Renee asked.

"Jackpot, babe," I said, folding the paperwork and stowing it in one of my pants' large cargo pockets. "It's a pallet-load of drugs destined for a new pharmacy opening in Henderson, Nevada. There are even two full totes of insulin. I'm not sure if insulin needs to be kept cool, but it's refrigerator-cold outside, so I bet it's still good. We'll take them regardless."

"Can insulin freeze and still be effective?" she asked. "Anything liquid is going to freeze if left in the trailer."

"Good question... I don't know. But we can clear some space in the Humvee and make sure it doesn't get that cold. I'll transfer a few ammo cans from the Humvee's rear storage area to the trailer."

I keyed the comms and asked Melissa to bring the trailer over to us.

"Roger that," she replied. "Give us two or three minutes and we'll be finished transferring the linens."

"Help me up there, and I'll lend a hand tearing off the rest of the shrink wrap," Renee said, looking up at me from the ground.

She held both hands up and I hefted her up into the trailer. Greta looked up at us in expectation of joining in the fun. "Sorry, honey, you stay and guard," Renee said. Greta thumped her tail and started surveying the area around us.

We made quick work of the pallet's shrink wrap and sat on two of the locked totes to wait for the trailer's arrival.

"I've got something to tell you, Jon," Renee said. "I've been waiting to be sure, but now I'm fairly certain. . . I think I'm pregnant."

I looked her in the eyes, but stayed silent as I digested the news.

"Renee—" I said a minute later.

"I've missed two periods now. I've never missed a period. Ever."

"Renee—" I said again.

"I think it happened when we were in Cabo," she said, eyes locked on Greta down below us.

"Renee, I think—"

"I have to be honest. Besides being in love with you, it's one of the reasons I wanted to come along. If we are pregnant, the child should grow up with both parents. Even if it's in shitty times like this."

Renee brought her eyes up and looked at me in question.

"Can I talk now?" I asked with a wide grin.

"You look happy. Are you?" she asked.

"I am. Very. And excited at the possibility of having our own little human running around the ranch."

I brought her in close and crushed her in a bear hug, whispering, "I love you, Renee. I'll do everything I can to make you and our child safe and happy."

"Let's not say anything to the others until we're sure," she said.

I leaned back, nodded, then asked, "Have you noticed any changes in your body?"

"My boobs are bigger and tons more sensitive. And I've been hornier than usual."

"Bigger, more sensitive boobs. And hornier than usual. It all works for me."

"Yeah, yeah," she said, delivering a light punch to my arm.

The Humvee drove by the trailer's rear door followed by our trailer. Monica and Kathy, and now with Kris, hopped up into our own trailer and, using Burt's headlamps, quickly rearranged and stacked the boxes of sheets and towels. Renee and I carefully handed down the pharmacy totes, and the ladies gently stacked and arranged them in the trailer.

I handed the two insulin totes down, said, "Leave those two there, please. I've got to make sure they haven't already frozen. If not, I'll clear a space for them in the back of the Humvee."

I jimmied both insulin totes open and found the bottles still in a liquid state. With Renee's help, we transferred ten ammo cans from the Humvee's rear storage area to the trailer. We loaded the two insulated insulin totes into the Humvee and returned to help finish transferring the other totes.

"Kris, careful now," I said. "Those Steri-Strips can only handle so much. So don't overdo it."

"I won't. Promise."

Five minutes later, we were finished transferring the totes. We had the cartons and totes leveled off, matching the height of the other boxes and supplies already in the trailer. The tarp was secured, and we were finished. We still had a good four feet of empty space in our trailer, more than that if we were to double stack.

Greta lifted her head and let out a low growl. Renee and I strained to see through the falling snow but saw nothing.

Ten seconds later, the comms came to life. "We have a vehicle approaching from the south," Susan reported. "Four hundred yards and slowing."

––––––––––––––––

"HEADLAMPS OFF, NVS BACK ON, ladies," I said. "And spread out and get prone like we practiced. Safeties on until I tell you otherwise."

"Turn on the red dots?" Renee asked.

"No. Good question, though. But it's too dark for that."

I strained to see the Cruiser and could barely make it out. It was covered by several inches of snow and could easily be mistaken for being abandoned along with the six semi-trucks.

"Susan, can you get over to us without them seeing you?"

"Negative. Going prone."

Kris was prone a yard or two to my left. She lifted her head, looked at me, said, "The ground is really cold."

"Fingers off triggers, ladies," I said. "Kris, get up and hop in the back of the Humvee. You're not armed, and the back seat is the safest place for you."

Headlights lit up the road parallel to our position. Susan was prone fifty feet from where the vehicle would pass, the rest of us a hundred yards.

"Jon?" Susan said, her voice sounding stressed.

"Stay there, Susan. How many occupants?"

"It looks like two, a woman driving with a child in the passenger seat. It's an older-model Bronco and towing a single-axle, open-sided trailer—like ours, but much smaller."

The Bronco slowed to a crawl, turned toward the Cruiser and semis, missing Susan by ten yards. It came to a stop, its headlights going dark, and the engine shut down. Aside from the engine ticking in the chilled early-morning air, all was quiet.

"Jon?" This from Susan again, now in a hushed, strained voice.

"Susan, I've got you covered."

"Roger that."

"Chill, everyone," I said.

"Chill? How about freezing," Renee responded.

"I could have said, stay frosty," I said dryly.

"You're all hilarious," Melissa said.

"Quiet now, everyone. And turn your comms volume down—I can hear someone's off to my left."

The Bronco's driver's door opened, and a woman emerged. She was short, maybe five-two or -three, slender, though it was hard to tell with the knee-length, puffy parka she was wearing. She had a black knit ski hat on with a Snowbird ski resort logo on the front.

The woman reached back inside the cab and came out with a long gun which she attached to a single-point sling. She stood in place and listened for a good sixty seconds. *She's a cautious one*, I thought.

Satisfied, she patted the hood and the passenger emerged, quietly closing the door behind him. Her passenger was a young boy, maybe ten or eleven, and was wearing a puffy jacket and similar ski hat, though logo free. He appeared unarmed.

She took his hand, and they walked side by side toward the Cruiser, stopping at the driver's door.

"I hope there's something to drink or eat inside, Mom."

"Me too, honey. Let's keep an eye and ear out for approaching cars."

"I will. I have good hearing."

"I know you do."

She was reaching for the door handle when I yelled out, "Stop right there, miss."

She immediately let go of the boy's hand and grabbed hold of the rifle.

I quickly closed the distance between us. It was pitch dark, snowing heavily, and I doubted they could see me. "Not a good idea. Let the rifle hang. There are several of us."

"We mean you no harm," Renee shouted, thirty feet to the woman's right.

Hearing a woman's voice must have been reassuring, for the new arrival let the rifle hang as instructed. She took hold of the boy's hand and peered out into the falling snow.

"Please, let us be on our way," she pleaded.

"Release the weapon from the sling, set it at your feet, then step back five paces," Melissa commanded, her voice booming out of the darkness, thirty feet to the woman's left. "We're going to send someone out to search you and the boy. It's for your safety as much as ours. Do you have any other weapons on you or in the Bronco?"

"No, this is our only weapon," she answered, her head swiveling right and left, trying to track the voices. But she released the rifle, placed it on the ground, and stepped back. "Please, let us be on our way. There's trouble following us, and you don't want any part of it."

"Susan, search them please," I said, walking out of the darkness to within ten feet of the two newcomers.

Susan stood and came up behind the woman and child. "Hi there," she said.

Both jumped in surprise at the voice behind them, the sound of Susan's crunchy footsteps evidently having mixed with my own.

"Open your coats and put your hands behind your head," Susan commanded. Using her one good hand, she patted both down.

"She's got night vision, Mom," the boy said. "Are you a member of the military, ma'am?" he asked, directing his question to Susan.

"Deputy sheriff," she answered.

"Cool," he said.

Susan stepped back. "They're clean."

"Check the Bronco and trailer, Susan."

"What are your names?" Monica asked.

"I'm Emily Talbot and this is my son Peter."

"I'm Jon and the young lady behind you is Susan. She is a deputy sheriff from Battle Mountain, Nevada."

"Are you by chance missing your driver-side mirror?" I asked.

"Yes, some asshole driving down the middle of the. . ." was as far as she got. "Uh oh, I'm guessing that was you?" she asked, after several seconds of uncomfortable silence.

"Pretty sure it was," I answered.

"Oh, sorry. We needed to retrieve Peter from my in-laws and my husband was going as fast as he dared. A neighbor of ours was able to get the Bronco working earlier today. We brought the trailer to haul his parents and their food stocks back to our place in Burns, but we stumbled into a bunch of people looting their house."

"No worries. Hardly scratched our fender."

"If you're not going to rob and kill us, can you spare some water and something to eat," she asked, voice filled with a steely resolve. "I haven't had water today and I'm feeling the effects."

I keyed the comms, said, "Monica, can you grab some bottled water and trail bars and bring them on over?"

"Roger that," she answered.

"Bronco and trailer are clear," Susan reported. "Trailer is empty as is the Bronco."

"Susan, pick up her rifle and place it in her trailer. Ma'am, you'll get that back once we part company," I said.

Monica appeared out of the dark with bottled water and a handful of trail bars.

"She has night vision too, Mom," the boy said.

"I can see that."

Monica handed over the water and bars. Mother and son chugged a full bottle of water each, then attacked the trail bars.

Between bites, the mother said, "Thank you. All of you. . . however many of you there are."

Renee walked out of the darkness. "You said your husband was driving. Where is he?" she asked.

Emily Talbot's steel resolve melted away and she started crying, taking huge breaths, chest rising and falling in an attempt to control her emotions.

"Dad was shot and killed at Gramps and Nana's house," the boy answered for her, wrapping his arms around his mom's waist. "They killed my grandparents, too. Gramps told me to hide in the barn's hayloft. I saw them kill him and my grandmother. When I saw the Bronco drive up, I ran and jumped in the back seat."

"I'm so sorry," Kathy said, emerging out of the darkness and coming to a stop in front of the pair. "We're living in bad times, and it's only going to get worse."

"You have a place to go?" Renee asked.

"We do. Our home in Burns. It's well-stocked and very defendable. We have neighbors that have banded together to protect our subdivision."

"What did you mean when you said trouble is following you?" I asked.

"The men that killed my husband and his parents are ten miles or so behind us. Brad killed four of them before they dropped him. Peter and I were in the Bronco waiting for him. He'd made it to the passenger door when he was hit. Peter held them off with the rifle while I checked Brad's vitals—I'm a physician's assistant—but he was gone. We had no choice but to hightail on out of there."

"How many are there?" I asked.

"Ten or fifteen," she answered.

"More like twenty," her son said. Looking up at her, he said, "Sorry for correcting you, Mom. There were a few behind the house that you never saw."

"Not a problem," she said, rubbing her hand across his shoulders.

"Where did this happen?" Susan asked.

"Five miles south of Blue Mountain Pass. A couple miles past where we touched fender and mirror."

"You know for sure they're following you?" I asked.

"They have four working vehicles, three older-model pickup trucks and an old VW Bug," she said. "They were behind us for several miles. I was watching in the rearview mirror when the lead truck must have hit an icy spot and went off the road and into a shallow drainage ditch where it came to a stop and flipped onto its side."

"The rest of them stopped to help try to flip it back up," Peter added. "I lost sight of them when the road dipped. When we came up the next hill, I couldn't see them through the falling snow."

"We wouldn't have stopped here knowing they're behind us, but we really needed to find something to drink. I was starting to have problems concentrating—I know that's a sign of severe dehydration."

"Do you know any of them?" I asked.

"I don't," the mother answered.

"I do," Peter said. "The two that shot and killed Gramps and Nana are workers at the ranch across the highway from their place. One is named Stuart and the other Izzy. Gramps and I went over there a bunch of times before the blackout happened and they were both there."

"Stuart and Izzy. You're sure?" Susan asked.

"Yes," Peter answered firmly. "I'm sure."

"Jon, can we help them?" Renee asked. "Help as far as doing something about the group following them."

"Best to allow us to get on home and you on your way," Emily answered quickly.

"Your tire tracks will be visible for a couple more hours," I pointed out. "Easy enough for them to follow you all the way to your place in Burns."

"Oh," she said, with a tinge of resignation, realization setting in.

"Ours too, if we were to leave now," Melissa added.

I stepped closer, said, "If you want, we could put an end to this right here, right now. Only question is: do you want them all dead or just this Stuart and Izzy."

"You'd do that for us? You don't even know us."

"He wouldn't offer if he wasn't serious," Renee said.

"Well, I guess the two that killed my husband and in-laws."

"We like to be democratic when it comes to situations like this. So, what say you, ladies?"

It was unanimous on helping mother and son.

"Okay. Drive your Bronco and trailer to the road and position it so that both lanes are blocked. Do it now. Then come back here."

Mother and son moved the Bronco, and soon both lanes were blocked with no way to get around either side.

Once they were back, I had both mother and son join Kris in the Humvee's back seat.

"Susan, please go with them."

"Jon, let me at least—"

"No arguments, please," I said, cutting her off. "Just take them. I need someone to watch over them."

"One thing, Mrs. Talbot. You said you're a physician's assistant?"

"Yes. I work under Dr. Candace Brunk in Burns. She's a surgeon specializing in female reproductive and oncological issues."

"Would you mind looking at one of our travel mates? She was taken and suffered knife cuts to her breasts. I cleaned and bandaged them as best I could, but it would be good to have a professional check my work."

"Of course."

"Thank you. She's in the Humvee."

I watched as Susan escorted the mother and son to the Humvee.

"The goal is to stop the vehicles and have a chat with the occupants," I told the women.

"Monica, Kathy, and Melissa, I want you three to position yourselves fifty feet south of the Bronco on the far shoulder. Monica, from there, walk three car lengths south and Kathy, two car lengths. Melissa, stay at the fifty-foot mark. Renee and I will be on this side of the Bronco. All three of you then pace off twenty feet back from the roadway and take a knee. Set your rifles to three-round bursts. Melissa, full auto. The lead vehicle will stop when they spot the Bronco blocking the two lanes. When I tell you, I want the three of you to run toward the four cars—Melissa toward the first car in line, Monica the second and Kathy the third. Point your weapons at them but do not fire. Renee and I will do the same on this side. I'll be on the fourth vehicle. When we're in position, I'm going to fire a sustained burst on full auto as a warning."

"At them?" Melissa asked.

"No, over them. Then I'm going to shout out commands. You cover the windows for any shooters."

All heads nodded.

"What if they fire on us?" Kathy asked.

"Then return fire. Don't even hesitate. We're way beyond trying to be nice. We all good?" I asked.

Again, the women nodded.

"Okay. Good. Go get yourselves five extra magazines, then take your positions. Not sure how long we're going to have to wait, but we'll give it a half hour and then reevaluate. Go."

"What do I do with Greta?" Renee asked, petting the loyal gal behind her ears.

"She stays by your side. She's trained for just this kind of situation. She'll be right beside you until you tell her otherwise.

"Let's ammo up."

———————

FIVE MINUTES LATER, WE WERE in position. And ten minutes after that, it was once again Greta who first alerted us to approaching vehicles.

"I see them. Four vehicles in single file," Melissa reported. "Three pickups and an old VW Bug."

"Okay. It's them. Safeties off."

"Renee, I'm going thirty feet down the road. You watch the passenger side of the first vehicle. I'll handle the other three. Everyone, watch windows for sudden heroes."

Thirty seconds after I was in position, the lead vehicle passed me. It was a mid-1950s pristinely restored Dodge Power Wagon. Sitting on the front bumper was the biggest winch I'd ever seen on a pickup truck. Thirty feet south of the Bronco, it came to a sudden stop.

I keyed the comms. "Approach now," I said, as I ran toward the third and fourth vehicles in line, a VW Bug and an older Chevy pickup. I raised the barrel of my rifle and fired off a full clip over all four vehicles. I dropped the empty mag and inserted a fresh one.

"You, in the vehicles, place your weapons at your feet then put hands on heads. Now!" I shouted. "Do not lower your hands until I tell you. If we find a weapon on you, not only will you die, but the one next to you will die as well. Do as we tell you, and you will not be hurt. Drivers, turn your headlights and engines off. Leave ignition keys in the vehicle."

All was silent until a single three-round burst from Renee took out the passenger-side front window of the second vehicle in line. A shooter had tried to stick his shotgun out the window. He was now howling in pain.

Renee approached the wounded man.

"Back off, Renee," I yelled, as I ran toward her. "Leave him to me."

"He was going to shoot. I had to—"

"I saw. You did good," I said, opening the pickup's passenger door and taking the guy's shotgun. The shooter, an older teenager in dirty mechanic's overalls, slid to the roadway and lay on his back screaming in pain.

I keyed the comms, said, "Ladies, pick a vehicle and approach. Watch the occupants. If any lower their hands, fire on them."

"Renee, you and Greta take up position between the lead truck and the Bronco. I'm going to bring these guys up to you, car by car. Have Greta guard like she did with Clint."

I started with the last car in line—the VW Bug. Four men were inside, and I had them exit after I opened both doors. I frisked each one and, with hands behind heads, walked them past the three trucks. I made them kneel in front of Renee.

While patting down the five men from the truck in front of the VW, one broke from the group and made a run back down the highway. Greta whined and pranced in place. Renee pointed her hand toward the runner, said, "Go."

The runner disappeared into the snowy darkness with Greta fifty feet behind. A human cry soon echoed out of the dark with panicked shouts of, "Stop it. Stop it!"

Greta then herded the runner back toward us, appearing out of the inky darkness, trailing the man who was massaging his left forearm. It wasn't until the man was standing next to his buddies, that Greta gave up her charge and rejoined Renee.

I had the rest of them out of the trucks and kneeling next to the Bronco a few minutes later. I counted twenty-one. I hadn't found any further weapons.

I dragged the one that Renee had wounded to a spot in front of the others. He was clutching his stomach and moaning in pain. He wouldn't last long.

I swung the M4 to my side, took out the Glock, and put a single round through his heart.

I turned and addressed the kneeling men. "I'm sorry I had to do that. But he was suffering and was going to die horribly."

"He aint a fuckin' family pet, dude," the driver of the VW shouted, visibly upset.

"You're responsible for the death of three people earlier today," I said, ignoring the comment. "You probably don't know their names, but they were Mr. and Mrs. Talbot and their son Brad. You point out the ones that did the killing, and I will let the rest of you live. You have my word."

A flurry of hands left heads and pointed to two men in the second row. I walked over and stood over the men.

"Names?" I asked the two.

"Dumb and Dumber," one of the men in the back row answered.

"It probably fits, but give me their real names," I said.

"Izzy and Stuart."

"Thank you."

I pointed the Glock at another man, this one much older than the rest, and asked if that was the truth.

"Yes, sir."

"And it was these two that did the killing?" I asked, pointing to the two men. "No one else?"

"That is correct, sir."

"Which one is Izzy?"

"The one in the red jacket."

"Fuck you, Jared," Izzy screamed. "You fuckin' pussy."

I backed off and stood next to Renee.

"Izzy and Stuart, come up here next to your buddy," I said, pointing to the dead man lying in the snow.

"Fuck that, asshole," the man in the red jacket shouted out. "You're goin' to just—"

A shot rang out and the man known as Izzy slumped over in the snow, blood squirting out of his neck and onto the man kneeling behind him.

Melissa had done it again.

"The man asks you to do something, you do it. Understood?" Melissa shouted at the crowd.

"Yes ma'am," nineteen men shouted out in answer.

"Stuart, get on up there. Now!" Melissa commanded.

Stuart stood and slowly walked up to me.

"Kneel." Which he did. "You shoot those people, Stuart?"

"No."

"Bullshit."

"Liar."

"He done it," were just a few of the many responses from his buddies.

"They're fuckin'—"

I pointed the Glock at Stuart's forehead.

"Please, mister," he pleaded.

"Did you give the Talbot's a pass?" I asked.

"Well, I—" he started to say.

I pulled the trigger, and Stuart slumped onto the dead window guy.

Twelve rounds left.

"The rest of you are going to walk back to that house, and you are going to bury all three Talbots. We'll give you eight hours to get it done. You'll stay there until we show up. We'll be there eight hours from now," I said, looking at my watch. "But first, I want you to throw your wallets up here. That way, we'll know where to locate you if we find that you haven't done what you're told."

Several wallets landed at my feet. The rest of them didn't have wallets, which I understood. *Who needs wallets anymore?*

They then sat in silence. None moved.

"Get going, now!" Melissa shouted, raising her rifle's muzzle and firing a quick burst over their heads.

That did it. They all stood and started running south down the highway, falling and skidding on the slippery roadway. It was almost comical.

"Are we really going to the Talbots'?" Melissa asked, once the group was out of earshot.

"Hell, no," I answered. "But they don't know that. Monica and Kathy, please gather their weapons and put them in the Talbots' trailer. Look for ammo, too. Melissa and Renee, please transfer the stuff they looted from the house into her trailer." Then, into the comms, "Susan."

"Yes?"

"Send Emily out here, please. She can help transfer supplies."

"She wants to bring her son out."

"I wouldn't advise it," I said, thinking of the three dead bodies on full display.

"She says he needs to see things as they really are."

"Okay then."

Mother and son showed up a minute later, and I put them to work helping Melissa and Renee. Emily walked past the three dead men and said nothing, didn't even glance down at them. The son stopped and stared at the three.

"My dad always said that you reap what you sow," he said aloud, staring at the bodies. "Thank you for handing out a little justice."

"You're welcome. You'll need to watch your mom's back."

"Gramps told me to take care of mom. I'm gonna do that."

"Will you do something for me?" I asked him.

"Sure. Anything."

I took out the permanent marker and handed it to him.

"On each man's forehead, write *killer of innocents*."

"Sure."

"You know how to spell innocents?"

"Affirmative," he answered, and set off.

The pickups were soon empty of the looted supplies.

I walked over to Emily, said, "Seems a shame to have these four working vehicles sitting useless. If Peter can drive, I suggest you take this Power Wagon and have him follow you home. I'll disable the other three."

"Peter drove his grandparents' ranch truck so he could help with chores when he visited them. So yes, he knows how to drive."

I opened the Power Wagon's driver's door. "It's a stick shift. Is his grandparent's a manual?"

"It is."

I started the engine and checked the fuel level. "You've got half a tank left. Should be plenty to get you to Burns."

"Peter, come on over here," his mother shouted. He interrupted his writing and hustled over to us. His mother pointed to the Power Wagon, said, "Merry Christmas, Peter. You're going to drive this back to Burns. Stay close behind me."

"Seriously?" Peter asked, climbing up in the driver's seat, putting both hands on the steering wheel and his feet on the clutch and brake pedals.

It didn't appear that his legs were long enough to push down the pedals. "You have enough leg to push down the brake and clutch pedals?" I asked.

He had to scoot up toward the dashboard to do it, but was able to depress both pedals. "This is what I had to do when Gramps let me drive the ranch truck."

"Good enough." It wasn't as if he'd be encountering rush-hour traffic. I went to work on the remaining three vehicles, removing ignition keys, raising engine hoods, and pulling spark-plug wires. Then I pulled every other wire I could see. I finished them off by putting a bullet hole in all three gas tanks. I dropped the spent one and inserted a new magazine. Twelve tires received a round each.

Peter finished his writing and handed back the marker. I held out my hand and we shook. "Stay frosty, young man. I have no doubt you'll be able to take care of your mother."

"Thank you for helping us, sir," he said, his handshake firm.

"You're welcome. Continue being strong for your mom.

"Melissa, drive the Humvee over to Clint's driver's door and tell Kris to get in our ranch truck and wait for me. We'll top off the gas tanks by siphoning diesel from Clint's tank to the ranch truck and Humvee."

"The ranch truck's out of gas," Kris shouted across the distance.

"It's not. I'll show you the second tank's switch lever."

Emily and her son gave each of the ladies a hug, before it was my turn.

"Do you have any idea what happened to the power?" she asked as I disentangled myself.

I told her what we knew.

"Oh my gosh," she said, putting her hand over her heart. "This whole power outage is the result of an attack? And from the Chinese? After Putin was put away, I really thought we were on the path to reestablishing relations with them, but then when Pelosi felt it necessary to fly to Taiwan, she just lit the match that was waiting to ignite. I guess it's too late now for any kind of reconciliation. Oh well."

"What is it, Mom?" Peter asked, seeing his mother upset.

"I'll tell you when we're home, son."

To me, she said, "You treated your friend's wounds properly. The larger cuts can't be sutured closed—it's too late for that. She'll need to have those cuts cleaned and tended by a wound specialist. It's going to take some time. You've got her on antibiotics, so that's good."

"Thank you for checking," I said.

"The person that did that to her has been dealt with?" she asked.

"Yes," I answered, glancing at the snow-covered lump in front of the semi-truck. "He'll never harm another woman."

"Good."

Mother and son turned and walked back to the Bronco and Power Wagon. The engines started, and they were soon underway, merging left onto northbound Highway 78 toward Burns where they quickly disappeared into the snowy darkness. The deep growl of the Bronco's big V8 could be heard for a minute longer, and then it too was gone. The snow was coming down heavier than ever, sometimes blowing sideways with the stronger wind gusts.

We'd been there long enough. It was time to head out.